THE WHIP

THE WHIP

Catherine Cookson

SUMMIT BOOKS
New York

For Lisa Mallen
whose youth was short but joyful

Contents

PART ONE

The Child

1

"Will the new medicine make Dada well?"

The enormously fat woman moved her head and her triple chins wobbled over the collar of her bright red voluminous cotton gown. "Oh, sure, sure," she said.

"The apothecary here is good, isn't he?"

"Yes, yes; he's very good." The chins wobbled again.

"Not like the one in Dewsbury."

"Oh, he was a good apothecary too."

"He didn't make Mama better, did he?"

"Oh, look down there." The fat woman pointed to where the carriages were drawing up before the Mansion House in the long beautiful street and she said, "Come, let's go and see the justices; they'll be trying the culprits this Monday mornin' again."

When they reached the Mansion House there were only a few people on the pavement and they were able to see the Mayor, the Town Clerk and the three justices ceremoniously entering the building.

"Will they send everybody to the House of Correction?"

"No, no." The fat lady shook the small hand reassuringly, adding as she began to walk on, "Just the bad hats. They're very good justices here; folks get a fair crack of the whip."

She opened wide her mouth which was small for such a large face, but the laughter that issued from it had a deep sound, like one would expect from a man, and looking down on the child, she said, "That was funny, eh? Fair crack of the whip. You can give a fair crack of the whip, can't you?"

"Yes, yes, I can. Dada's gona make me a full-size one when he gets up. I ripped the peg out yesterday with mine."

"Did you now? Did you now? Well, as I've always said to Mr Travers, you have the makin' of a show lady, every inch of you."

"Dada says I'll be as good as him one day. But nobody could be as good as Dada with the whip, could they, Mrs Travers?"

The question was solemn and the fat lady answered in a similar tone, "No, no one could be as good as your dada with the whip." And then she added by way of good measure, "Or with the knives. Ah!" She brought the child to a stop at the bottled-glass window of the apothecary's shop, exclaiming, "Here we are, and I'm going in to get this wonderful bottle of medicine for your dada. In the meantime, you go down to the pastry shop and get a sugar dolly. Here!" She thrust a halfpenny into the small hand, and the child, looking up at the enormous bulk of flesh, said on a high note, "Oh ta, Mrs Travers. Oh ta." And on this she turned and scampered down the long street.

When, a few minutes later, she returned with the pastry untouched and held triumphantly in her hand, Frances Travers was waiting for her on the pavement, and looking down on her she said, "You've got it then."

"Yes. Ta."

"Well, aren't you going to eat it? It's for eating, isn't it?"

The child now broke off a leg from the pastry and, handing it to-wards the bulbous stomach, said, "There's one leg for you and I'll keep one leg for Dada."

As the fat fingers closed round the tiny leg the woman said, "It's a good child you are, Emma, a good child. Come, we'll take a dander down to the market before going back, eh?"

"Oh yes." Then looking up wistfully, the child said, "We never see the market when it's goin', do we? 'cos it's on a Saturday. But do you think we'll see the big fair?"

"Huh! haven't we got a fair of our own? Doesn't that satisfy you?"

"Yes." The child laughed now. "But . . . but it isn't like the big fair, is it?"

"Big enough. Don't start turning up your nose at our fair, Emma Molinero."

Emma knew that the fat lady was teasing her and she did a little skip along the edge of the pavement and the cobbled road; then returning to her companion's side, she put her head well back as she looked up at her and asked, "Will we be here for the St Leger?"

"Ah now, now, that's a point. That's not until well into September, and here we are still in August and been here two weeks already. There's a saying, you can get too much of a good thing you know, and so we've always made it a policy to keep movin'. Two to three weeks, three at the most."

"But Dada is sick."

The fat lady made no answer to this, and it was some seconds before Emma broke the silence between them by saying, "I like it here, I like

Doncaster. It's a lovely place, nice and clean, not muddy." She looked down at the pavement. "And the people are nice; even the rich ones, like Mr Casson. He lets us have the two fields, doesn't he? And the horses can gallop. Some people don't like you to let the horses gallop, do they?"

"No; you're right there, Emma, they don't."

"Do you think Dada will let me go on the full show tonight, Mrs Travers?"

"Well, well now, I couldn't say about that. He's not for you going on the full show. You might as well know he's not even for you doing your bit before the tent, so I shouldn't set your heart on him being talked round. He's got his own ideas, an' rightly I suppose, but," she ended, muttering to herself now, "can't see the harm in it. It's got to come."

They had walked almost the mile length of the main Doncaster street and were now on the towpath by the river and in sight of the first field where stood a jumble of tents, one large and four smaller ones, together with three caravans and two flat carts, their shafts resting on the ground. In a further field five horses were grazing.

A number of people, seven in all, could be seen moving between the tents in the first field. And these made up *Travers Travelling Show,* not counting the man who lay dying in the first of the two caravans, or the fat lady and the child.

The fat lady was panting visibly and audibly as she entered the field, and almost immediately her husband, a tall thin man, approaching her, greeted her with the words, "Good for business that is, with a stone of grease running down you. Why couldn't you let Charlie go?"

"Because," retorted his wife curtly, "he needs to keep in shape more than I do." Her stumpy arm, seeming to shoot out, pointed to where a youngish man was pummelling at a bag of sand strung between two poles.

Septimus Travers, looking from his wife to the child, said, "Flogging a dead horse." Then turning abruptly, he walked away, and the fat woman and the child went towards where a middle-aged woman was talking to four dogs. The animals were of indiscriminate breeds and size: they were lying on the ground, front paws straight out before them, and on each one's back sat a tabby cat.

Addressing the end one, the woman commanded, "Stop that clawing, Betsy." The cat sheathed its claws and the dog on which it was sitting opened its mouth and yawned. Then the woman, putting her hand to her shoulder on which sat a rook, its feathers gleaming like polished black-lead, said, "Hooky," and the bird flew lopsidedly, owing to its clipped wing, from her shoulder and alighted on the back of the first cat, then proceeded to jump from one furry back to another. This done, the bird dropped on to the grass and began pecking vigorously, only to be brought up by the trainer's voice yelling, "Round, Hooky!"

On this, the bird circled the company of dogs and cats before finally coming to a standstill in front of them.

As the fat lady passed them she said, "He's comin' on fine, Martha. You're a marvel, a real marvel."

For answer, the small woman wagged her head from side to side: she knew she was a marvel and she knew she was fitted for better set-ups than this. Oh yes, the time would come when her strange ability was not advertised on a strip of canvas bearing the words: *Martha Newbourn, Amazing Animal Trainer,* but would be on a wide board emblazoned in gaslight, advertising the acts of a circus, and she would perform under a big tent which would be full of people.

The fat lady came to a stop at the foot of the steps leading into the first of the three caravans. She did not attempt to go up them but, poking her head forward into the doorway, called, "I got it, Georgie."

The voice that came back to her was thick and weak saying, "Thanks, Frances."

"She's enjoyed her trip to town."

Again the voice said, "Thanks, Frances."

Taking the medicine bottle from her basket, Frances Travers handed it to Emma, then pushed her up the steps and into the caravan.

José Layaro Molinero, known among his companions as Georgie, or Mollo, turned slowly on to his side in the bunk and held his hand out to his daughter, and she, placing the medicine bottle in it, said, "This'll make you better. When you drink it all, it'll make you better."

He did not look at the bottle but laid it behind him on the narrow bunk; then touching her arm lightly, he said, "Sit. . . . Sit, my Emma."

Emma sat on the stool at the head of the bunk, her face on a level with her father's, and she smiled at him as she said, "It was lovely in the town. The sun was shinin' and everybody was nice to us and no one called after Mrs Travers today. But that was perhaps 'cos the boys were all at school."

"Wouldn't you like to go to school, my Emma?"

Her head to one side, the child thought for a moment, then said, "Some time, but not all the time, not when I'm practising. Did you hear that I whipped out the pegs?"

"I heard. . . . I want you to go to school, Emma, and learn to read and write."

"But you learned me. I can do my name."

"Your name is nothing, it is only the beginning. I had the chance to go to school, but I scorned it. I, too, preferred the whip, but . . . but it was a big mistake. The whip leads you nowhere, only to the end of it, and the end stings. You understand? No, no, you don't. But my Emma, me . . . I want you to learn, to learn your letters. And a lot more things. You are like me, you would be quick to learn. I was quick to learn what I thought was all I needed, and that was the language. I was but ten when I came to this country, but ten, three years older than you are now, but I . . . I learned the language. I speak good, don't I?"

"Yes, Dada, you speak good."

"But"—he shook his head slowly now—"I do not speak too good. There is another way to speak and I want you to be learn-ed that way. . . . Do you know you have a grandmama?"

Her eyes widened and her lips moved into a smile as she nodded at him, saying, "Yes, you have told me, in Spain."

He hitched himself slowly up on to his elbow now and brought his face close to hers as he said, "You have another grandmama, Emma. She is here in . . . in this country."

"Here?" Her eyes grew wider, and he nodded at her and repeated, "Here. She is your mama's mother."

"My mama's mother? And she is here?" Emma now looked towards the open door of the caravan, and he put in, "Not here, but not so far away."

"We are going to see her?"

"No, not me. I not go to see her, but you go. She . . . she doesn't like me." He smiled faintly now.

"Then I don't like her."

He patted her hand, saying softly, "She has good reason. My Eliza, she ran away from her mother to marry me, and her mother never want to see her again."

"She don't want to see me then."

"Oh, I think she will."

"I won't go to see her without you. And anyway, I can't go 'cos Mr Travers is learnin' me to get right for the fair day. When the big fair comes we will join them like last year, and Mr Travers says. . . ."

"I don't want you in the big fair day."

"But, Dada."

"No more. No more." He closed his eyes and shook his head. *"El latigo,* it is finished for both of us."

"The whip? Why?"

"Because, my Emma—" he was holding her two hands now on top of the striped blanket and he pressed them down into it as he said, "Better things, better things for you besides the whip, or the knife."

Slowly he eased off his elbow and lay back, and his breathing became heavy, accentuating the silence that had fallen between them.

Presently, she said softly, "Dada." And he answered, "Yes, my Emma?"

"I would rather go to my grandmama in Spain."

He made a sound like a throaty laugh now and he raised his eyes up towards the painted roof of the caravan just above his head as he said, "And so would I, my Emma, so would I, but . . . but it cannot be. Spain is too far away, and . . . and your Spanish grandmama . . . well, she would be too old to bother. She will be nearing . . . oh—" he screwed up his eyes as he reckoned his mother's age, and then said, "coming up to seventy years, my mother will be."

Turning his head, he gazed at his daughter. "You have her eyes, kindly eyes," he said, "but"—now he pursed his lips slightly—"you have her temper too. Oh yes, my Emma, you have her temper too. You smile, but yes, you are your Spanish grandmama's other self. Your mama, she had no temper, my Eliza had no temper, she was. . . . What was she, my Eliza? She was agreeable. Oh yes, agreeable. And you too are agreeable." He nodded now at Emma. "You have her hair, like the chestnut shell when rubbed, only darker." He put out his hand and stroked the thick long waves that fell below the child's shoulders and he said now, "Always look to your hair. Wash it. Whenever you come to a river, wash it, 'specially if the river is runnin' fast. And. . . ."

Of a sudden he began to gasp, and she stood up and, bending over him, said, "Take some of your new medicine, Dada, it will make you better."

After a moment he gasped, "Bring . . . Robert . . . or Annie."

She scrambled down the steps of the caravan and ran to where two young boys, looking startlingly alike, were practising tumbling on the grass and she called to them, "Andy! Billy! where is your Dada?"

They stopped and together they pointed to the next field where a man was riding a horse bareback. One minute he was sitting on it, next standing on its back, and the next minute he had done a back somer-sault and landed on his feet, and all the while his wife held the horse by a long rope.

Running to the gate of the field, Emma called, "Uncle Tummond! Auntie Tummond! Dada wants you."

They both stopped, turned, and looked at her; then the woman, going to the horse, unloosened the rope and followed the man towards her.

They did not ask her any questions but they passed her, and she fol-lowed them. She liked the man she called Uncle Tummond, but she was a little afraid of his wife who could eat fire. She was a fearsome sight, his wife when eating fire. And she was teaching her sons, too, to eat fire. At present, though, they were just tumblers.

She did not follow the couple into the caravan but sat on the steps and listened to their voices. Her father's voice came to her, distant, saying, "You sent it off?" And the answer came, "Yes Georgie, six days ago. It caught the Edinburgh mail that would drop it off at Newcastle. The coach went out on the dot, like every day, at six minutes afore two. It would be in Newcastle that night and get to that place beyond Gateshead Fell the next day."

"There's been time to answer."

"Perhaps they cannot write." It was Auntie Tummond speaking now, and her husband answered, "They could have got a preacher or somebody."

"That's if they ever see a preacher up there in the wilds."

"Don't be silly, woman! How far did you say it was from the town, Georgie?"

"Oh." Her father's voice came faintly now, hesitantly saying, "About five miles from the city of Newcastle. Beyond Gateshead Fell there . . . there was a village . . . Fell-burn. Yes Fell-burn, above that. Above that."

"Well then, the letter should have got to her all right. Perhaps she has died, Georgie."

"Perhaps . . . but no, no. Alive she was when Eliza died. And she can write. I sent letter to her then, an' she return a bitter letter. No, I do not think she died. . . . Robert."

"Yes, Georgie?"

"I don't want my Emma to travel; I . . . I want her to grow up in a . . . a home."

"There's worse homes than this, Georgie." It was Auntie Tummond's voice again. "She'd be well looked after, we'd see to that."

"I know, I know, Annie, and I . . . I do . . . do thank you, warmly I do, but I promised Eliza she would never go into the show. Play the whips, yes; learn to use 'em, yes; but not for the show. Eliza, she's very upset when I show Emma how to throw the knife, but Emma take to both the knife and the whip."

"Aye, she's amazin' for her age. An' Georgie, that's why Sep wants her in the show; just for this once when the fair comes. You see, you're a big miss, Georgie, like Eliza was. Things haven't been goin' too well. It . . . it would do him a favour if you let her go in just this once. I would see . . . in fact I promise you, Georgie, it'll just be this once."

"No, Robert, no. I . . . I know you are not askin' for yourself, if it were so I would say yes, because I owe you, always have, and now you give me shelter to die in."

"Nonsense. Nonsense." Annie Tummond was speaking again. "It's share and share alike. The lads like sleeping under canvas and so does Emma. Oh yes, she does, she prefers the canvas to this any day. You know yourself she'd rather sleep outside than sleep in your wagon. . . . Oh! now, now; don't distress yourself."

When Emma heard the sound of her father's harsh coughing she rose from the steps and looked towards the open half of the door, and when the coughing subsided she leant forward towards the lower half of the door and strained her ears to what her father was now saying. But the words came muddled and all she could make out of them was, "Promise me, Robert, promise me." And Mr Tummond's voice answering, "It'll be as you say, Georgie, it'll be as you say."

2

The people of the town were very kind: some sent flowers, some even followed the small cortège to the graveyard. The remarks they made about the Spaniard were all kindly: some of them could look back over the fifteen to twenty years that the Travers Travelling Show had come each year to join the big fair, besides putting on its own displays. The Spaniard had always seemed a handsome-looking man and strong. He had no spare flesh but people were amazed at the strength of his arms as he manipulated the whips, some only three feet long, others ranging fifteen to twenty feet. They recalled how the women in the audience would squeal when the whip trapped the legs of a husband or brother, never of themselves, but so gently that the captives felt no hurt.

And they recalled too how he threw the daggers all round the lovely young girl who was his wife. It had been a great pity, they said, and very strange that she too should die in this very place only eighteen months back. He was being buried on top of her. Now wasn't that unusual? Not unusual for townsfolk but for travelling show people. Well, it was something to remark on.

The townspeople also remarked to each other that all the members of the Travers Travelling Show were superior-like people, that is superior to gypsies and such. Some had even warned their children not to tease the fat lady, although she seemed so good-natured that she didn't appear to mind.

But what surprised those townspeople who were following the coffin which was laid on the flat cart and draped with a many-coloured shawl, the whole being drawn by a horse, was that the travelling people had allowed the child to be present. The little girl, they noticed, was walking between the fat lady and the fire eater; and she wasn't dressed all in black, but in a brown coat and a green bonnet. For that matter, none of the travelling people were in black. Of course it was understandable, they supposed, black clothes cost money, and the travellers usually dressed gaily even if the colours were faded with many washings.

Emma was crying. She knew she was crying inside but her face was dry. There was a terrible pain in her chest and also a feeling of resentment. This latter was centred round the apothecary: she had laid such stock on that bottle of medicine and she had seen that her dada had taken every drop of it. But it hadn't helped, he had died. Like her mama had died.

When she stood by the graveside and watched the long plain box going into the ground and listened to the parson's voice, she knew that he was telling lies. If her dada was going into heaven he wouldn't be going into the earth, they would have put wings on him like in the windows of Christ Church, the one with the tall spire. She had been in there; Mrs Travers had taken her when out for a dander one day. She had liked the church. It was very nice and very big, but it made you seem smaller than you were. No, she didn't believe this parson. There was something wrong somewhere.

The clods were dropping on her dada, hitting him. No one had ever hit her dada; they were frightened to because he could use the whip so well.

Something exploded in her chest. She heard someone yelling. She didn't know it was herself until Uncle Tummond lifted her up, saying, "There, there. There, there," and carried her away.

She cried on and off for three days, while those about her kept talking, talking. When she finally stopped crying she slept for a long while, and when she woke up everybody seemed different. They spoke to her in low voices, their words kindly, and she knew they were saying good-bye.

Auntie Tummond woke her up one morning from the straw pallet at the head of the caravan, told her to dress, and then gave her a mug of milk and a shive of bread, after which both she and her husband sat on the edge of the bunk and, looking at her, said, "Emma, you're going to your grandma the day."

She made no reply, just swallowed the mouthful of bread and continued to look at them. And now it was Uncle Tummond who said, "Your dada wanted it, we . . . we didn't. We wanted you to stay, everybody wants you to stay, but Georgie made us promise to send you to your grandma's. She . . . she lives on a farm and it'll be very nice, animals and all that. Your dada wrote to her, so—" he gulped in his throat before ending, "so she should be expecting you, likely waiting for you." He looked at his wife as if for confirmation, but Annie Tummond was staring at the child and it was she who now took from the pocket of her voluminous skirt a little leather pouch and placed it on the stool in front of her. She shook it gently and from it there sprayed a number of golden sovereigns.

"This is your dada's savings. He . . . he wanted you to have it. There are fourteen sovereigns. It is quite a bit of money and you must take care of it. I'll pin it to the inside of your bodice. And don't let anyone know it's there until you get to your grandma's."

Emma looked down at the golden coins; then silently she picked up one in each hand and then extended her arms towards the couple sitting on the bunk, and at this they both shook their heads vigorously, saying, "No, no! It is for you."

"Dada would have given you them."

"He has given us enough, his cart and horse and odds and ends. . . ."

"Not the whips and his knives?"

"Well"—Annie Tummond shook her head—"he didn't say anything about them."

"I want them, please. Please."

She leant towards them, and Robert Tummond, putting out his hand, patted her arm, saying, "All right, all right, you'll have anything you want, but they'll be a bit of weight."

"I can carry them." Now rising to her feet, she asked simply, "How do I go?"

"Well, we've been talking about it," said Robert Tummond. "There's two ways: either by the express from London which calls at the Reindeer and then goes on to Newcastle, but it comes in here on three in the morning. And then there's the Highflyer. That stops at the Black Boy and that's a bit later, just on five, but it only goes as far as Durham, and Charlie who knows these parts says it's longer from Durham to Fellburn village than 'tis from Newcastle to the village, so we think the earlier one would be better for you. We don't know exactly what time it goes out but we'll have to be there close on three. And don't worry"—he put out his hand—"you'll be in the charge of the guard, and they are nice fellows. And there'll be lots of people travellin' and they'll look after you. You'll have the address of your granny pinned on your coat, and when you get to Newcastle, well"—he blinked now before adding—"the guard will likely put you on another coach or carriage. Oh he's sure to put you on something that'll take you to the village. Now"—he forced a grim smile to his face as he ended—"it'll be a great adventure. Don't you think so, Emma? A great adventure."

She stared back at these two dear friends, then pushing the stool aside, she threw herself towards them, and again she was crying.

*

They were all there with the exception of Septimus Travers for, as he said, somebody had to stay and look after the camp. But then Emma knew he wasn't pleased that she was going to her grandma's. And she also knew it would have been fruitless to tell him that she too wasn't pleased that she was going to this strange grandma's. But if her dada said she had to go then she must obey her dada. She had always obeyed her dada. . . .

She was the last to enter the coach. Dawn was just breaking and through her blurred gaze she saw all their faces, and like her the women were crying, even Miss Newbourn, and she had never seen her cry but once before. That was the day her new dog, a greyhound, had run after the performing rabbit and killed it, and Miss Newbourn had taken a stick and beaten the dog till it was almost dead too, then she had hugged it to her like someone does a child and cried over it. And the men had to pull it from her and Mr Travers had shot it. But she was crying now and Emma felt that it was because she had liked her as much as she had liked the greyhound and all her animals.

She would miss the animals. But then Uncle Tummond had said there'd be lots of animals on the farm, big animals and little animals, lambs. They'd never had a lamb in the troupe.

A gentleman had been sitting in the corner seat but he had moved up to let her be near the window.

The last faces she saw were those of Auntie and Uncle Tummond, for they ran alongside the coach until it reached the main road when the horses started to gallop.

When, with the sudden jolt, she almost slipped off the edge of the seat the gentleman next to her put his hand out and steadied her, and she turned and looked at him. He was a young man; his face was clean, he had no beard; his clothes were black, and he had a high white collar. These things she took in, and when he said, "You have a lot of friends. It's good to have a lot of friends," she did not answer because the lady on the end seat opposite who had joined the coach when she did leant towards the gentleman and in a whisper said, "She's from the circus. Well, it's a kind of circus, travelling players. Her father died and she's going back to his people I think." She made a motion with her head, then tapped her chest which indicated the label pinned to Emma's coat, and the gentleman said, "Oh. Oh, I see." And he turned to Emma once more and smiled down at her. Then bending forward he read what was written on the label:

I am Emma Molinero.
I am going to my grandmother's,
Mrs Crawshaw at Boulder Hill Farm,
Near Fellburn Village,
Close by Gateshead Fell.

Now the gentleman, smiling widely into her face, said, "Well, well, we are for the same destination, for I too am going that way."

"Taking up a new parish, reverend?"

Emma looked at one of the two men sitting next to the woman, then at the gentleman at her side, and she now remembered what the high collar represented. He was a reverend. She listened to his voice saying, "I'm taking over the parish of St Jude and the vicarage is in the village of Fellburn."

"Interesting. Interesting." The gentleman nodded his head, then seemed to lose interest, and the one who had turned into a preacher which was different from a gentleman, smiled down at her again, and this time she took more stock of him. He had a nice face, but he was very young for a preacher, he didn't look as old as Charlie . . . Charlie Lamb the boxer, and Charlie was young. In a way, he didn't look unlike Charlie for his chin was square, but Charlie said his had been knocked square with the punches from the locals. Anybody could fight Charlie for a shilling a go, and sometimes he let them win and they had their shilling back and another for winning.

The preacher had grey eyes, his nose was large and his mouth wide. She noticed he had a crossed tooth in the bottom set. Her mama had had a crossed tooth. She couldn't tell if he was tall or short but he was very thin because she noticed his knee bones pressing up out of his tight trousers.

The lady opposite started asking him questions now. Her voice was monotonous and made her sleepy because she had been awake since the middle of the night. She heard the preacher's voice, and it was like no other she had ever heard, say, "I had a curacy in Kent." Then, "Yes, this is my first fully-fledged living." Then, "Oh, Chester-le-Street. That isn't so very far away. I hope you will come to St Jude's for a service sometime."

His voice was very low. Likely he didn't want to disturb the gentleman who was snoring, and when the man gave a big snort at the same time the coach lurched she jumped slightly, then she felt an arm go about her and her cheek came to rest on the rough serge of a coat that smelt of smoke, not wood smoke or pipe smoke, just smoke, and it wafted round her and then lay heavily on her and she went to sleep.

3

She was standing on the pavement outside the Queen's Head in Newcastle. When the coach had arrived the parson had taken her inside and given her a meal while waiting for her grandmother to come.

But now the parson's own conveyance had arrived in the shape of a gig driven by a man with a beard who for the third time was saying, "Shall we be on our way, Parson?" And the parson for the third time looked down questioningly on Emma, and now bending his knees, he brought his face closer to hers, saying, "Does your grandmother expect you? . . . Does she know you are coming?"

"I don't know. Dada wrote to her."

"Did your da . . . father have a reply? Did he . . . did he have a letter from her?"

She shook her head, and on this the parson straightened himself and looked at the man who was standing impatiently at the horse's head and said, "You will know Boulder Hill Farm, I suppose?"

"Oh aye, I know Boulder Hill Farm. But the folks aren't called Crawshaw. Jake Yorkless works that place, has done since his old man died, and he had worked it afore him, and again his father."

"Do you know anyone called Crawshaw who lives near there?"

The verger shook his head, saying, "Not that I can recall, it's . . . it's a way out. Yet wait. There's a woman there. She comes in with the farmer and his family now and again. Feast Days like, but I don't know her name. It's a scattered parish as you'll find out, Parson. You wouldn't get half of them in on a Sunday if it wasn't for the gentry comin' and them being their landlords."

"You're a cynic, verger. Anyway, what are we going to do about this child?"

"None of our business, I would say, Parson."

"You would?" The young man looked at the older one: his head was thrust slightly forward, a big question not only in his words but in his eyes, and now his voice soft, he added, "Suffer little children, eh verger?"

John Haswell stared back at the new vicar. Huh! it looked as if they were in for something here. Holier than God, this one was going to be. Parson Crabtree had kept his sermonizing for the pulpit, and he had shovelled out hell fire and brimstone from there, but that once done, he became an ordinary man an' he let folks get on with it, except for burials when he sent them off, destination unknown. He had been a tactful man, old Crabtree, made friends with those who had money to support his church and reprimanded those who hadn't, and closed one eye, both eyes at times, when it suited him, spirit-wise, so to speak. But here was this one not five minutes on the ground and holding up things because of a little urchin that looked as if she had just stepped out of the poor house, or was about to step into it.

"It doesn't look as if anyone is coming for her, not at the moment, so we'll take her to this farm. Will it be much out of the way?"

Reluctantly the verger had to admit they would pass the bottom of the road leading to it, but as he watched the young fellow lift the child into the gig and he himself took his seat he said, "Not taking the gig all the way up from the coach road, Parson. It's rutted and it rained all last night, the animal would be mud up to the hocks. Anyway, it isn't all that far."

Emma had taken in the whole of the conversation. The outcome of it was that she liked the parson, but she didn't like the driver, Mr Verger.

As they crossed a fine bridge over a river she looked down on the ships both lining its banks and those with sails set gliding beneath the arches, and she turned an ecstatic look on the young parson, saying, "It's a big river, isn't it?"

"Yes, it is, a fine river."

"There was a river in Doncaster"—she nodded at him—"but it wasn't like this one. 'Tis a fine river."

They smiled at each other and he said, "Indeed, indeed it is."

As they left the bridge and entered another town, she said, "What's this place?"

"I understand it is called Gateshead but"—he bent down to her—"I'm almost as ignorant of the vicinity as you are."

"Oh." She continued to look at him and smile, and she took it that what he meant was he didn't know very much about the place either.

Having passed through the township they were now in open country with cultivated fields stretching away into the distance. Then once more they were running between houses, a village this time. And Emma's remark was, "Nice."

"Yes, it's a nice village," the parson said and then he added, "I can from now on call it my village."

"Your village?" she nodded at him. "It's your village?"

"Well, in a way, since I shall be its pastor. You know what I mean?"

When she made no answer he said, "The vicarage is just beyond, over there, see." He bent down towards her and pointed. "In front of those trees."

"Oh, it's a big house."

"Yes, too big. And now—" he looked towards the verger's back as he added, "you will soon have to alight, my dear. Do . . . do you think you can manage to carry that bag? It looks very heavy."

She smiled broadly at him now as she said, "No, it isn't, not really. There's only two petticoats and a dress, and a pair of shoes, besides Dada's knife belt and the whips."

He screwed up his face at her as he repeated, "Whips?"

She nodded her head. "Dada was very good with the whips, catch even a moth in the air. Yes he could." She nodded as if expecting a denial. "And I can take out pegs."

"Really?"

The gig had stopped now and, getting down from it, he held out his arms and lifted her to the ground; then taking the cloth bag from where it was lying at the side of the verger's feet, he tested it with his hand, saying, "Are you sure it won't be too heavy?"

"No, no, mister . . . Parson, it won't be too heavy. And ta. Thank you. Thank you for the ride."

"How far is the farm up that lane?" The parson was speaking to the verger now, and the man replied, "She'll be there in five minutes, ten at the most." The young man stared at the verger for a long moment as if he was about to say something; then he turned to the child again, saying, "Well, good-bye, Emma, for the present. We shall meet again very shortly."

"Good-bye mister . . . Parson." She bobbed her head to him, then looked at the man seated and, remembering her dada's teaching, she inclined her head towards him too, saying, "Ta. Thanks, mister." Then she turned away, the cloth bag held in her arms against her chest in an effort to show the kind man that it wasn't heavy at all. And she had gone some distance before she heard the wheels of the gig grinding on the road. It was then she stopped and dropped the bag to the ground and looked about her.

There were fields on all sides of her. In some the corn had been cut and stooked, but it was still standing in others. There was no sight of a habitation of any kind. She turned round and looked in the direction the gig had come, but she could not even see the village. She bit on her lip, her face began to crinkle, and she was suddenly filled with fear, because for the first time in her life she was alone. Always before she had been in the midst of people. Always she could put her hand out and touch someone. When it had rained or the weather was very cold they had shared the caravans, sleeping side by side. All except Miss Newbourn, because she wouldn't leave her animals. And anyway the dogs and cats kept her warm. But here she was in the great open space, no houses to be seen, no people to call to, to touch, let alone laugh with. And no Dada to run to.

She gripped the bag now with both hands and at a stumbling run she went along the endless lane until of a sudden it sloped gently upwards between the two hedges, and when it turned to the right she stopped again and, dropping the bag to the ground once more, she stood still and gazed down at the farm about a hundred yards away.

She could see the yard with the outbuildings flanking two sides, and the square-looking house at the head of it, and there were hayricks in the yard and cows moving about, but more important there were people there, a woman and two men.

She did not attempt to run now but, still holding the bag up to her chest, she went slowly forward through the gap in the stone wall; then came to an abrupt stop and in not a little fright because ambling towards her were a number of cows, and they were making for the gap in the wall.

Darting now to the side, she pressed herself against what appeared to her like a contorted piece of iron work. Then when the cows had passed into the lane the boy who was behind them stopped and looked at her. He took her in from her bonnet to her boots; then glancing over his shoulder to where a man and woman were standing in the middle of the yard, he thumbed towards her before continuing on his way after the cows.

She walked now towards the two people. What she noticed first was that they were both very tall. The woman tall and thin, the man tall and broad. When she was standing quite close to them she had to put her head back to look up into their faces, and her eyes settled on the woman as she said softly, "Are you me grandma?"

"*What?* What did you say?" The woman's voice sounded strange, thick, guttural, the words running into one another.

She repeated, "Are you me grandma? I'm"—she now tapped the piece of paper pinned to her coat—"I'm Emma Molinero."

When the woman made no answer but turned and looked at the man, fear and loneliness swept over her like a wave and she began to gabble.

"He said this was the farm, the parson man. They brought me on the cart to the bottom. I was set off the mornin'. It was very early, I got up in the middle of the night. I didn't want to come an' they didn't want me to come, but Dada wished it because of Mama. . . ."

"What on earth." The woman now bent down and, her voice not unkind, she said, "You're at the wrong place, hinny. I'm not your grandma. What did you say your name was?" She now bent forward and read the label. Then straightening up, she gazed at her husband for a moment before muttering under her breath, "My God! Lizzie. This one's Eliza's. He was a foreigner, wasn't he, down at the fair, with a name like that?" She was pointing down to Emma's chest. "And she's known about this, the bitch! Remember the letters? Well! Well! Well!" She drew her chin in. "She's going to get a gliff, isn't she? She wouldn't tell us who they were from . . . the letters, but I guessed it could only be connected with Eliza, or her man, Eliza now being dead."

"Where is she?" It was the first time the man had spoken and his voice came to Emma like that of the woman, thick, guttural, and the woman answered him, saying, "Doing her stint for the painter. She should be up about now. Well! Well! Well!"

The woman now bent down again to Emma and what she said was, "Don't cry. Your granny lives here. Well, not here"—she jerked her head back to the house—"but over there." She pointed beyond the outhouses. "She works for us an' Mr Bowman in the cottage." She now pointed in the opposite direction towards the open gap in the wall and the lane beyond. "So you'd better come away in and wait for her. Here, give me the bag."

As she lifted the bag she said, "My! my! this is heavy. What have you got in here, stones?"

"No"—Emma's voice was small—"it's me dada's whips and his knife belt."

"God above!" The woman was now looking at her husband as she spoke. "Whips and knife belts. Huh! We've got somethin' here. Well, come away in."

Emma followed the woman across the yard and round the corner of the house, through a back door and into a room that seemed chock full of all kinds of things.

"Sit yourself down there." The woman pointed to a stool near an open fire with bars across and an iron spit dangling above it. She was hot and tired and thirsty; the last place she wanted to sit was near a fire. The room seemed stuffy and it was filled with a number of smells she couldn't put a name to because none of them represented onions, or herbs, or wood smoke, or wet grass.

She was deciding she didn't like this woman or the man very much when the woman said to her, "Would you like a drink of buttermilk?"

"Yes, please." She knew what buttermilk was, she'd often had it from the farms at which they stopped to buy eggs and vegetables.

She accepted the mug of buttermilk thankfully, and when she drained it almost at one go the woman said, "By! you were thirsty." Then looking towards the open door she exclaimed to the man who had now taken a seat at the end of the wooden table which was placed in the middle of the room, "Here she comes."

Emma imagined she had stopped breathing and that her chest was swelling because it was getting tighter, and it wasn't until the woman crossed the threshold, then came to a dead stop and stared at her, that she let herself gulp at the hot air.

"You've got a visitor, Lizzie. Didn't you know you were gona have a visitor? She mistook me for her granny." The farmer's wife now gave a deep chuckle before going on, "The wages of sin, and in the flesh an' all."

Emma almost started from the stool as the woman now rounded on her mistress, crying, "It was no sin, she was married. She sent me the marriage lines. You saw them."

"Mind your tongue. Mind your tongue, Lizzie Crawshaw. You forget who you're talkin' to." All the banter had gone out of the farmer's wife's voice now, and the woman standing in the doorway came back at her, crying, "I'm not allowed to forget that ever, am I? Thirty-nine years out of me forty-five I've been reminded of it every day with one and another."

"Well! well! do you hear her?" The tall woman turned to her husband, and he replied, "Aye. Aye, I hear her. Steppin' out of your boots, aren't you, Lizzie?"

Emma looked from one to the other, noting that the man's voice wasn't as unkind as his wife's. But her eyes came to rest on the woman in the doorway. She was much shorter than the farmer's wife and inclined to be plump. She was wearing a linen bonnet with a frill at the back. The strands of hair showing on her cheeks were fair. Her eyes were a vivid blue and full of anger. . . . And this was her grandma, and she was saying, "Put beggars on horseback an' they ride to hell."

The farmer's wife's voice now startled her, crying at her, "Get up out of that and go with your granny!"

She did not immediately obey the command but looked towards the smaller woman as if waiting for her to speak. And after a matter of seconds she did speak, saying, "Come away with you."

Quickly she lifted up the bag and walked towards her grandmother who without looking at her, for her eyes were on the farmer's wife, placed her hand in the middle of her back and pushed her forward into the yard. Then moving ahead she muttered something which Emma couldn't catch, but she followed her, having to trot to keep up with her, past a row of cow byres, some stables and a large barn, then round a corner and by two pigsties. These were placed at the head of a field in which there were long hen crees. After crossing a space strewn with old farm implements, both wooden and iron, they came to an open flat piece of ground on which stood a cottage.

Even to Emma it looked a very small cottage. It was made of rough stone which had been cemented together haphazardly. There was a window, and a door, in the front of it. It had a slate roof out of which a chimney stuck.

Once inside the room, Emma blinked her eyes in order to take in her surroundings. She noted there was another window, a smaller one, and a door at the far end of the room, and on the wall to the side of it was a big cupboard. To the right of her, and seemingly stuck in the corner of the walls, was a fire grate with a round iron door above it, and in the middle of the room stood a small wooden table. It had one chair under it and to the side of it was a rocking-chair. On the wall to the left of her was a low narrow cupboard with shelves above it, and near it a ladder leaned against the wall. There was no sign of a bed.

They stood confronting each other in the dimness, Emma staring at her grandmother and her grandmother staring at her.

Emma wanted to speak, she wanted to touch the woman in front of her and, in some extraordinary way, comfort her.

Her grandmother was the first to break the silence. She said, "He shouldn't have done it. He had no right to send you."

"He's dead. My dada is dead."

"I know that, else you wouldn't be here. But still I say he had no right to send you. You've got no claim on me. I washed me hands of her when she went off with him. Slaved to bring her up decent, then to go off with a fair man. . . . Scum."

Up till now Emma had not heard the word scum, and did not know its meaning, but she gathered from her grandmother's tone that she hadn't liked her dada. And so she said in a voice that trembled but held defiance, "My dada was a good man. Everybody loved him, and he was clever. He could stand in for nearly everything except the fire-eatin'."

She watched her grandmother now close her eyes and turn her head away. Then turning back to look at her again, she said, "What am I gona do with you? I'm past takin' on responsibility of another one. And she'll make you work. By God! she'll make you work. Do you understand that?" She poked her head down towards Emma.

"I can work."

"You can work? . . . Huh! What would you know about work goin' round with a circus, a lazy, thieving crew?"

"They weren't. They weren't." There was no tremble in Emma's voice now. "They were all good an' nice and I didn't want to come."

"Then why did you?"

" 'Cos Dada made Uncle Tummond promise to send me to you."

"Oh, dear God." Emma now watched her grandmother shake her head wildly from shoulder to shoulder, then sit down in the rocking-chair and, gripping the sides, rock herself backwards and forwards for some minutes before stopping suddenly and saying, "Well, you're here. Get your things off, and the quicker you know the ropes the better it'll be for you."

Emma took off her coat and hat, and when she went to open the bag her grandmother said, "What have you in there?"

"Dada's whips an' mine, and his knife belt."

"*What?*"

Lizzie Crawshaw now watched this new granddaughter of hers lifting out from the bag what looked like a piece of polished black wood about fourteen inches long around which was twisted a leather thong, thick in parts then tapering off to an almost threadlike end. This was followed by two similar ones but on a smaller scale. Next, she brought out a roll of soft leather from which protruded a number of wooden handles.

"God in heaven!" Lizzie's head was moving in small jerks as she asked softly, almost in awe, "What were those for?"

Emma's face looked bright as she answered, "To throw. He could throw them all around Mama, an' me an' all. And I can throw them. He was showing me. Only mine didn't always stick." Her smile broadened. Then thrusting her hand down into the front of her dress, she struggled for a minute as she unpinned the chamois leather bag.

Holding it in her outstretched hand, she went towards the rocking-chair, saying, "These are for you, you can have them." She watched her grandmother look down at the bag before taking it into her hand; she then moved it up and down as if weighing it; after which she undid the string and tipped the contents into her palm, then sat gazing down on the twelve sovereigns. Her lower jaw slowly sinking, she looked from them to the child standing before her, the child who showed no resemblance to her daughter. And now she muttered, "Sovereigns?"

"There's twelve of 'em. There were fourteen, but I gave one each to

Auntie and Uncle Tummond, because Dada liked them and they were very kind. They said these were mine, so you can have them."

Emma now watched her grandmother's eyes close tightly, then her chin droop down towards her chest as she muttered something. But it was so low that Emma couldn't catch the words until her grandmother lifted her head again and said, "Twelve sovereigns, over two years work. Twelve sovereigns." Then nodding towards Emma, she went on, "Do you know, I've never seen so many at once in all me working days. It all had to go home until he died, me dad, three years gone; then the following year I went mad and spent all me earnings, five pounds in one go." She closed her eyes again and shook her head, then muttered, "What am I sayin'? But child"—her voice changing, she eased herself towards the front of the rocking-chair and she put her hand on Emma's shoulder, only to take it off again as if it had burned her, and she swallowed deeply before muttering, "Don't mention this money to her, the missis. Don't mention it to anybody. Do you hear?"

"Yes."

"But do you understand?" The hand came on her shoulder again and this time it stayed. "If they thought I had this much they'd have it off me one way or another. You know somethin'?" She screwed herself back on the chair now, saying, "I could up and walk out of here this minute."

There followed a silence during which Emma waited for her grandma to go on and she watched her smiling to herself, before of a sudden her chin drooped again and she murmured, "But I wouldn't, I can't, I'm tied, in more ways than one I'm tied." And now she rose to her feet and, going to the table, she stood with her hands flat on it looking down on them, and Emma stood looking at her.

Presently her granny asked, "Are you hungry?"

"Yes."

"Well, there's mutton an' bread in the cupboard an' milk in the jug. It's over there." She pointed. "Go and get it; the sooner you make yourself useful the better. . . . By the way, what do they call you?"

"Emma."

"Emma . . . well, that's plain enough. And here, before you do anything else take that label off your coat. And in future don't call yourself by that name."

"Not by Emma?"

"No, your surname, the foreign name. I don't want to hear it. From now on you'll be known by your mother's name, Crawshaw, Emma Crawshaw, you understand?"

No she didn't, not fully, and she liked her name, but she wanted to please this grandmother. Yes, she did, she wanted to please her because she felt in time she could like her, so she said, "Yes, Grandma."

On the name the woman again closed her eyes.

4

During the next few days Emma was introduced into a new life. She learned that she had to call Farmer Yorkless's wife missis, and Farmer Jake Yorkless mister. The twelve-year-old twins she could call Barney and Luke, and after her introduction to these two she realized that she liked Barney but she didn't like Luke. The eleven-year-old Pete and the ten-year-old Dan she looked upon as being almost her own age for, whereas Barney and Luke were tall, the latter two appeared undersized.

Billy Proctor the cowhand she saw as an old man because of his side-whiskers. Her grandmother she saw as an old woman, yet she had no wrinkles on her face.

On the morning following her arrival she had been given her place in the farm. The farmer's wife had evidently arranged it overnight. She was to get threepence a week. The tasks allotted to her were odd jobs in the farm kitchen such as sweeping the floor, scouring the pans and washing up the crockery, all under the supervision of her grandmother. Outside, she had to attend to the hens. Besides gathering their eggs and replacing the straw in the boxes, she had to scrape the floor of droppings. This would be made easier she was told if she would take the ashes from the hearth and sprinkle them in the crees. Apparently this job had previously been in Dan's domain.

She took to the work and she learned fast. She liked working in the hen crees best of all because this took her outside, for during the time she spent in the kitchen she felt she couldn't breathe properly.

Then there was their form of eating. Her grandma helped to prepare dinner but neither of them sat down at the table; instead, their meal was ladled into a bowl by the farmer's wife and they took it across to the cottage and ate it there. The same procedure applied to Billy Proctor, only he hadn't any cottage. He, Emma discovered, ate his meal in the smelly room where the pig boiler was, that's if it was raining or cold, otherwise he ate it where he slept in the loft above the stables.

As it was still summer everyone returned to the fields after the evening meal. The stooks had all been brought in but now there was raking and gleaning to be done, and Jake Yorkless saw that the last wisp of straw was lifted: he was apt to reiterate in a sing-song voice, "Waste not want not, for there'll come the day when you'll need that lot."

In the fields the farmer was a jolly man. He would slap his wife on the buttocks and call her Dilly, and cuff his sons around the ears and make them laugh. And he would joke with Billy Proctor. The only one he didn't joke with and didn't laugh with was her grandmother.

She was slightly afraid of the farmer and his wife, and of Luke too; that was until she used the whip for the first time when the fear left her and defiance took its place.

She had now been at the farm for five weeks. The weather had changed: the keen winds were coming in from the sea, there was a slight rime on the grass in the mornings, and when she went over the yard to the hen crees she ran to keep herself warm.

She had got into the habit of talking to the hens. They were a mixture of White Leghorns and Rhode Island Reds, and all dominated by one cock. He was a fine fellow and he had got used to her approach for he would strut towards her when she came through the gate. With the exception of two, she liked the hens. These two were thickly feathered Rhode Island Reds and they had almost stripped a White Leghorn of its plumage. The poor bird's head and behind were quite bare, and on this morning when she entered the field she saw that they had started on their victim again, tearing at its breast now, and the poor thing was running round in circles squawking its head off.

As she ran to separate them she shouted at them, "You'll find yourselves in the pot, you two, if you're not careful. Leave her alone! Poor Betsy."

When, after being chased away, one of them returned and attacked its victim again, there crossed Emma's mind the picture of Miss Newbourn training the rook. She would lasso it to bring it back into line, for Miss Newbourn could also use the whip. As she had explained to her, you had at first to get them to do what you wanted, but you had to do it gently.

Well now, that's what she would do with these two beggars, she would train them to behave themselves.

Running, she made for the cottage, not towards the door but round to the side where a broken and rickety ladder led through a hatch into a space below the roof which couldn't, under any circumstances, be given the name of loft for at its highest point it was only five feet, tapering to two feet at each side. And this was where she slept. Her grandmother slept in the big cupboard bed that let down from the wall in the room below; she wouldn't have her sleeping with her, she had said so on that first night, and she had taken a bale of straw up into the roof space, where apparently at one time she herself had slept. Inside the cottage you entered the roof space by the other ladder and a trap door.

Through bits and pieces her grandmother had let fall she had gathered that the tiny cottage had at one time been attached to the original farmhouse that had stood here, and that part of the cottage had been used for the animals. A fire had destroyed the main building and most of the stone had been used to build the present farmhouse. That was nearly a hundred years ago.

She didn't mind sleeping in the confined space because she could push the hatch outwards, and lie on her side and look up into the sky and it was just like sleeping in the tent.

Now she scrambled up the ladder, crossed the roof space on her hands and knees to where her cloth bag was lying and, delving into it, she brought out the smallest of the three whips. Untying the thong from around the handle, she worked her wrist back and forth to get the leather into play again for it had become twisted when rolled up. It had never been out of use so long since her father had made it for her.

Down the ladder once more, across the yard and into the field she went. The two bullies were at their victim again. Standing some little way from them, she began to manipulate the whip. At first her wrist was stiff and as her small hand weaved this way and that, she told herself she must practise or else she would forget all her dada had taught her.

Suddenly it seemed that the six foot thong came alive. It flicked low down over the ground, its end curled and the Rhode Island Red's legs were tied together and the bird let out such a squawk that the cock, giving voice, came flying to her assistance. Then the whole company of fifty hens set up such a cackling, screeching, and squawking that she yelled at them, "Shut up you lot! Shut up!"

She had not noticed Luke's arrival on the scene and as he stared at the big red hen lying on its side, its legs held by the end of the whip, he yelled at her, "What do you think you're doin'?"

And she yelled back at him, "Training it. It's pickin' Betsy to death. Look." She pointed with her other hand.

"Let it go. You're barmy, you can't train hens."

Still shouting above the chorus of the hens, she cried, "You can, you can train anything. Miss Newbourn said so."

"Da! Da!"

She heard his voice calling now and saw him standing on the low brick wall that edged the field.

In the next minute it seemed to her that the farmer must have sprung the two fields that divided them; and Luke's yelling had also brought his mother from the house, together with Dan from the barn.

"God in heaven! Let go that hen."

Taking small steps, her arm still taut, she circled the squawking hen while looking up at the farmer and saying, "It was pickin' Betsy to death." She indicated the almost nude Betsy with a sideward movement of her head.

"Let go the bloody thing." The farmer made to grab her hand and her arm jerked and the hen, being pulled some inches along the ground, became hysterical.

Now Jake Yorkless was gripping her wrist as in a vice, but he had to force her fingers from the handle of the whip and in this he was aided by his wife who was now holding her, crying as she did so, "You little vixen you! There'll be no whips used here unless it's on you, madam. Oh yes, unless it's on you. And that's what you want. I've said so from the beginning."

Emma stood aside now holding her wrist that seemed to be broken, and as she watched the farmer take the handle of the whip and bring it across his raised knee, her teeth became tight in an effort to stop herself from screaming.

The tears were raining down her face as he flung the broken whip at her feet, yelling, "You use that again, me girl, and I'll take it across your back. You hear me?" Then looking at the hen that was now staggering on its feet, he said, briefly, "One of the pullets." And his wife answered, "Yes, a good layer."

"Will it be all right?"

"I doubt if she'll lay after this fright. We'll see when I try them the night." And nodding now towards Emma, she finished, "If she doesn't lay regular you'll pay for her eggs with your threepences, miss."

Threepence a week, Dilly Yorkless reckoned, amounted to a shilling a month. She was no fool was the farmer's wife where counting was concerned. Moreover, with regard to the hens she knew how many eggs were to be expected each day, for on the previous evening she would make the rounds of the hens, trying them, as she termed her method of feeling how far the egg was ready to lay, so there was no chance of anyone helping themselves.

As they left the field, the farmer's wife's last words to Emma were, "You'll go short on rations the day, me girl. That'll learn you. An' wait till your granny comes up from the cottage, I'll have something to tell her."

The only bright spot in the day was when Barney came slyly up to her and with a broad grin on his face whispered, "Is it true you roped one of the hens an' set up a hullabaloo?" When she made no reply, only bowed her head, he went on, "I wish I'd seen it. You must be clever with a whip 'cos hens are sprightly on their feet when they want to be. And it was one of ma's best, the Rhodey." He started to chuckle now, then ended, "You're a funny little lass, aren't you?"

She raised her head and looked at him. He had brown hair, brown eyes, and a big mouth. It was a slack mouth but looked kindly. She liked Barney. She answered him sadly now, "They'll kill Betsy, the big ones; she has hardly any feathers on."

"That happens, it always happens with hens, they pick on the weakest. It's the same with all animals, you can't do anything about it."

She wanted to be cheeky and say, "Can't I?" because she was feeling angry inside. But what could she do? And they had broken her whip; her dada would have been so upset if he knew. Anyway, she still had the thong and she could make another handle, and she would. She was nodding to herself. Yes, she would, she'd make another handle and she'd practise on the quiet. She'd show 'em.

She had a mental picture of herself plying her dada's whip and bringing it round Farmer Yorkless's legs and when she saw his feet leave the ground and he fell on to his side, like a horse brought down by Uncle Tummond, she smiled to herself. Then the smile gave way to laughter, and now she was looking at Barney and on a giggle, she said, "It squawked louder than the pigs, it did." And on this he pushed her gently in the shoulder, saying, "You're a funny little Spanish onion."

The action of his hand told her she had at least found one friend in this place, but his words brought home the fact that she was different. How or why she couldn't as yet work out.

The missis and her granny were in the kitchen talking, and she sensed it wasn't nice talk. Although the words seemed ordinary they were talking about her. The missis was saying, "Anyway, you're more use up here."

"You're late in finding that out." Her granny's tone conveyed temper.

"No, I'm not late in findin' it out, but there was no other to take your place. Now there is, things are different."

"She's but a bit of a bairn."

"She's an old-headed bit of a bairn, if you ask me. And she's got to learn, anyway; she's on eight and you started when you were six, if I remember rightly."

"We both started when we were six, if I remember rightly."

"Oh yes, you remember rightly, Lizzie; you always remember rightly about that."

There was a short silence; then her granny's voice came again, saying, "She can't bake and make a meal for him."

"I'm not expectin' her to do it the day, or the morrow, but you'll take her with you for the next few weeks an' break her in. She can do the housework, what there is to be done, 'cos as you've said yourself he won't let you touch anything in his paint room."

Again there was silence; then her granny's voice said, "You know what you are, Dilly Tollett, you're a vindictive bitch."

"Don't you use that tone with me, Lizzie Crawshaw, or I'll have Jake speak to you."

"Oh you will, will you? And what will he be able to do?"

"He could take your job away."

"Huh! I can see him. I can see him and havin' to house someone decent, and feed them decent, and pay them decent. Oh . . . I can see him doin' that. And anyway, I'd still be on your doorstep, I'd still be in the cottage. You can't do anything about turfing me out of there, because it's in black and white. Payment to my mother for services rendered to the dirty old bugger his father was. And let me tell you, Dilly, if everybody had their rights this is the house she should've been in with me standin' where you are the day."

"Get yourself out afore I lose me temper."

"Oh, that'll be a pity. That's when you show your true colours, isn't it, when you lose your temper. You manage to cover them up most of the time, I must admit."

"Get yourself away. Go on, get yourself away."

There was a long pause before Emma heard the kitchen door bang. Then a minute later she saw the missis standing in the pantry doorway. Her face looked red, her lips were pressed tight together, and she wagged her head from side to side before saying, "Get yourself out of that and go with your granny. Leave it! Leave it!"

Emma dropped the cloth with which she had been wiping down the pantry shelves back into the bucket and went out, drying her hands on her coarse apron. But she had to squeeze past the missis in the doorway because she hadn't moved, and when she looked up at her she couldn't see her face for the quick rising and falling of her bust.

Her granny was in the cottage and she made no remark on her appearance except to say, "Take off your apron and roll it up. And go and put a comb through your hair."

As Emma now hurried towards the ladder her granny's voice halted her, saying, "Don't go up there, there's not time. Come here." And reaching to the low mantelpiece, she took down a black comb and for the first time in their acquaintance she touched her grandchild's head.

The combing wasn't gentle but it wasn't rough because when her granny came to a tat she held the upper part of her hair in her hand while she combed through it.

It was a nice feeling having her hair combed, it was nice to feel her granny's hand on her hair. It came to her suddenly that she could like her granny, in fact she did like her, and she imagined what it would be like if her granny were to put her arms about her. Oh, that would be nice. She would like that.

Without further words they left the cottage and went out, but not through the farmyard; her granny led her round by the back of the farm buildings. Their journey took them across three fields until they came to a cart track, and it was as they stepped on to this that her granny began to talk. With no lead up, she said, "Behave yourself in front of Mr Bowman, he's a gentleman. An' whatever you see or hear when you're in the house, don't repeat it, ever." She turned her head sharply and looked at Emma, adding, "You understand?"

Emma nodded her head, and her granny went on, "You likely heard what went on back there, you've got ears. You know somethin'?" She now stopped in her tracks and stared down at Emma. "Her and me were brought up together, played together, worked together, were young lasses together. Now would you credit it? She was brought up in the cottage where we're going to now. Her da was the ploughman, mine the shepherd. Old man Yorkless, his wife had died so my mother saw to the house . . . an' to him. Aye and him. Jake fancied me. Aye he did. But that one"—her head jerked backwards—"got her hooks into him and saw to it that he had to marry her. Anyway he was no cop, big gormless lout, and I mightn't have had him had he offered, even with all that was tagged on to him. I didn't mind her having him, not at first. Some of us have got to be lucky I thought, until she started to play the lady, imitating the Hudsons." Her head jerked to the left. "They're the big farmers over yonder. Visits them she does, him and her. And goes to church on Sundays. My God!"

Her last statement seemed to swing her from the ground and she was hurrying forward again, Emma having to trot to keep up with her.

They had come in sight of a stone cottage situated seemingly at the end of the cart track on one side and fronted by a road on the other when her granny spoke again, saying almost to herself, "She can't stop me seeing him. I'm finished at seven. Then there's Sunday."

Emma had noticed the pony and trap standing in the shade of a tree at the other side of the road before her granny had. The sight of it caused her granny's step to slacken, and when they came abreast of it she stopped and looked at it, then turned her gaze on to the front door of the cottage. It was open and while she paused before going towards it there appeared in the doorway two figures. One of them Emma recognized immediately as the parson who had been kind to her on the day of her arrival. And the recognition was mutual for the parson, stepping on to the rough path, smiled broadly towards her, saying, "Well, well, my companion of the coach. How are you?" He came up to her as she answered, "Quite well, sir." He looked towards Lizzie, saying now, "And this is your granddaughter?" It was a question and when Lizzie didn't answer immediately, Emma said, "Yes, sir."

The parson was speaking to her granny now, saying, "I've been meaning to come and visit you, and I'm just getting round to it now. The parish is very scattered and the days fly." He paused a moment before adding, "I am sure that you are delighted with your granddaughter; she is very good company."

Still Lizzie did not speak and there seemed no need, for now the parson had turned to the other man saying in a different tone, "I'll call on my way down again, Ralph." Then he added, "This is the greatest surprise and pleasure I've had for many a long day."

"Me too, Henry. Me too."

Emma decided that the one they called painter man had a nice voice. They both had nice voices, different from them at the farm. She couldn't understand some of the things that were said up there, especially when the boys were talking.

The parson was looking down on her again, saying, "You haven't been to Sunday school yet, have you?"

"No, sir. No, sir."

"Well, you must come on Sunday. I understand that the farmer's boys attend; you must come with them. I'll look forward to seeing you."

Emma noticed that he hadn't asked permission of her granny. But he was speaking nicely to her granny now, he was even shaking her hand as he was saying good-bye to her. Yet her granny hadn't opened her mouth to him.

Emma watched him get into the trap and when he lifted his hand to wave good-bye she was in the act of responding when her granny muttered, " 'Tisn't for you." And looking to the side, she saw the painter man waving and of course she knew she had been wrong to think that the parson was waving to her. Still he had been nice to her. She liked him, she liked him very much. Would her granny let her go to Sunday school? What was Sunday school? She'd have to find out.

She was in the cottage now. It wasn't really unlike their own cottage, only much bigger and it had furniture in it. An oak table was set under one window, and a big leather chair stood to the side of an open fire which was set in a high grate with an oven next to it.

Fronting the fireplace was a brass fender and a brass stand from which hung a long pair of tongs and a poker. Two wooden chairs and a stool completed the furniture in the room. However, what drew Emma's eyes straightaway was the colour that seemed to flood the room, for there was hardly an inch of wall space that was not covered with frameless pictures, all set higgledy-piggledy yet seeming to fit one into the other like a puzzle.

The man was looking at her now and smiling; then dropping on to his hunkers, his face level with hers, he said, "Hello, Emma."

Her eyes flickered up to her granny, then back to him, and she said, "Hello, sir."

"What's your other name?"

"Emma"—she paused—"Crawshaw."

He now brought his face forward until it was only inches from hers. She could see that his eyes were bright and laughing as he said, "Your real name, your dada's name?"

Again she was looking at her granny, but longer this time. Her granny though made no indication of how she should answer, so she answered in the way she wanted to and with pride as she said, "Emaralda Molinero."

He repeated her name, "Emaralda Mol . . . in . . . ero. That's a beautiful name, much nicer sounding than Crawshaw." He glanced up at Lizzie, and on this she swung round and went down the room and passed through a doorway.

Rising from his hunkers, he pointed towards the wooden stool, saying, "Sit down."

Obediently she sat down, and he now seated himself in the leather chair opposite and stared at her, his head slightly to the side. He stared at her until she began to feel hot, and then he said, "You're beautiful. Do you know that, Emaralda?"

She was about to say no, when her granny's voice rang in her ears, crying, "Don't talk like that to her, her head'll be turned soon enough. And there's no room for beauty in her life and what it'll bring."

"There's room for beauty in everybody's life, Lizzie, and all the sourness in the world won't drown it."

"She's but a child and. . . ."

"Well, the sooner she learns to appreciate the beautiful things in life the better for her."

Emma stared somewhat apprehensively at the painter now. He

sounded angry, and he looked angry; his blue eyes had lost their laughter. She watched him take his hand and ruffle his thick hair that was very long, almost on to his shoulders. He wasn't very tall, something of the height of Charlie Lamb the boxer. She often likened people to Charlie Lamb the boxer, she didn't know why. But then Charlie had been thickset and strong. This man was thin, thinner than the parson, and his face looked pale. But it was a big face, and he had a big mouth an' all. All his features appeared large, yet in her mind they seemed to fit his face because he looked nice, not bonny nice, just nice.

Her granny, grabbing her hand, almost whipped her from the stool. She took her through the door into the other room. This she recognized as the kitchen, but it was a very small kitchen. Besides the fireplace and oven, it held only a little table, a pump which stood over the stone trough, a plate rack on the wall, and a small delf rack and cupboard. Through the open back door she could see a paved yard, with outhouses of some sort beyond. One thing more she noticed in the kitchen was a ladder attached to the wall, and this she guessed was used to reach a roof space similar to the one in their own cottage, but bigger of course.

Her granny was speaking to her now, saying, "Put that apron on and then peel eight taties out of that basket"—she pointed down towards the side of the sink—"and a turnip an' some carrots, an' don't take all day over them. If you want water you pump it." She now pushed the handle of the pump up and down, and a spurt of water fell into the sink. Next, she tied a rough coarse apron over the white bibbed one she was wearing, and went into the other room.

Emma had to concentrate on peeling the potatoes for she found she was continually glancing out of the small window above the sink. The fields beyond stretched endlessly away. Some were bright yellow, some brown, some black. Her eyes grown used to the distance, she espied a ploughman and a host of seagulls trailing behind him.

She was telling herself that she liked this cottage, it was a much better cottage than theirs, and she liked the painter man, when his voice came to her, saying softly but loud enough for her to hear, "Don't worry about me, Lizzie." The tone sounded impatient. "I get along five days in the week, don't I? No, six days in the week, counting hours, and I'll be pleased to have the child."

She stopped what she was doing and put her head to one side in order to hear her granny saying, "You won't miss me then?"

"Oh, Lizzie. Lizzie."

"You didn't always say my name like that, your memory's short."

"Oh, Lizzie; the years are going on, I'm no longer the sick boy needing comfort and you're no longer. . . ."

Emma dropped the carrot into the dish and waited, and her granny's voice came almost in a whisper, a bitter sounding whisper, "I'm getting old, I've hit forty. I'm past it, that's what you think."

"No Lizzie, no, that's not what I think. I'm still fond of you. You know that. I'll ever be grateful to you for all you did for me years ago, and have continued to do."

"But you don't want me to continue any more."

"*No! No!* You get me wrong."

"Oh yes; you can say what you like. But you've no objection to the bairn taking over. If I can't come here during working hours there's only the late evening or Sunday, and it only needs them out for their walks to see me here on a Sunday and the tongues'll wag. And Dilly and Jake, pious as they are now, will be on to you to move."

"I doubt it." The painter's voice sounded calm now. "As you've so often pointed out, the two shillings a week I pay for your services pays your wages up there. And who else would pay six pounds ten a year for a place like this? Oh no, they won't ask me to go and they can't turn you out, so I don't think you need fear in that quarter."

"That being said, you don't mind if you don't see me again?"

"Oh Lizzie, how can you say such a thing?"

In the ensuing silence Emma put the cleaned potatoes, turnips, and carrots into fresh water. Then she dried her hands and stood looking about her before moving tentatively towards the living-room door, and there she stopped, brought still with mouth agape by the sight of her granny standing with her arms around the painter, and he holding her. And her ears seemed to stretch as she listened to her granny saying in a voice that she had never heard her use before, "You're all I've got in life, Ralph, don't throw me aside. I'd die. I tell you I'd die. Seeing you is all I live for, there's nothing else."

"You have the child now." The painter's voice was soft.

"Oh that, she means nowt to me. She's but the sperm of that Spanish circus man."

"She's a beautiful child and an engaging one, the little I've seen of her."

"Yes. Well, it won't do her any good; looks like she's got never does, together with her temper."

"She's got a temper?"

"I'll say she has, I told you about the hen business. Well, she stood up to Luke the other day an' all. She doesn't like him. I don't meself.

He's a bully of a boy yet she stood her ground with him and he didn't like that."

"Good for her."

"But us, Ralph; you'll never say you don't need me, will you?"

"No, Lizzie, no; I'll never say that."

Emma's eyes spread wide as she watched her granny hold the painter's head in her two hands and put her mouth to his. Her mouth was still on his when she turned back to the kitchen and stood against the sink biting hard on her lip. She had seen her dada and mama kissing and somehow that was right, but her granny was an old woman. And the painter man . . . was he old? No, he wasn't old, not like her granny.

Her granny said she hadn't to let on about anything she saw or heard down here, but it came to her in a puzzling sort of way that the missis up at the farm already knew. And that was why she was sort of happy in stopping her granny from working for the painter.

She didn't know whether she was sorry for her granny or not because she had turned into somebody else, somebody who was no longer an old woman.

5

She had been seven times to Sunday school. She would go down to the village walking behind the boys, on two occasions tramping knee-deep through the snow; this very much against her granny's wishes.

Although by her granny's own words she now knew that she meant nothing to her, it had not altered her own feelings towards her and she kept trying to please her. She obeyed her in most things, yet when she had tried to stop her going to Sunday school she had raised a fuss, even going to the length of using a form of blackmail by saying she would ask the missis for permission instead, and she'd let her go. This had caused her granny to stare at her in a very odd way and say something that she didn't fully understand, which was, "Your brain's too big for your head, and your head's too big for your body, miss, and it'll explode on you one of these days."

She had got her own way that day, and now she was once more tramping through slushy snow on this particular Sunday on her way to St Jude's.

Apart from what she learned in Sunday school she liked going through the village for the people spoke nicely to her, but most of all on a Sunday she liked talking to the parson.

Emma hadn't had any experience of churchmen of any kind so she wasn't to know that this parson was very unusual: he wasn't pompous as most parsons were, he wasn't always talking about heaven or hell as most parsons did, and he didn't insist on the boys sitting separate from the girls in Sunday school. But Miss Wilkinson didn't approve and as soon as the parson had finished his lesson she would split them up and in no gentle way. The children would wait for this and giggle and laugh during the change-over.

Sometimes Emma would try to walk with Barney, but when she did so Luke would take his place on the other side of her. She had come to recognize that everything the twins had they shared. Not so Pete and

Dan; these two fought continually, and not in fun but often with a viciousness that left them scarred in knees and shins.

Moreover, besides the pleasure of learning her letters and the Bible, which in a way seemed secondary except that she liked some of the stories, she had met other little girls like herself: Lily Mason the butcher's daughter, Angela Turnbull the grocer's daughter, and Jane Tate, whose father kept the inn, they were all nice to her. Angela Turnbull nearly always gave her a sweet, and this she looked forward to.

The room behind the vestry was cold and the breaths of the children rose like steam. She was sitting between Barney and Luke, and Luke kept nudging her with his hip which distracted her attention from what the parson was saying. He was telling the story of Jesus and about Him liking little children.

When an extra strong nudge came from Luke, Barney put his hand behind her and pushed at Luke, and Luke just grinned at him. But he stopped his nudging.

Then the parson was saying: "Miss Wilkinson is going to take you for your letters. I hope you have done a lot of work on them this week. I'll be looking at them later. God bless you all." And they answered in chorus, "God bless you too, Parson."

Immediately he left the room Miss Wilkinson's arm came out, her finger pointing, and it scrambled them as a fork might have done eggs. And now Emma was sitting next to Angela Turnbull and Angela pushed something into her hand and when she looked down at it her eyes widened with pleasure for the gift was a coloured sugar stick. She had the desire to put her arms around Angela and kiss her, but she knew you mustn't put your arms around people and kiss them; it was bad. She hadn't thought it was bad until she had seen her granny and the painter, because in the travelling show, which life now seemed to have taken place some long, long time ago, people often hugged each other, especially if there had been a very good audience. Or they'd had a fine meal and some bottles of beer. But what she said to Angela was, "Oh ta, thanks, thank you. You are kind." And Angela smiled her plain round-faced rosy-cheeked smile and basked in the gratitude of her dark, bright-eyed companion who looked different from all the other children in the village.

After the lesson was over in which they had learned to spell Bible, Jesus, Mary and Joseph, Holy Land, and lastly, an absolute puzzler, a frightener to both the tongue and the hand . . . Jerusalem, they all scrambled thankfully outside, there to be greeted by the parson who patted each one on the head and gave him a word. As usual he left

Emma to the last, and today, bending over her, he said, "How are we getting along, Emma?"

"Fine, Parson. Fine."

"You like coming to Sunday school?"

"Oh aye, yes."

"Have you a book at home?"

"A book?" She narrowed her eyes and then shook her head, saying, "No Parson, I haven't got a book."

"Well then, I want you to take this." He now handed her a small parcel, saying, "It's a little book of simple stories, together with a writing pad and a pencil."

"A real pencil?"

Her mouth was wide and he nodded at her, his wide too, saying, "Yes, a real pencil, not a slate pencil, a vine pencil."

"A vine pencil?" She made a small movement with her head that indicated incredulity. "And I'll be able to draw like on slate"—she now indicated the church with her thumb—"back there?"

"You will indeed, just like on the slate."

"Oh, thank you, thank you, Parson."

"You're very welcome, Emma. I'm sure you'll make good use of it."

During this exchange the four boys had been standing a little apart looking on as they usually did when the parson spoke to Emma. They couldn't quite understand why he always kept her till the last and why he wanted to talk to her. They had remarked on this to their mother and her explanation had been that the child was ignorant, much more ignorant than others, and wild with it, and the parson was trying to calm her down, make her normal like. So they stood watching the parson making Emma normal like. They all noticed how her face shone, and they were all touched by something they couldn't as yet explain to themselves. Perhaps Luke understood the tangent that was attached to this feeling, and the tangent urged him to destroy the cause of the feeling, and this he attempted to do on his way home.

They hadn't gone far along the road when Pete said, "Open it, Emma, and let's have a look."

"When I get home," she answered. "I might drop it and it'll get all slush."

"You haven't got butter-fingers, have you?"

She turned and glanced at Luke, saying primly, "No I haven't got butter-fingers, but I don't want to open it till I get home."

"Leave her alone." It was Barney speaking to Luke now; and Luke replied, "I'm not touchin' her. But she's Parson's pet an' she sucks up to him, else why didn't he give us books and pencils, make us all alike?

'Taint fair. 'Taint fair. Anyway she's nowt but a charity bairn. That's what Ma says, she's a charity bairn."

"I'm not! I'm not!" Emma didn't know exactly what the term charity bairn implied but that it was something detrimental was conveyed by Luke's sneer.

Saying, "Yes, you are!" Luke thrust out his hand to grab the little parcel, and when she pressed it to her with both hands and cried in childish retaliation, "Leave go or I'll slap your face mind," he bawled at her, "You'll what? I'll show you."

And now he was wrestling with her amid the cries of the three brothers, Barney protesting but Pete and Dan egging him on.

When the little parcel was wrenched from her hands and it fell into the mud, they sprang apart and looked at it for a moment; and now there arose in Emma a feeling that turned her into a vixen, a trapped vixen, and in this moment it was well that she hadn't the whip in her hand. But without it and against this big boy her hands seemed useless; yet as always when in a fix she was finding her mind would hark back to the company and it did at this minute. And as this fix was a fight her thoughts concentrated on Charlie Lamb the boxer. She had watched Charlie practising but never in the ring because her dada had never allowed her to go into the boxing tent. But she now recalled a particular movement of his; he doubled his fists tight, pushed his left arm straight out, then swung his right arm in a curve, she now did just this, and had her head been on a level with that of Luke's she might have caused him more damage than she did: her left fist coming with almost lightning speed caught him unawares under the chin. He had his mouth open and his lower jaw being suddenly pushed upwards, caused him to bite his tongue. And as he went to yell out, Emma's small right fist coming upwards caught him on the side of the nose, and when the blood spurted both from between his lips and down his nostrils there was consternation.

The bleeding wasn't heavy but it was enough to stain the pocket rags of his three brothers, and when he began to run homewards his brothers followed him, even Barney deserted her, and she was left standing in the muddy road looking down at the little parcel that had now been trampled on.

After picking it up she made no attempt to clean it but held it tightly to her, oblivious of the mud marking her coat, and she too made her way home.

She was trembling in every limb as she approached the farmyard. She was very sorry now for hitting Luke. But he had hurt her and nipped her in different places as they struggled for the parcel. She shouldn't have hit him so hard to make him bleed though; but anyway, he was bigger than her and older than her. She looked down at her small mud-covered hands. She'd get wrong: the missis would likely go for her.

The missis certainly did go for her. She was awaiting her approach outside the kitchen door and she didn't give Emma any time to defend herself against the accusation, but crying, "You wicked little bitch you!" she grabbed her by the coat collar and hauled her into the kitchen, and there before the staring eyes of the family she tore the parcel from her now limp grasp and threw it into the heart of the fire. Then taking a leather shaving strop that was hanging to the side of the fireplace beneath a small mirror, she again grabbed hold of her before bringing the strop viciously around her legs between the top of her boots and the bottom of her coat.

Although Emma had woollen stockings on, the leather stung her into a dance and as she howled out in pain Dilly Yorkless yelled above the narration, "I'll learn you, if nobody else will; you're not gona bring your circus tricks here. You're a wicked ungrateful little bitch." She now threw the strop down but, still holding Emma, she hauled her outside into the yard and as a final gesture she brought her hand in a sweeping slap across the side of the child's face.

It should happen that Billy Proctor had just come out of the cowshed and, seeing what was happening, came hurrying over, saying, "Let up, missis. Let up."

"You mind your own business, Proctor."

"Me business or not, she's but a child, you could have knocked her deaf."

"And that I will. I'll knock her brains out if she as much as raises her hand again to anybody in my family. You should just see what she's done to Luke."

"Luke? Huh!" The cowman was laughing. "Her go for the big 'un?"

"Yes, she went for the big 'un, as you call him, and he's bleeding from the nose and mouth."

As Emma, now swaying on her feet and crying loudly, staggered past the cowman, Billy gave one glance at his mistress before turning with the child and leading her out of the yard and towards the cottage. There he explained to Lizzie the little he knew, ending by saying, "I heard the bairn screamin' in the house when I was inside the sheds. She must have been at her there."

"What did she do to you?" Her granny was bending down to her now and Emma, still sobbing, pointed down towards her ankles.

Lizzie pushed her towards the cracket and when she was seated she pulled down one stocking to reveal a number of weals and scratches, some oozing blood; then looking up at Billy Proctor, she said bitterly, "My God! She'll answer for this. She will that." Then turning to Emma, she commanded, "Stop it! Stop that snivelling and tell us what happened."

Brokenly now Emma related the incident as she recalled it, and when she ended Lizzie said, "Well, where's the thing that caused all the trouble?"

"She . . . she put it in the fire."

Lizzie was looking up at the cowman as she said slowly, "If ever there was a spiteful bitch in this world, she's one, Billy." And he, nodding down at her, said, "You're right there, Lizzie. Put the devil on horseback and he'll ride to hell, but when he has a skirt on he goes twice as fast. Never you worry, lass, I don't, I just keep tellin' meself I'll see me day with them, for they're a mean lot. And hypocrites, into the bargain: sitting in church every Sunday mornin' and old Crabtree closing a blind eye to all that was going on as long as his share was left in the vestry. But this young one's different." He now bent over Lizzie and laughed into her face as he said, "They're all up a gum tree, they're shakin' in their boots 'cos he doesn't take it. Milk or water's his drink and he's put it over from the pulpit an' all, the evils of strong liquor." Billy's shoulders were shaking now as he went on, "In The Tuns last night they were on about it. Even George Tate's belly wobbled until he had to give over laughing. Of course it would be a good thing for his custom if it was stopped, but they might as well try to stop the tide comin' in, eh Lizzie? . . . I wonder what the young parson would say if he knew what he was sitting on, or preaching on, 'cos it must run right under the pulpit."

" 'Tis a pity somebody doesn't tell him, if it was only to potch that lot over there"—she jerked her head to the side—"because he's got a well-stocked cupboard. . . . For two pins. . . ."

"Aw now, Lizzie." The cowman straightened his back and, his face grave, he said, "Never do owt like that. Don't even think 'bout it, 'cos you'd have the village down on you, most of 'em anyway. And then there's the House. Mr Fordyke's in on it you know, and even does a run when he's down from London town. And you know something?" He grinned at her now. "I think Miss Christina Leadbeater, Spinster, likes being handled. If she'd had half the men lifting her in her lifetime as she's had since lifting her headstone, she wouldn't have remained a spinster long, eh?"

"Enough of that. Look, hand me that dish with the water in, there, till I clean these legs, and then I'm goin' over there. And if you're in the cowshed, Billy, and the door's shut you'll still be able to hear what I say."

As the cowman went out laughing Lizzie said quietly, "It's all right, hinny, I won't hurt you. It's just that I must get the black hairs from your stockings out of these scratches or else you'll have trouble later on."

Emma sat quiet now for replacing the terror and pain that she had recently experienced was a warm feeling which encircled her, for her granny was speaking kind to her. She didn't mind if her legs did get bad, in fact she hoped they would because her granny would then see to them.

PART TWO

The Friend

1

Emma had been on the farm for two years now and she had learned many things and managed to create some pleasures for herself, secret pleasures that could only be enjoyed in the night. For the rest she had been forced to understand the difference in position between the boys in the farmhouse and herself. This situation had come about after the time the farmer's wife had thrashed her. From that day she had been given to understand that she was a servant and the meanest of the type; consequently, when her granny wasn't present the treatment was rough. The boys were forbidden to speak to her, and they didn't, with the exception of Barney who would sometimes give her a word on the sly. But this didn't stop Luke or the two younger ones from setting traps for her, such as laying trip ropes or attempting to push her over when she was in the pigsty, all without uttering a word and so obeying the commands of their mother.

But during the last year she had found a way to come back on them. Should they succeed in knocking her down she would no longer cry, but from where she lay she would twist like an eel and throw handfuls of pig slush at them, and her aim was nearly always direct.

During this time Emma had acquired three staunch friends: one on the premises in the form of the cowman Billy Proctor. Then there was Mr Bowman the painter. They had become talking friends. Although at times she couldn't grasp the meaning of what he was saying, he made her laugh. And then there was the parson. Oh she liked the parson. When he visited the farm he always went out of his way to see her. If she should be working in the barn or down in the hen field, he'd make a point of having a word with her, and sometimes he would say, "I've left a little parcel for you in the cottage, Emma." And she knew it would be a book with holy pictures in it or a pad and pencil. Last Easter he had given her a picture made up of pressed wild flowers, and she had nailed it to a post in the roof.

Then there were her secret pleasures, and they *were* secret, no one knew about them, not even her granny, least of all her granny. For had her granny known that on certain nights she got out of the hatch door and clambered down the broken ladder that had three rungs missing, she would have undoubtedly torn the ladder from the wall and nailed up the hatch.

Her granny was a heavy sleeper and was in the habit of snoring so she never made her escape until the snores were deep. And she also pushed some straw into a hump under the blanket because she knew that once or twice her granny had come up the indoor ladder and poked her head through the trap door, but had not as yet ventured further, for this would have meant crawling on her hands and knees across the floor to where the pallet was.

When first the urge came on her to walk in the moonlight, she hadn't thought of taking the whip with her, until one night, having wandered the length of the farm, she had come to the wood that separated the farm boundary from the Fordyke land. It was called Openwood. Her granny had explained that the land yon side of the wood had once been common land, open to the people of Fellburn village and thereabouts to graze their cattle on, and when Mr Fordyke claimed it as his, he had railed it in. But he hadn't railed the wood, perhaps because it was a dirty wood, being full of scrub, yet it held some good big trees and the villagers gathered kindling from the twigs and there would have been a hullabaloo had he gone the whole hog and railed it in an' all.

It was just as she crossed the border of the wood, for she was really fearful of entering it and so hadn't as yet plucked up the courage to do so until this night, that she had, as she put it, almost jumped clean out of her skin when she saw shadowy forms passing before her. She was too terrified to scream and had become immobile; and this likely had saved her from being noticed, for with her dark head and black cloak she had merged into the scrub against which she stood.

However, so great was the fright she got this particular night that it put a stop to her wanderings for some weeks. But the next time the moonlight became irresistible she took with her the small whip for which she had painstakingly made a new handle. What she hoped to achieve with it were she surrounded by a group of men didn't enter her mind, she only knew she felt safer carrying the whip.

Her second pleasure was a daylight one and it was her discovery of the river. She had been six months at the farm before she really saw the river, and it only two miles away. It was Billy Proctor who took her down one Sunday afternoon, and as she stood on the bank and looked at the different kinds of ships, forming a panorama that stretched away along both banks and made up of scullers, keel boats, barges, small sailing vessels, and large ones that looked gigantic to her eyes, she had been speechless. Even when Billy had said to her, "Don't you think that's a bonny sight?" she hadn't replied until he came back with, "You don't like the river then?"

Then she had cried, "Oh! yes. Yes, it's beautiful, lovely. I've never seen so many ships."

"Oh, this is nowt," Billy had said; "it's dead on a Sunday. But from the morrow morning at five o'clock when it comes alive, you've never seen owt like it." Then he had ended somewhat sadly, "I wanted to go to sea as a lad, but they wouldn't let me. They were gettin' old and had to be kept, an' when they both went I was too old for change, too old to run up a riggin'."

Emma realised he was talking about his parents and was sad because he hadn't been able to go to sea. She liked Billy; she wished she could make him happy in some way.

On that particular Sunday, Billy had walked her back through Openwood, and she had become excited, running here and there, trying to recognize the paths she followed in the moonlight. It didn't look so nice in the daytime, and not all that big; in fact, when the trees were bare you could see through it from one end to the other and into the field beyond. One thing in the wood appeared new to her, and that was the big oak. She couldn't remember seeing a tree as big as that before. Yet some of the trees she did recognize and they looked smaller in the daylight.

As she stood looking at the trunk of the oak tree there came into her mind a picture of her dada throwing knives at such a tree. He had marked a head and body on it that was almost a replica of her mama's and his aim was accurate, each dagger striking the tree two inches outside the chalk line. It came to her that she would like to practise with her dada's knives. She knew she could throw straight but she also knew there was a great difference between throwing a ball or a stone straight with a flick of the wrist and the strength of the wrist needed to throw the knives. But it was just a thought, and it slipped out of her mind as quickly as it had come in.

But from that day, whenever she could, with or without Billy, she went and looked at the river and the boats, and so used did she become to the short cuts across the fields and through the wood that she told herself she could find her way there blindfold.

*

For the past six months she had taken over her granny's duties for the painter. Two mornings a week she went to the cottage and cleaned it, all except the paint room; she peeled vegetables to make his broth, and she cooked him pancakes, but as yet she didn't bake his bread. The missis sent him down two loaves a week for which she charged him tenpence, and ninepence a dozen for his eggs, some of them only pullets', which her granny said was downright robbery because you could get them anywhere else for fourpence a dozen or sixpence at the most.

There were times when the painter took a day off and strolled to the fish quay on the river and he would bring back a dozen or more fresh herring. She would get them, bone them and, after rubbing them with sage leaves and salt, would roll them up and put them in a dish in the oven. She liked these days for he would say to her, "Tuck in, Emma," and she tucked in because she loved herrings; moreover, she always felt hungry.

This morning she was on her hands and knees, a bucket by her side, scrubbing the stone floor of the living-room, and when the painter stepped over the clean part to stand on the step of the cottage she paused a moment in her scrubbing to look at him because he was speaking.

"It's a beautiful morning, Emma," he said. "Too nice a day to be buried, and Henry's burying his grandfather today."

Henry, she knew, was the name of the parson and she had heard that his grandfather had died and he had gone back to his home to take the burial service.

"Nice fellow, Henry. He should never have been a minister." He turned and looked down at her. "Last person in the world I would have thought would have taken the cloth. A rip when he was a lad, up to every kind of mischief and trick you could imagine. He was up to us older ones. Me, I could give him six years but I always looked upon him as an equal." He smiled down at her, then looked out again as he went on, as if talking to himself, "Life's queer and yet it has a pattern. There we were, brought up within a few miles of each other in that picturesque village and we went our different ways. I, of course, went mine long before he went his and now here we are, come together like two immigrants in a foreign country, because you know, Emma"—he was glancing down sideways at her now—"this is a foreign country, a rough alien foreign country, where the folks appear kind on the surface but are devious beneath. Oh yes, Emma"—he was nodding at her—"devious, that is the word. Your mistress up above"—he thumbed in the direction of the farm—"and her man, they are good examples. And the farm worker, all the farm workers, whether they be quiet or loquacious, they're all devious. They look at you and they can tell you weren't born here, so you are somebody strange, somebody to be taken down in one way or the other, someone to drag a penny out of. But there again, that streak doesn't run through only one class. Oh . . . oh no. Your For-dykes are another example, only they go one better, they don't wait to do the foreigner, they take it out of the skin of their servants and all those under them. Yet they are not as bad as the mine owners. Oh, no, no, Emma. You know something? If I want to draw a leech or a tyrant I think of a coal owner getting his pennies out of children's sweat. . . . Have you ever been down a mine, Emma?"

"No, Mr Bowman."

"Then you're fortunate. Do you know that? You're fortunate to be scrubbing that floor. And yet at times when I see you scrubbing that floor I want to drag you up from it. But then I say to myself, well if she doesn't scrub the floor Lizzie will come down and scrub the floor. And do I want Lizzie to come down and scrub the floor? No; I would rather have Emma." He was grinning at her now. Then turning about, he ended, "Life's very complicated, Emma, very complicated." And with this he stepped again over the clean part of her floor and was making for his studio when a giggle turned him round and he stared at her, his eyebrows raised, his mouth pulled down at the corners in an expression of enquiry.

"You're laughing at me, Emma?"

"I like to hear you talk, Mr Bowman."

"And you find what I say funny?"

"No." Her face became serious as she thought of an answer. "Not what you say but somethin' in your voice," she said.

She hadn't known what he would say to this but what she didn't expect him to say and in a loud voice was, "Hold it. Keep like that."

She found it difficult to obey his command because one hand was on the scrubbing brush on the floor, the other was splayed over the stone slab and her head was up and to the side. What was more, a beam of sunlight coming through one of the small glass panes in the window was shining right into her eyes. And now he was saying in a loud voice, "Remember just how you're kneeling, and what you're doing, can you?"

There was a long pause before she said, "I'll try, Mr Bowman."

"Then get up; bring that bucket and your brush and come in here."

She had never before been in the paint room; she had caught glimpses of it as he opened the door to go in, but all she had seen was the bare floor. Now he was propelling her into the room.

She put down the wooden bucket and quickly looked about her. It was a much larger room than the living-room which she now realised was really the original kitchen. To the side of the window was a large easel with a canvas on it and round the walls, four and five deep, similar canvasses were stacked. There were rafters in this room, as in the kitchen, and across them lay boards and on them what looked like rolls of brown material. There was a fireplace but no fire in it, and the only furniture in the room was a long wooden table, half of it covered with trays of paint. The other half held a slanted drawing-board with a stool on the floor in front of it.

"Get on your hands and knees again, Emma. Now remember how you looked next door."

She did as he bade her. Then he was squatting in front of her pushing her hand here, turning her head this way and that, scraping the wooden bucket to different positions on the floor. And then he said, "Don't smile."

She didn't feel like smiling, she felt cramped.

"Look at me. Can you think of something sad?"

"Oh yes." She could think of something sad, she could still recall quite clearly the last time her dada spoke to her.

He made her start when he cried, "That's it. That's it. Now just stay like that, Emma. Just stay. Just . . . stay . . . like . . . that."

He had rushed to the table and taken up a large pad; now he was squatting in front of her and he began to draw quickly.

She still tried to keep her thoughts on her dada and what he had said to her on that last occasion they were together. But other things began to intrude, such as what would her granny think when she knew she had been in the paint room? And she hoped the sun wasn't shining where the Parson was burying his grandfather, because it would be better to be buried if the sun wasn't shining.

"Just a minute more, that's it. Don't move your head."

The minute seemed to stretch into an hour before she heard the painter cry, "That's it. Enough to start on. . . . *Child with a bucket,* that's what I'll call you. *Child with a bucket.*"

She sat back on her heels now, asking, "Can I finish me floor?"

"Yes, finish your floor, Emma." There was laughter in his voice. "And do all the work you've got to do in the house today because on Thursday I want you to sit for me. Oh"—he laughed out loud as he saw the expression on her face—"not on your knees again, you can sit on a cracket." He pointed down to the floor. "And I just want to get your face as I saw it today."

She smiled at him now; then she asked a question.

"Can I tell me granny?"

His mouth formed a large pout now and he brought his chin into the soft collar of his shirt as he said, "No, Emma. No, don't tell your granny. This is just a secret between you and me. Eh? . . . Right?"

She smiled at him before she repeated the last word, "Right." She didn't add "Mr Bowman", and the thought entered her mind it was a good job her granny wasn't here, else she'd get a shaking for not minding her manners. Yet her granny didn't mind her manners when she was with the painter, she talked back at him, like the mistress did the master up at the farm. This would only happen of course when she herself was out of the way, but she had good ears and she kept them open. There was some deep connection between her granny and Mr Bowman that she couldn't quite explain to herself; in fact, she didn't want to explain it to herself, because she knew that once she found the explanation she wouldn't like it for it had to do with her granny kissing the painter. And she wanted to keep on liking her granny. Her granny was kind to her at times. She had given her a penny to spend on fair day down in the village. She had debated whether to buy a hair ribbon with it or some cinder taffy, and the cinder taffy had won. But she hadn't enjoyed the fair day because it reminded her of the company, and the people at the fair didn't seem nice like the members of the company. She hoped that the company would sometime come this way. But Mr Travers had always worked the circuit into Yorkshire and beyond. It appeared that people expected them at certain times and saved up for their coming. . . .

Her work finished, she knocked on the paint room door and when after a moment Mr Bowman's voice called, "Yes?" she said, "I'm off, Mr Bowman." And to this he answered, "Go on then. Go on then." His voice sounded short, full of impatience. Her granny had told her never to disturb him when he was in the paint room.

On her way back she had reached the second field when she saw Barney. He was mending a fence. Barney was now fourteen years old, he was growing not only tall but broad with it. Emma thought he looked nice. But Luke who had the same colouring and similar features with the exception of his mouth, which was thin and straight, didn't look nice to her. She thought his face looked mean, like his character.

Barney had stopped hammering the post in some time before her approach and when she came up to him he was standing, his arms by his sides, the hammer gently swinging backwards and forwards from one hand.

"Finished?" he asked.

She nodded at him before saying, "Yes."

"Do you like workin' down there?"

"Yes."

"Better than up here?"

What could she say to that? If it had been any of the others she might have lied, but to Barney she could say, "Yes, it's cleaner."

"You shouldn't have to see to the pigs. It's Dan's job, and he would do it, I know he would . . . only. . . ." He wagged his head in some embarrassment. And she put in quickly, "Oh, I don't mind, I like Fanny an' she knows me; even with the litter she never goes for me."

"No, she doesn't." Barney said this with some surprise in his voice as if the knowledge had just come to him, which it must have done because he went on, "When you come to think of it, she doesn't, and she's a bitch is Fanny. She's lifted Pete clean over the railings afore the day, an' she can't stand the sight of me da. You going to the river on Sunday?" He was looking down at the swinging hammer now, and she answered, "Perhaps, if Billy's goin'."

Her granny had made it an unwritten law that she didn't go anywhere by herself, especially to the river, for as her granny had once prophesied she could wake up on one of them boats out in the ocean and not know how she got there. Funny things happened on the river bank between Newcastle and Shields. What her granny would say . . . or do if she knew that she had got within sight of the river on a moonlight night only last week didn't bear thinking about. She still sometimes felt afraid on her midnight jaunts, but not so much now when she carried the whip with her.

"I might be going down to the river on Sunday meself. They say there's a great sailing ship in, one of the biggest yet. Masts almost touching the sky."

"Really?"

He nodded at her. "Aye, that's what they say. Tony Hudson was telling me. His da and granda had not only seen it, they'd been on it. They know the first mate."

"It must be wonderful to be on a boat, a big boat with sails."

"Aye." He nodded at her, then said thoughtfully, "Sometimes I wish I could go on a boat."

"You do? You don't like being on the farm?"

"Oh"—he wagged his head now—"sometimes; but sometimes I'd like to get away, be on me own you know. But . . . but there, I never will."

"Why not? People go away; they run away to boats."

"Aye, so I've heard." He was laughing at her now. "But I don't think I'm the runaway kind, haven't the gumption."

"Oh"—she was strong in his defence now—"yes you have the gumption. Yes you have, Barney. You're the best of the bunch."

He looked at her for fully a minute before he said, "I'm glad you think that, Emma. Aye I am. Eeh! well, better get on." He turned abruptly now and, lifting up the hammer, banged it down on top of the post, and she went on her way up to the house.

Barney was nice. There were a lot of nice people in the world to sort of make up for the other kind.

2

It had been stifling hot all day, but the wind had risen in the evening and had cooled things down, except under the roof. Emma knelt on the straw pallet and opened the worm-eaten hatch below the roof and let the wind waft round her. Her calico nightgown was sticking to her skin. She would like to go out, but it was a very dark night and the moon wouldn't be up till later.

After easing her nightgown from her body in several places she suddenly twisted round on the pallet, tore off her nightgown and, grabbing up her shift from the floor, she pulled it over her head, then drew on her print dress. Quickly now she pulled on her stockings and got into her boots, and finally, stretching up, she unhooked her black cape from a nail in the rafter post. She never went out at night without her cape, even as now when she only intended to go down by the burn. The water in the burn was very low but it still trickled over the stones and even the thought of it cooled her.

A few minutes later she was pushing herself backwards out through the hatch door and her feet were groping their way down the broken ladder and on to the rough grass.

The wind was stronger than she imagined for it billowed her cloak into a balloon so that she had to gather the two ends and hold them tight in front of her.

Surprisingly, the night wasn't as jet black as she had imagined and when her eyes grew accustomed to the darkness she found her way easily to the stone wall bordering the first field, then over this, across another field and so to the stile beyond which was the coach road.

She did not cross the stile but continued along the border of two more fields. When she came to the darker blur of a group of small trees she knew she had reached the bank of the burn with Openwood beyond.

It wasn't until she had taken off her boots and stockings and was standing in the cool of the water that she realised she hadn't brought her whip with her because she had been in such a scurry to get out.

Well, it didn't matter tonight, because she would be going straight back.

When the wind lifted her hair and brought it over her eyes she almost stumbled, then giggled softly to herself. That would be it, wouldn't it, if she fell in the water and wet her dress? How would she explain that to her granny? Then she told herself practically that even if it should get wet she could hang it up and, with the hatch left open, it would dry in the draught by the morning.

Gingerly now, she stepped on to the bank and after sitting down she tucked her feet up and dabbed them dry with the hem of her dress; then she pulled on her stockings and laced up her boots and was on the point of rising when she became transfixed into stillness by a muffled sound coming from further along the burn. It was a strange sound, not recognizable, like footsteps yet not like footsteps. One minute she could hear it, the next minute she couldn't. She was frozen with fear. Was it ghosties?

When the wind swirled the sound towards her once again she knew it wasn't ghosties, and like lightning now she scrambled up the bank. But immediately she realised she couldn't make her way home because she would have to pass the noise. So what she did was to run into the thicket that surrounded the trees of Openwood, and there she almost did die of shock for no sooner had she crouched down than she knew she was not alone, for she was touching something, and as the lesser of the two evils seemed to be the approaching noise she had opened her mouth to scream when a hand was clapped over it, and her back was pressed against a body. She then felt a hand going over her hair. It was a gentle touch which told her immediately it belonged to no one from the farm, not even to Barney, because there was no farm smell from whoever was holding her.

Now she was aware that the noise was coming nearer and she distinguished it as the careful tramping of a number of feet.

As she stared fixedly before her through the thin screen of bramble the burn bank became faintly illuminated by the dispelling clouds across the rising moon. The light wasn't strong enough to show up individual shapes but what she saw appeared to her imagination like a long animal with weird-looking humps on its back. It wasn't until the tail end of the animal had almost disappeared from her view that the moonlight becoming stronger showed her a man with a box on his shoulder.

The weird procession had passed some while before she felt herself drawn from the bushes. The hand was still around her mouth and when the fingers left her face and a head bent over her and a voice said softly, "Emma," she almost did yell out, but not any more in fear, just in sheer amazement because she recognized the parson. When she went to repeat his name it came out like a grunt from her throat. Then he was bending down to her, the dark blur of his face before her as he whispered harshly, "What on earth are you doing out at this time of the night, child?"

She gulped deeply before she could whisper back, "I was very hot, sweatin'. I came down to the burn to put me feet in."

She heard him sigh, then say, "What do you think would have happened to you if those men had seen you?"

"I don't know, I forgot me whip."

"You forgot your . . . ? Oh, dear Emma, your whip wouldn't have stood you in good stead tonight I'm afraid. Do you know who those men were?"

She surprised both him and herself now when after a moment's hesitation she said, "Yes, I think I do; they are smugglin' the liquor from the ships."

She saw his shape stretch upwards in the dim light of the moon; then he said, "Well! Well! And what more do you know about these men?"

"Only that those who help get a share of the bottles."

He now reached out to her and took her hand, saying softly, "Come, we'll sit down by the burn and have a little talk, for you seem to know as much, if not more, about these gentlemen than I do. And since you've been the means of stopping me finding out any more tonight, perhaps you'll tell me what more you know, eh Emma?"

When she was seated side by side with the dark-cloaked parson the moon came fully out and she turned and looked at him. His face looked very grave and his eyes large and dark, and she said to him, "The moonlight's nice on the water, isn't it? Coolin' like."

"Yes, yes, Emma, the moonlight's very nice on the water. But now, as we cannot remain here for very long because I'm sure that at least some of those gentlemen will be returning this way to their ship, I'm going to ask you again to tell me what more you know about their activities."

She gave a long audible sigh as she set herself to think. What did she know about the liquor running? Only that everybody seemed to know about it, well everybody of her acquaintance. And she said this.

"I don't know nothin' more than t'others, Parson; everybody seems to know about it an' that it's stuck in a place where the customs would never dream of lookin'."

"And where's that?"

"Oh, I don't know, except that it's in. . . ." She stopped and, her head going back, she screwed up her eyes as she peered at the scudding clouds now passing over the moon. What was it Billy had said to her granny that time the missis had knocked her about, something about the parson standing on the place, or some such?

His voice broke into her thoughts, saying with some urgency, "Yes, Emma, it's in where?"

"Well, I don't know, except Billy said to me granny about you standin' on the place where it was, or something like that."

"You mean the stuff is hidden near the church?"

"Yes, an' there was a name they mentioned but I can't remember it, Parson."

She watched the parson now put his head back and look up at the moon the while he talked to her, saying, "I've been on their trail three times of late and they mostly, I notice, pick a dry night to bring their catch in from the river, where I assume it is stored by the gentlemen who return this way because I've seen them coming back before. They are all very cute, Emma, very cute. I have kept watch on several nights but tonight was the only time I have been fortunate enough to watch them on their way inland. Then you, Emma"—he now glanced down at her—"almost frightened me to death when you appeared from nowhere and trod on my feet."

"I'm sorry, Parson." She didn't add that she herself had nearly died of fright.

"Well, the incident has its compensations for never have I enjoyed sitting by the burn like this before. But I'm afraid we must cut short this idyll. You must now hurry back and get into bed before your granny discovers you're missing."

"She won't, Parson; I hump the blankets up and she never comes through the let, just pokes her head in."

"You're a wicked child, Emma." His voice denied what his words implied and she laughed gently as he went on, "And what would she think of me keeping you standing out here, when I should be taking you by the collar and yanking you home?"

"Oh, she wouldn't say anything to you, Parson, because she thinks you're too good to be true."

Now it was the parson who made a strange sound in his throat, and after a moment he said, "Your granny thinks me too good to be true?"

"Yes, Parson; she's not like the rest of 'em, she has a good word for you."

"Indeed, and . . . and who do you mean by the rest of them?"

"Well. . . ." She felt slightly embarrassed now and didn't wish to go on in case she should implicate anyone in particular, but when he said, "Yes, Emma?" she muttered, "Well, them on the farm and down in the village and about."

"And what do them . . . they say about me?"

Her embarrassment grew; she felt she was telling tales, yet it wasn't really bad what they said about him and so she told him, "Well . . . well they say you seem to know everything that's going on in heaven, but . . . but you don't see what's goin' on under your nose."

"Is that what they say, Emma?"

"Yes, Parson."

"Well, well."

The moon was fully out again and she could see he was smiling as he asked now, "Is there anything else they say about me, Emma, that might help me to mend my ways and enlist their favour?"

She thought a moment, then said, "Well the only other thing they've got against you is you use big words. Old Parson Crabtree, the one that was afore you, they said called a spade a spade, and he only used big words when he had the bottle, I mean when he was drunk. Although I didn't know parsons got drunk, do they, Parson?"

"Some do, Emma; but go on."

"Well, that's all I can think of, Parson, except that Billy . . . Billy Proctor's for you, because he said you might be a fool, but you're no idiot."

She was now somewhat amazed at the sound that came from the parson, it was as if he were choking; and then bending down to her, his face close to hers, his eyes looking startlingly bright, he whispered, "You know something, Emma? I think the good Lord directed me here tonight precisely to meet you, and for you to enlighten me as to the measure my parishioners have of me. And not only that; I think He wanted to establish that we are going to be friends, firm friends. Will you be my friend, Emma?"

She had no hesitation in saying, "Oh, yes, Parson. Oh, yes, I'd like to be your friend."

"Then that is settled. And as a friend you will keep me informed of the opinion my parishioners continue to have of me, whether it changes for the better or for the worse. Will you, Emma?"

"Yes, Parson, but on the quiet like."

"Oh, yes." He chuckled now and repeated, "On the quiet like." Then his voice changing, he said, "One more thing, Emma, before we part, I want you to read all you can, use every spare moment you can to read and learn to use big words too. Any fool can call a spade a spade, Emma, even an idiot can call a spade a spade, but you have to be of a certain intelligence before you can use big words coherently. Now there's a word to set you puzzling . . . co . . . her . . . ent . . . ly.

Once a month I will give you a new book to read, and once a month I will test you on the big words. You understand?"

"Yes, Parson." Her voice sounded flat, she wasn't very enamoured of having to learn big words. She liked reading stories but up till now she had skipped the big words.

"Go now, child." He pushed her gently from him, then quickly caught hold of her shoulder, saying, "Do be careful when you come out at night, child. I would rather you promised me that you'll never take up this escapade again, but I feel it would be too much because your blood would drive you into the open. But go now, go now, and God bless you."

She went without further words and puzzling over why her blood should drive her into the open. That was a funny thing to say.

Once again, as she later said to herself, she almost jumped out of her skin when, having skirted the small barn and about to run across the open space to the cottage, she saw a movement in the yard. Through the dim and flickering moonlight she made out the tall figures of Farmer Yorkless and two of the boys, but from this distance she couldn't tell which two. And she shivered from the top of her head to the soles of her feet as she imagined what would have happened if the master had been in that trail of men and they had caught sight of her. He would have whipped her raw; if not he, then his missis would have done so.

Although they had now disappeared into the house she waited until the moon was hidden again by the clouds before she scurried towards the ladder and up through the hatch. And she was still shivering as she pulled off her boots and clothes and climbed under the blanket. But lying secure once more, her thoughts, now calm, traced back the happenings of the last hour, and what emerged was the highlight: the parson had asked her to be his friend. Oh, she liked the parson, she liked him better than anyone else on earth. Besides the honour of being friends with the parson, in some way it formed a barrier against hell.

It was as she was dropping off to sleep that the word Leadbeater came into her mind. And it was still there the following morning when she awoke. And she remembered where she had heard it. Billy had been telling her granny about it being on a headstone and her mind, groping back to the conversation, knew that the name was connected with the place where the liquor was hidden.

Now that would be something to tell the parson, wouldn't it? But she'd have to wait till Sunday.

*

It was on this day that Emma became aware of her body. The first instance took place in the grain shed. She had gone in to get some boxings to make the crowdy for the hens, and Luke happened to be there getting the horse fodder. She never spoke to Luke and he never directly spoke to her, but he talked at her whenever he was near her. This morning, however, his approach was different.

She knew he had gone towards the door and when he shut it and came back up between the wooden bins that held the grains she straightened herself and looked at him. He was a good head taller than her and he seemed to tower over her as he said, "Growin', aren't you?"

She made no reply, and he went on, "Ma says that you're black underneath, it's only your face that's become tanned with the sun, bleachin' it like. Are you black underneath?"

"No, I'm not!" Her voice was indignant.

"I don't believe you."

"I don't care if you believe me or not. Let me by, I've got to make the crowdy."

For answer his hands shot out and pulled the tin dish from her and threw it to the side so that the boxings sprayed out all over the stone floor, and as she gasped he said, "You can tell Ma that you tripped. She'll skin you 'cos they're good boxin's, an' she'll stop your pay for weeks."

She was still gasping in her throat, as she imagined the reaction of the missis, when he said, "Tell you what. I'll say it was an accident an' I dunched you if you let me see if you're black or not."

"Let me by." Her voice was trembling now.

"Who's stopping you?"

He had moved his hand to the side but in order to get past him she'd have to squeeze her body between him and the stanchion post of one of the bins and when she made no move to do so he moved, now almost throwing himself on her, his upper body pressing her backwards over the bin. While the palm of his left hand was tight under her chin thrusting it upwards and so preventing her from screaming, his right hand was pulling up her long skirt. But as his hands groped above her ragged garters that held up her black stockings and on to her bare flesh, there came into her small body a power bred of desperation.

She fought him with the strength of someone equal his size and age. When her back seemed to break, her hands left his hair and her nails found the flesh of his face and tore at it, and as the pressure on her chin was suddenly released she let out a piercing scream, and it seemed that the same instant she was tumbling backwards, legs over head, into the bin of soft boxings.

Almost choking from the boxings in her throat, she coughed and spluttered while clawing herself up the wooden frame, and as she gripped the edge and hung over the top she saw Barney and Luke facing each other in the corner of the grain shed. And Luke was saying, "I was only havin' a bit of fun with her."

"It looks like it by your face!" cried Barney. "If you weren't my brother, by God! I'd—" She saw Barney's head move from side to side, then he finished, "We've got on till now, but this I'm tellin' you, our Luke, you touch her again like that and that'll be the finish atween us. Mind, I mean it, I'll have no more truck with you. I've said it afore but I mean it this time."

"She's a troublemaker: there's been no peace since she came. And you've always taken her part."

Luke now moved towards the door, dabbing at his face with a piece of hessian, and Barney came towards her and, putting out his hands, he helped her out of the bin, and when she was unable to stand he put his arms about her and held her to him, saying, "There, there, it's all right. Don't cry."

She lay against him gasping and spluttering, "It wasn't me, Bar . . . Barney; he came at me and he spilt the boxings, and . . . and. . . ."

"It's all right. It's all right, Emma. I'll make it right with Ma, don't worry. . . ."

"My God! Let go of her."

Emma wanted to spring away from Barney's arms but at this moment she hadn't the strength; nor did Barney thrust her from him, but quietly pushed her against the support of the bin and turning, he faced his enraged mother, saying, "You can't blame her."

"Get out of here; I'll deal with her."

"Oh no, Ma, fair's fair."

"What did you say?"

"I said, fair's fair. It was Luke's fault; he was at her, trying it on."

"She egged him on, he's just told me. That chit"—she thrust out her arm, her finger now almost touching Emma's face—"egged him on. That's her Spanish blood comin' out. Shameless they are, those women."

"Ma—" He had moved so that he was standing in front of Emma now. His voice slow and his words emphatic, he said, "You would like to believe that. I'm tellin' you I saw him. He had her bent double over the bin, in fact she fell into it. He had his hand up her clothes."

"Shut up you! Get out of here."

"No, I won't, Ma. Oh no, I won't."

"My God! boy. Do you know who you're talking to?"

"Yes, Ma, I know; and I'll do what I told you an' me da I'd do only a few weeks ago, I'd up and go off to sea if there was any more trouble. That's what I'll do."

He watched his mother take in one long deep breath; then she spat at him, "You're but a boy."

"I'm doin' a man's job here, Ma, and I could do a man's job on board ship. Many've done the same thing afore me. Aye, many have."

At this point Lizzie appeared in the doorway and, taking in the situation at a glance, she said, "Come on, lass. Come on, hinny. I'm glad you left your mark on him. I hope you went deep enough for the scar to remain there as a reminder."

"She's a dirty little slut and I won't have her in my house. For the future she's outside and in the dairy. Do you hear?"

"I hear. And that suits us both. As for being a dirty little slut, one has to be trained in that line, don't you know, Mrs Yorkless? Both me and me daughter, although she was foolish enough to run away, we were both married without our bellies being full. But that's something we won't go into the day."

Lizzie's voice was so tantalizingly calm that the farmer's wife looked as if she would have a seizure at any moment, but she managed to cry, "Mind your tongue, Lizzie Crawshaw, or you'll be. . . ."

Lizzie was leading Emma towards the door now but she stopped and, turning about, asked enquiringly, "I'll be what?" She waited; and when all the answer she received from her mistress was a grinding of the teeth, she said, "Oh yes, if it wasn't for my cottage I know where I'd be, but I have my cottage and you can't do anything about it, or, by the way, me bit field that goes with it, the bit that your husband has turned into barley, I'm told I could ask for rent on it. We'll have to go into that."

They were out in the yard now and crossing it in silence, which lasted until they entered the cottage. But here Lizzie's attitude changed: her calmly irritating voice was replaced by agitated tones as she said, "In the name of God, child, what happened?"

When, between gasps, Emma had related exactly what took place, Lizzie said, "There's one thing sure, lass, he was just a young groping lout afore, the need could be seen in his every look an' action, but from now on you can take it from me he'll be a groping man and he'll not rest until he has his own back on you. I know him, I've known him from a nipper, he bears malice over the least thing. Now I'm gona say this to you an' before God I never thought I would 'cos I don't hold with whips and such, but whenever you go out to the river or for a dander on your own take one of them with you, 'cos you're gona need protection. And likely not only from him, the way you're blossoming out. You know what I mean, lass?"

Lizzie was bending down to Emma who was sitting on the cracket, and Emma, looking up into her face, said honestly, "Well no, Granny."

"Oh God in heaven!" Emma now watched her granny straighten up and walk over to her bed and back again before bending towards her again and saying, "You haven't got to let anybody touch you, any man. Don't you understand?"

"Oh yes, Granny, I understand that." She didn't go on to say what she didn't understand was about this blossoming out.

Letting out a long almost painful breath, Lizzie sat down on the rocking chair opposite and said, quietly now, "Has anybody ever tried to touch you before . . . in that way I mean?"

"No, Granny. But . . . but I know what you mean, and I'll never let anybody touch me, never."

"Never's a long time, hinny. But until you're grown up see to it that nobody does. Now I've got to get back or else I'll have me mistress after me." She gave a wry smile and shook her head while still looking down at Emma; then she added, "Wash your face, comb your hair and tidy yourself up, and then go down to Mr Bowman's. You're well past your time."

"But . . . but the hens, the crowdy, he knocked the dish out of me hand and it went all over the floor and. . . ."

"Don't worry about the hens' crowdy, I'll see to that the day. Go along now."

Ralph Bowman seemed in very high spirits. She had hardly got through the back door than she heard him coming out of the paint room; and then he was in the kitchen, holding out his hand to her saying, "Come here; I've got something to show you." He didn't seem to notice that there was no smile on her face this morning and that her manner was subdued but, taking her by the hand, he almost ran her through the living-room and into the paint room, and there, putting her before the easel, he said, *"Child with a bucket. Child with a bucket."*

She was looking at a picture of a girl about her own age kneeling on a stone floor, a big wooden bucket at her side, a scrubbing brush in one hand, her other resting on the stones while she looked up at someone above her.

Her head poking slowly forward, she screwed up her eyes as she stared at the face. It looked like her, the bit that stared back at her from the cracked mirror above the razor strop in the farm kitchen. Yet it wasn't her; that girl's face was bonny.

"Well?"

" 'Tisn't me, is it?" She was looking sideways up at him.

"Of course, it's you, you dunderhead. Who else would it be? You sat for it, didn't you?"

"Yes, I know"—her voice was as brisk as his now—"but I don't look like that."

"Who says you don't look like that?"

"Well, I don't . . . do I?"

The question at the last was subdued, and now dropping on his hunkers before her, he put his hands on her shoulders as he said, "Emma Molinero, that is you . . . yet not you, because I couldn't do justice to a face like yours, ever."

She liked the sound of her name, it was a long since she'd heard it. She smiled at him, but not her usual smile, and noting that she was different this morning, he said, "What's the matter with you? Aren't you well?"

"I'm not bad," she answered; "but I've had an upset."

"What kind of an upset?"

She lowered her eyes and turned her head to the side; it was difficult to talk about her upset to a man. And he repeated, "What kind of an upset?"

"It was with Luke, I—" She now turned and looked into his eyes before ending, "I had to scratch his face."

"Oh." His mouth formed the roundness of the word and, slowly rising to his feet, he said, "That's how it is? And what happened to Master Luke?"

"His face was bleeding. But . . . but the mistress blamed me."

"She would. Of course she would, that's understood." He was nodding at her. "But Emma, my dear, you've got to expect things like that happening to you."

"I have?" Her voice sounded indignant.

"Oh yes, yes; and it'll happen more often as life goes. . . ."

"It won't, they won't." She had stretched her neck upwards now. "I'm gona use the whip; me granny says I've got to take it with me. I'm gona practise it an' all, the big one."

"Your granny says you've got to practise using the whip?"

"Yes, she did."

"Well, well." His face was straight now. "It must be serious when your granny says you should practise the whip because she's not for whips, is she?"

"No, she's not . . . she wasn't, but . . . but she is now. . . ."

"Hello! Anyone there?"

The painter hurried towards the door, crying, "Henry! Come in. Come in."

When the parson came into the room he said, "Well, well, 'tis Emma," as if he hadn't seen her for weeks and not just last night; or was it this morning? So many things had happened.

"How are you, Emma?"

Before she could answer, Ralph Bowman said, "She's not very well this morning, Henry, but . . . but we won't talk about it yet. Look at this though. What do you think?"

Henry Grainger stood in front of the portrait. He didn't speak for some long while, but then he looked down at Emma, then at his friend, and he said very softly, "Perfect. It's the best thing you've ever done."

"I think so too." Ralph's voice was also soft.

"What are you going to do with it?"

"Nothing; it's already sold."

"Sold?" Henry's voice was high now.

"I had two visitors yesterday from the Hall." He jerked his head towards the wall. "Very honoured, indeed."

"You mean the Fordykes?"

"Yes, James and his lady, as ever was."

"And they bought it?"

"Yes, she did. Apparently she is very interested in art, brought up with it. She's the daughter of Peter Rollinson, and it's going to his house."

"How marvellous! I hope you charged them a good price for it."

"Thirty guineas."

"Huh! thirty guineas. It would have brought a hundred in London."

"Perhaps. But we're not in London, and thirty guineas is not to be sneezed at. Yet at the same time I didn't want to part with it." He looked down at Emma now, adding, "But we've got the model here, and she'll sit for me any time, won't you, Emma?"

"Yes, yes, Mr Bowman."

"Do you think you could make us a pot of tea, Emma?"

"Yes, Mr Bowman." She left them and went through the living-room and into the kitchen; and she knew they had followed her for their voices came to her low but distinct and by what she heard she knew that Mr Bowman was telling the parson what had happened to her. But when she took the tea into them Mr Bowman changed the conversation to talk about a book he was reading and the parson said nothing, he just looked at her and his face had a sad look.

She returned to the kitchen and began to prepare the vegetables for Mr Bowman's dinner. She could hear them talking again, but so softly that she couldn't catch what they were saying until, the conversation changing once more, they were discussing the book that the painter had mentioned when she had taken the tea in. The name of the man who had written it sounded very plain, Sydney Smith. There were two Smith families in the village; Peggy Smith came to Sunday school. She heard Mr Bowman say, "You put me very much in mind of Sydney." And the parson answered laughingly, "Oh, that's funny, it's the woodman being compared with the king, and to me he is the king of satire and of humour. When I am very down and feeling very much alone and asking the great why, I read one of his pamphlets and I seem to get some kind of an answer. I think there are times when God sends such as him to show a new concept of religion, that the ingredients for the preparation for the after-life do not consist of the fear of hell and of continually keeping the smell of brimstone in one's nostrils. You know, Ralph, I never wanted to be a minister, the church was the last thing I thought of and I'm surprised to find myself in it . . . and you know too, I think so are my parishioners."

She didn't fully understand what he was on about but she liked to hear the parson laugh, he had such a nice deep laugh, a happy laugh; and he was saying as he laughed now, "But what strikes me as rather unfair is they expect so much from their pastor, he has to give twenty-four hours a day service. Twice last week I was called out of the dead of night to help Mrs Brigham in the passage from this life to the next, but just as she was about to step over she changed her mind . . . both times. I don't think she liked what she saw, at least it wasn't what she had envisaged all her life, and this morning when I called she was sitting up and eating raw eggs."

She could hardly hear the rest of the sentence for Mr Bowman's laughter. His was a different kind of laugh, almost a bellow, and it rose as the parson ended, "She sucks them from the shell. It has to be seen to be believed. Of course I don't think that's her only sustenance because there was a strong smell of rum when I entered the room this morning."

There was more laughter and more conversation that she couldn't distinguish, until she heard Mr Bowman say, "And the plate, is it any heavier these days?"

"No, about the same. They expect services of all kinds but they are dilatory in paying for them. I'm finding difficulty in keeping up that huge old house, and the services of Miss Wilkinson. I don't know how on earth my predecessor managed to bring up eight children on his stipend."

"Oh, from what I can gather, Mr Fordyke senior helped out a lot there. But when his son married he left the Hall and now, I understand, he lives out Jesmond way. But he pays frequent visits here, for I've seen him now and again stalking the hills. Of course, he was up to his neck in the smuggling business and likely kept old Crabtree and his brood supplemented because of the storage provided by your said predecessor. Which reminds me, have you found out anything more?"

"Not really, except that I'm held as a fool by some of my parishioners but not quite an idiot."

He was repeating what she had said to him last night; and as this thought came to her it also revived the name of Christina Leadbeater. She stopped peeling the potatoes and dried her hands on the hessian towel, then stood looking towards the door that led into the living-room, asking herself: should she tell him? Or would it do any good if she did?

As things stood now she mightn't get the chance to go to Sunday school, the missis might do something to stop her, and then she wouldn't see the parson. Unless he came up to the farm.

She stood in the doorway and said, "Parson."

"Yes, Emma?" He turned quickly towards her.

"I've remembered somethin' about the rum-runners."

"You have?" He came quickly towards her, and then drew her towards the middle of the room where Mr Bowman was sitting, and she looked from one to the other now, then back to the parson before she said, "It's to do with a headstone."

"A headstone?"

"Yes; Billy said to me granny that the headstone was called Christina Leadbeater, or some such name, and it was often lifted from the wall."

Henry stared at her for a long moment, then turned and looked at Ralph Bowman and saying quietly, "There is a headstone with the name of Christina Leadbeater on it. It dates back to sixteen hundred. It's quite a large headstone, and it's lain there so long it's sunk into a groove. A number of the old headstones are lying against the north transept." Then turning and looking down on Emma again, he said, "And I'm supposed to be sitting on top of the stuff. That's it, Emma, isn't it?"

She hesitated before saying, "Yes, something like that, Parson."

She was startled as Mr Bowman, jumping up from the chair, cried, "Of course! Henry, that's it. There's no crypt there, but there must be a cellar or some kind of place they used as a store room. Oh! Emma.

Oh! Emma Molinero." She felt herself swiftly lifted off her feet and held up and her face was in front of the painter's. Then he kissed her and cried, "You're not only a beautiful model, my dear Emma, you're a God-given solver of liquid mysteries."

She was very red in the face when she hurried back to the kitchen. She felt disturbed in a strange way. It had been a most strange disturbing morning. It had been a disturbing time altogether. It had really started last night when she had become a friend of the parson's. Then she had experienced the awful feeling of Luke putting his hands on her, and the gentleness of Barney's arms. And now Mr Bowman had kissed her; he was the first man to kiss her since her father died: she didn't count the kisses of the members of the Travers Travelling Show the morning she left.

This is what her granny must have meant by blossoming out.

3

Emma did indeed blossom out over the next four years. She was now thirteen years old, tall for her age, her figure already developing, her features, set in a mould under the creamy tanned skin, combining to make her face one that was so different from any in the neighbourhood as to set her apart. Mothers of sons saw that she was someone to be slightly wary of; mothers of daughters looked on her with envy; and the daughters, those with whom she attended the Sunday school, with the exception of two, Angela Turnbull the grocer's daughter and Peg Hall whose father was the blacksmith, took their opinions of her from their mothers.

On the farm the atmosphere towards her had changed but slightly, except that Dilly Yorkless had been forced to subdue her feelings under the threat from Lizzie that she would send Emma into service. And Emma had become a very good worker: not only could she attend to all the business of the dairy, see to the pigs and chickens, but she could also help with the milking. Without Emma, Mrs Yorkless knew she would have to employ a full-time hand and wouldn't get half the work out of her. Moreover, she knew the parson had taken an interest in the girl, lending her books and some such, and as much as she would like to stop this she knew she couldn't, because Jake wanted them to stand well with the parson for the parson stood well with those up at the House: not only was he invited there to dinner once a week when the family were at home, but they also loaned him a horse for the hunting.

Then there was the painter. When she had first found out that he was painting the little hussy and selling his work she had objected strongly, and she had made it known to him through Lizzie that the girl was paid for work and not sitting. And Lizzie had made it known to her that the painter was interested in moving to another cottage for there was one vacant on the Hudsons' farm, and Jane Hudson would jump at a tenant like him, paying through the teeth in rent, not forgetting what he had to fork out for household services twice a week.

So, much against the grain, Mrs Yorkless left things as they were. But she kept a sharp eye on her sons, warning them what would happen if she ever caught one of them talking to the hussy.

Lizzie's time was taken up cleaning the eight main rooms of the farmhouse, scouring the stone-floored pantries and store rooms, and helping with the cooking and curing. When she did manage to get outside it was into the fields because there were now only three of the four boys working, Dan the youngest of the family having two years previously contracted the chest complaint so that he now spent most of his time lying in bed in the back bedroom; only on days when it was warm and sunny did he venture outside, then he was wrapped up almost to the eyes in winter clothes.

Should Emma happen to go round the back of the house she would always look up at Dan's window, and should his pale face be near the pane she would wave to him and he would wave back. It was he who had first lifted a hand in salute, and she had answered it immediately, standing gazing up at the blurred image behind the pane. They could never have a word because the window was tight closed, but she often mouthed a message to him, mostly appertaining to the weather. If it was sunny she would point up to the sky, if it was cold she would hug herself.

When he had been about the farm she hadn't cared much for Dan for, like his brothers with the exception of Barney, he didn't speak to her. And Barney only spoke when they met away from the farm, or they happened to be in either the byres or the barn and no one else was there. And then his words were always stilted: "How are you, Emma?" he would say, to which she would answer, "I'm fine, Barney. How are you?" And to this he would answer, "Me an' all."

Barney was a big fellow now. He and Luke were both about the same size, only Luke was a bit thicker in the shoulders and perhaps better looking; but he was still nasty. She couldn't stand the sight of Luke; nor he of her apparently, for he always turned his head away when she was near. She hoped he would soon leave the farm for he was courting the verger's daughter, Mary Haswell; she was seventeen and rather pretty. Her granny said the missis wasn't for the match, Mary was too dollified and the verger and his wife had spoiled her, and that she would have to change her ways when she became a farmer's wife.

She never bothered about Pete. Pete was a dour kind of fellow. He didn't talk much. Her granny said it was because he was the deep kind that took all in and said nowt, but he did what he was told without question. There was one man on the farm though that she was afraid of, even more than she had once been afraid of Luke, and that was the farmer himself. Like his son Pete, he, too, hadn't much to say, but it was the way he looked at her. She always felt she had done something wrong when he stood looking at her. Sometimes he would turn away with a shake of his head. But a few weeks ago he had really frightened her. It was the morning after there must have been a liquor run for he came into the cowshed and his hair was all wet where he had been holding his head under the pump and he had almost knocked over the bucket of milk she had just taken from Daisy Bell. And he had gone to kick it; then realising what he was about to do, he had stopped and, putting his hand to his head, had stared at her, and as she looked back at him from the stool he had said something very strange.

"You know what, you young Spaniard?" he had said. "You're going to cause more bloody upset and trouble than all the customs in the bloody country. You know that?" And she had looked at him squarely as she answered, "I don't cause any trouble, mister. I do me work and mind me own business; you can't say I cause trouble."

He had seemed a little surprised at her stand and after a moment of gaping at her had muttered, "You've got a tongue like your granny. As for not causing trouble, you were made for trouble. Do you know that? You were made for it, cut out for it. Aye." He turned his head away now and he paused before he repeated, "Aye, cut out for it." Then he had walked up the byre, leaving her puzzled and frightened and feeling very exposed to whatever it was that emanated from him.

Away from the farm she never felt frightened for she had got into the habit of carrying the whip with her. She always concealed it inside her skirt, the handle just visible above the waistband and in line with her elbow, the thong wrapped in such a way below the butt of the handle that it would unwind once she flicked it.

From the time her granny had warned her to carry the whip she had practised whenever the opportunity presented itself, which was mostly late at night when the farm animals were bedded down and the members of the family inside. Then she would take the big whip out beyond the field and flick and twist and twirl the long leather thong until now she could almost, as her granny said, make it speak.

It always amazed her that her granny liked to watch her antics with the whip. On the other hand, though, she didn't like to see her practising with the knives. But there was really no place to practise the knives around the farm except for throwing them at the wooden beam that ran up the side of the cottage.

It had taken her some long time to get the hang of throwing the knives. She tried to remember all that her father had done with them. But watching and doing were two different things: the art wasn't only in having a good eye, it was in the strength of the wrist, and knowing how to use it. She had chipped a knife badly on the stone of the cottage during her early practising, but now she never missed the beam. It didn't, however, give her enough scope, not like the oak tree in Openwood. But it was very rarely she had the time to visit Openwood in the daylight, and so it was only on a strong moonlight night that she could attempt to do any throwing.

But if the weather held and it didn't rain there would be a lovely harvest moon tonight, and she'd go into the wood and practise. She hadn't been going out at nights very often. Sometimes she was too tired; once she lay down on her pallet she would be fast asleep and when the cock crowed at five o'clock in the morning she always felt she hadn't slept for five minutes. What was more, a lot of the excitement had gone from her night strolls. When she first came here and had slept in this enclosed roof space she had imagined she would suffocate, and all she longed for was the open air. But now she had got used to being closed in. In fact, on winter nights what she enjoyed most was sitting on the mat in front of the cottage fire roasting potatoes in the ashes while her granny sat knitting in the rocking-chair. Sometimes her granny talked and told her of things gone by and how it was when she was a young girl. It was then that her voice and manner softened, and she understood her more than she did in the daytime when for no apparent reason she would go for her, while warning her of dire things to come. Only last week she had cried at her, " 'Tis a good job that parson's getting married, 'tis that." Now why had she said that? And she herself hadn't known the parson was going to be married. She had been surprised how the news had affected her; she had felt upset and when he had spoken to her after Sunday school and asked her what she thought of her latest reading by Sir Walter Scott, he had appeared to her just the same, not a bit as if he was going to be married. But how did you appear if you were going to be married?

She was impatient this morning to get down to Mr Bowman's to hear the latest news, because she could talk to Mr Bowman, ask him questions, just like she could the parson.

She doubted, if the parson was going to be married, that he and Mr Bowman and herself would laugh together, like they did sometimes, for instance like they did over the parson finding the liquor store. Oh, how they had laughed about that.

The parson and Mr Bowman had gone in the dead of night and moved the stone that bore the name of Christina Leadbeater on it and there, behind, was a flat slab and when they moved it, it showed a hole only big enough to allow one man through it. But there were three stone steps leading down into a goodly sized passage running well under the church, and on each side were stacked bottles of liquor, each one covered with a straw cap.

They had replaced the stone that night, and the following day had decided on a course of action. At the bottom end of the churchyard there was a vault that held the body of John Freeman Ellis. It hadn't been opened for years until the vicar went in when he first came to the parish. He had obtained the key from the vestry, and he still had it. Another quiet visit to the vault gave him the idea where he could store the liquor, and the very next night they transferred seventy-eight bottles, but left the straw covers standing as if there were still the bottles underneath them.

It was almost a week later when the rumpus broke out in the village. It was kind of a secret rumpus but nevertheless evident. Billy had said to her granny there was one thing sure, it was somebody in the know, and when they found him, or them, because one man couldn't do the job alone, he would be skinned alive.

On that particular Sunday the parson preached a sermon on trust and on man loving his neighbour; he had used a lot of big words, and she'd had a hard job not to splutter.

Mr Bowman had warned her not to let on to anybody, including her granny, about what had happened. Amidst laughter he told her that he had been very tempted to help himself to a few bottles, feeling he had deserved them for all the work he had put in. But then her granny had a nose, he said, and a mind for prying, so he had ended, discretion was the better part of rum valour! . . . The parson and he had laughed a lot.

And they had all laughed until their sides ached when the parson described the looks on certain faces in the congregation as he admonished them to love their neighbours, knowing full well what their thoughts were regarding their neighbours at that present moment.

She had taken the news to them the following week, having gathered from Billy's and her granny's conversation that it was suspected the culprits had come from *The House,* likely the butler and the footman or some high-up servants had got their heads together and now had their own private store of French brandy and Jamaican rum.

It had come to Emma some time ago that Mr Bowman and the parson in some ways treated her as a grown-up, while other people treated her as a child, and those on the farm as the lowest form of servant. She had sometimes thought if it hadn't been for the parson and Mr Bowman she would have run away before now. But then her good sense had asked her, to where would she run? To whom would she run? She had no one, only the parson, Mr Bowman and her granny. But when it was summed up that was a lot. And she was thankful, oh yes she was, because as her granny had once said when in a temper, she was lucky that she hadn't been brought up in the poorhouse over the bridge in Newcastle for then she would now be in the mines, for no matter how hard this Mr Ashley tried to stop the bairns going down he might as well try to spit against the wind, for the owners maintained the pits would close if the bairns' labour was withdrawn. She didn't know who this Mr Ashley was but he must be a nice man, and somebody high up too. And yet her granny only heard of him through Mr Bowman.

Mr Bowman read the newspapers and he talked to himself about them, sometimes raging up and down the room when a thing didn't please him. And when the parson was there they both talked ninety to the dozen. Sometimes about heaven and hell and things in the Bible. It was then that they would argue; but they generally ended up laughing.

She had finished her morning chores and was ready to go down to Mr Bowman's. She hurried across to the cottage and, going to the end of the room where a tin bowl stood on a block of wood, she took up a hessian towel and, having dipped the end into the water in the bowl, she wiped her face with it, rubbing well round her nose, the part of her that seemed to attract splashes of glar from the piggery. Following this, she took off her rough coarse apron and put on a white one, the hem of which reached to the bottom of her skirt. A bib was attached to the apron and she pinned the top to the shoulders of her blue serge dress near its frayed collar. She was feeling ashamed in this frock as it was no longer decent because she was growing so fast the hem didn't reach the top of her boots and the sleeves were half-way up her forearms. But she consoled herself she would soon have a new one. Last November her granny had gone to the shoe fair in Gateshead and she got a big gentleman's cloak and a lady's blue cord dress for ninepence from a woman who was selling old clothes. Her granny had spent a good part of the winter turning the cloak into a working frock for her, and she said she would make a blouse of the lining. She wished she had started on the cord dress first because it was such a pretty colour: the material was very good, but the lady who had worn the dress must have walked through a lot of mud for the bottom of it was badly stained. Still, her granny said she would get more than enough to make her a Sunday frock. But it took a long time to make a dress and she had the thought that she would ask her granny to cut it out and she would get at the sewing herself, 'cos she wasn't a bad hand at sewing, her stitches were nearly all the same size except here and there and when they went out of line it was mostly when the candle was guttered because of the wind coming down the chimney, or when she was dog-tired. Finally, she took a comb from the corner of the mantelpiece and combed the front of her hair under her white linen cap.

She always felt a kind of elation when she went to Mr Bowman's. It was like entering a different world. And it was a different world for she was beginning to liken her life at the farm as being in the house of correction where the warders had been struck dumb. Very often the only voices she would hear in the course of a day were those of the animals. She loved the animals, especially the pigs. Oh yes, she had a special feeling for the pigs. But children in the village called each other dirty pigs, yet she had found that pigs weren't really dirty; they got wet and their feet churned up the ground into clarts, but they did their business in a special place. Oh, she liked the pigs, and she suffered agonies on slaughter day. Last year was the only time she hadn't cried her eyes out. Instead, she had run to the far end of the chicken field and had stuffed her fingers in her ears to shut out their squealing; and she had prayed for them, prayed that they wouldn't feel it. She could understand the mister and Luke killing the pigs but not Barney. But Barney always helped.

She purposely made her way round the back of the farm this morning, and there she saw Dan at the window. She stopped a moment and smiled and waved her hand, and he waved back. His face looked smaller today. She was so sorry for Dan; he was going to die. It was awful to die when the sun was shining like it was now, so warm that it got right through your clothes to your skin.

She half turned her head away and, looking upwards, she pointed to the sky, then looked back at him, and he nodded at her. He knew she was saying it was a nice day. She wondered why they didn't let him outside when it was so warm; her granny said the fug in the room would knock you back and there was a nasty smell there, a kind of scenty smell that spoke of death. Poor Dan. She waved to him again, walking a few steps backwards as she did so; then she turned and hurried towards the wall and the beech hedge that cut off the yard. When she knew she would be out of his sight she slowed her step.

She was finding it pained her to look at Dan yet somehow she felt that he needed company, outside company. She wondered where he would go when he died; would it be straight to heaven? Or would he have to suffer in hell for the things he had done, such as laying traps for the rabbits and the fox and clubbing half of Bonny's litter with a wooden mallet? She had cried all night over that. Even when her granny had explained they only kept the best of a litter to be trained to look after the sheep, and what would they do with eight dogs running round the place.

She would ask the parson where he thought Dan would go when he died.

The parson was going to be married. . . .

She had just come in sight of the bridle-path when she saw the parson. He was driving his horse and trap and seated beside him was a lady. She knew that he had espied her for he drew the horse to a stop, then hailed her with his hand.

She was walking by the border of the field that was full of corn and she had to keep to the edge of it until she came to the bank and could drop down into the road, and she had to watch her skirt going down the bank because it generally rolled up to her knees. Then she was standing on the road looking up at the parson and the lady. The lady was nearer to her. She was young and pretty, she had a round face and a pink skin, her eyes looked clear without colour and she had curly brown hair which showed under her bonnet. She wasn't smiling.

"This is Emma, Christabel. Emma, this is Miss Braintree."

Emma bent her knee, then said politely, "Good-day to you, Miss Braintree."

Miss Braintree, besides not smiling, didn't speak, she merely inclined her head. And the parson spoke again. His voice seemed extra loud to Emma; it was as if he imagined her to be in the middle of the field, and what he said was, "Emma's a very bright girl, Christabel. She's one of my brightest Sunday school pupils. She can read and write as well as I can and I'd like to bet she could get up in the pulpit and preach a sermon." He laughed, and Emma smiled, but with her lips tightly pressed, knowing that the parson was making a joke, but Miss Christabel Braintree still neither smiled nor spoke. And the parson now said, "You on your way to Mr Bowman's, Emma?"

"Yes, Parson."

"Well, you'll find him in high fettle this morning, he has sold another one of your pictures. What do you think of that?"

Her mouth opened widely now and she said, " 'Tis good to know, Parson."

"Surely 'tis good to know." She knew he was imitating her way of speaking.

"Well, we must be off and you on your way. I shall see you on Sunday, Emma."

"Yes, Parson. Good-bye, Parson. Good-bye, miss." She again bobbed her knee and the young lady inclined her head; and then the trap was bowling down the road.

Funny, she had never opened her mouth, not even to say, "Pleased to be seeing you," or " 'Tis a fine day," or anything like that. She was pretty though. But why had the parson been so hearty? She had never known him be so hearty, he must be pleased.

She entered the cottage by the back door as usual and she hadn't had time to put on the table the coarse apron she used for kneeling in before she heard her name being called: "That you, Emma?"

"Yes, Mr Bowman."

He met her at the kitchen door, saying, "I've news for you."

"Yes I know, you sold another picture." She grinned at him.

"Oh!" He always did a funny thing with his mouth when he said, "Oh!" like that. He pushed it out almost like a pig's snout and it always made her want to laugh. But she wasn't feeling inclined to laugh this morning, not very much anyway.

"Did you come upon them?"

"The parson, you mean?"

"Yes, the parson and Miss Christabel Braintree. My God!" He turned from her and walked into the room saying, "She's as much fitted for a parson's wife as . . . as. . . ." She watched the back of his head moving as he searched unsuccessfully for words to explain the antonym of a parson's wife. He turned to her again, saying, "Far better if he took Miss Wilkinson. She might be a few years older but she's got some sense in her head; and she knows how to stretch a penny. But that one will need a servant to dress her. He's mad . . . mad." He was shaking his head again. "And he hasn't been courting her six months. Met her of all places at his brother's funeral. That's four deaths in that family in as many years. He used to be the second youngest, now he's the second eldest. But that's where he met her." He looked down at her, saying slowly now, "I don't know what's come over him these last few months; he's even questioning his religion. Now I'm allowed to question his religion, and any religion, but he's in it up to the neck. And now the transubstantiation is bothering him. Well, not exactly bothering him but he's taking it to pieces, if you know what I mean. . . . And you don't know, do you?" He poked his chin out at her. "Oh, Emma, what a pity it is you've got to grow up; and you're doing that at a gallop. Do you know that?"

She answered him solemnly, saying, "I know I'm getting too big for me clothes."

"Huh!" He let out his bellow of a laugh as he said, "As long as you don't get too big for your boots." Then appraising her, he said, "I've been thinking. My next of you is going to depict you as a young lady, a sixteen-year-old. I'll drape your top." His hand went out towards her now but it didn't touch her, it made waving movements around her shoulders as he said, "White silk with a rose or two just there." His finger was pointing to the nape of her neck. "Not too much flesh showing, your hair loose." He now went to whip off her cap and she gave a startling squeal as the pin in the back tore at her hair.

All contrition now, his hands were on her head and he was repeating, "Oh! Emma. I'm sorry, I'm sorry. I'm an unthinking brute. Did I hurt you? Oh! Emma, my dear."

"It's all right. I . . . I've got to pin it."

"Of course, of course. Oh, I'm sorry." He was nodding at her now. But then his thoughts jumping to the posing of her again, he added, "No, no; your hair must be piled up high, not loose, not loose. . . ."

"Are you havin' the rabbit stewed the day, or do you want it roasted?" She watched his head suddenly droop forward on to his chest then jerk back on his shoulders, and again he was laughing and talking to the ceiling, saying, "Do I want my rabbit stewed today, or do I want it roasted? Come down to earth, Ralph Bowman. Come down to earth." Then he lowered his gaze and now said quite seriously, "I think I'd like it roasted, Emma. Then get through your chores as quickly as possible, I want to make a sketch of you. And by the way . . . here—" He turned towards the window under which was a small table with a drawer in it and, pulling this open, he took out a sovereign and a shilling. Going to her, he lifted one of her hands and placed the sovereign in it, saying, "For your secret hoard;" and then putting the shilling into her other hand said, "Hoodwink money for your granny."

She smiled at him. "And it is hoodwinkin' her, Mr Bowman, and I feel awful."

"But she takes the shilling, doesn't she?"

"Yes."

"Well, if she knew you got a sovereign she'd take that too. And Emma—" He now took a step towards her and, bending until his face was on a level with hers, he said, "Some day you're going to need money, perhaps to take a journey to fly away, and this I know, anything anyone wants to do is always made easier by money. How much have you got in your hoard now?"

"I've got thirteen sovereigns. This will be fourteen. It's a fortune. I . . . I really wouldn't know what to do with it, not all that money. And I know me granny at times would. . . ."

"*No! Emma. No!* That was a bargain between us, wasn't it? You don't tell your granny what you're getting for sitting for my pictures. Your granny is taken care of, she's not left without an odd shilling, but she spends it, and that's her business how she spends it."

She knew how her granny used her extra money, she used it for buying liquor on the quiet. The rum-running still went on, but she had no idea now where they stored it, but she gathered from Billy it was difficult to come by and that the price had gone up. She only knew that what they bought came through the blacksmith and the verger. She also knew that the knowledge that the verger was in on the game made the parson angry. He could make allowances for the others but not for the verger. He had called the man a smarmy hypocrite when talking to Mr Bowman, and she had been surprised that the parson could not only sound angry but look angry; always when he talked to her his voice was kind, even when he was reprimanding her for not reading as much as she should. With regard to this, he didn't seem to understand that she had only late night-time to read and she got very tired and all she wanted to do was climb the ladder and roll on to the pallet. Sometimes she was so tired she didn't take her clothes off, and once or twice she had been too tired to eat the evening meal and had fallen asleep. But missing a meal didn't worry her because it was usually just wishy-washy stew which she often had to force herself to eat. The only meal she liked was the rough porridge in the mornings. Eaten with fresh milk this filled you up for hours. If there was any over she would have it later when it was cold and almost solid. There was always plenty of porridge because her granny could help herself in the mornings, though for the other meals, the missis doled them out. But the twice a week down here at the cottage she had nice food because there was always left-overs. Mr Bowman didn't seem to eat much, likely because he stuffed himself between meals with cheese and bread and beer: there was always a big platter in the paint room holding a loaf and a big collop of cheese, and one of the Stoddart lads from the village trudged up every day with beer from the inn. It was Willy who was doing it at present, and it was a long way for a little lad. But still he got a penny a week and that wasn't to be sniffed at. Georgie had done it afore him, and Bill afore that, but they were both working five miles away in Birtley now. One in the Brine Spring from where they got the salt, and the other was down the pit; and neither of them was ten yet.

He had gone into the paint room and she had returned to the kitchen but his voice reached her clear, saying, "I had a visit from Madam Yorkless yesterday. Smooth as butter she was. Wanted to know if I was still comfortable and if I was satisfied with your service. I answered both in the affirmative. She surprised me by saying she had an interest in pictures. Now would you believe that? Our Mistress Yorkless turning to the arts! She was breaking her neck to get into this room, and I had a strong desire to break her neck. Can't stand the woman; she's like an elongated snail."

As his voice went on and on Emma smiled to herself: he could talk for half an hour on end and not expect an answer. She liked to hear him talk; although he jumped from one thing to the other she always seemed to learn something fresh every time she came down here. She didn't do much talking herself, simply answered his questions.

At first she had been in the habit of jabbering to him about the doings on the farm, but one day, having told him what the usual routine of her day was, he had become angry. And later that week her granny had gone for her and told her to keep her mouth shut about what she had to do because the painter, being the kind of man he was, wouldn't be above telling the missis what he thought of her expecting a child to work twelve to fourteen hours a day. And so now, she mostly just listened.

She had skinned and prepared the rabbit. She didn't mind handling the rabbits when they were dead because then they couldn't feel any more; and when she took the skin outside and laid it on a bench ready for scraping, salting, and stretching, she paused a moment and looked away across the fields. It was a beautiful day; she wished she could turn about now and walk and walk right down to the river, or perhaps just to the burn and through Openwood, just walk. And as she stared over the wide countryside there rose in her a feeling, like a compelling urge, to get away, to go on until she came to a village, a different village like Birtley—funny, she had never been to Birtley—then onwards, through Chester-le-Street to the city of Durham. She knew all their names, she had learned them from a map in a book that the parson had loaned her. Durham seemed the end of the world one way, but t'other way was the even greater city of Newcastle, and it was surrounded by villages, with names like Gosforth, Jesmond, and Lemington. She liked the sound of the names; she had a different picture in her mind for each one.

Billy had told her about the towns that bordered the river right down the south side to a place called Shields from where the sea opened out and covered a great expanse of the earth. Billy said it was a wonderful sight and, one of these days, he said, he would take her down on a Sunday river trip.

She didn't hold much to Billy's promises because he never seemed to have any money, for whatever he had he spent at the inn in the village. And when he couldn't go to the inn he was very testy. Often on these occasions she had given him the penny that her granny gave her back when she handed her the shilling she had received for sitting for the picture.

It was at times like this when the urge came upon her that she thought of the travellers and wondered what had happened to them. A big fair, she knew, came to Newcastle every year, and there were little ones an' all in between; but she knew none of them would be Mr Travers's company, for each fair had what it called its circuit, and there was always trouble if anyone crossed into another man's. She could remember vaguely a big disturbance when a troupe from a foreign country had set up on one of Mr Travers's sites.

Sighing deeply, she turned to the bench and the rabbit skin and, taking up a hammer and a few tacks, she nailed it to a board.

A short while ago she had thought it was a beautiful day, and it being so she should feel nice, but she didn't feel nice: she didn't like this rushing, churning, urging inside of her, it made her discontented. And then there was the parson: he was going to be married and she knew she wasn't going to like his wife.

It wasn't a nice day. Even though she was down here with the painter, it wasn't a nice day.

The restlessness of the day had crept into the night. She was sitting with her knees drawn up under her on the pallet, looking out through the open hatch. The full moon was low in the sky and hazy; there was a feeling of storm in the air, and when it came it would likely be heavy for they'd had no rain for the past three weeks.

She was still in her day clothes except for her boots and stockings; it was no use lying down for she knew she wouldn't sleep, her mind was too active, and strangely she didn't want to go out.

What did she want?

She looked at the words in her mind as if they had been spoken by someone else and she bowed her head because she knew the answer but felt too shy to voice it, even to herself. And even if she had voiced it she wouldn't have been able to say that she wanted company, someone of her own age or thereabouts to walk with, someone like Barney. She liked Barney, if she liked any of them, yet she kept telling herself he was still the son of the mister and missis and neither of them was nice, so how could he really be nice. And yet he was; he was nice to her. And last Christmas he had slipped her a handkerchief. And she still had it; she hadn't used it, it was in the box on the floor in the corner over there. It was the first present she had received since she left the company, the first from those on the farm. She had four books, though, which were all her own and which the parson had given her.

What's to become of me? There was the voice in her head again.

But there was no answer in her mind, except that some part of her refuted the idea that she would spend the rest of her life on this farm.

The haze had left the moon now and the land looked bright and beautiful, almost like daylight. . . . Bright enough to practise the knives.

No sooner had the thought come to her than she twisted around on the pallet and crawled two paces on her knees over the wooden floor and, reaching out, picked up a pair of rope sandals. These were what her granny had made for her. Her granny was good with the rope; she could make mats and things. The sandals had a thick sole of plaited rope, with a band to hold the toes and a larger one to go over the ankle. Two pieces of rope were attached to the heel. These came round the ankle and held the sole in place. They were light on the feet and she often wore them at night like slippers.

Having put on the sandals, she now picked up the middle whip of the three that were lying on top of the box at the foot of her bed. Then on her knees again, she reached to where the knife belt lay rolled up and, extracting two knives from it, she stuck them in two roughly made rab-bit-skin sheaths and pushed them down the band of her skirt. Lastly, she pulled her black hooded cloak from a nail in a beam and, putting it on, she poked her head slowly through the hatch, looking first to right then the left. Because the moon was low this side of the cottage was in deep shadow and she knew she could be unobserved while going down the ladder; but once away from the cottage she would be in open ground until she reached the wall. She guessed it was close on twelve o'clock and in consequence there was very little likelihood of any occu-pant of the farm being awake, with the exception perhaps of Dan, for they all had to rise at five o'clock.

And she had no fear now of meeting up with the rum-runners, for since the business in the graveyard they had taken another route. But she was wary of meeting a poacher or a tramp: sometimes a road tramp passing through made off with a chicken.

Having reached the wall she bent low and hugged it until, the field dropping into a hollow, she was lost to the cottage and the farm build-ings as a whole.

She stopped now and drew in a long breath of the cooling night air. It was wonderful to be out again. It must be all of nine months since she last took a midnight walk. That had been in the autumn. The air had been crisp and there was a wind that had caused the clouds to race across the moon. And she had raced too. Like a wild March hare she had run hither and thither over the bottom field. And then she had lain on the earth and laughed to herself. But after that night she had questioned whether it was a normal thing to do and if there was something wild in her that should be restrained? Because if anyone had seen her they would have surely thought she was mad.

But she didn't feel mad tonight, in fact she was feeling sad.

She came to the burn, but didn't go down to it and put her feet in the water: her body urge was for some form of activity; not the sort that would make her run wild like a hare again, yet one that demanded action, excitement, yes excitement, something different to break the monotony of her days and nights. At this moment she even hoped she would come across a string of the rum-runners again.

The moon had misted over once more and she would have to wait until it was clear before she started throwing.

Her step slowed before she entered the wood: she was questioning herself again, asking if this wasn't as mad a thing to do as what had happened on the autumn night last year; in fact, in a way more mad, throwing daggers at an oak tree in the moonlight. What if her granny got to know?

This question raised a slight titter inside of her. She could even hear her granny crying, "They'll have you locked up, girl. They'll have you locked up." And yes, they did lock people up for doing odd things: if you were considered unnormal they tied you up and put you in the madhouse with chains round your ankles.

The thought brought her to a stop within the deep shadow of the wood. Eeh! she'd better go back. She had been mad to come out anyway; if she came across a tramp even her whip wouldn't save her because some of the tramping men were hefty. They weren't really tramps, just hungry men who couldn't get work. And they were known to come this road on their way to the city. Well, not exactly this road, not through the wood, they travelled by the coach road or the bridle-path.

But anyway, if she went back now without doing anything she'd just feel the same and might as well have never come out, and as she had got this far she would have one or two throws. There was no harm in it. And what was more, she liked throwing the knives even better than practising with the whip. You needed more skill throwing the knives.

There was an open space around the big oak and in the spring it was covered with the remaining acorns that lay on the winter leaves that had been mulched into a carpet by the feet of the wood animals as they emptied the acorns. But now, at the height of summer, the ground round the oak was almost bare and the great trunk of the oak was clean except where it was shadowed by some stunted holly and brush that grew between its roots. These caused a shadow over the lower part of the trunk but where she would aim for was now lit by the low full moon.

As she came off the narrow path and rounded a bank of low scrub she put her hand under her cloak and withdrew a knife from its sheath. Then taking up a similar stance to that which she had seen her father assume so often, she half closed her eyes, lifted her arm, bent her wrist back, and let the knife go.

The scream that rang through the wood almost lifted her clear from the ground. Her mouth wide open, her eyes staring out of her head, she now saw two figures spring from the foot of the oak, stand for a moment transfixed before apparently grovelling on the ground, then flying in opposite directions as if through the air. One she took to be a woman who was still screaming, the other a man, whose legs looked starkly white and who was, as far as she could make out, wearing only his shirt.

It was some seconds before she was brought to herself through the pain in her hand. She was clutching a briar bush and all she could say to herself was, "Eeh! did I hit them? Eeh! did I hit them?"

After a moment spent standing, gasping for breath, she slowly approached the tree. There above her head shone the handle of the knife. It was almost six feet from the ground, and they had been lying down. She couldn't have hit them. But that woman screaming, she would have woken the neighbourhood up, at least those down on Hudson's farm.

Reaching up, she pulled out the knife and quickly tucked it into the sheath in her skirt band.

Scurrying now, she made her way out of the wood; then almost bent double, she ran along by the walls and the hedges until she came to the hollow in the field below the cottage, and there, dropping on to her knees, she gasped for breath. And in this position there crept into her mind the picture of the two people scrambling to their feet, both half-naked, the woman with her mouth wide open from which emitted the awful screams, and the man whose hair seemed to be standing on end, although it might have only been tousled. As the picture presented her with a pair of bare legs disappearing into the trees there passed through her body a quiver that turned into a muttering shudder which escaped her lips in the form of a series of huh! huhs!

When the sound grew louder she threw herself face down into the grass, pressing her mouth tight to the earth in an effort to stifle the convulsions of laughter that were rocking her. Presently, her body still shaking and aching, she pulled herself round into a sitting position and adjusted her cloak and the hood over her head, and she rocked herself gently.

Who had they taken her for? The devil? And who were they anyway?

She hadn't been able to make out their faces because they had been so distorted, only that the man must have had very thick hair.

Oh dear me, she had a pain in her side. Anyway, she felt better, not sad any more. It had been worth going out. But eeh! what would happen to the woman? She must have been misbehaving because if she had been married she wouldn't have needed to be carrying on under the oak tree, would she now? And her yelling had given her away. But perhaps she had got home without being stopped. Eeh! she had screamed; it was unearthly, like somebody coming up out of a grave.

But enough, she herself would be in a grave if she didn't get back under the roof and quick. It was a good job the moon had hazed over again.

Pulling herself to her feet, and again bent double, she scurried up by the wall, then ran across the open space to the corner of the house.

The shadows had moved now and because she knew that the old ladder would no longer be quite so shielded she cautiously put her head round the corner of the wall. And then it was she who almost screamed, for there, standing at the foot of the ladder, was the figure of a man looking upwards.

Unconsciously she gasped, and the sound brought him around; then almost in a spring he was standing beside her, towering over her. She had closed her eyes and was waiting for a blow or the sneer of Luke's voice or his arms coming about her, but it was Barney's voice she heard saying, "What do you think you're up to, Emma?"

"Oh! Barney." She opened her eyes. "I . . . I wa . . . was"—she was stammering now with relief—"I wa . . . was just taking . . . I mean . . . I . . . I had just been for a str . . . stroll."

"At this time of night!" His voice was a hissing whisper.

And she answered, "It was very hot up there."

"Did you hear somebody scream a little while back?"

Again she closed her eyes and it was some seconds before she said, "I heard something but I thought it was . . . was an animal trapped like."

"That was no animal, I . . . I thought it could be you."

"Me?" Her eyes were wide now as she looked at him.

"Yes, you, out on one of your night jaunts."

Barney had known she went out at nights and he . . . he hadn't split on her. Oh, Barney was nice.

"How . . . how did you know?"

"Oh, I knew; you're not the only one who likes to wander."

"You never let on."

"I . . . I didn't want to frighten you, or stop you from having a little . . . well, freedom, sort of."

"Oh, Barney, thank you, thank you."

There was a silence between them, and for all they stood in the shadow she could still make out his face. His eyes were soft and kind and now his voice came soft and kind as he asked her a question: "Do you like me, Emma?"

She had no hesitation in answering, "Oh, yes Barney I like you, I like you best of the lot. I always have."

"You're only thirteen, Emma, and I'm eighteen. I'm . . . I'm ready for a wife. You understand, Emma?"

She did, and she didn't, so she remained quiet, and he went on, "But . . . but I'm willin' to wait. I'm gona wait for you, Emma. Do you understand?"

Her mouth was dry, she gulped in her throat, gathered some spittle, wetted her lips with it, then said, "You mean, till I'm ready for courting like?"

"That's about it."

She felt warm, nice, protected; but that was only for a moment. "Your mother?" she said.

"My mother can't rule me life, an' she knows it, as does me da. I'll pick where I want to."

"But she wouldn't have me here, she'd go mad."

"There's other farms in the world and I've got a pair of hands on me. I know I'm no scholar, not like your other friends the painter and the parson, but I've me wits about me and could always make a good living for us both. What do you say, Emma?"

"I say, thank you, Barney."

His eyes were very bright, his lips were shining with moisture, his head was moving from side to side in small movements, and his voice sounded thick as he said, "It'll just be between us then, nobody to know only you and me?"

"Yes, Barney."

He put his arms out now and when they came about her and she was pressed close to him, her stomach seemed to whirl upwards and lodge against her throat. She felt she was going to choke; she didn't know whether she was happy or afraid.

His mouth was on hers; the lips were closed, as were hers, and they remained there for what seemed a long time, long enough for the feeling of fear to subside and a warm glow to take its place.

They were standing apart now and he said, "Go on, get up that ladder, and no more night jaunts. I've got to get back to old Dobbin."

"Is he bad?"

"Aye; I don't think he'll see the night out, he's had his day. He's twenty gone and he's been worked out. That's what they do on farms, Emma, they work you out. But they're not going to work me out, and they're not going to work you out. I'll see to it."

He leaned forward now and looked round the corner; then taking her hand, he drew her to the foot of the ladder.

When she had mounted it and was about to go through the hatch she looked down at him, and he smiled up at her and raised his hand.

A few minutes later she was lying on the pallet bed staring at the rafter that sloped steeply over her head. She had wanted adventure, something to happen, and it had happened. She was named. Barney had named her. Somehow it didn't matter about the parson getting married now, at least not so much.

Emma had come to the end of the last milking for the day. She lifted her head from the soft belly of the brown cow, sat still for a moment on the stool, let out a sigh that spoke of weariness, swivelled round and was about to rise and pick up the wooden bucket when her attention was caught by the sight of the missis standing in the opening of the cow byres talking to her husband who had just been leaving the byres with a pail in each hand. The missis had on her Sunday bonnet and her black beaded Sunday cape which she wore when she went visiting; and this wasn't often, but today she had been into Gateshead Fell and had apparently stopped in the village on her return for now she was saying, "I tell you the village is agog with it. Midnight they say when she came screaming down the road. Woke up the Turnbulls and they are some distance from her cottage, which is yon side of the graveyard. In fact, as Ann Turnbull said, she thought the dead had risen. Anyway it brought the parson out. He was in his study writing. Miss Wilkinson says he's sometimes there till one o'clock in the morning. She spluttered to the parson . . . I mean Peggy MacFarlane did, that she had seen the devil and he had thrown a dagger at her and just missed her heart. He was of a great height with horns and was black from head to foot."

"She must have been drunk."

"No, she wasn't, not Peggy MacFarlane."

"Then she's going off her head. Anyway, what did she want traipsing out at that time of night for? And her man's away, isn't he?"

"Aye; he's drovin' some cattle down for Hudson and Crosby."

"Aye, so he is . . . Crosby . . . so he is. Well now, what did she want out at that time of night, I ask you? And up near the Openwood, you say? Oh! oh!" The farmer now laughed. "I'd like to bet Eddy 'Farlane's aware what she gets up to when he's out of the way an' managed to slip back and take a shot at her. And I don't blame him."

"Well, there could be something in that, but I don't think so, 'cos he's been gone over two days, and if he had been back here somebody would have spotted him. He'd have a job to hide himself, would Eddy MacFarlane, the size he is. Anyway, she's in a state an' she says the knife was as big as a spear and it shone in the moonlight, an' when she ran the devil ran after her an' tried to catch her. But as soon as she reached the churchyard wall and clung on to it he disappeared, he couldn't come near holy ground."

At this Emma swung herself round on the milking stool again and once more her head was pressed against the warm belly of the cow, but now her hand was tight across her mouth. Eeh! the devil; and a knife as big as a spear; and the devil chasing her to the churchyard wall. When she lifted her face up it was wet. Quickly drying it on her apron and now assuming a solemn look, she rose and picked up the bucket of milk and went down the byres. The farmer and his wife were still talking and they had to move to one side to let her pass; but she was stopped by Dilly Yorkless suddenly stretching out her hand and touching the bucket and, her thoughts back to the business of the day, she said, "That from Primrose?"

"Yes, missis."

"It's down, isn't it?"

"Yes, a bit, missis."

"Haven't been stuffing yourself, have you?"

Emma straightened her weary back and looked straight at her mistress as she said, "I never touch the new milk; I don't like it warm, never have."

"Go on with you, and no backchat."

Emma went on and the farmer's wife's words followed her, saying, "Getting too big for her boots, that 'un. Wants taking down a peg, and I'll see to it, surely I will. . . ."

Later that evening, Lizzie had hardly put down on the table the dish of mutton stew that she had brought from the house before she said, "Something going on in the village; her ladyship came in full of it. You know Peggy MacFarlane, the drover's wife, who lives in the cottage down in the dip yon side of the church? Well, she's supposed to have seen the devil last night. And what I say is, it's about time he paid her a visit an' all; the antics she gets up to when her man's away. Anyway," Lizzie chuckled, "whoever the devil was he was up to her capers. I wonder who her partner in crime was this time? Hudson, while supposedly on his last rounds? Or it could be that son of his, Anthony, for he's a spark all right. It could even be Joe Mason; he thinks he's got enough charm to kill, does Joe. Not satisfied with knocking his beasts on the head, he serves them over his counter with a smile on which you could slide. Oh, it could be anyone of them. . . . What you doing up there? Washing yourself away?"

It was a moment before Emma turned from the tin dish and said, "I'm coming, Granny."

Quickly now, she dried her hands on the towel, wondering as she did so what Barney would make of the news. Would he be bright enough to put two and two together and make four? He just could, because he had his wits about him, wits enough to make him pass her a number of times the day without a word. Only once had he looked at her, and then his gaze was soft and had a kindly message.

As she went to the table she wished she could tell her granny. Oh she did; she wanted to have a good laugh.

She had a good laugh the next morning. She was somewhat late arriving at the cottage; the missis had been in a funny temper and had kept her at it until the last minute. Ten o'clock was the time she was supposed to be at the cottage and at half past nine the missis had come into the dairy and complained that the pans hadn't been scrubbed properly; she said there had been stale cream on one of the rims. Emma knew that was a lie: she couldn't have left stale cream on one of the rims because she always ran her hand round it when she finished, and if it wasn't absolutely smooth she went over it again. So it was almost on ten before she left the farm, and she'd hardly had time to tidy herself up, and she had run all the way and was panting for breath when she reached the back door.

She knew the parson was here because his trap was in the road, and so she went into the kitchen very quietly.

She paused a moment to get her breath and was pushing back the hair that had escaped from her cap when the two figures appeared in the kitchen doorway. It was as if they had been waiting for her. And she was a little startled by their manner.

It was Mr Bowman who spoke first. "Ah-ha!" he said; "what have we here? A young lady or a demon? Come here, miss."

He was beckoning with an outstretched arm and slow-moving forefinger, but as she moved towards him her eyes rested on the parson who had his head bowed and his chin pulled into his stiff white collar; and his eyes were turned up, almost seeming to disappear beneath his eyebrows in a questioning manner. He looked very funny. But when she neared them it was Mr Bowman who said in a deep voice, "Emma Molinero, what have you got to say for yourself?"

They both now backed away from her into the living-room, and after hesitating a moment she followed them, her teeth tight pressed down on her lower lip, her head thrust forward. And now she was staring at the slabs on the stone floor, unconsciously taking in the fact that they weren't very dirty and would just need to be washed this morning and not scrubbed, as the weather had been so dry there were no mud marks to be got off.

"Come here, Emma."

The parson was now sitting down on the chair by the window, and when she was standing in front of him, their faces on a level, he asked quietly, "What have you got to tell us, Emma?"

She looked from the parson up to the painter and, her voice very small, she said, "You mean about the devil?"

"About the devil, Emma," the parson said, "about the devil. He was dressed all in black and threw a spear at a defenceless woman."

Her teeth dragged in her lip again and, her head bending further down now, she muttered, "It was very hot and I went out for a walk." Her head jerking up now, she looked at the parson, adding quickly, "I hadn't done it for a long, long time." Then her glance taking in the painter as well, she said, "I . . . I wanted to do something . . . well, not just walk. I don't know." She shook her head. "Anyway, it being a bright moonlight night, I thought I could practise throwing the knives. I don't get much chance otherwise and they remind me of Dada. They sort of bring him back because"—again her gaze was centered on the parson—"he gets dim in me mind. I can't remember what he looked like at times. But when I touch the knives or the whip he comes back, and so I . . . I took a couple of knives and went into the wood, and I just threw one." Her mouth opened wide now, her eyes stretched, and she made a gasping sound in her throat as she looked at the painter who had dropped on to his hunkers by the side of the parson. They seemed almost as one, and now she was spluttering as she said, "I'd . . . I'd hardly thrown it, it just left me hand, and . . . and I didn't hear it hit the tree 'cos she yelled. An' then they were all mixed up scrambling around, and . . . and then they ran dragging their clothes. . . ." Her voice trailed away on the word clothes; she couldn't go on to tell about the man with bare legs.

Her head was down, her body was shaking when two pairs of arms came round her and she was clasped between the parson and the painter, and their combined laughter filled the room.

When she was standing alone again the painter was sitting on the floor, his head almost between his knees, and the parson was rubbing his face vigorously with a handkerchief, and he muttered, "Oh, Emma, Emma, what are we going to do with you? You have caused the devil to walk, and . . . and after all, though I say it, it may not be such a bad thing, my congregation may swell on Sunday." Then impulsively he reached out and caught her hand and, his voice changing, he added, "Oh, Emma, in more ways than one you bring brightness into life."

"That I endorse," said the painter getting to his feet. "That I endorse. And come, let's drink on it, eh? Tea, Emma, and I'll see if there's something left in the bottle to strengthen it. All right! All right!" He now nodded towards the parson. "You can have it plain, but I like mine polished."

She was running back into the kitchen, only to be stopped at the door by the painter's voice calling, "The man, Emma, did you see him?"

"Oh yes, I saw him, Mr Bowman."

"Would you know him again?"

She thought a moment, then shook her head, saying, "No; only his hair."

"His hair?"

"Aye, it was very thick. Well, I mean it seemed to stand up from his head a long way and looked light, not white, not old hair, just light."

"Huh! That's a very good description, Emma."

As she went into the kitchen she heard the painter say, "Not old, light and thick, describes our neighbour Hudson's head. What do you say, Henry?"

And she heard the parson's voice answering jovially, "I would say you have an artist's eye, Ralph. Thick and fair and standing straight up. . . . I bet it was standing straight up. What do you think?"

Again there was laughter, rollicking and deep now; and then she heard the parson say a strange thing: "I shouldn't be in the church, Ralph, not with my mind. I shouldn't be in the church."

No laughter followed this, but the painter said, "That's another thing I endorse, Henry, and wholeheartedly."

As she made the tea she wondered if the parson hadn't been a parson, what he would have been. She couldn't put a trade to him. But still, if he hadn't been a parson she would never have met him, and if she had never met him that would have been a great miss in her life, even if he was going to be married.

4

Routine is subject to the weather, it is lengthened or shortened by it. Now at the beginning of December the cock didn't crow so early, the hens didn't lay so early, pigs grunted later, the horses didn't neigh for their first drink of water before the light showed; only the cows seemed to be indifferent to the seasons, and at times their bags were painfully full to overflowing before they were relieved.

The farm didn't waken till six o'clock during late autumn and early winter. Even with this respite the pallet dragged at Emma. She would descend the ladder in the bleak flesh-shrinking mornings and have to grope towards the table for the candle and the matches because her granny wouldn't allow her a candle up in the roof, it would be too dangerous. Often she would find her granny curled up like a ball under the blanket and the sheepskin mat and it would take a great deal to waken her. Sometimes she let her lie until she had the fire going and a cup of hot milk ready. They didn't often have tea; it was only at Mr Bowman's that tea seemed to flow like water in the burn, always there when you needed it.

But this morning Lizzie was up and dressed and had the fire going. They didn't usually exchange more than a sentence or two in the early morning, but this morning, Lizzie, pointing to a tin dish which was set before the stool in front of the fire, said, "Put your foot in that; it's a bit hot, but the hotter the better."

"But it's all right, Granny, it's healed over."

"You were limping last night."

"Well, it's just a bit sore on the scab."

"It was a rusty spike, wasn't it?"—her granny's voice was harsh now—"and near the big toe, and anything near a big toe or a thumb can cause lock-jaw. Put your foot in there and do what you're told."

Although the hole pierced in the sole of her foot by the nail which had also pierced her boot had healed over, it was, as she said, still sore. And so she was warmed by her granny's concern. She was also warmed right through by the hot water covering her foot and to add to it she put her other foot in the dish; as she did so looking up at her granny through the candlelight and saying, "No use wastin' good hot water."

Lizzie made no reply to this light jest but, going to the fire, she took off the black iron pan full of porridge and ladled half a dozen dollops into a bowl, and after pouring some milk on to it she handed it, together with a wooden spoon, to Emma, saying, "You sitting for a picture for him these days?"

"No; he hasn't done any painting for weeks, not since his cough got bad again. He sits over the fire most of the time." She stopped abruptly because she knew that her granny knew he sat over the fire most of the time, because she sometimes slipped up there at nights. But apparently he didn't tell her what he did during the day, and she hadn't had the extra shilling for some time now.

Emma's mind went to the niche in the rafters where the little bag of sovereigns lay, and she felt guilty and somewhat mean. What could she do with the money? She couldn't even buy a ribbon, and oh, at times how she longed for a new hair ribbon! Her desire didn't range as far as a bonnet or a coat, new clothes were something that were bestowed on the children of the gentry; or on Mary Haswell, or on Miss Kathleen Hudson, Farmer Hudson's granddaughter, they seemed to be dressed in different clothes twice a year.

" 'Tisn't going to be an all-day job." Her granny brought her thoughts back to the present and so she hurriedly wiped her feet, then reached out to the fender where she had laid her stockings and boots to warm. She put them on before she started on her breakfast.

Ten minutes later she began her day's work, and the only comfort during the following four hours of grind before she made her way to Mr Bowman's was the warmth in the cow byres and in the chicken run.

She was limping quite a bit when she arrived at the back door of the cottage, and she was surprised when she entered the kitchen to hear voices coming from the living-room. The other one she recognized immediately as that of the parson, and the absence of his gig outside pointed to him having walked. Twice recently she had seen him walking, but at a distance.

She couldn't hear exactly what he was saying until she unwound the woollen scarf that covered the hood of her cape, when his voice sounded clear in her ears as he said, "I know it's for the best yet I feel guilty. Part of me though is relieved; but the greater part of me feels disappointment, rejection and not a little foolish."

"Best thing that could have happened." It was Mr Bowman's voice, thick and husky as he went on, "I told you at the beginning, and it would have been a catastrophe if it had gone through. You're well out of it, and she was wise to realise this. . . . Man, she stuck out like a sore thumb. If you were so badly in need of a wife far better you had taken Miss Wilkinson because she's been apprenticed to the job for years, she would have fitted your situation like a glove and. . . ."

"Don't be silly, Ralph. To me Miss Wilkinson is a spinster lady of uncertain years. She's almost forty if a day."

"Well, what's ten or eleven years between friends?" The painter began to cough now, and the parson said, "You should get away from here, Ralph, the air's too harsh."

"Yes, I should. . . . Yes I should." The words were said between gasps. "And if pigs and paupers could fly, I'd be away tomorrow."

"I wish I could help."

"You do, you do, more than you know. Oh yes, more than you know, Henry. Anyway, I'm not worried, I've got over worse spells than this. And I don't intend to die, not for a long time."

"Have you had the doctor recently?"

"Yes, Henry, I've had the doctor recently, and he assures me it's not the consumption; bronchial tubes and other bits of odds and ends stopped up, that's all. Once we get the winter over they'll all empty. It's as simple as that."

"Nothing's simple."

"Well, perhaps you're right, except perhaps the truth when one is honest enough to face up to it. And I can tell you this, Henry: you face up to the truth in yourself and you'll find you're damned glad to have escaped."

She had by now put on a clean apron, smoothed the front of her hair from her forehead, taken off her muddy boots and put on her rope sandals, and all done quietly. But now she clattered the pan in the bottom of the dish that was standing on the little table, and the painter's voice came from the other room saying, "That you, Emma?"

The next minute the parson was looking at her through the kitchen door. He did not speak immediately; when he did his voice sounded ordinary as he said, "Nasty morning, Emma."

"Yes, Parson; where the ice has thawed on the road it's very muddy."

"I found it so."

She smiled at him. It was a smile of greeting, it was as if he had returned from being away for a long time: she was seeing him now as she had seen him before the threat of marriage hung over him, or over her. She couldn't work it out; she only knew she was glad that young woman wasn't coming into the parish, and into his life. She must have given him the push. Well, whichever one had done it, she was glad.

She walked towards him now and he moved aside to allow her to enter the room. Going straight up to Ralph Bowman, she stood in front of him, saying, "How are you today, Mr Bowman?"

"As you see me, Emma. As you see me."

"I've a message for you from Billy."

"A message for me from Mr William Proctor? Well! well! Let me hear it."

"Well"—she nodded her head towards him—"he says you could be rid of your cough within a week or so if you rubbed your chest every night with goose fat and sucked some houghhound, or put it in some hot water and drank it."

"Well now. Well now. Is that a fact?"

"That's what Billy says. And it's worth tryin', houghhound's cheap enough, and I could get you the goose fat."

"What do you think of that, Henry?" The painter was looking up at the parson, and Henry said, "Sounds a very sensible cure to me, especially the houghhound, for I think you've already tried the goose fat."

"Not for a long time—couldn't be bothered—but this combination sounds very good. Henry, the next time you're in Gateshead Fell, for I don't suppose the village shop would stock it, you could get me some houghhound. Houghhound ginger, that's the term, isn't it, houghhound ginger?" He appealed to Emma.

"Yes"—she was nodding at him now—"houghhound ginger, or houghhound candy, it's the same thing."

"Talking of cures, Emma, how's your foot?"

"Oh, it's nearly better, Mr Bowman, thanks."

"Emma trod on a rusty nail. It went through the sole of her boot." Ralph Bowman was again looking at Henry, and he, all concern, turned to Emma, saying, "I thought you were limping. Have you had it seen to?"

"Oh aye. Yes. It's all healed. It's just when I step on it at the side like. . . . Shall I make some tea?" She had spoken to Ralph Bowman again and he said, "Yes, Emma, make some tea."

While she busied herself filling the kettle and preparing the tray for the tea her ears were alert to the conversation in the next room, but it didn't bring her to a stop until she heard the parson's voice low and angry-sounding saying, "Utter scandal, the way they have her working on that farm, and she but a child."

And now Mr Bowman's voice answering, "I agree with you in part, but you know, Henry, what's escaping you and has escaped me till recently is that our Emma is no longer a child; at times she is even no longer a little girl. The last picture I did of her, which is all of seven months ago now, even then I saw the young woman emerging. In a couple of years' time she could be married."

"Oh no! No!" The words sounded vehement.

"Oh, yes, yes. There's three hefty fellows on that farm and you can't tell me that they've closed their eyes to her. Henry, you go around with your head in the clouds and your eyes on the stars, you don't see what's below your nose."

"That isn't right, and you know it. I'm no star gazer, Ralph, and I know what goes on under my nose, only too well, and that has made me uneasy, so uneasy that I am every day questioning my position. I've told you before I feel I'm in the wrong job so to speak. But as for Emma being fit for marriage in two years. . . . No!"

"Oh, Henry." There was a long pause now before the painter went on, "You've always seen Emma through coloured glass. She's a woman in the making and, let me tell you, she's going to be a very disturbing woman. As for not being ready for marriage, what about the latest stir in the village with your little Nell Highpen, fourteen years old and about to give birth, and they don't know whether it's her father or her brother or one of the customers from The Tuns from whom she was seen begging pennies. . . ."

"There's a difference between that poor child and Emma. Emma has intelligence, she can read and write, better I should imagine than any of the children of the gentry, better I do know than John and Peter Fordyke. I've seen their hand with the pen, and their mother's too, and she a lady in her own right. That kind of thing will not happen to Emma, except . . . except. . . ."

"Yes, Henry?"

"Well, you know what I mean, unless it is forced on her."

"And that could be. Yes, it well could be. She thinks she's only got to carry that whip in her waistband and she's protected from the devil himself. But you let some determined big lout get. . . ."

"Be quiet, Ralph."

"All right. I'll be quiet. The only thing I'll say is, the quicker she's married the better for all concerned, Henry . . . for all concerned."

A deep silence followed this statement during which Emma stood still near the table, her ears strained towards the next room from which there came no sound of movement, and she imagined that the two men might be standing looking at each other.

For herself, she was looking out through the little window into the bleak day and she was feeling slightly indignant that these two friends of hers, and she did class them as friends although one was her employer and the other a parson, should, in a way, be arranging her life and that the only escape they saw for her was through marriage and that as soon as possible. Well, she wasn't going to get married just to escape. . . . But what about Barney? She was promised to Barney. But that wouldn't happen for a long time, well, not until she was eighteen, or nineteen, or perhaps twenty years old. . . . Would Barney wait that long? Barney had said he'd be quite willing to wait until she was ready, and she would have to be very ready before she married, 'cos it was a frightening thing. She knew that already, yes a very frightening thing, for Miss Wilkinson let her read some of the Bible stories to the Sunday School class now, and last week she read about the Marriage at Cana. And afterwards, Kate McGill collared her outside and started telling her about what happened when their Mary got married. They all worked on Mr Crosby's farm and they'd had a big tea and dance and great do's in the barn; then when they were all rowdy they had carried both Mary and her Tommy half a mile down the road to the cottage and pulled their clothes off them and stuck them in bed together. But it didn't matter because Tommy had been too drunk to do anything to their Mary.

That was marriage.

She wanted none of it, not even with Barney.

She took the tray of tea into the room. They were talking to each other now about the Houses of Parliament up in London town and a Mr Peel doing something about corn.

She returned to the kitchen and went about her work, and decided it wasn't a nice morning at all, and her foot was hurting her worse than ever.

It was just turned twelve when she left the cottage. The weather had worsened, the wind was blowing now and there were specks in it. Her hands were freezing. Her granny, she knew, was knitting her some mittens for Christmas; she wished she had them now.

She had left the bridle-path and was beginning to cross the second field when she saw the riders in the distance. There were two of them. The hunt often crossed this way, but there was no hunt on today that she knew of; they were just two men, she supposed, out for a gallop, and they were galloping in her direction. She kept on walking, hurrying now to where there was some low scrub and an outcrop of rock, thinking that they wouldn't come near that. The only reason she wanted to be out of their way was that the horses kicked up so much earth she would be spattered with it.

When she reached the rocks she paused and looked to the side. The riders seemed to have changed their course and to be riding away from her; then of a sudden they wheeled the horses about and came galloping straight towards her, and she gasped and was on the point of yelling when they brought their horses to a skidding stop close to the outcrop and almost to her side.

Looking up at the riders, she saw that they were Masters John and Peter Fordyke from the House; she had seen them in the hunt, and also the time when they had accompanied their father to the farm. But that was a good two years ago, and then they had appeared like two young lads but now they looked like young men. The elder must be all of seventeen, if not more, and it was he who spoke to her, shouting at her, "You're the girl from the farm, aren't you, Yorkless's?"

She nodded.

"I hear tell you're out of a circus?"

She made no answer to this.

"Have you lost your tongue?"

"No sir, I haven't lost my tongue."

"Oh, she's alive." The elder turned his head and looked at the younger rider who now spoke, saying, "They said when you were little you used to do fancy tricks with the whip. Can you still do them?"

"Yes, if need be."

They both stared at her now while their horses pawed the ground and tossed their heads.

What happened next was so sudden that she was taken off her guard, for the older boy, flicking his riding crop towards her, shouted, "Catch that!"

The short lash flicked across her eyes and her hand coming up swiftly grabbed at it, and as the rider jerked at the other end of it the leather seared the skin of her palm. But at the same time it also revived in her the old flashing rage and with the sudden twist of her wrist she caught hold of the lash and the next minute the stock had been wrenched from the young man's hand, and almost in one movement she swung it round and towards his leather-booted leg. But such were her feelings and the unbalanced stance she was placed in because of her sore foot that she missed her aim and the crop stung the animal's flank and the next minute it was rearing on its hind legs, only to plunge downwards, bringing its rider toppling over its head.

There was a sickening thud, and her eyes became fixed on the inert figure now lying between the rocks. The younger man had dismounted and was shouting unintelligible words; he had already caught his brother's horse and tied it to a stump of a tree. When he knelt down on the ground beside his brother, Emma was still standing staring: her life seemed to have stopped; she felt no beat in her heart; a great dread had frozen her body and fixed it to the ground; the only thing that was left alive within her was her mind. She had unseated the son of the House and he looked dead.

"Help me to lift him!" The shout from the younger boy brought life back into her and it jerked her forward.

Without hesitation she put her arms under the shoulders of the prostrate figure and helped to pull him clear of the outcrop of rock and on to the flat muddy ground of the field. When he was straightened out she stood with her back bent looking down on the still form, watching the younger boy shaking his brother gently while pleading, "John! John! Come on, wake up."

When there was no answering movement to his plea he turned and, staring up at Emma, said, "You . . . you see what you've done! You've killed him. Go and get help. Go to the farm and get help!"

Again the boy's command seemed to bring life back into her and she was already racing over the field. The mud, clogging her boots, impeded her, and once she fell forward on to her hands but was up again in a second. And she didn't take the back way which would lead her first to the cottage, she made straight for the farmyard yelling, "Mister! Barney! Pete!"

She hadn't called Luke's name, but it was he who appeared in the yard first, and she came to a running stop a few yards from him and cried, "One of the young masters is hurt, they want help. Fell off his horse, near the crop stones in bottom field."

Jake Yorkless was by now looking down on them from the hay loft and he shouted, "What is it? What's the nuration?" And Luke answered him, "Young master, he's had an accident. In bottom field."

Jake now turned to Emma, demanding, "What kind of an accident?"

"He . . . he's hit his head; he hasn't come round."

"Better take the old gate." Luke was calling to his father as he ran towards the barn, and Jake Yorkless, who had come down into the yard, shouted after him, "Give Barney a call. He's mending west fence, he'll hear you through top loft."

"What is it? What's the nuration about?" Dilly Yorkless was in the yard now, with Lizzie behind her, and the farmer, thumbing in Emma's direction, said, "She says young master's been hurt: fell off his horse; lying in the outcrop."

"Fell off his horse?" Dilly Yorkless looked at Emma, then said, "How did that happen?"

Emma remained mute: they would know soon enough and then the heavens would open above her.

"Well, answer me, girl. Were you there or weren't you?"

"I . . . I was there." But she was saved from going on further by Luke appearing in the yard with the gate, for his father, taking hold of the other side, said, "Well, let's get going. And you"—he was nodding towards his wife now—"you'd better come along. Bring a towel and things in case they're needed."

Without further ado his wife turned and hurried back into the kitchen; then reappeared within seconds it seemed, her coat on, a shawl over her head, and a bundle of towels under her arm.

"Will I come an' all?" It was Lizzie asking the question, and Dilly Yorkless answered abruptly, "Can't see the need, and there's plenty to do inside. As for you!" She nodded at Emma. "Get about the day's business; you've wasted enough time as it is."

The yard empty, Lizzie looked at Emma, saying now, "You're as white as a sheet, girl. What happened?"

Before she could answer, Barney came running into the yard calling to Lizzie, "Something wrong? What's our Luke yelling about?"

"There's been an accident to the young master of the House, so I understand. He's down in the bottom field among the outcrop. They want you down there."

"Oh. Bad?"

"I know nothin' about it. Emma here has just brought the news."

"Is he bad, Emma?"

Her mouth opened to say, "I don't know," but there was a great heave in her stomach and she turned from him and ran towards the cowshed wall and, leaning her head against it, vomited.

Barney made to go towards her, but Lizzie stopped him, saying, "I'll see to her; you'd better get along with the rest, they need four hands on a gate."

"What is it?" Lizzie was speaking quietly now as she bent over Emma, and Emma, lifting her apron from between the folds of her coat, wiped her mouth and, looking at Lizzie, all she could say was, "Oh! Granny; I . . . I did it."

"*What!*"

"He . . . he went to hit me with his crop for no reason, and I grabbed it. . . . Look"—she held out her hand—"it burned it, so . . . so I pulled it from his hand but . . . but—" She put her hand over her mouth as if she were going to retch again, then finished in a rush, "I missed me aim, I . . . I lost me balance 'cos of me bad foot; I went for his leg and I hit the horse and it up-ended and threw him."

"In the name of God!"

Lizzie groaned aloud now; then taking Emma's arm, she said, "Come on into the house." And like that she took her through the yard and to the cottage.

When Emma was seated shivering before the banked-down fire, Lizzie, looking at her, said slowly, "Trouble seems to follow you, girl, as the sparks fly upwards. What'll be the outcome of this only God knows. You and those whips! I'll burn 'em. I will, so help me God! I'll burn 'em. And what if he dies? Child"—she bent right down to her—"what have you done? And to the son of the House. My God! It's well Fordyke doesn't own this farm or else him and her and the rest of them and you and me together would be out on the road this very day. But you . . . it's more than likely they'll see you on the road, me girl, after this business. Nothing I could say will change their tune concerning you from now on. I can bet me last halfpenny on that. And where will you go, she won't give you a reference for service? There'll only be the pits, and likely you're too big to go down there now, it's the little 'uns they're after. Oh God!" She began to pace the room now, her hands to her head, and all the while Emma sat staring at the dull embers of the fire.

Her mind was racing. She already knew what she would do if she was sent away; she would find the company and join them. But her granny's next words shattered that hope as if it had been struck by lightning, and, as lightning sears, so was her brain seared by the words: "If he dies, they could hang you, girl. That, or at best send you to Botany Bay, you're not too young for that, or put you in the house of correction for life. Oh! God in heaven, why am I to suffer this? All my life I've been plagued: work and disaster, that's all I've known, and a love that turned sour. . . ." She caught herself up on the last words; then slowly coming back up the room she stood before Emma again and quietly now she said, "Stay put here. One or t'other of them should be back shortly, likely her. I'll stand the brunt of it before they get at you, and I'll pray to God, and you do, too, that he's still alive."

It seemed to Emma an eternity of painful lifetimes until at three o'clock when, going to the cottage door for the countless time, she heard the commotion in the yard and knew they were all back. She heard the missis's voice raised high; then her granny's voice even higher; but she couldn't make out what they were saying, yet the substance of it she knew only too well. Standing against the stanchion, she pressed her head back and closed her eyes tight while her joined hands were gripping the front of her dress.

Her eyes sprang wide when she heard the steps coming round the side of the house and when Barney appeared she let out a long shuddering breath.

Quickly he came to her and, standing against the opposite stanchion, he said, " 'Tis all right, he came round. He was concussed and his head split open at the back, but he'll survive. 'Tis all right, 'tis all right, don't cry. Oh, Emma, don't cry; you've been through enough. What did he do to you?"

She couldn't speak because of the enormous lump clogging her throat, and he went on, "His brother said you struck out at him with a crop."

Spluttering and choking and her head moving up and down, she muttered, "It was hissen. He brought it across my face and . . . and I grabbed it." She held out her hand and showed him the weal. It had turned blue now and there were two parts where the skin was broken and the blood was oozing through. "I . . . I pull . . . pulled it out of his hand and went to . . . to. . . ."

" 'Tis all right, don't distress yourself any more. But you've got to face up to it, they'll likely send for you."

"Who?" The question came from high in her head.

"Them up at the House; they are not the kind to pass it over. But you stand up for yourself. Do you hear? Stand up for yourself. . . . I've got to go now."

As quickly as he had come he disappeared around the side of the house, and within seconds her granny came from the other direction, and all she said was, "One thing, you've been saved from the gallows. But don't think you'll get off scot-free; if she never had it in for you afore, she's got it in for you now, and somethin' to hang on to. Anyway, go on and get about your work. Keep out of sight if you can. I've told her what'll happen if she lays a hand on you, so you needn't be afraid of that. But I don't know which is the worse, her hand or her tongue, and that's gona flay you if I know her. Still, don't answer back. There's only one thing I hope." Lizzie nodded to herself and finished on a private note as she said, "I hope God lets me live long enough to see me day with them. That's all I pray for."

5

Three days later she was summoned to the House. The message was
brought by a groom, by word of mouth. Riding into the yard, he looked
down disdainfully on the farmer's wife as he said, "Your girl, one
Emma Crawshaw, is to be at the Hall at eleven o'clock this morning."
And on this he turned away, having showed more arrogance than his
master might have done.

Almost joyfully, Dilly Yorkless took the message to Lizzie. Without
preamble, she said, "She's for it. They want her up there at eleven
o'clock."

Lizzie rose from her knees where she had been scrubbing the short
stone passage leading from the kitchen into the hall and, drying her
hands, she said, "Aye, well, she'll need company, and she's having
mine."

"Oh, no she's not!"

"But oh, yes she is. She's not goin' up there alone to be eaten alive."

"If anybody's goin', I'll go with her."

"No, you won't. You're no kin to her, you've got nothing to do with
her."

"I'm her mistress. That's kin enough in the circumstances." Dilly
Yorkless ground her teeth together as she looked at her life-long opponent; then she ended weakly but harshly, "If you insist on leaving your
work I'll go and tell Jake."

"Do that. Do that." Lizzie picked up the bucket, went to the side
door and threw the slops into the yard; then placing the empty bucket
to the side of the door, she looked again at her mistress, saying, "Yes,
do that. And tell him to come and try and stop me. Do that, Dilly."
And on this she went out and walked steadily across the yard. But once
clear of it, she scampered towards the chicken runs where she knew
Emma would be at this time of the morning, and opening the door she
knew a moment's sadness as she saw the thin figure of her grand-

daughter scraping the hen droppings from the top of the egg boxes over which ran the roosting barks.

Emma was using the scraper so hard that she hadn't heard the door open and not until her granny's voice said, "Emma, you're wanted," did she turn and go towards her.

"You've been called to the House. You've got to be there for eleven. It's ten now; get inside and give yourself a good wash and put on your good frock." She was walking by the child's side now and she added, "Don't worry, I'm comin' along of you."

"You are, Granny?"

"Aye, I am."

"Oh, ta. I . . . I'd be terrified on me own."

"You'll be terrified in any case. I don't suppose they'll let me into the House. Still, we'll wait and see. . . ."

Fifteen minutes later they left the farm. They did not take the short cut along the bridle-path but went by the coach road, and it was five minutes to eleven when the lodge keeper let them through the iron gates and they walked up the drive, and for the first time they saw the front-age of Head Hall. From a rise above the coach road only the chimneys could be espied standing out above the surrounding trees, but from here the House was a monument of imposing stone, with a pillared front and turrets at one end.

Knowing better than to approach the House from the front, Lizzie drew them to a stop for a moment. To the left of her she saw a path skirting a high hedge, the top of which had been cut into the shape of birds, and she drew Emma along it. As she had surmised it led to the side of the courtyard.

Emma's life was mostly spent in the farmyard and its surrounding buildings, and so she gazed in amazement at this space which was four times the size of the farmyard, with a whole row of horse-boxes flanking one side, most of them showing horses, their heads bobbing over the half-doors. But her amazement at the size of the yard was nothing to that as they entered the kitchen. Her granny had knocked on the door and it had been opened by a girl of Emma's own size but dressed, oh so differently, for she was wearing a light blue print dress, over which was a stiff white bibbed apron, and over that a waist apron of dark blue ma-terial. She had a cap on her head that had a goffered front, and under it her face was round and red-cheeked. She smiled at them but it did noth-ing to reassure Emma, for here she was standing in this wonderland of a room, and she could count five people. They were all working, yet at the same time they were all looking at her.

A cook spoke to them. She was of medium height, round in the body, and her tone was not unkindly as she said, "You can sit down there." She pointed to a settle set back in the fireplace alcove. Some form of meat was being grilled above the large open fire. Then turning to a young girl, she said, "You Lily, go and tell Mrs Atkins they're here."

The cook now came and stood in front of Lizzie, saying, "I can't offer you a sup of anything 'cos you could be called any minute."

At any other time Emma would have loved a sup of anything, but now she was feeling sick and trembling inside. Yet she was taking in all the things in this enormous kitchen, the beautiful things: the shining pans, the great steel and brass fender, the huge black oak dresser that stretched into the far dimness of the room and which was weighed down with china, all beautiful coloured china. And then there was the ceiling of the kitchen. This end of it seemed to be covered with bunches of herbs hanging from hooks, while further along were other shapes which she couldn't quite make out. The floor was stone, she saw, like the farm kitchen, but this was clean as a new pin. And then she saw why, all of them in the room were wearing slippers.

Of a sudden she was on her feet, and her granny too, for there, coming towards them, was a black-dressed figure of a lady. Well, she looked a lady.

After looking at Emma for a long moment, she spoke to Lizzie, saying, "I'm Mrs Atkins, the housekeeper. The master is ready for her."

"Can't I come an' all?"

"No."

The thin trimly dressed woman turned to Emma and said, "Come." And Emma, glancing at her granny, hesitated. But then both the housekeeper and her granny spoke together, the housekeeper saying again, "Come," and her granny muttering, "Go on."

She followed the housekeeper up the kitchen, through a green-baized door into what looked like a small hall with a lot of doors going off, and from one a young boy in a dark green suit poked his head out and stared at her. Then they were going through another door, and she was in a big hallway in which two uniformed men were standing and to her eyes they looked gaudy, like the men at the fair dressed sometimes. The housekeeper spoke to the taller one, her voice in a low mutter, and he, bringing his gaze to bear on Emma, let it rest there for a while before lifting his hand and crooking his little finger, which seemed to press his head back and bring his chin out.

Now she was walking just slightly behind the imposing figure and having to suit her step to his. They mounted a staircase that curved round and which was so thickly carpeted that she could feel the softness through the soles of her heavy boots. And at the head of the stairs it was as if the butler had been thinking about her boots for, pausing, he brought his dignified gaze round and on to her bonnet for a moment before it lowered itself, seemingly against its better judgement, to her feet. And there it rested for some seconds before it caused him to take a sharp intake of breath. Then again they were moving on down a corridor that had windows on one side and marble heads of men on stands set between them; through another door, along another corridor, and then they stopped.

As she watched the gingery-brown-clad arm lift and knock twice on the door Emma felt her knees were about to give way and her mind gabbled a prayer: at that moment, the worry that was churning her stomach wasn't so much concerned with what was about to happen to her, but that she wouldn't be sick on these lovely carpets.

The butler had opened the door and now was standing aside with his hand on the knob, motioning her inside.

Ten seconds could have been counted before she crossed the threshold and when she heard the door close behind her she jerked her head to the side, but the grandly dressed man was no longer there.

She was staring wide-eyed at the occupants of the room: she took in first of all the younger of the two riders, then a man of medium height, youngish but inclined to be stout. These two were both standing, but sitting in a wheel-chair was a man with white hair and a white moustache, and his face looked thin and his body looked thin, what she could make out of it, under the rug that was over his knees. Part of her mind wondered why he needed a rug because the room was stifling; yet in spite of this she was shivering.

"Come here." It was the plumpish man who spoke, and now she walked slowly until she was standing with her toes pointing towards the head of a tiger, whose skin was set in front of the hearth like a rug.

"Your name?"

"Emma Crawshaw."

The three pairs of eyes were fixed on her. And then the man spoke again: "Do you know that you nearly killed my son?" he said.

She gave no answer, but the man in the wheel-chair made a sound like a grunt.

"If justice was being done, you'd be in court this very morning being tried for your crime, but . . . but because my father-in-law considers your age we have decided to treat you with some leniency." He now looked down on the older man. But there was no movement from the figure in the chair who continued to stare at Emma, and so his son-in-law went on, "We have brought you here to see what punishment is fit for people who act like wild animals and attack riders. . . ."

"I never did."

The words were loud and out before she could stop them, and her chin, like the butler's, was thrust upwards. And now having spoken, she repeated, "I never did attack them . . . he did me."

"You struck out with a crop and hit his horse."

She was glaring at the youth now, and as if he were an opponent who was her equal she cried at him, "I had no crop of my own, 'twas his. He brought it across my face and I grabbed at the end and pulled it out of his hand."

"You mean to say that you grabbed the end of his crop and pulled it out of my son's hand?" The plump man had his head poked out towards her, and defiantly she answered him, saying, "Yes, I do. And look, that's what happened to me hand." She held the palm upwards and the man's head came further forward as he looked down on it through narrowed eyes. Then he turned and looked at his son. Neither of them spoke, but their heads were jerked round, as was Emma's, when a voice like a deep growl came from the chair, saying, "Here! girl."

Slowly now, she skirted the tiger's head, then stepped gingerly on to its back and walked towards its tail and stood within a foot or so of the chair.

"Your hand." It was another growl.

She turned her hand palm upwards towards him, and the man brought his upper body forward in the chair and peered at it. Then turning his head slowly towards his grandson, his voice even more gruff now, he said, "This is a different story. Did John or did he not strike at her?"

The youth glanced at his father, looked down at the carpet and was about to speak when the old man bellowed now, "Answer, boy! Yes or no. Did John strike at her first?"

"He . . . he just flicked his crop, Grandfather."

"Across her face?"

The boy swallowed deeply and said, "I . . . I couldn't see from . . . where . . . where I was."

"But you could see that she retaliated and hit back, you could see that, couldn't you?"

"Yes, Grandfather." The voice was small.

The old man stared hard at the young one's bent head before turning and looking at Emma again and asking, "How did you manage to get the crop from my grandson's hand?"

Emma looked into the sunken blue eyes for a moment. The skin round them was very wrinkled but the eyes themselves were bright, and as she held their gaze a little of the fear in her subsided, and almost brightly now she said, "It was with a flick of me wrist, sir, like that!" She demonstrated.

"Where did you learn the trick?"

Before she could answer the plump man put in, "She's of gypsy stock."

"I am not. I am not of gypsy stock."

The plump man seemed to swell before her eyes, his face assuming an expression of instant anger, his mouth opening wide, but before he could utter any reprimand the old man forestalled him by saying, "Of what stock are you?"

Her breathing had quickened and she had to swallow before she said, "Me father was Spanish, sir. He worked in a travelling show. He was a great man with the whips and the knives."

"And he taught you to use the whips?"

She moved her head downwards, saying, "Yes, a bit sir. He . . . he died when I was seven, and I was sent here—" she thumbed over her shoulder now and ended, "to the farm an' me granny."

The old man surveyed her for a long moment. "Did you purposely hit out at the horse with the intention of unsaddling my grandson?"

"No, I did not, sir; I went to aim for his leg. And I wouldn't have hurt him, 'cos he had a leather boot on, but I have a bad foot where a nail went through the sole of me boot an' I didn't have a good balance an' . . . an' what's more"—her voice sank—"I was afeared."

The old man took his gaze slowly from her and let it rest on his son and his grandson. Then addressing his son, he said, "What have you got to say to this? Has the boy got nothing to do in his free time but to search out menials to taunt? This settles it: no more school, it's the army for him."

She watched the plump man's head droop downwards. Then the old gentleman was saying to her, "Does your hand hurt badly?" and she answered, "No, sir."

"Could you show me how you use your whips?"

The widening of her eyes seemed to have affected her lower jaw for it dropped open and it was on a gulp she said, "Show you, sir?"

"That's what I said."

For a moment she forgot about the other two occupants of the room and she smiled at the old man and said in an almost light tone, "I'd be pleased to, sir."

"What kind of whip do you want?"

"I can swing anything up to ten feet, perhaps a little more. I haven't had much practice lately, not with the long ones."

She watched the old man turn and nod towards the mantelpiece, and his grandson, who was nearer to him, put his hand out and pulled on a thick red cord. Within seconds there was a tap on the door and the butler entered. Bowing slightly, he waited, and the old man barked at him, "Have an assortment of whips sent up from the stables."

She had turned her head towards the butler expecting his mouth to fall agape at the strange order, but he again merely moved his body forward before turning and going out.

"Do you throw knives too?" The question came at her as sharp as a knife, and she jerked her head round so quickly that her neck bones seemed to crack as she answered, "I'm not so good at them, but . . . but I think I could split a peg from here to there." She pointed towards the foot of the wall to the left side of her on which she now took in the wild animals' heads and glass cases holding stuffed birds.

"Do you think you could hit that animal's nose?" The old man was pointing to a big horned beast's head nailed up on the wall.

Emma studied the head for a moment, then said, "It's higher up than I usually aim at, but if I stood there"—she pointed to where an oblong table about three feet long was placed at the end of a couch—"I'd likely hit it from there."

"See to it." The old man was nodding towards his son-in-law who now went to pull the bell rope, but the old man's bellow stayed his hand as he cried, "Move it yourself, man, there's two of you. It won't bite or break your back."

Emma saw the plump man's face turn from pink to red and then to an almost purple hue as he walked towards the table, from where he motioned to his son to take the other end of it.

The old man spoke again. "Take the knife out of its sheath," he said, pointing to a leather pouch hanging on the wall next to a large wooden plaque.

It was the youth who obeyed this order. However, when he went to give the knife to his grandfather the old man didn't take it, instead he pointed towards Emma, and the boy, turning about, offered it to her. She took it without looking at him.

She stood weighing it in her hand for a moment before looking at the old man and saying, " 'Tis heavy, heavier than two of Dada's put together."

"What did your father do with the knives? What did he aim at?"

"Mama. She stood against the board and he threw them round her, thirteen of 'em."

"Thirteen of them?" The old man's eyes widened, and when she nodded, he repeated, "Thirteen of them? Handy man. Handy man. Well now, see what you can do with that bison."

She now looked from one to the other of the three men, then down at the knife in her hand. She took the handle between her finger and thumb and swung the knife gently backward and forward. The blade seemed long, much longer than her dada's knives. She now went and stood at the end of the couch, and looked at the far wall. The animal's head was really much too high for her and the knife was too heavy. She swung it again between her finger and thumb, then let her wrist sway back and forward taking its weight. Of a sudden she brought her elbow up on a line with her chin; then her hand hanging just behind her ear moved twice from the wrist before letting the knife go. There was a pinging noise as the point of the blade pierced the tight drawn skin of the animal and entered the head at a point between the nose and the upper lip.

She turned slowly and looked towards the old man. His wrinkled face had moved into a grin; his lips were pressed together, his nostrils had widened showing more clearly the hairs growing out of them. It was some seconds before he spoke, when he said simply, "Good." And then, looking at his son-in-law, he said another word which overshadowed the first, "Remarkable."

Another knock on the door and the butler returned carrying a number of whips, the handles tucked under his arm. The expression on his face had altered somewhat and Emma couldn't put a name to it, except that she thought he hadn't liked being sent for the whips.

"What's the longest one?"

"I don't know, sir."

"Then find out, man."

The butler stooped his stiff back and, taking what appeared to be the longest handled whip, he stretched out the thong.

"That's the four-in-hand," the old man said; "should be . . . should be twelve feet. Think you can manage that, girl?"

Emma moved a step forward now and, picking up the whip from the floor, she said, "Yes, sir. But there's not much space here."

The old man now looked round the room and grunted before he said, "You're right, you're right, not much space here. Take up a smaller one."

She now took up a whip with a thong measuring about five feet and, weighing it in her hand, she said, "This is a nice one." She had directed the words to the old man and it seemed to her in this moment that there were only the two of them present in the room, the others had ceased to count. And, strangely, all fear had left her. She was experiencing a new sensation, one which told her that with some people she could hold her own, people that were like the old man.

She was quick to recognize that the master in this house was the old man and not his son-in-law, yet everybody took Mr Fordyke to be the boss. She also took in the fact that Mr Fordyke stood in awe of his father-in-law. She guessed that in a way he must be rather weak and as fearful of the old man as she had been of himself when she had first set eyes on him. But she was afraid of him no longer. She wished her granny was up here to see this all happening; she wouldn't believe her eyes. Oh, and how she wished the missis had come with her. Oh, she did. Mrs Yorkless fully expected that she would be sent along the line, she had said so only yesterday, and that alone had kept her awake most of the night.

She was flicking the whip now, making it curl above her head. She made it form an S then an O; then stopping suddenly she looked towards the chair and said, "I can whip a peg out of the ground, but I cannot show you here."

The old man twisted slightly in his chair and looked about him, then said, "You see that wooden idol, that statue on the table there." He was pointing now. "Could you whip that off there without breaking it?"

She looked at the wooden idol. "I can whip it off," she said, "but I don't know whether it will drop to the floor or not, because when I take out the pegs I've got to swing round to keep them going, then pull them into me." She demonstrated with her hands now as if she were plaiting rope.

"Take one of the short ones." He pointed to the floor, "Try it."

As she moved towards the whips lying on the floor she caught the look of the youth. His eyes were round but not in admiration, the look in them was more akin to that in his father's eyes, which was a mixture of disdain and arrogance, yet threaded with something she couldn't name and wouldn't have credited it to be fear.

Having taken up a whip with a four-foot thong she went towards the table and looked at the idol; then stepping back some paces, she set her wrist into a circling motion which grew larger and larger; then a wide flick of her wrist sent the thong outwards. The tip curling around the wooden idol brought it off the table in a flash; but it was much heavier than she had imagined and it was dropping to the floor when she raised her arm with her wrist still moving and brought the piece to her chest. And there hugging it to her, her face in a smile of triumph, she looked towards the chair and the old man. He was smiling too, his mouth open wide now showing a row of brown discoloured teeth at the bottom of his mouth and three brown stumps in the front of his upper jaw. Then of a sudden the smile disappeared from his face as he looked at his son and said, "Well, court's over, send me daughter to me."

For the first time since Emma had come into the room James Fordyke made an open stand against his father-in-law, saying, "Something's got to be done with her, she's got to be taught a lesson, you can't just. . . ."

"I should think she's taught you a lesson." The old man's voice was a growl again. "What you want to do, James, is to teach your sons a lesson, teach them how to deal with the peasantry. Tell them there's a difference between them and the animals, although—" his voice changed for a moment as he interspersed, "some animals are far superior to any human. Still, there's an estate to be run here, so I gather, and Master John should be old enough now to have some sense of responsibility and not run the earth playing tricks, spiteful tricks, on children. As I said, send my daughter to me."

When James Fordyke turned abruptly and walked down the room, the youth now said in a very subdued tone, "Have I your leave to go, Grandfather?"

"You have; but remember what I've said, the same applies to you."

The two Fordykes were followed by the butler; and now she was left alone in the room with the old man, and there returned to her a feeling of apprehension. He was a terror, he seemed to have everybody frightened. Did he frighten her? Funny, not much, but she knew she'd have to be careful or else he'd fly off the handle.

"Sit down."

"What?"

"Are you deaf, girl? I said sit down."

"On there?" She pointed to the velvet-covered high-backed chair at the other side of the fireplace, and now he laughed again, and his voice changing, he said, "Yes, on there."

Gingerly she planted herself on the edge of the chair, her black boots sticking out below the long skirt of her blue serge dress. She was hot. She wished she could take her coat off. If she'd had a nice frock on underneath she would have asked his permission.

"Tell me about yourself . . . your father, your mother."

She hesitated for a moment, then began to talk, recalling what she could remember of the travelling show. She went on to tell him of her work on the farm and what she did at Mr Bowman's, and how she sometimes sat for him. She had just come to the point when she was about to mention the parson when the door opened and a lady entered. She was of medium height with brown hair and wearing a gown which almost matched its colour. The skirt was very full and as she walked into the room there came a rustling sound from beneath it, like when you rubbed the heads of ripe corn between your hands and the grain fell out.

The lady paused for a moment and looked at Emma, and the look brought Emma to her feet and she bobbed her knee. Then addressing the old man, the lady said quietly, "So what's the verdict?"

"Not guilty."

"Somebody would be displeased."

"Somebody was, my dear. Anyway, the cause of all this narration"—he now waved a bony blue-veined hand towards Emma—"has been entertaining me for the last half-hour and I think she needs some reward. What do you say?"

"Whatever you wish, Father." The lady now turned and looked at Emma and she smiled, and her smile was kindly. She had the same colour eyes as the old man.

Now changing the subject and seeming to forget about her, the old man brought his daughter's attention round to him again by saying, "He's going into the army." And to this she answered, "I'm glad."

"This business has settled it."

"Then I should say it is well it happened."

Again the old man changed the topic by pointing to the wooden idol that was now reposing back on the table and saying, "She whipped that off and didn't drop it. What do you think of that?"

"Clever. Very clever." The lady was nodding towards the idol; then she added, "What would have happened if she had? Would your luck have broken?"

"Probably, probably. But it isn't my luck I think about nowadays. Anyway, she has given me the brightest half-hour I've had in some long time. Arrange that she'll come back when I need her, will you?"

"Yes, Father."

"Well now, I think a hamper of some kind; from what I gather from Pearson, those Yorklesses are a tight lot. The girl lives with her grandmother, fed on the side. This I've learned from her." He nodded towards Emma without looking at her. "So a hamper. Eh?"

"Yes, Father."

"But don't leave it to Atkins. Send Bella to the kitchen to supervise it; there's nobody stingier to the working class than the working class. Funny thing that is, isn't it, Kathleen?"

"Yes, Father, 'tis a funny thing, but only because it's a part of life, and life is a very funny thing."

Emma now watched the lady put out her hand and touch the stubbly cheek of the old man before turning towards her and saying, gently, "Come along."

Before obeying the lady, Emma took a step towards the chair and, dipping her knee more than usual, she said, "Good-bye to you, sir. And thank you. I'm glad you liked the whips."

"Good-bye, child. You must come again."

"Oh"—the word seemed to come out of the top of her head—"oh, that I will, sir. Yes, that I will." She dipped her knee again, then walked backwards for two or three steps before turning and almost bumping into the lady.

Once outside the room, remembering her manners, she kept two paces behind the lady until they came to the big passage that was filled with the carved heads of men, and there the lady met another lady. This one wore a plain grey alpaca dress with white cuffs and collars, and the lady spoke to her saying, "Take this little girl down to the kitchen, Bella, and see there is a hamper made ready for her. Her grandmother I understand is in the kitchen; and so make it sufficient that they can carry it between them."

"Yes, ma'am."

The lady now turned and looked down on Emma, and Emma, who had hardly been able to believe her ears, bobbed her knee and said, "Thank you, ma'am. Thank you most warmly." And the lady smiled and inclined her head towards her, then motioned her to go with her companion.

The woman called Bella waited for her to come alongside her, and like that they walked down the main staircase, across the hall, through the corridors and into the kitchen.

Immediately her granny sprang up from her seat and looked towards her, and in this moment it came to Emma that her granny looked old. Her face was drawn and her lips were trembling, but when Emma, going towards her, smiled at her widely, saying, " 'Tis all right. 'Tis all right," Lizzie's anxiety left her features and she whispered, "Thank God. Thank God." Then they both turned and looked to where the lady in the grey frock was talking to the housekeeper and the cook, and the housekeeper was saying, "A hamper, Miss Noble?" And the lady in the grey frock answered, "Yes, that's what I said, Mrs Atkins, a hamper. And Cook, bring a small ham out, will you please? And some pressed tongue, and—" She put her head back now as if thinking; then nodding, she brought it forward saying, "A basin of brawn and some jars of preserve."

There was a long pause before the cook turned away and went through a door into a larder, when Miss Noble, looking at the housekeeper, said, "The fruit loaves. You always keep a number to hand, don't you, Mrs Atkins? I think the hamper will hold one, say a medium size, four pounds, and a little sugared fruit. You always have a store of that, haven't you?"

Emma's ears detected a soft persuasive note in the grey lady's voice, but it seemed to cover a sternness that the others recognized, because now the housekeeper obeyed without any question, except by the look on her face.

When the hamper was eventually filled, Miss Noble turned to Lizzie and Emma who were standing side by side in front of the settle and she said, "Do you think you can carry this between you?"

Emma almost answered for her granny because it seemed such a long time before she said, "Yes. Oh yes, Miss. And . . . and thank you very much. Oh, thank you indeed. All that stuff! Well, well." She laughed, a shaky laugh, then added, " 'Tis for us and not for the missis?"

" 'Tis for you, or at least for your granddaughter to share as she thinks fit. It is the mistress's orders."

"Well, will you please thank the mistress most warmly from . . . from me? Please do. Oh yes indeed, please do."

Not only the staff from the kitchen but others, a number of them and all dressed in different uniforms, were gathered at the top of the kitchen watching their departure. Then in the stable yard there were men standing outside different doors and Emma realized that they were all looking at her as if she was the devil or something. She was glad to get out of the yard.

They had only gone a little way down the drive but out of sight of the house when Lizzie eased her end of the hamper down on to the ground and Emma did the same, and Lizzie looking at Emma, a look she had never bestowed on her before, said, "How in the name of God did you do it, child?"

"I'll . . . I'll tell you all about it when we get home." And with this Emma picked up her end of the basket again, and Lizzie had to do likewise, and it seemed in a way in this moment that Emma had come into her own. Fortune had turned its face towards her, she no longer felt the least of all the creatures, nor, no matter how the Yorklesses treated her in the future, would she imagine herself to be of no consequence.

6

The village was agog. It had spread around that Emma Crawshaw had been accepted up at the House, not by Fordyke, no, but by the real boss there, Sir Peter Rollinson, the man whose daughter had married James Fordyke and had saved his place from being sold up. Three years ago when his ancestral home yon side of Durham had been burned down she had brought her father and all his trophies they could save to live at the House. He was known as a great hunter in his young days, and a great gambler in his middle life, and admired as such, but not so his son-in-law: James Fordyke was known as a gambler, yes, but also as a woman chaser, a chaser of very young women. Two young servants had been dismissed from the House not for the simple reason that they had obliged him, but because they had showed evidence of it with full bellies. Yet he went to church every Sunday and sat in his sheltered pew, and the villagers bowed their knee to him. One thing they did know and it was said openly, if the outcome of the incident had rested with him, young Emma Crawshaw wouldn't have been stuffing her kite and that of her grandmother up in the cottage after the visit to the House, but would have been along the line in one way or another.

And it was said . . . and she said herself, that she had been invited back to show her tricks to the old man. Did you ever hear the likes of it? It had come down through Mr Winters, the butler, that she had done her tricks up in the old man's private apartments, throwing knives at buffaloes and deers and such animals that were stuck on the wall, and roping all the vases and things. Did you ever hear the like? What were things coming to? And to think of those two having all that special food when ordinary food was as scarce as gold dust owing not only to the bad harvests but to the flood of Irish who were coming over in their boat-loads at fourpence a head and working for next to nothing, so doing the honest Englishmen out of their rightful work. Hams and tongues and all kinds of luxury they were stuffing themselves with, and all because that young Spanish-looking Emma Crawshaw brought the young master down from his horse. I ask you, they said, what was the world coming to, it had turned topsy-turvy.

So too thought Emma, for there had come a lightness on her life, and she sang whilst about her work, except when in the cow byre or the yard. Her granny and she joked together and they ate their fill for nearly a month from that hamper.

The news even seemed to affect Mr Bowman's chest, for his cough had eased off. As for the parson, on the following Sunday, after gazing at Emma as if in wonder, he had said, "Of all the people to captivate Sir Peter . . . the giant on the mountain, the dragon in his den, the bane of—" he paused, then finished in a mutter, "a certain person's life. You are a female incarnation of Saint George, Emma."

She liked to listen to the parson when he rambled on like this, and although, like when she listened to Mr Bowman, she didn't always understand clearly his every word, she got the gist of what he meant. Then he had ended, "From now on, Emma, I think you can consider yourself safe, and have no need to carry your whip on your"—he had leaned towards her and whispered—"evening treks. You have come under the protection of Sir Peter and so you have nothing to fear."

And Emma thought that too, that she had nothing to fear from anybody any more. But she was mistaken, and it was brought home forcibly to her one morning in the new year when Luke deliberately kicked her bucket of milk over the cow-splattered dirty floor of the byre, after which they had stood glaring at each other.

The morning was deadly cold, the ice seemingly inches thick on everything. Her hands had just thawed out on the warm flesh of the last cow. She had lifted the bucket of milk to the side and was rising from her stool when Luke's tall figure darkened further still the entrance to the stall and after staring down on her for a moment he had lifted his foot and kicked the bucket over. As it clattered on the cobbled floor it hit the cow's hind leg, and the animal jumped, its motion overbalancing Emma and she fell back on to her bottom, her hands splayed out in the slush. But no sooner had she hit the ground than she was up, yelling now, "You beast! That's what you are, you're a beast. I'll tell her, the missis."

He stood aside, laughing at her as she grabbed up the bucket, and as she made for the door he called, "Tell her, an' see what you get."

With that particular rage that she hadn't experienced for a long time filling her, she ran across the slippery yard and without ceremony pushed open the farmhouse kitchen door and definitely startled both Jake and Dilly Yorkless who were finishing their breakfast at the table and, presenting them with the empty bucket, she cried, "He kicked it over on purpose. He came in and kicked it over on purpose."

"Who?" The farmer had risen to his feet, and she cried at him, "You know who, your Luke. And I'm not gona stand it. Do you hear? I'm not gona stand the blame. I'll go. I can you know. I'll go." She was repeating what her granny had said to her only recently: You needn't fear that 'un, meaning Dilly Yorkless, any more, 'cos she won't get anyone to do what you do. And what's more, she'd be afraid of what you might say up at the House to the old 'un, for in a way they're still dependent on the House, 'cos they've got only thirty acres of freehold land and that includes my patch, the rest is rented from Mr Fordyke.

Emma had turned towards her mistress as she spoke, and now Dilly Yorkless cried at her, "Get your mucky self out of this kitchen. Look at you!"

"Yes, look at me." Emma held out her filth-covered hands. "But . . . but 'twasn't my fault, so there. Don't blame me."

She turned and marched into the yard, and Jake Yorkless followed her and on the sight of his son going into the stables he called, "You Luke!" and when Luke turned towards him, he demanded, "What's this? You kicked her bucket over?"

"Kicked her bucket?" Luke came slowly towards them. "She's at it again, spinning her yarns. She slipped with the bucket in her hand."

Now Emma was almost screaming at him: "If I'd slipped with the bucket in my hand, I'd be covered with milk. What you did knocked me off the stool. And look!" She turned her back to the farmer now and thrust out her bottom. "I would have been flat on my back but my hands saved me." Now she was thrusting her hands out towards him.

Jake Yorkless stared at her for a moment right into her face; then he said in a quiet voice, "Get about your work."

"Yes, and don't think because. . . ." His wife's voice was cut off by him now almost barking at her, "Shut up! woman. Shut up!" And on this he almost pushed her back into the kitchen and banged the door.

Emma was left in the yard with Luke, and as she marched past him making for the yard pump, he stood still and his lips didn't seem to move as he said, "I'll get you one of these days. See if I don't."

The parson had said she'd no need to carry the whip any more when she went out on her midnight jaunts. He might be right there, but she knew now that it would be wiser to carry the whip during the day when in the vicinity of Luke Yorkless, for no matter how often she told herself she wasn't afraid of him, she knew that deep down he created a feeling of terror in her.

Every Sunday following this incident she prayed a special prayer that

Luke would get married soon and leave the farm. She felt she could only give the matter detailed thought on a Sunday when kneeling in the side pew and looking up at the parson, because he was the nearest thing to God she knew, and he looked at her so kindly when his eyes lit on her from the pulpit. During the week there was no time for praying, she was too busy and too tired at night and often too cold to think of anything but the need for sleep and warmth.

Dan Yorkless died early in March and the day he was buried the snow was so thick on the ground that the horses couldn't get through and the men from the village came and helped to clear a path from the farm down to the coach road, and a similar one to the churchyard.

Even so, a roughly made sledge had to be used to convey the coffin; they had tried to harness a horse to it but the animal had slithered so much and they were fearful that should it fall they'd never get it up again in the narrow path. So Dan was pushed to his final resting place on a door nailed on skids.

The farmer's wife's attitude to her son's going puzzled Emma, until her granny explained, but kindly for once when speaking of her mistress, that why she wasn't crying or wailing aloud was because she was relieved of a burden, because the boy had been completely bed-ridden for four months now and bleeding from inside, and she had had her hands full with him. As for the boy, he was now at rest and, as her granny said, would be glad of it.

She had cried about Dan, he seemed so young to have to die. You shouldn't have to die until you were old, as old say as Sir Peter. But then she hoped that he would live for a long time yet; she hoped she would soon have a call from him because she had a number of new twists to show him. Practising was very difficult: the only free times she had to herself were one whole Sunday in a month and half a Sunday for the rest of the time. Sometimes it would be in the morning when she could go to church, other times in the afternoon when she could go to Sunday school, but always for some time on a Sunday she would sit on the floor in the roof and practise with the whip.

She couldn't practise outside on the Sabbath day, and it had been a long winter and she had never ventured out at nights, but still, as she assured herself, she was keeping her hand in. Even so, it wasn't like having plenty of space. The only time she had played the whips outside was one day last year when the mister and missis had gone into the market on the dray cart, and Luke and Billy had driven in the cattle that were for sale. That day she had gone round to the back of the house because she knew that Dan would be sitting up, and she had done her tricks for him, and when she was finished she put her fingers to her lips and he had responded in the same gesture. She could have liked Dan as she liked Barney.

But now Dan was being buried. They said if you lay deep enough in the snow you got warm. She hoped he'd be warm always.

Yesterday the missis had ordered her into the kitchen to help prepare for the big funeral spread. It was years now since she had worked in the kitchen, and she hadn't been in it half an hour before she knew she wouldn't like working inside ever again. After the hall kitchen it seemed a poky place, nothing to be proud of; but the missis, she knew, was very proud, not only of her kitchen, but of her whole house.

She had peeled vegetables for broth, she had scraped the meat off the bones and chopped it up together with onions and herbs ready for the meat pies. She scored the skin of the newly dressed pig and rubbed salt into the cuts. She hadn't liked doing this for she knew which pig it was, she had called her Nosey because she always pushed her snout into her hand like the dogs did.

Between times she had washed pots and pans, kept the fire going, scoured the steel knives and forks with bath brick then washed them ready for the table, and lastly towards the end of the day, Dilly Yorkless took her into the main room where the meal was to be served. It was a sitting-room but two trestle-tables had been placed in it to seat the mourners. It was the first time she had been in this part of the house and before her visit to the House she would have considered it lovely, but now she saw it as a very ordinary room, stuffed to suffocation with furniture, and all ugly. A black horsehair couch, two black horsehair chairs, unrelieved with cushions or antimacassars. The walls were dark with pictures all in black and white like photographs of people long dead. The mantelshelf above the fire, which was set for lighting on the morrow, was weighed down with ornaments, the like she had seen at the fairs, while the front of it was draped with a long piece of red material tucked up here and there like a lady's overskirt.

Pointing to the thin carpet that covered the stone floor, Dilly Yorkless had said, "I want you to wash it."

"Wash the carpet?"

"That's what I said. You're not deaf, girl, are you?"

"But how'll it get dry? I . . . I mean for the morrow."

"When you're finished put a match to the fire. It'll be dry all right."

"What'll I do it with?"

"Don't be stupid, girl. What do you usually wash with? Hot water'n soda."

Emma stared down at the carpet. Its background was grey with what had once been a blue flowered pattern on it and when some minutes later she started to scrub it she told herself it wasn't fair, she had done a long day's work, twelve hours so far, and she couldn't work harder, and she likely wouldn't work half as hard if she had a job in the House kitchen, or even, as her granny feared, down the mines.

At nine o'clock that night when, bone weary, she entered the cottage she said as much to Lizzie. But Lizzie, who had been on her own feet the same number of hours and was tired to the heart of her, suddenly sat down in the rocking-chair and, her hands joined on her knees, she said, "Don't talk so, girl. I've enough to put up with in me life without you goin' off now."

So Emma knew that was that: in her own way, her granny was telling her she needed her. So she was stuck here, and would be all her life until . . . until her granny died.

The thought dragged on her legs as she climbed the ladder to her bed.

She had been ordered to stand at the door and take the men's coats, and this she was doing. She looked at them standing out black against the snow, each one as he came to the door kicking his boots against the wall and scraping the sole on the iron footscraper that stood to the side, then coming in and stamping his feet on the roped mat. She had noticed that men never seemed to wipe their feet properly, they banged them up and down instead of rubbing them backwards and forwards like women did.

And some of them, after she had taken their coat tugged at it in her hand in an endeavour to extract a flat flask or a half bottle from the inside pocket, before proceeding into the front room where the missis was sitting all in black on one of the horsehair chairs awaiting their condolences. In all, the mourners numbered twenty-two.

From what she had heard, a funeral tea always started like this but ended like a wedding. That's what the bottles were for, she supposed.

The front door closed, she was going into the kitchen when she met Lizzie bearing a tray full of food, and Lizzie said, "Go and see to the animals, they'll be burstin'."

And at this she whispered back, "But I've got me good frock on."

"Then change it. It's his orders."

She had a great inclination to disobey the order as she stood looking down at her good frock over which was tied a clean white apron. She didn't want to get into her stiff smelly working clothes again; what was more, she had washed herself down from head to foot before the fire the night before last. This, of course, was after her granny had tucked herself in bed and was almost asleep before her head touched the pillow. She had felt wonderfully clean, her body glowing warmly in the firelight, and she had paused a while to compare the skin of her hands with that of her rising breasts. Her hands looked ugly, red and chapped, with the nails broken down to the quick. Her nose had wrinkled at the comparison and she determined from then on to rub goose grease into them every night, if not, some pig fat. . . .

But here she was now in her everyday clothes again with the routine as usual.

She collected the buckets from the dairy and went into the cow byres. One good thing about it, it was warm in here. Two of the cows were bellowing: there was a shuffling and snuffling and rattling of their tethers, and as she passed them she said, "All right, all right, I'm here."

Her thoughts were still rebellious as she settled down to the milking and she was half-way through it when she heard the byre door open. She turned a startled eye towards it, for this she imagined was just the time Luke would put in an appearance while everybody else was busy in the house. But it wasn't Luke, it was Barney, and she stopped her milking and rose to her feet. It was very seldom they had a minute alone together.

When he stood in front of her she saw that his face looked sad, and he sounded sad as he said, "I'm going to miss Dan."

To this she answered simply, "You liked him?"

"Yes." He nodded. "Best of the bunch really. Oh! Emma." Of a sudden his arms had come out and he was holding her close to him. Their breaths were wafting across each other's eyes dimming their vision, and when he said, "Oh, how I wish I could put a couple of years on you this minute," she made no reply for of a sudden she didn't want the years on her for that would mean. . . . Well, what would it mean? It would mean being held like this tightly, but in a way that brought no comfort, only a kind of fright. This was only the second time she had been in his arms. She had liked it the first time, now she wasn't sure. Yet she liked him. Oh yes, she was quite sure of that, she liked Barney. But not the way he was looking now. Her body seemed like a reed pressed into the middle of his; one of his hands was on the lower part of her back and the other between her shoulder blades. When he closed his eyes and the colour seemed to leave his red cheeks she forced herself away from him, muttering, "Eeh! Barney, what if they come in."

He was standing with his head down now, his eyes closed. "You still like me?" he said.

"Oh, yes, Barney. Yes, I still like you."

He raised his head and, the colour seeping back into his cheeks and his eyes looking straight into hers, he said, "Remember I'm gona go on waiting for you, till you're ready."

She nodded her head once, swallowed deeply, then said, "I . . . I know Barney."

Smiling quietly at her now, he said, "That's all right then. I . . . I'd better be gettin' back."

He made a move to go, then turned, saying quietly, "We'll have to try to arrange to meet on the quiet somewhere, eh?"

She made no answer but again nodded her head once.

Sitting down on a milk stool again, she did not begin milking straight away but leant her head against the cow's flank and pondered why she was feeling like this, frightened of the years that were coming on her and what was in them for her. She wished she could talk to somebody about them: she should be able to talk to her granny about such things but she couldn't. This only left the parson and Mr Bowman, and she would as soon think of jumping in the river as talk of feelings like this to them.

She felt miserable. It was a long time since she had felt as miserable as she did at this minute; but it wasn't miserable enough to wish she was dead. No, she wanted to live, but . . . but . . . how could she put it? . . . have a say in her own life. Yes, that's what she wanted, to have a say in her own life. But Barney was waiting for her and, in his words, she would be ready for him in a couple of years.

At one time years seemed to have been made up of endless time. You didn't think about them as years, just seasons, and between one season and another there were months, weeks and days. And the days were endless; twelve to fourteen hours of endlessness, distinguished only by your body sweating or freezing. But over the past year time had changed; it was moving faster. And next year, it would move faster still. And the next. . . .

What was the matter with her anyway? She didn't know which end of her was up at the moment. Marriage. Marriage. Gettin' married. . . . Would the parson marry her? *What was she saying?* She had meant, would the parson marry her to Barney?

She stared at the flank of the cow, and then her hands shot out and gripped the teats so tightly that the animal kicked, and at this she said, "I'm sorry. I'm sorry."

Really, as she had just said to herself, she certainly didn't know which end of her was up when she could think a thing like that.

PART THREE

The Wedding

1

Now fifteen and a half years old, Emma appeared like a fully grown young woman. She carried her five foot four inches very straight, her hair had lengthened considerably and had darkened to a shining black, the process making her skin appear like warm cream. In contrast, her eyes, which at times appeared too big for her face, were a deep brown and heavily lashed; her eyebrows were almost straight and did not follow the curve of the eye sockets. Her lips were red but not over full, and her teeth looked strong and evenly spaced. And she was, as she had heard the parson remark to Mr Bowman, well above average intelligence for her class.

When she first heard him express this opinion she had experienced a feeling that, to say the least, spoke of annoyance. He was her friend, yet obviously to him she was still of an inferior class, even though she could read the same books as he read. Of course, she couldn't speak in a foreign tongue nor could she understand any of the Latin phrases that sometimes appeared in a book. Perhaps you had to know such things before you could rise from your class. She pondered these thoughts at such times when she couldn't sleep at nights, and this was often of late, for she knew the time was almost upon her when she would be ready for Barney. Besides the other troublesome feelings she had on the subject, the thought his declaration would have on his mother caused her at times to close her eyes tightly. The woman would go mad, as would his father.

Tempers were short enough on the farm. There had been torrential rainstorms which had flattened the fields of barley, and the place had been a quagmire for weeks. Farming all round was in a bad way: the average price of wheat was eighteen shillings for five pecks, and last year flour had gone up to three shillings and sixpence per stone, and all other grains and meals in proportion. Then potatoes were selling at one shilling and sixpence per stone, and beef and mutton reached eightpence a pound. Moreover, to make matters worse there were frequent although small outbreaks of the cholera. There had been one in Gateshead and the missis hadn't taken anything into the market for a month, and the mister had gone for her saying it was merely diarrhoea, and anyway, towards the end of the year people's bowels always became slack.

Emma had heard the painter reading from the newspaper that the guardians of the poor in Gateshead Fell had been appointed to distribute bread and soup tickets in order to allay further disease caused by malnutrition among the poor. But the parson had come back at him saying they might as well take a bucket and try to scoop the River Tyne dry, for the damage was already done, people were living in filth and squalor, their only relief being beer and raw spirit, and they didn't mind what manner of means they used to provide the money to acquire it.

Emma liked to hear them talking; it sounded like arguing at times, but they still nearly always ended up laughing. Besides discussing the daily news, they talked of all kinds of things. She could now picture what the parliament in London must be like. First, she had imagined it peopled with courtly gentlemen, but from what she could gather and the way the gentlemen shouted at each other it seemed more like The Tuns on a market day.

But today was fine, the sun was shining and shining hotly, so much so that the earth was steaming. It was half past ten in the morning. She was in the big barn breaking a bale of straw with which to replenish the nest boxes in the hen cree when Barney came round the partition and put his arms around her.

There were two partitions in the barn where once the horses had been stalled, and now he pulled her down behind the end one until she was on her hunkers, and he whispered to her, "Come out tonight, Emma." And to this she whispered back, "I can't. I . . . I'd better not."

"It'll be dark, the moon won't be up."

"I'm . . . I'm afraid."

"What of? You . . . you've done it afore."

Her head went down, and then she muttered, "All right."

He pulled her face towards him and his mouth fell hard on hers, and for a moment she was lost in his kiss; and he too, or he would have heard the footsteps even on the straw that was strewn on the floor. The next minute an almost unearthly cry overbalanced them and Barney found himself yanked back by the collar; then his mother was screaming, "I knew it! I knew it! I knew there was something on with that bitch. . . . *You!*"

As the tall woman sprang towards where Emma lay, Barney regained his feet and gripped hold of her from the back; then swinging her round, he stood between her and Emma, bawling now, "Leave her be, Ma. Leave her be. She's mine. You might as well know, she's mine."

"*Never! Never as long as I breathe.*"

Barney pushed his mother from him now and still yelling, he cried, "You can't keep me here. The world's wide; I'll go and she along of me."

"You won't get a penny, nor a rag. . . ."

"I will though." He was now yelling as high as she. "There's what's owing me, years of labour."

"Not a penny. And you'll rue the day you ever took her. She's bad meat, that 'un, bad meat. Things have never been the same here since she entered the gates. But you, you sneakin' young swine you!" Her rage brought her hand, fist doubled, up above her head, but she held it there. Then they both turned and looked towards the door where Pete was hissing at them, " 'Tis a groom from the House, he's in the yard, and you screamin'."

Dilly Yorkless brought her clenched fist slowly down from above her head; then after glaring at her son she turned her eyes on Emma, who was leaning against the partition, her hands tight pressed against it, and she spat at her, "I curse you! Do you hear? And your offspring. You'll live to regret this day, you foreign bastard you!" And on this she went out.

Barney now turned towards Emma. Her face was drained of colour and her head was hanging, but still her hands were pressed tight against the wood of the partition, and he said, "If I go, you'll come along of me." It wasn't a request but more of a command and she lifted her head and looked at him, saying, "There's me granny."

He now shook his head at her, saying, "She's got to let you go sometime."

"I'm . . . I'm not yet sixteen."

"What difference does that make?" His voice had begun on a bawl but suddenly dropped, and he repeated, "Susan Croft down in the village, she had a bairn last year and she but fifteen then an' married."

"She had to get so." Emma had taken her hands from the wood now, but had them pressed tightly together in front of her chest, and she said, "It wouldn't be that way with me."

"I know, I know." His voice had a soothing note to it; but then almost bitterly he went on, "Don't I know! I . . . I want you, Emma, I need you. Here I am, a man twenty years old and never yet have I taken anybody. I'm as clean as you because"—he gulped deep in his throat—"I . . . I love you, Emma. Have done, always. You seem to have been in me life from I can remember, not from when you just came. . . . Oh, Emma." As he put his hand towards her and repeated again, "Oh, Emma," Lizzie's voice came on them also saying her name: "Emma!" But it had a harsh sound and Emma sprang from behind the partition and looked down to where her granny was standing in the barn doorway.

Seeing them, Lizzie looked from one to the other; then the rising of her shoulders indicated her great intake of breath before she said, "You've been called up to the House."

Emma's eyes stretched wide and her lips moved into the words, "The House?" but made no sound.

After her visit to await sentence on that memorable day she had waited to be called again, but as time passed and no bidding came from the House she knew it had been a thing that happened but once. She had gone on though practising for a time with the whips and the knives whenever the opportunity allowed, until some months ago when, realizing the futility of it, she had stopped after asking herself what use it was anyway, she had learned all the tricks she could with the whip and she'd never really be expert, not like her dada, with the knives. You had to have the strong wrist and accurate eye of a man to be able to cut string with the point of a dagger, and that's what her dada had been able to do.

Barney followed her up the barn and when they both came close to Lizzie, she looked from one to the other as she said, "You've let hell loose, the pair of you, haven't you? And where's it gona end?"

"It'll end, Lizzie, where I always knew it would end, she'll be me wife. She's known for a long time she's gona be me wife."

Lizzie had turned but, looking back at him now, she said, "And I've known for a long time what the game was atween you, and I've just been waitin' for this day. Now it has come and I can't see the end of it. But go, you"—she had turned to Emma—"and tidy yourself. An' change. And you'll have to go alone as I can't go with you, I'm . . . I'm needed here."

Emma walked on past her granny saying nothing, but minutes later, having washed herself and about to put on her other dress, she felt in a way as if God had stepped in and saved her from some catastrophe.

As she went to put on a clean cap she suddenly stopped and looked at it in her hand; then with a gesture almost as fierce as that which had been shown by her mistress a few minutes earlier she flung it aside and, tearing off the apron that she had just tied to her waist, it followed the cap. Then she took the bone comb from the mantelpiece and pulled it through each side of her hair. Following this, she sat down and almost ripped off her big mud-covered black boots and, reaching out to the side of the fender, she picked up her rope sandals and put them on. Then her defiance carrying her forward, she made her way through the farmyard in view of her master and mistress and her granny who were in loud conclave outside the farm kitchen door.

Her passing brought them to silence, and then Dilly Yorkless screamed, "Where does she think she's going like that!"

"The House, I would think." It was her granny speaking.

"Come you back here and dress decently, you slut!"

"Leave her be: I wouldn't attempt to stop her if I was you. She won't be long here anyway. You can't keep her, she's not bonded, and neither is your son."

Dilly Yorkless's reply came as a jumble of enraged words to Emma as she walked into the road, but she hadn't got far along it when her defiance flowed from her as if a lock-gate inside her had been lifted, and her body slumped and she began to tremble through fear not of her mistress so much as of what her granny's words had implied: "She won't be long here anyway, she's not bonded, and neither is your son."

She wanted to go away, to get away from the farm, but not with Barney. The truth was, she didn't want to marry Barney.

She became sick with the knowledge that she had dared to give voice, if only to herself, to her true feelings. . . .

When she reached the lodge gates she was very hot and she took her one and only handkerchief from the cuff of her dress and dabbed her face with it.

The lodgeman had closed the gates behind her before he said, "You've got to go to the front lawn, the old master is out there."

"Where is that?"

"Take that side path"—he pointed—"it'll bring you through the shrubbery and the rose garden, and then there's the lawn. You can't miss it." He smiled at her.

It took her all of four minutes to reach the lawn. She came on to it from a tree-shaded walk, and there at the head of it, just below the steps leading from the second terrace that edged the wide drive approach, sat a muffled figure in a wheel-chair. He was sitting in the shade of an awning and there was a table to his side with jugs and glasses on it. At the other side of him sat his daughter and standing some distance behind the awning were two liveried servants. Hesitantly, she walked across the lawn, but stopped when she was about five yards from them, and she remained still until the lady beckoned her forward with the lift of her hand. Then she was standing once again looking at the old man and he at her.

He had shrunk, he wasn't as she remembered him. His eyes looked like pin-points, and the skin of his face was hanging in flaps at each side of his jaws. He was changed; and apparently he must have thought the same about her, for when he mumbled something to his daughter she leant towards his ear and said slowly and clearly, "It is the same girl, Father, but she has grown."

When he muttered something else the lady looked at her and said, "You didn't bring your whips with you?"

"No, ma'am."

"Do you still use them?"

"Yes, ma'am."

"Bennett." She had turned her head to the side and the name immediately brought one of the menservants to her, and to him she said, "Bring an assortment of whips from the stables."

The old man now shuffled in his chair and, bringing his head forward a little, he said in a voice like a croak, "Grainger tells me you are a scholar. Tell me, what do you know?"

She looked from him to his daughter somewhat perplexed. What could she answer to that? What had the parson meant by saying she was a scholar? She could only read and write, and so this was the answer she gave him: "I can read and write, sir, that's all."

"What does she say?" He turned to his daughter who, putting her mouth again to his ear, said, "She claims that she is only able to read and write."

"Enough. Enough." He was nodding at her. "What do you read?"

She thought a moment. She often kept one of the parson's books a month or more because her granny only allowed them one candle a night after which she had to read by the firelight, and sometimes in the morning her eyes were red. One night, the moon had been so clear she had been able to read up in the roof, but it only happened the once and because in that particular book the print was larger than usual.

She began to recall the books she had read over the past year or so. Speaking loudly, she answered him: "Books. Er . . . *Mansfield Park*. This was written by a lady, Jane Austen. And er . . . *The Lady of the Lake*. This though was written by a man named Walter Scott." When she seemed to have finished, the old man made no comment for a few minutes, and then not to her. Turning to his daughter, he repeated the two titles, then went on, "A pig girl reading! And reading a book by Jane Austen and *The Lady of the Lake*."

"Yes, it is amazing," his daughter said. Then looking at Emma, she smiled at her and asked quietly now, "Do you like working on the farm?" And after a moment's hesitation, Emma replied quietly, "No, ma'am."

"What does she say?"

The lady turned to her father again and said, "She doesn't like working on the farm."

"Understandable. Understandable." The skin on his jowls flopped up and down. "What do you want to do?"

She shook her head as she said, "I don't know."

He seemed to have got the gist of her reply for he repeated, "You don't know? . . . Go into a circus?" His face moved into what resembled a smile and she nodded brightly back at him, saying, "Yes, sir. Yes, that would be nice. I should like that, to go into a circus."

And yes, she would like that. Oh she would, to travel from one place to the other, to be in the open air most of the time, the clean open air, no more smell of cattle. She didn't really mind the smell of the cattle though, but the cesspit behind the house, that smell she couldn't stand. And part of her job was to empty the slops that were left in buckets in the yard on to the heap, until it went ripe enough, as Farmer Yorkless termed it, to take to the ground.

The servant had returned with the whips and laid them at her feet. She counted ten, and one looked almost as long as that which her dada had used. She picked up a medium-size one first; then looking at the lady, she said, "Do you think, ma'am, I could have some pegs or pieces of wood?"

Again the servant was given an order, and until he returned she played the whip into rings and snakes and twirls around her head, and lastly she skipped through a loop.

When the servant came back once more he laid at her feet an assortment of pieces of wood: four six inch pegs, a number of ordinary clothes pegs and some odd pieces of wood that were like kindling. She took the four large pegs first and after placing them some distance apart, going directly away from where she now stood, she proceeded to whip them from the ground. This completed, she looked at the old man; but he was looking at his daughter and saying in an almost excited tone, "She's like Rad, you know, I told you when you were small about Rad."

"Yes, Father. Yes, I remember."

"Well, she's like Rad. His was just a rope, but he could throw a loop over a running beast as easily as she whipped out those pegs. Rad. Rad." He shook his head and, now looking back at Emma and his voice seeming stronger, he commanded, "Well, go on. Go on."

And she went on. Sometimes she misjudged her distance or her stance wasn't right, or her wrist wasn't working properly, and the trick didn't come off; and at this she would look at him apologetically, but he always jerked his hand upwards and she would go on and have another try.

It was as she was demonstrating what she could do with the longest whip that the lady signalled her to stop, and when she looked at the old man his head was bent forward and he looked asleep. The lady now rose to her feet and one of the servants came and drew the chair gently from under the awning, but as he did so the old man raised his head and, looking about him, said, " 'Tis finished?"

"Yes, Father."

His gaze came to rest on Emma and with a weary gesture he beckoned her to him, and when she was standing by his side, he looked at her kindly, saying, "Do something with yourself, girl. You understand?"

Yes, she understood, and she nodded at him, saying, "I will try, sir."

He nodded back at her and, turning to his daughter, said, "See to her."

Emma watched the men lift the chair up the steps and push it across the drive before she turned and looked at the lady. She too seemed to have got much older: she wasn't beautiful but she had a nice face, a quiet face, like her voice, and she was speaking to her now, saying, "Thank you for entertaining my father. He enjoyed it."

"I'm happy he did. May I say, ma'am, he seems a grand gentleman."

The lady's eyelids blinked and her head moved slowly now as she said, "You're right, he is a grand gentleman." Then she added, "Now what would you like? Some food, or would you prefer money?"

"It doesn't matter about either, ma'am, I was just pleased to do it."

"You must have something, he wished it."

"Then if you don't mind, ma'am, I'd rather take the food."

"Very well. Have . . . have you got someone with you?"

"No, ma'am; I came by meself."

"Oh. Then you won't be able to carry a hamper. I will see that it is sent down for you."

"You're very kind, ma'am."

"Good-bye, and thank you."

"Thank you, ma'am." She stood still while the lady turned away. To her eyes, she looked like a picture out of a book. She was wearing a pale lemon-coloured summer dress. The material was very soft, for the skirts billowed gently as she walked up the steps, and there was no breeze. At the top of the steps she saw the lady pause when a man approached her from the side of the drive. The exchange between them was very short and the lady walked on while the man came down the steps towards her. She recognized him immediately as Mr Fordyke. He was more plump than when she had seen him last and she was about to turn away when he spoke.

"Up to your tricks again?" His voice wasn't unkind; she knew it was meant to be a joke and she looked at him, saying, "Yes, sir."

He came to a halt about a yard from her and he stood saying nothing but looking at her. Although his eyes were on her face he seemed to be looking all over her and he said now, "You've grown somewhat since last we met."

"Yes, sir."

"Still working on the farm?"

"Yes, sir."

"Not much future in that, is there?"

She made no reply. She was beginning to experience a strange sensation, her skin was pricking and it wasn't with the heat. She knew at this moment that she would rather have this man angry with her than smiling at her as he was doing now. "I've . . . I've got to be getting back, sir. Ex . . . Excuse me."

"I haven't given you leave to go." The smile had gone from his face. "You don't seem to know your place."

She was even surprised herself as she heard her voice saying, "My place is on the farm, sir. My master too is there."

As she watched his colour change she recalled that once before she had seen it look like this. And now, his voice and manner of the haughtiest, he said, "You're insolent, girl."

"I didn't mean to be, sir. I was merely pointing out that I don't work for you, so therefore I cannot be expected to obey your orders." Eeh! she was talking like the parson, or like some character in the book she was reading just now.

"Get out! Get off my land, and don't let me see you here again. Do you hear? No matter who sends for you, don't let me see you here again."

She backed from him, then turned and only just stopped herself from scurrying like a rabbit across the lawn. With an effort she kept her head up and her shoulders straight and her walk steady, at least until she got into the avenue of trees, where, as it had done earlier in the day, her body sagged.

Two rumpuses in one day. It was too much, and now she was likely walking into another one. What would her reception be when she got back to the farm? Oh, why had things to happen to her like this? There was that in her that wanted to run and skip and laugh and be happy. She knew that she could tend the animals and do all the work that was laid upon her and still be happy if it wasn't for people. Yes, that was the trouble, people: the mister, the missis, and Luke, even Barney. Oh yes, Barney. Barney was assuming a different kind of trouble in her mind.

She skirted the farm and went straight to the cottage and changed into her working clothes.

She found the farmyard empty. The whole place seemed quiet, but as she was about to enter the byres Luke came out.

"You're back then, me ladyship," he greeted her. "And I suppose you'll be pleased to know that you've put me mother to bed. The first time in her life she's taken to her bed in the day, but you've managed to do it, as you've managed to hook our Barney. But there's somethin' between hookin' and gettin' the fish out of water. You've got to play the big 'uns; a lot can happen in between times."

She slid past him into the byre and made for the far end where she stood with her back to one of the partitions and closed her eyes tightly. Of a sudden she wanted to cry. . . .

She hadn't finished the milking of the second cow when Barney came into the byre, and standing over her as she leaned forward on the stool, he asked quietly, "How did it go?"

"All right," she mumbled. Then lifting her eyes to him, she said, "Your mother's in bed?"

"Yes, 'tis the diarrhoea; she's had it for a few days. But her temper brought it on worse."

"It wasn't just the row then that's made her bad?"

"No, no." He shook his head. "She came back from church on Sunday with it." He laid his hand on her shoulder now, saying, "Don't worry, things will plan out, you'll see. One way or another they're gona be all right for us, you'll see."

And on this he turned and went out, and she repeated to herself, "All right for us," and then went on with the milking.

It was as she reached the end of the byre and the last cow that Pete poked his head through the doorway, shouting, "Emma, there's a fellow from the House wants you."

When she went into the yard she saw a small brake and a liveried man lifting a large hamper down from it, and as she neared him he looked at her and said pleasantly, " 'Tis for you."

"Thank you." Then his voice lowering and his head poking towards her, he said, "You're lucky to get it; the master was for stopping it, but the mistress said you had to have it, an' what she says in the end goes." He nodded at her, and then after looking at her enquiringly for a moment, he said, "Got on the wrong side of His Highness, did you, lass? I saw him as he came up from the lawn, he looked like a frustrated bull. But then that's nothin' new for him. Anyway you amused the old boss, and that's something, 'cos he's never been out of doors for almost a year. He used to be very lively at one time. I worked over at his place, you know." He jerked his head. "I came to the Hall when he did, he asked for me. A fine man he's been in his time. You should have seen him when he came back from abroad. Strappin' he was, strappin'. Been a great hunter, you know"—again he nodded at her—"and that's why he likes your tricks I think." Then he added somewhat sadly, "But he's going downhill fast, he'll be lucky if he sees another year out. Anyway" —he thumbed down towards the hamper—"you've got stuff in there that'll last you a week or more. Miss Noble saw to its packing, so I understand. If it had been left to Mrs Atkins or Cook you would have had short shrift, I'm tellin' you. Every man for himself up there. Times are changin' and you'll likely live to see them, lass. Yes, they're changing. Well, I must away."

"Thank you, and"—she moved towards him as he mounted the brake —"please thank Miss Noble, will you?"

"Aye. I won't be able to see her meself, but I'll get word into her that you're grateful."

"I am. I am."

As the brake was turning in the yard before moving away, Lizzie came out of the farmhouse door and as she looked towards the hamper her face brightened for a moment; then without any preamble she said, "We better get it across." And she taking hold of one handle and Emma the other they went out of the yard and into the cottage. But after they had placed it on the table, Lizzie didn't immediately go to open it but, looking across at Emma, she said, "She's right bad, it's the diarrhoea. She's had it for days but wouldn't give in. I've told him he should get the doctor. You see"—her voice dropped—"Billy told me there's a rumour of cholera going round in Gateshead Fell, and in Gateshead itself. It's come over from Newcastle, and if it gets a hold there could be a repeat of what happened in the thirties. All over the country that was, and they were dropping like flies in Newcastle and about. Anyway, I've told him he should have the doctor, so it's up to him what happens now."

What happened after that Emma looked back on as a nightmare.

The doctor came to visit Dilly Yorkless the following morning and at first he diagnosed just a fever and a touch of the autumn bowel epidemic, but the following day he brought another man with him, and when he left they knew that the cholera was among them.

Emma had never seen her granny run, but when she came running from the house across the yard and met her as she was emerging from the hen field, she asked, "What is it?" And Lizzie replied, " 'Tis as was feared."

"Oh, no, no!"

"Aye. An' look. Listen, girl, don't you come near the house, nor me. I've got to be over there. You see to the animals, an' you've got enough stuff in that hamper to last you for a week or so. Scour all the cans. I'll wash all the kitchen utensils that's needed in the house, and I'll get the lads to empty the slops. You're not to touch them, do you hear?"

"Yes, Granny."

"Now do as I bid you: see to the cows and the animals but keep to this side of the yard, don't come near the house, no matter what anybody says, him, or anybody else. Do you hear me?"

Again she said, "Yes, Granny." Then putting her hand out towards her, she said, "But you . . . you could get it."

"I won't get it, I'm as strong as a horse. But listen to me. Once you've finished your work don't go out of the door, stay in the cottage and keep washing yourself. And don't go near the middens unless you have to. Take your slops down to the burn and throw them in there."

"But Granny, I . . . I wash me hair in there at times."

"But you can still wash your hair in it, girl, it's running fast. But now, do as I bid you and don't come near me. If you want me for anything, shout across the yard. Now do you hear, lass?"

Emma nodded and stared at her granny for a moment, and the tender look on Lizzie's face made her want to put out her arms to her, she wanted to hold her, and be held; she wanted to talk to her, ask her what she should do about Barney, ask her about . . . marrying . . . and after, but what she said was, "Take care, Granny, please. Please take care."

"I'll take care, lass. Don't worry about me." And the glance they exchanged now was full of tenderness and simultaneously they both turned away from each other.

For four days Emma kept to her side of the yard and whenever she was in the open she looked across towards the house. One time there was an argument going on between Barney and Pete about the buckets of slops standing outside the door. It was apparent that Pete didn't savour the job of emptying them.

She was becoming bone weary, for she was rising at four o'clock in the morning and staying on her legs till nine at night. The only one she spoke to was Billy. He too had been ordered to stay away from the house and, like hers, his work had almost doubled.

On the sixth day of her working isolation she saw the parson. It was late in the evening. She was making her way to the cottage, almost dragging her feet, when she saw him through the dusk coming from the direction of the field. She reached the cottage door and opened it expecting him to come in, but when he was still some feet away from her he stopped and said quietly, "I won't come any nearer, Emma. I just wanted to know how you are faring."

She looked at his face. It had taken on the hue of the coming night and looked grey, his eyes were red-rimmed; and he did not look spruce as he usually did. "How are you, Emma?" he continued, and she answered, "I'm all right."

"You look very tired."

"I am a bit."

"You mustn't get over-tired because the. . . ." He put his head down as he stopped speaking. When he lifted it, he added, "It's a terrible time."

"How are they farin' in the village?"

"There have been two more deaths today. Katie McGill died."

"Oh no!" She put her hand to her mouth. She had liked Katie McGill. Her father was a shepherd and they lived in a cottage no bigger than this one, and there were eight of them altogether. Poor Katie.

"And Mr Collier you know."

Her mouth opened and closed and she shook her head. "That's six," she said.

"Yes, six. And . . . and I'm afraid there may be more. But it is much worse in the towns, although they tell me they've got it under control in Gateshead. I wish we could say the same for the village and hereabouts. And I'm sure you will be sad to know that Sir Peter Rollinson died last night, not from cholera, it was old age."

Her hand was pressed tightly across the lower part of her face now and she leant against the stanchion of the door and closed her eyes. That lovely old man, the only man of the class that had given her a kind word. The rest galloped past you and bespattered you with mud from their horses; or when coming out of church a look from them would push you aside to give them a straight way. But that old man had been so nice to her on the two occasions she had met him, and his daughter too.

"Emma."

The parson had taken a step nearer to her, and he was within two arms' length of her when she brought her attention to him and saw that he was in some agitation. And when he spoke his voice was low and had a tremble to it: "I, like everyone else, am in God's hands," he said; "I don't know my hour. I am visiting the sick, so therefore my call may come any time, and, Emma, I would not like to go to my maker without first telling you that I . . . I hold you in high esteem, in the greatest esteem. I've had your concern since I first made your acquaintance on the coach, but over the years I have come to care for you deeply. Whatever God wills I would like you to remember this, Emma."

She was aware that her eyes were wide and wet and that large slow tears were running down through the sweaty grime on her face, and her heart was aching with the pain that was new and strange and beautiful, the pain that she wanted to hug to her, to press it so hard into her body that it would increase until she was enveloped in it.

"Don't cry, Emma. Don't cry."

She opened her eyes and after a moment said, "Take care. Don't . . . don't—" she was about to say die but changed it to, "don't run risks."

"There are so many brave people running risks at the moment, Emma, my part is very small, and as I said, we're in God's hands, but what His purpose is I don't know." He shook his head as he looked down at her and added, "I dare at times when in the depths to question His motives, but I've told myself perhaps He has sent this scourge to make those in authority aware of why these things happen, aware of the conditions that breed them."

His head was moving slowly now as he finished, "I don't know. I don't know. Anyway Emma, I say to you, take care, great care and keep away from the house. And by the way, Mr Bowman wishes to be remembered to you."

"Is . . . is he all right?" Her voice sounded like a croak.

"Yes. I have called to him from the gate, and he seemed well enough yesterday. But he is very concerned for you and your grandmother. . . . Good-bye, Emma."

She brought herself up straight from the support of the stanchion and, her lips trembling, she muttered, "Good-bye, Parson," and in a gabble she added, "I too hold you in high esteem." Then turning about, she rushed into the cottage and closed the door, and, throwing herself down on to the mat in front of the dead fire, she laid her arms on the seat of the rocking-chair and buried her head in them and gave way to a paroxysm of weeping, all the while muttering to herself that she would never marry Barney, never marry anyone. Never. Never. And if God would only keep the parson safe, she would do anything He asked of her.

2

The morning was heavy with rain. It had rained incessantly for twenty-four hours. The yard and everywhere about was like a sea of mud, and, as her granny would have said, her spirits had dropped to her boots. She had now been eleven days on her own and she was filled with worry, not about being alone but about her granny. She had seen her last evening across the yard. Her face had looked drawn, her shoulders rounded and there was no life in her voice as she called, "Are you all right, lass?"

If her granny took the cholera, what would she do? She pushed the thought out of her mind and went on scraping the cow dung from the floor of the byre.

When she heard the door open she turned about and saw Barney standing there. He did not come towards her, nor did she move towards him, but when he said, "Ma's gone, Emma," her whole body jerked and she let go of the rake and it dropped on to the slime of the floor.

In a normal way, she knew she should be terribly sorry, and she was feeling sorry, but not because she had any liking for the woman who had treated her worse than she did the animals, she was sorry that the excuse she had for not marrying Barney had been taken from her by death, for she had made up her mind to say to Barney, "I can't come between you and your ma, I couldn't live with it." It would have been a lie, but it would have been the gentlest way of telling him that she wasn't for marrying. Now that excuse had gone.

"I'm sorry to the heart, Emma. We didn't get on all the time and she stood in my way, but she was a good mother, she brought us up well." He was speaking with his head lowered, but when he lifted it he spoke with a voice that sounded full of authority as he said, "There'll be changes, Emma; the way'll be clear now." Then he swung round and went out.

She turned slowly and looked into the face of a cow, and it opened its mouth and gave a small moo that sounded like a moan, and it could have come from her own lips at this very moment.

They buried Dilly Yorkless two days later. There was no long cortège to this funeral, no big spread in the farmhouse; in fact there was no meal at all for the men in the farmhouse for Lizzie had gone sick.

It wasn't, she assured Emma from her bed in the cottage, the cholera, it was just that she was tired, for she couldn't remember when she had last had a night's rest. The men, she said, had all taken their turn, but after all, they were men and no good at nursing. But now it was over, a day, two at the most, and she would be on her feet again.

Lizzie seemed to have forgotten that she wanted no contact with Emma, but when your master says to you, "If you're going to be bad, Lizzie, you'd better get to your own bed," what could she do?

When the diarrhoea started to get real bad, Emma cried aloud as she emptied the buckets, "Oh, no! God. Oh no! Don't do this. Don't do this."

The doctor came on the third day and he heartened her by saying that her granny would likely pull through; there had been no deaths in the village for over a week now, and those who were sick were recovering. The scourge had worn itself out.

The parson came and he no longer stood a distance from her but he walked into the cottage and sat down by Lizzie's bed; and he talked to her, but strangely not about God or heaven or anything like that, which somewhat surprised Emma. He told her she'd soon be on her feet and she must get well for she was needed in the farmhouse now. "You can't expect four big men to look after themselves," he said. But her granny hadn't spoken at all, she had just lain and looked at him.

When he was about to take his leave he beckoned Emma outside, and there he said gently, "She'll survive. With God's help, she'll survive, as I have done, Emma." Then his head slightly bent, he said, "I'm sorry I disturbed your mind that night past, but things were very bad and people were going like flies, and of course being merely a human being in contact with them I was fully expecting my call to come any time. I . . . I hope I didn't worry you."

"No, no, Parson," she answered; "you didn't worry me."

"Good. I . . . I shall call again tomorrow. Good-bye, Emma."

As she returned into the room she knew that the parson wanted her to forget what he had said on that past night.

She went to the bed and, kneeling down by its side, she wiped her granny's brow with a piece of wet rag; and as she did so Lizzie made a sound like a laugh. But no muscle of her face had moved, and, her voice slow as if each word was an effort, she said, "Men wanting me in the farmhouse. After all these years. I . . . I could come into me own, what . . . what should have been mine in the beginning; but now I'll never do it. 'Tain't fair. Life ain't fair. No"—her voice sank deep in her throat—"life ain't fair."

She closed her eyes for a moment and Emma stopped wiping her face and went to rise from her knees. But Lizzie spoke again, saying, "Marry him lass, Barney, and you'll come into what should have been mine. It'll be justice . . . justice. I might rest easy knowing that you were reaping the benefit of me havin' been cheated; for she cheated me. Oh aye, barefaced she was, barefaced." Her voice trailed away, and Emma turned towards the fire and leant her head against the wooden mantel-shelf and the tears rolling down her cheeks made tiny pinging sounds as they dropped from her chin on to the hot ashes on the hearth.

The parson wanted her to forget what he had said . . . and implied. And he *had* implied. She wasn't a fool, she knew what he had implied as plain as if he had put it into words. Somehow she had always known how he felt about her; she had always known how she had felt about him. And her granny wanted her to marry Barney. . . . Her granny thought she was going to die. Oh, no! No! No! She mustn't! *She mustn't die.*

Dropping on to her knees, she began to beseech God for her granny's life.

Lizzie didn't take as long to go as Dilly Yorkless; three days later she was dead.

Emma couldn't take it in. She had tended her up till midnight. The diarrhoea had eased off and she was lying quiet. Her face had looked pink in the candlelight and Emma had said, "You look better, Granny, you've got over the turn."

Lizzie hadn't answered but had taken her hand between her own two and given it a weak grasp, and so it was with a feeling of relief that Emma had sat in the rocking-chair that was pulled up to the side of the bed and in utter weariness she had fallen into a deep sleep.

It was the cock crowing that woke her up. The room was dark and was dead cold; the candle had guttered itself out, as had the fire. Pulling herself awake, she scurried about getting a candle. When it was lit, she placed it on the box to the side of the bed. Her granny looked peacefully asleep. Next she blew up the fire and put the kettle on and, having filled a little pan with some milk, she placed it to the side of the hob.

Going to the bed now, she gently straightened the bedclothes under her granny's chin. It was then, for the first time, she noticed the stillness about her.

Her hands trembling, she touched the pale cheek; then she was kneeling by the bed, both hands now on Lizzie's face, crying, "Granny! Granny! wake up. Granny! Granny!" But Lizzie was past waking.

Emma lifted up the candle the better to see. It looked as if her granny was smiling one of her rare smiles.

"*Oh! no. No! No!* Granny. *No!* Granny." She was wagging her head from side to side, talking aloud now. "You were better last night. Oh no, no, don't be gone. Oh Granny. Granny."

The sound of the kettle spluttering and the milk boiling over brought her to her feet and she rushed to the fireplace and retrieved them both from the flames and put them on the hearth, then she turned and stood looking towards the bed, her hands joined in front of her face, her teeth biting down on her two thumbnails.

The cock was still crowing. She now turned to the door and, taking a cloak from the back of it, she pulled it around her and went out. The wind was driving a thin rain before it and as she entered the farmyard she saw the kitchen door open and Jake Yorkless emerge.

"Mister."

He stopped when he heard her voice. Then lifting the lantern he had in his hand, he said, "What's up? Stay where you are."

She came to a standstill some yards before him, saying, "Me granny, she's . . . she's gone."

He did not speak for a moment but she saw him turn his head to the side and bite hard down on his lower lip. Then he uttered one word: "God!"

Now he was looking at her again, saying, "Get back to the cottage. I'll tell them down at the village; they can come up and get her."

As he was turning to go back into the house she said, "I . . . I want her buried decent."

He swung round and lifting the lantern again, he asked, "Where's the money coming from?"

"I've . . . I've got the money."

"You've got the—?" He stopped and took a small step towards her. "Where did you get the money, enough to bury her?"

"It was given to me. It doesn't matter. And . . . and me granny should have some an' all. I brought it with me when I came here. I gave it to her."

"Begod! you did." There was high surprise in his voice. And she heard herself answer, "Yes, begod! I did."

It must have been the manner of her answering him that brought his head poking forward and moving from side to side as if he wasn't sure it was she who had spoken. And he was standing like that as she turned away and went back to the cottage. . . .

The parson came at ten o'clock.

She had washed her granny, laid her out in a clean calico nightgown that Lizzie had sewn many years back and had kept for this very purpose. She had combed her hair. And now her head rested on a piece of clean sheeting that she had laid over the striped tick of the feather pillow.

Yesterday she had washed and managed to dry one of the three twill sheets they possessed, and now it covered her. Following this, she had opened the two windows, and the door too, and let the cold damp air sweep through the room, for the smell in it was beginning to make her feel sick. Lastly, she had brought a bucket of water from the stream and washed her own face, arms, and feet in it. Then she had cleaned up the room as best she could, so when the parson arrived everything was as tidy and as clean as she could make it.

As Henry Grainger looked at this girl, this budding woman, his heart was so filled with sadness that the usual words of comfort he kept for the bereaved would not come to his lips. He only knew that if anything should happen to her, if she should follow the woman on the bed, then his faith in God would be snapped entirely. He had for some time been in great agony of mind over the infallible ways of the Lord. He could understand Him taking the old but not the young, not those to whom he had given life and whom he had allowed to glimpse the waters of spring but had then forbidden them to taste them. But this girl before him, who had been destined to work so lowly and who was now left without a guardian and at the mercy of men, and those men near at hand, one at least of whom was known to be a licentious creature even though he was promised to a young woman in the village, what was to become of her? What were God's plans for her? This was a big question mark in his mind.

His voice sounded ordinary as he asked, "How are you, Emma?"

"I'm well, Parson, but heart sore. She . . . She was all I had, and . . . and we got on together." Her voice broke as she ended, "I . . . I think, under her roughness she was fond of me."

"She was more than fond of you, Emma, she loved you. I know that."

After staring at her lowered head for a moment, he walked up the room and, kneeling down by the low bed, he began to pray softly. Using ordinary words, he asked God to accept this hard-working woman into his care and to give her a place in heaven where she would find rest for all eternity. . . . That last was a phrase that sometimes troubled him. Eternity was long, and could a soul rest forever in it? That is if it was to carry any of its earthly character over the border of death.

When he rose to his feet, Emma was still standing where he had left her and she said to him, "I want her to be buried decently, Parson, not in a common grave. I can pay for it, I have money."

He said nothing, but at the look of enquiry in his eyes she reminded him that Mr Bowman paid her for the pictures, and she added, "I think me granny might have something in her kist, I haven't looked yet. But anyway, there'll be enough for a decent coffin and a grave."

"They'll . . . they'll want to take her tomorrow, Emma."

"Yes, I know; but Mr Farrow would surely have a decent coffin on hand."

"Yes, yes, perhaps so, Emma. Anyway, I'll talk to him. But don't worry, she'll be put away decently. I'll see to that."

"Thank you, Parson.

"Parson."

"Yes, Emma?"

"Will you tell Mr Bowman?"

There was a pause before he said, "I'll tell Mr Bowman, I'll go right there now. He'll . . . He'll be very sorry."

They nodded at each other and he went out, and slowly she sat down on the rocking-chair and looked towards the bed. Mr Bowman would be sorry. Had he loved her granny? She didn't know; that he had used her at one time she did know, but she also knew that usage and love weren't the same thing.

3

It was a week since Lizzie was buried, and no one had invited Emma
into the farmhouse. There was no woman at all in the house, the men
were looking after themselves. And now this morning, shamefacedly
Barney stood in front of Emma admitting that they tried to get someone
from the village to see to things indoors, but that no one would come
near the place.

Two women had died here within a short time of each other, and
they were women who had been hale and hearty. So, no mothers were
offering to come up and give a hand, much less allow their daughters to
take up work on this particular farm.

With her eyes cast down Emma listened to him saying, "In a way,
Emma, it could be a good thing, a godsend because they'll have to have
you in, in the end. The place is like a pigsty and beginning to smell like
that an' all, and we haven't had a decent meal since me mother went.
None of us were made to cook, Pete least of all." He smiled weakly at
her, then he ended, "You've only got to bide your time."

On this she turned to him, bringing his face stretching with something
akin to amazement when she added, "I mightn't want to bide me time.
I'm free, I can up and go, and that's what I'm thinking of doin' an' all,
the way I've been treated here. Dogs have a better life and I don't have
to put up with it any more. I'm going to talk it over with the parson and
see what he says."

Barney's mouth opened and shut twice before he said, "What's come
over you? I . . . I thought you wanted it as much as me. And . . . and
there's a chance you could . . . yes you could"—he was nodding vigorously at her—"you could be mistress over there one day. And if you
want to know anything, I've already spoken to the parson, yesterday."

It was her turn to stretch her mouth, and she barked at him, "Well,
you shouldn't! You shouldn't!"

"Why? We've been promised, haven't we?"

"I don't know." She shook her head from side to side now. "I was but a bairn, well just a young lass. I'm no longer a young lass, I'm coming up sixteen and I'm not going to be tret like a black slave any more. I read that all the slaves aren't treated the same, some have kind masters. Well, it hasn't been my lot, has it? So I'll make up me mind later and let you know." And she surprised him still further by swinging round and throwing the empty milk bucket against the byre wall, then marching out across the yard to the cottage.

There she sat down at the table and, joining her hands on it, she beat them up and down on the bare wood as she asked herself, could she go to the parson and ask his advice? Slowly she shook her head. No, not about getting married to Barney, she couldn't. But she could go to Mr Bowman. Yes, that's what she would do, she would go to Mr Bowman. She would get cleaned up proper, not to do his work, because he had likely been managing these past weeks himself, but to ask if she could talk to him, because as she saw it now he was the nearest thing to her granny she had left.

It was half an hour later when she went across the fields and dropped down on to the bridle-path. She had seen no one, not even a farm cart rumbling along the coach road; the mail coach she knew had passed some time before. But as she approached the cottage she saw that someone had arrived before her, as the parson's trap was outside in the lane.

Quietly now, she let herself in the back door and as quietly she closed it behind her. The door leading into the living-room was open and the voices came as clear to her as if she were facing the men who were speaking. It was Mr Bowman's voice that was saying, "Don't think it hasn't entered my head, Henry. Oh, yes, yes. And you may not believe it, but I have my own standard of morals and every time I have looked at her with desire in my heart I've had Lizzie before my eyes. You're under the idea that God gives us life, Henry. Well, for my part I think if that is so He's a creature with a wry sense of humour: He turns our hearts to things that are good to look upon, but when the years touch those things and the skin wrinkles and the temper frays it is not our hearts that are touched but the dark depths within us and we want rid of the things that we once loved, or thought we loved. You see, Henry, Lizzie was very good to me when I first came here. I didn't expect to last long, but here was this woman, a pretty woman in her early thirties, not old enough to be my mother but old enough to act like one to a twenty-one-year-old sick lad, and I've got to admit she created in me a desire to live and to take up the painting again. And, as you guessed, from the beginning she became my spare-time wife. At what stage I became tired of the situation I don't know, perhaps it was as I said when age began to gallop on her. Man is a mean thing, Henry, no real gratitude in him. Emma came as a blessing in disguise, at least I thought so, for she would curtail Lizzie's visits. But then Lizzie found a way. I was cruel to Lizzie, Henry, more so I think when I saw her granddaughter growing into a thing of beauty. So Henry, unless you want Emma to become another Lizzie under this roof, don't press me to take her on as my little housekeeper and nurse, for the inevitable would happen. Oh yes it would. Your faith in me is misplaced, my dear fellow, very misplaced. . . . But now, there's you. What about you?"

"It's impossible, I've told you."

The parson's voice came to Emma like a thin whisper on the air, and she screwed up her eyes against it. But her ears were wide to his next words: "Apart from the villagers not accepting her, my stipend barely keeps me alive."

"You could get rid of Miss Wilkinson."

"No, no, Ralph, I couldn't. It is expected that one has a housekeeper or a maid of some kind in the parsonage; the parson's wife has a number of duties that would keep her occupied. Then . . . then there might be a family, and I've had experience of how these are brought up in some parishes, the farm worker's children are better fed than many of them."

"Can't you ask the bishop to supplement your stipend? It's known that he lives like a rajah up in Auckland there. Or what about applying for another parish? There's some rich ones kicking around the North. Doesn't the Hall pig in?"

"Mr Joseph did a little, but I doubt our present Mr Fordyke is inclined that way; from what I can gather his interests lie in other directions."

"Yes, yes. I've gathered that too. But look, Henry, nothing could be worse for her than the life she leads up there. And it's not going to be much better if, as you say, she marries young Barney, although he appears to be the best of the bunch."

"It's out of the question, Ralph. And what's more, she's so young, and here am I thirty-two, almost seventeen years her senior."

"Oh! God almighty." The painter's voice faded away from Emma and she knew he must be walking up the length of the room. Then, his voice becoming clear again, she knew he was approaching the kitchen door and so, swiftly, she let herself out.

Standing with her back to the cottage wall she looked up into the sky. The clouds were high with puffs of white down resting on patches of pure blue and she wished from the bottom of her heart that she was up there, alongside her granny. There they were back in the room discussing her as if she was something that could be weighed, and then sold. . . . And then there were those up at the farm waiting for her to be cleared of the plague so that she could be taken into the house and work fourteen hours a day after the four of them, and be expected to be thankful. Six men, three of them supposedly loving her, one of them hating her as deeply as the three loved her and the fifth one indifferent, because Pete seemed too dim of mind to show emotion one way or the other. And then the mister. She could not put a name to his feelings for her, but at times he frightened her almost as much as Luke did.

What was she to do? The painter couldn't have her, the parson wouldn't have her. That hurt her most, it was like one of her dada's knives grinding beneath her ribs. But like a salve in the hurt was the indignation she felt: she wasn't a thing to be pitied, she was her dada's daughter, and she wasn't bad to look upon. Moreover, she could read and write and she had gathered a little knowledge from the books she had read. No, she wasn't a creature to be pitied and bargained over like something in the market at the shoe fair. The feeling of indignation brought her from the wall. She'd be mucked about no longer. There was one channel open to her and that was to marry Barney, and if the mister didn't marry again she would, as Barney had said, one day be mistress of the house. She would aim for that, yes she would, and once inside that house she would see to it that they got somebody else to look to the pigs and the animals.

With this thought she checked herself: she was never happy encased in the house, she preferred to be outside amongst the animals. Well then, her mind came back at her, you can't get everything you want in this world, as her granny so often had said; you plumped for whatever was at hand, you sorted out the grain from the chaff, and the grain in this situation was Barney.

She turned about and with a great to-do she thrust open the kitchen door, quickly passed through the little room, then faced the two men who, surprised at her entry, stood staring at her.

Looking straight at the parson, she said in as formal a tone as she could muster, "I'll be sixteen on the first of February, Parson, and I aim to marry Barney. I gave him me word two years gone, so would you kindly put up the banns from that day please?" And looking at the painter, she said, "I hope I find you well, Mr Bowman? Now I must get back. Good-day to you." And she jerked her head first to one, then to the other before turning about and hurrying from the room.

When they heard the back door close, Henry Grainger looked at Ralph Bowman and, his hand gripping his chin, he said, "She must have overheard us. In . . . in some way she must have overheard us. Oh, my God!"

4

"I cannot take the service, Ralph."

"But you've got to. It's your church, your parish."

"Well, I can't do it. I'll have to make some excuse. My father hasn't been well lately. I . . . I can ask the Reverend Blackett from Gateshead Fell to officiate."

Ralph surveyed the man before him. He was thirty-three years old, a tall good-looking, virile man, but a man who looked more capable of working with his hands than he did preaching from a pulpit. He said quietly, "Is it as bad as that?"

"Yes, it's as bad as that. But once she is married, things will be different."

"You hope."

"Oh yes, they will." Henry nodded emphatically now. "Once the marriage is consummated I will know it is done and that'll be that."

"You know, Henry, what I think? I think you're much too clever to be a parson and too much of a fool to be a man."

"Yes, perhaps you are right. But tack the latter to the former and there'll be more truth in it. I was a fool ever to enter the church, because in it black is black and white is white, there's no allowance for grey, and life is made up of grey."

There was silence between them for a moment; then on a laugh Henry said, "You know something? This'll surprise you more than anything that has gone before, I think. Last week I drank a glass of spirits, the first in my life."

Ralph put his head back and let out his usual bellow, which hadn't been heard in the cottage for some time now, and he said, "Well, well! the man's beaten the parson. What about trying it again?"

"I wouldn't mind, although were it to become known it would ruin my reputation, and the only good quality I have in the eyes of my parishioners is that of being a staunch teetotaller. They tell me that I'm the only parson in Northumberland and Durham that doesn't resort to the bottle."

"Well, your secret's safe with me."

"But not with Miss Wilkinson; she watches me like a hawk. I bought a small flask of spirits when I was in Newcastle and, believe me, I had a job to know where to hide it. I have locked it in a drawer with my sermons."

Again Ralph laughed loudly as he cried, "That should put some spirit into them."

"Oh, Ralph, I think you could do better than that. Still, it's adequate because I'm afraid there's very little spirit in what I have to say these days from the pulpit. I see that crowd of faces looking up at me; I know things about every one of them; I know the majority of them come only out of habit, and that the things they are praying to God to forgive them for, they will continue to do as soon as they leave the church, such as slander, spite, not forgetting fornication. If I were a real man of God, I would forgive them all these things, but looking down on them I am thinking as I talk to them, you are a band of hypocrites and you are not alone, as I am your leader. And at times I think of all that liquor reposing in the vault. . . ."

"Yes, yes, I do too. Somebody's going to get a haul someday. Now there's an idea, instead of buying the stuff why don't you go in and . . . ?"

"Never! I'm bad enough as it is . . . oh no!"

"Oh, laddie. Here! drink that. You're too hard on yourself. As you said, you shouldn't have entered the church. No, you shouldn't, you should have gone into a monastery, the strictest order."

Henry was sipping on the raw spirit and he spluttered now and choked before he was able to say, "What! and frizzle up inside with the thoughts that consume me?" Then looking tenderly towards the painter, he said, "I'll tell you something, Ralph, and please don't sneer, but each night I thank God for your friendship. Without it, I don't know what I would have done in this place. You, to me, have been my father confessor. Not the bishop. Oh no, not the bishop. I'm very wary what I tell the bishop."

Ralph did not answer, he put his hand out and gripped the shoulder of the younger, tormented man in front of him, saying as he did so, "Well, for my part I'll tell you, I may not pray at night, but every time I see you, Henry, I welcome you in my heart, for I too don't know what I would have done over these years without your friendship, and the openness that is between us, no sham, no pretence, just plain speaking. Well, here's to however long it lasts."

Gently they touched their glasses and in an embarrassed silence they finished their drink. Then Henry, picking up his hat to take his leave, said, "If you should see her just before the day wish her well for me, will you? Tell her that I've been unexpectedly called away."

"I'll do that, Henry. But I must say this, Emma's no fool and if she hadn't guessed before, she'll know now the reason why you won't perform the ceremony."

"It won't come as any surprise to her, Ralph, she's known since the time of the cholera." On this he made a small motion with his head, then turned about and walked out. And Ralph, watching him from the doorway, muttered, "The fool. The fool."

Emma was so changed that in some ways she didn't recognize herself. She still knew fear, mostly of Luke and not without cause. She still knew apprehension, apprehension concerned with her coming marriage. But as far as respect went and bowing her knee, even metaphorically speaking, to the four men on the farm, this was now a thing of the past, and she wondered why she hadn't stood up for herself before.

That the men were aware of the change in her was shown in their individual attitudes towards her. She remained the same only to Billy Proctor. Billy had told her that she had given him more laughs of late than he'd had in his whole life on this farm, and he wished at her age he'd only half the spunk that she had now.

She didn't look upon her attitude as spunkish, she only knew inside herself that she wasn't going to be messed about any more. Yet at times, as her wedding day drew near, she lay in the dess bed, the bed in which her mother had been born and in which her granny had died, and she cried, often well into the night.

For weeks now she had only glimpsed the parson at a distance. She hadn't been to Sunday school nor church since the cholera, and her absence was put down by the villagers to resentment that no one had gone near the farm because of the plague.

A fortnight after her granny was buried, Barney had come to her and said, "Me da wants you indoors, Emma." He spoke the words as if he had achieved a victory for her, but he was soon disillusioned by her saying, "If mister wants me to go into the house then he must come and ask me himself, and arrange me pay."

"Now, look here, Emma." He had taken a manly stand before her. "Don't look a gift horse in the mouth; the very fact that he's sent word for you to come over is a battle half won."

Again she surprised him by looking him straight in the face and saying, "To add to your knowledge, Barney, the battle hasn't even begun. Now you can tell that to your da in any way you like. And remember, I'm free, and I can walk out of here this minute if I want to. And I can get work; they'll have me up at the House, or anywhere."

This last she knew was just wishful thinking, because the House was the last place she would go for work, remembering who was the real master there now, and she knew that however kind his wife was, she could expect no favours from him.

What Barney said to her then and slowly was, "Have you gone out of your mind, Emma?" And she answered him, "Yes, I have. And I've come to me senses, and not afore time. Me granny put up with this life because she had to, but I'm not me granny and as yet I have no ties."

Barney had stared at this new being. The old Emma was no more. The girl who'd had to defend herself with a whip could do it more effectively with her tongue now. He didn't like it, and he wanted to tell her so, but he held his tongue because their wedding day was nearing and he was athirst for her. Always he was athirst for her. She had, in a way, got beneath his skin and he couldn't think of anything else but her. Even in his sleep he now dreamt of her, and he hadn't been given to dreams. . . .

So Jake Yorkless came to the cottage late in the evening and knocked on her door, and mockingly, when she opened it, he doffed his cap deeply to her, saying, "You sent for me, ma'am?"

But the grim smile left his face and there issued a bawl from his mouth when she said, "You needn't come funny with me, mister."

"Begod! no, I'm not comin' funny with you, Emma Crawshaw, I've come to tell you, you come to the house the morrow mornin' at half past five and get going, or else you go."

"Well, I can do that an' all, and if I go Barney goes with me. I suppose you know that? And what's more you'll get nobody from the village, because it'll be some long, long time afore any woman puts her foot in your door, because the smell of the plague is now joined by the dirt of the lot of you."

She knew she had gone too far and a wave of fear swept over her when his hands came out like claws towards her, but she cried at him, "You touch me, mister, and I'll flay you." She sprung back into the room and picked up from the table one of the whips that were lying there. She had only a few minutes earlier brought them down from the roof, wondering what she would do with them because she couldn't see her being allowed to take them into the house, and if she left them here, one or the other would surely come in and destroy them, even perhaps keep one to use on her. She wouldn't put it past Luke. Oh no.

"By! God, I never thought to see the day." Jake Yorkless was almost foaming at the mouth.

And now, the whip gripped tightly in her hand, she dared to answer him, saying, " 'Tisn't afore time, mister, and I'm paying back something that you owed me granny, for you never stopped your wife from taunting her, and you knew full well she should have been in her place."

As they glared at each other in the fading light she was amazed to see the fury drop away from his face. Then slowly lowering his head, he said grudgingly, "If your granny had had your spunk, she would have been." But his head quickly jerked up again and he added, "But that's not sayin' you're coming the high and mighty with me, miss. If you're coming into my house, you'll keep your place."

"And what is that to be?"

For a moment he seemed lost for words, but then, his lower jaw moving from side to side, he said, "Remains to be seen how you act."

"Well, that'll depend on how I'm treated."

"Oh, God almighty!" He now held his brow in his hand and, closing his eyes, rocked himself backward and forward, saying, "In all me born days I've never listened to anything like it. If our Barney hadn't gone mad, I'd. . . ."

He stopped, took his hand from his head and stood looking at her in silence.

Then he turned and was about to move away when she said quietly, "I can't be expected to do all the work meself. It took the missis and me granny all their time, and me outside. I can't do three folk's work, I'll have to have help."

He stopped and looked at her. Then, his voice low and his words slow, he said, "Well, I'm afraid you'll have to try, because if I could have had anybody from the village I wouldn't be standing here putting up with your claptrap. Do you know that?"

"Yes"—she nodded at him—"I'm well aware of that. But . . . but I know somebody who would come."

He pulled his neck up out of the rough collar of his coat and said, "You do?"

"Yes. Mrs Petty."

"Mary Petty?"

"Yes."

"But she's got a squad."

"They look after each other, so she says. She could come from eight till five, but only for me."

"Well! Well! Well! You've got it all worked out, haven't you?"

"I do better than most."

Again he was staring at her in silence. Then he almost flung himself round and marched off into the darkening night. And she went back into the cottage.

Holding her hand tightly against her chest, she pressed it as if to assist her breathing while she asked herself, how in the name of God had she dared to make that stand? What was in her? Something was happening . . . had happened. Six months ago she would as soon have thought herself capable of throwing knives at him as of stabbing him with her tongue as she had done. But she had won. In a way, she had won, but as she had said to Barney, the battle hadn't yet begun, and it wouldn't till she was married and had some kind of status. That's what she wanted, some kind of status to make up for the rejection of others.

These others she didn't name, not even in her mind.

5

"Eeh! you look bonny, lass," Mary Petty said; "I've never seen any-body look so bonny. And your frock's a right picture. Fancy you makin' it yourself. You are a clever lass, Emma. Altogether you're a clever lass. I used to say to my Katie, Emma Crawshaw's a clever lass and she shouldn't be used like she is on that farm, and now in two hours time you'll have come into your own, you'll be a missis. Huh—" the little flabby-bodied woman grinned now as she said, "an' that's what I'll have to call you, no more Emmarin', but missis."

"Oh, Mrs Petty, there'll be no need."

"Oh, aye there will. Mightn't be from your part but from—" She now thumbed towards the bedroom door. "He'll see to it. If not Mr Barney, his da will. I thought he was a bit of an upstart, Jake Yorkless. You know I worked outside alongside your granny all those years ago, an' if everybody had had their rights she should have been in here. But then the Lord decides, an' you wouldn't have been who you are with York-less for your granda. You certainly wouldn't look like you do the day 'cos you're past bonny. And this is to be your bedroom." Mary Petty looked round the room, nodding as she went on, "And you've got it nice. It's a decent size, you can get round the bed. That's a nice chest you have there; an' what's that little door next to it?"

"It leads into the roof, it's used as a store room. There's another door at yon end of the house, you'll have seen it. I think they used to put the winter feed up here afore they had so many outhouses."

"Aye, an' I've seen somethin' like it down at Tilson's old mill. . . . Well lass, you're ready." She now gave her full attention to Emma who was standing in the middle of the room dressed in the first new article of clothing she'd had since coming to this place. The dress was of white linen, stiff enough to allow the skirt to billow a little; she hadn't had enough material to make it full and fashionable. The bodice was not fitted to her shape because she was conscious of her fast rising bust, so she had made the upper part of the dress in the form of a blouse. But both the skirt and the blouse were drawn into her narrow waist by a belt of the same material and on the front of which she had embroidered a bunch of forget-me-nots. And it was forget-me-nots she was to carry as a small nosegay.

Although the May day was bright it was still chilly, but she had prepared for this with a soft pink, shop-bought shawl. The extravagance of this purchase which had cost four shillings and sixpence had given her a guilty feeling, but she had told herself it was only once in a lifetime you got married. Following quickly on that thought had come the ardent wish that something would happen before the promised day which would make it impossible for her to go through with the ceremony; the thought of the parson joining her to Barney created in her a feeling that if persisted in she knew would erupt in sickness.

But it was only yesterday that she knew she was going to be spared that ordeal, that on the previous day he had been called away to attend his father who was ill. This news convinced her that God could be kind when He liked.

The painter had given her this news. He had given her a wedding present of her own picture, the one where he made her sit by the fire and pretended she was sewing. In fact she had sewn during that sitting, she had hemmed him a handkerchief from a piece of fine lawn that had once been the back of one of his shirts. He didn't seem to care how he dressed on top but he had two drawers full of good shirts and underwear.

He had wished her happiness, he had held her hand between his two and stared into her face as he said, "I wish your granny could have been alive to see you tomorrow. She was a good woman, your granny. She had her faults, but then who hasn't? And although you may not have known it, Emma, she loved you."

She had wanted to cry then, she had wanted to lean against him and feel his arms about her like those of a father. She wished he would have given her away.

Then he had given her the message Henry had given him some time ago. And he had gone on, "Henry is grieved that he cannot officiate at your wedding because he is very, very fond of you, Emma."

She had said nothing, but she had looked hard at him, and his gaze had dropped from hers. Then without further words she had turned about and left the house, carrying the picture. And now it was hanging on the wall to the side of the bed.

Mary Petty was still chattering: "There'll be a lot of villagers there; they're all looking forward to seeing you wed. 'Tis a pity you have no soul of your own, you need a woman relation at a time like this. Anyway, you won't be in for a rough night 'cos there's going to be no big do after. 'Tis a pity in one way, I mean about the do, not about the rough night. Oh no. I can remember the night I was married. They carried us both into the room and practically tore the clothes off us. Drunk as noodles they all were. And Ned too, he was so drunk he couldn't tell which was top or bottom of me." She now put her arms round her waist and her body shook with laughter; then she added, "He soon found out after, as my squad proves. But you're gettin' a better start than I had, lass, or many another like you that has been brought up on the farms, one-room hovels were our mansions. Our Letty and Jane think they're in clover now 'cos they've got two rooms an' a scullery, but they are still mud-floored. I suppose I should be thankful to God that I'm not still living in Newcastle. That's where I was born, you know lass, in Newcastle. But as I've said to himself time and again—that's when I get fed up with me life—the only difference is that the midden is now at the back of the house instead of in the gutter as it was when I was a bairn in the city. Life's a funny thing. Aw, well now, lass, you're ready. By the way, I wouldn't expect your new brother-in-law to be at the church, 'cos from what I can gather he was in The Tuns last night shoutin' his mouth off. He left on Laura Nixon's cart, and you're old enough to know what that means."

When Emma shook her head slightly, Mary said, "You don't? You don't know about Laura Nixon from outside of Birtley township? Oh, Laura's known far and near. She lost her man in the first year she was married, but she hasn't gone short since. Didn't you know she was the cause of Mary Haswell giving Mr Luke the push? Her brother followed him one night and there was a fisticuffs show up. He lost a good thing there because old man Haswell isn't without a penny, 'tis known."

"I'm ready, Mrs Petty." Emma was getting a little weary of Mary's chatter. However, she was grateful for the last piece of news, but most of all she was grateful that there would be no big do afterwards; she had heard more than once what happened to the bride and bridegroom, and she felt the whole thing to be indecent, besides being embarrassing. She had often wondered how the bride could stand it. Yet she also under-stood that by the time they were ready for bed, the bride was often so full of mead the happenings meant little to her except to make her gig-gle. Well, she wouldn't be full of mead; but then perhaps it would be better if she were.

Jake Yorkless was standing in the kitchen awaiting her and he stared at her as she walked the length of the room towards him. His jaw was slack, his eyes veiled, he uttered no word but looked her up and down for perhaps thirty seconds, and in complete silence; the break in it came when he turned abruptly and walked out of the door into the bright hard sunshine.

After a moment's pause Emma followed him.

He did not help her into the trap and she had to gather her skirt well above her new slippers in order to take the high step, and she had hardly seated herself when he set the horse in motion, and she had to grab at her small straw hat. She had come by this only last week on a second-hand stall in the Gateshead Fell market. She had walked all the way there and back and so saved the price of the hat which was tuppence.

Besides Billy Proctor who was to give her away, there were a number of people standing outside the church and she recognized them as members of families that weren't God-fearing, such as the Farrows, the Hobkirks, the Charltons and the Wheatleys. Wheatleys and Charltons were notorious characters: the Charltons were drovers, the Wheatleys helped with the tanning over at Chester-le-Street. Mr Wheatley had the nickname of 'the skinner', and he was so mean about standing his turn in The Tuns that it was said he would skin a louse for its hide. But all these people waved to her. Their expressions were kindly and some of them called, "Good luck, Emma. Good luck. Happy life, Emma. Happy life." And their warmth almost brought her to tears.

The church was dim and there were a number of people in the pews. Miss Wilkinson was playing the organ, and the pumping of the bellows worked by Tommy Price interspersed a wheezing sound in between the notes. It sounded no different today than from any Sunday, yet she was more aware of it. She had once told the parson that the organ sounded like someone with a bad chest attempting to sing soprano, and that made him and the painter laugh. But the painter hadn't come, he said he wouldn't. She was sad about that.

The man who was standing where the parson usually stood at the top of the two steps leading to the altar was short and plump. He looked so well-fed; likely he had come from a town parish. She did not look at her bridegroom although she knew that Barney was staring at her.

While they were kneeling side by side in front of the strange parson her mind took a great jump and she thought, will I have to take me frock off and do the milking when I get back? Because it's only twelve o'clock now and the tea should be over by about three as there's only six outsiders, and they include Billy.

The others were Anthony Hudson who was now standing to the side of Barney, acting as his best man, Farmer Hudson himself and his wife, and Mr Haswell the verger and his wife. As regards a wedding it would be classed in the village as a shabby one; but then she knew a lot of the villagers wouldn't have accepted an invitation if they had been sent one, for, after all, who was Barney marrying? A nobody, just a farm skivvy when he could have had the pick of a number of lasses in Fellburn village or even as far away as Gateshead proper on the one side, and Birtley or any of the hamlets around on the other, because he used to get about, did Barney. And she had to admit he wasn't at all bad-looking and was well set up in his body.

At this point her mind flew off at a tangent again. If during the past weeks the travelling show had happened to come this way, she was telling herself now, she would have run off with them like her mother had done; but not to marry someone, just to work among them. She would have loved that. She didn't want to marry anybody, she. . . .

"Barnabas, wilt thou have this woman . . . ?"

"I will." Barney's voice was low but firm.

"Emaralda—" the parson seemed to stumble over her name—"wilt thou have this man . . . ?"

She was brought back to the present with a start when she became aware that Barney's elbow was nudging her gently, and she said, "I will."

He was leaning towards her, putting the ring on to her finger. She listened to the parson's voice mumbling on, he didn't speak clear like Henry. Her whole body jerked. That was the first time she had ever thought of the parson as Henry. . . .

She was married now, she was Mrs Yorkless. She didn't like the name. She hadn't liked Crawshaw, but she liked Yorkless even less.

They had signed their names in the vestry and she had walked down the church aisle, her arm through Barney's. Now they were outside with most of the people from the church milling about them. Some shook their hands and others patted Barney on the back. The verger was saying to Jake Yorkless that he and his wife would be along later as he had to see to the Reverend Blackett.

They were in the trap again: Jake Yorkless was driving and she and Barney were sitting behind. Barney was holding her hand tightly. It had a reassuring feel. For the first time she had turned and looked fully into his face and she smiled at him. She was his wife, she would do what duty was expected of her, and he would be good to her. She felt sure of this. He would stand up for her and not let her be abused. She drew comfort from this. Life mightn't be too bad. There were things in it you had to remember and things in it you had to forget, but it was difficult to forget the things that you wanted to remember, and that was a task that lay ahead of her.

*

It was nine o'clock in the evening of the same day. She had long since changed out of her wedding dress and laid it in the bottom of the mahogany three-drawer chest that stood to the side of the window. The bedroom had once been Dan's. Luke had refused to move out of the larger one where he and Barney had slept together since they were children. And although she had opened the windows wide in this room, whitewashed the walls and scrubbed the floor boards a number of times, to her mind the smell of death still lingered about it. Moreover, the bed, though not a single one, was yet not a double one and its size suggested close proximity, whether one wished it or not.

There had been no merriment at the wedding tea, only stiff and polite conversation, and as soon as the guests had gone, which wasn't very long after they had finished eating, Jake Yorkless, who was now her father-in-law but whom she still addressed and would go on addressing as mister, had turned to the bridegroom, saying, "Well, as our Luke doesn't intend to put in an appearance or lift a finger and those animals are blaring for release, an' Proctor doesn't seem to be doing much about it, 'tis best we get our glad rags off, eh?"

Barney had looked at his father, a hard resentful look, then he had turned his gaze on Emma, and she had given him no sign, except to droop her head, before walking out of the kitchen to go to her room and change. But as she left she heard Barney say, "You couldn't make allowances even for today, could you," and his father answered, "What is there to make allowances for? You've got the night to come, haven't you?" . . .

And the night had come, almost. The lamp was burning on the centre of the kitchen table. For the past hour or more, Jake Yorkless and Pete had sat at the table drinking. Pete hadn't drunk as much as his father, but enough to make him fuddled-headed, giggly and thick-tongued.

Jake Yorkless too was thick-tongued, and his tongue had become loose for he was talking incessantly at Barney where he sat on the settle, a mug of beer to his hand. Barney was far from drunk for he had taken little, and he had said little, he just sat listening to the prattle at the table, until his father, addressing Emma, said, "You know, girl, you're lucky. Or maybe you're not. It all depends on how you look at it. But if this was happening in me grandfather's time, or even in me father's, you would be in the barn now being tried out. 'Twas the custom for the father to break in the bride. Still goes . . . still goes some places, an' I don't see . . ."

"Shut your mouth! Da."

Barney had risen to his feet and was now looking down at his father. "Now get this, an' you're not so drunk as you don't understand what I'm sayin', she's me wife and as such she's due for respect. And what's more"—his voice was low now, but more telling than when he had shouted—"let anyone lay a hand on her, and I'll do for them. Do you hear? Kith or kin, I'll do for them."

"What the hell's up with you? Who's touching her? . . . Who wants to touch her? Not me, or any other bugger on this farm, except yourself. Your brother who's close blood of your blood can't bear the sight of her. An' when you're on about respect, let me tell you this. I'm still master here, but she's not mistress, and it won't be past me to take another to me bed, an' not afore long. And then she's back where she was."

"Never! Get that into your head, Da, never. You marry again and I go out. I've said it afore and I repeat it, the world's wide and I've got a pair of good hands on me, and she's proved she can work as good and as long as two women. By God! she has."

"Huh!" Jake Yorkless lay back in his chair and thrust his thumbs into his trouser pockets and glared up at his son as he said, "You know somethin', Barney boy? You've gone soft an' you'll regret it. 'Twill come a day when you'll regret it. You've taken on a dark horse and once you straddle her she'll ride you to hell. Remember that, she'll ride you to hell."

Barney glared at the man who had sired him but for whom he had never had much liking, and now that little was no more. Turning about, he walked to where Emma was standing in the shadows and, taking her arm firmly but gently, he turned about and walked her out of the kitchen, across the small hall and up the stairs into their bedroom. There he lit the candle; then taking her by the shoulders and pressing her gently down on to the side of the bed, he sat beside her, saying softly now, "Take no notice. They're ignorant, they've seen nothin' but the land, they know nothin'. I don't know much more, only this, I love you, Emma, and always have done, and in a way it's cleansed me an' softened me and learned me that there was something more to this living than mucking out animals. Although I've learned an' all that animals are cleaner than men in many cases. And I promise you this, Emma, I'll always be good to you, and I'll wait for the day until you can look me in the face and say, 'I love you, Barney.' Because you've never said it, have you Emma, you've never said, I love you?"

An emotion was oozing itself through her pores. She could give no name to it because it wasn't a feeling, like she had for the parson, it wasn't like any feeling she had ever had before. She couldn't put the name compassion to it, she only knew that all fear of this night had gone from her, and she remained still and pliable under his hands as he loosened her clothing. And when she eventually laid down beside him his flesh brought her comfort.

PART FOUR

The Mother

1

"Well, you'll just have to get on with it, won't you?"

"Yes, I suppose I will, Mrs Yorkless." Ralph Bowman laughed at her; then added, "But she gets on my nerves, she never stops chattering."

"Well she brings you all the village news, doesn't she, and that from up above?" Emma jerked her head backwards.

"Yes, you're right there, she does. But if she tells me once she tells me the same thing six times over with hardly any variation. The woman hasn't the smallest amount of imagination."

"Then you'll know what she's telling you is true."

"Clever. Clever." Ralph Bowman now put his head on one side and said, "How long do you think it'll be?"

"What are you asking me, how long is it afore it's born or how long is it going to be before I'm comin' back here?"

"Both."

"Well, I give meself three days at the most to when it's due; as for when I'll be back, it all depends how I feel. If I'm able I won't leave it long, a couple of weeks or so."

Ralph Bowman looked at the young woman standing before him. The only part of her still recognizable from the girl he remembered before her marriage was her hair and eyes, for her face was puffed and her stomach was a miniature mountain suspended from her waist, while her ankles were swollen over the top of her shoes. And that was the outside of her. Inside too there had been a change. But of course he knew this was a natural thing. In the ordinary way, marriage changed a woman, or a girl, or a child as he had thought of her—it seemed only a short while since she sprang through the kitchen door and said she was going to marry Barney. He wondered if she knew how many lives she had affected on that day. Materially she had affected his because after her marriage she came down to him only once a week, when she cooked for him and sometimes did a sitting. He had done a picture of her with her stomach high. In a way she didn't look unlike Van Eyck's "The Marriage of Giovanni" in which the maiden looked already pregnant. But all told, he was grateful that he saw her at least once a week; more often if he was sick, for she was tender to him in sickness, and he was always worse in the winter. He had continually been amazed after spring would arrive and he was still here to see it. He should have been dead years ago. What kept him going he didn't really know. Here he was, stuck in this isolated part of the world, isolated in spite of all its industry. But the whole country seemed isolated, and nobody of his acquaintance seemed to bother about the world outside. Beyond this island the world was raging with revolutions, crowned heads were being torn from their thrones, men were dying in their hundreds and thousands. Yet life strolled on here, the classes keeping strictly apart, the owners defending their place in society and seeing that the lower classes kept within the boundaries they were told God had destined they should live . . . and be content.

In his early days in London and Paris he had raged with those of like mind against the conditions of the workers, especially of the young children, and had longed to join up with the pioneers. . . .

"You're miles away."

"What, Emma? Oh." He laughed. "Well, you set me off. Anyway what are you hoping for, a boy?"

"Doesn't matter."

"What does Barney want?"

"He says it doesn't matter."

"Do you ever wonder, Emma, what he or she is going to grow to be in this strange world of ours?"

"Yes, I have wondered; but as long as they're healthy, and as happy as life affords, then I'll be satisfied."

"As happy as life affords. There's a bit of cynicism there, Emma. You know what I mean?"

"Yes"—she poked her head towards him—"if you're asking what cynicism means, I do. And I didn't mean my words to be like that. I was only thinking whatever job he or she has to do they'll be happy in it."

"And I hope so too. And being your child, Emma, she'll, or he'll be happy. I have no doubts on that. Anyway you'll let me know, send some word down?"

"Yes, Mr Bowman."

"Emma, how long have we been friends?"

She hesitated for a moment, then said, "Well, I suppose since shortly after I came here, when my granny brought me down. Ten years, I should say."

"Yes, 'tis ten years. And don't you think it's about time that you used my christian name and called me Ralph?"

"No I don't." Her voice was loud. "How could I? I think of you as Mr Bowman or"—she laughed now—"the painter."

He was laughing too as he said, "You do? You think of me as the painter? Well, call me Painter."

"Don't be silly."

"You sound like a wife, Emma." He was smiling, but she wasn't as she turned to him now and said, "And that's what I am."

"Yes, yes, of course." His face was solemn, and he repeated, "Yes, yes, of course." Then on a lighter note he added, "Well, let me know how things go. Send the big mouthpiece down."

"I'll do that. And take care of yourself. Don't go outside without a shawl around you, the wind is keen."

He was about to say, "You still sound like a wife," but checked himself, and quietly watched her put on her cape and pull the hood over her head and smile at him before going out of the door.

Going to the window, he kept his eyes on her until she disappeared around the bend in the road, and all the while he cursed himself for the fact that he couldn't call her wife. Why hadn't he taken the risk last year? She would have understood the business between him and her granny, the main ingredient of which had been over and done with years ago. He was thirty-nine years old and, even with his chest trouble, there was still life in him. She would have renewed that life. True, she hadn't been in love with him no more than she had been with Barney. What her feelings were towards Henry he couldn't really gauge, only Henry's for her, and they were a torment to the man, while his own were but a longing ache and a void. Still, he could look at her from time to time and he could even touch her as he arranged for a sitting. And then there was her face staring at him from the canvasses he was supposed to have sold. He had sold the first half-dozen but the rest were carefully wrapped in oil sheeting and lying across the rafters in the roof. At times he would bring them down and look at them, and each picture of her face told him he had loved her as a child, and then as a girl, and now, but they could not convey the strength with which he now loved her as a wife and a mother to be. Had she any idea of the effect she had on a man? He doubted it. She was so unselfconscious about herself. He even doubted if she realized how beautiful she was.

*

After the heavy frost the road was slippery, and a late February sun had not yet melted the thin layer of ice that lay on the puddles in the road. There had been no snow for more than a fortnight now, but that didn't mean there wasn't more to come. However, those lambs that had been born and had survived the last heavy downfall should be inured to what was to come. They had lost eight sheep and ten lambs in the drifts, and Dobbin had slipped and broken his leg and had to be shot. She had been so upset about that. When she suggested putting the leg into splints, the mister, as she still thought of her father-in-law, had bawled at her, "Don't be a bloody fool!" And for the first time in her life she had used a swear-word and yelled back at him, "Don't you bloody well bawl at me." That night in bed Barney had hugged her with no intention of leading up to loving her, he had just hugged her and with his head on her breast he had laughed until the springs of the wooden bed had almost given way. He said it was the funniest and most surprising thing he had heard in many a day, and that the look on his father's face was a picture, because his mother, although rough-tongued with everyone else, had never dared to swear at her husband.

Barney had been kind to her and her feeling for him had grown deeper. Into what, she couldn't actually say. She sometimes asked herself if this was real love and that the feelings she had for that other person just the outcome of a young girl's romantic fancy. Whatever it was, it was a growing comfort to her.

She was also aware that if it wasn't for the presence of Luke in the house there would be a sort of family happiness here. Pete in his way had taken to her, and the mister, although he never gave her a word of thanks, seemed to appreciate her cooking and the different order she had brought into the house. She had opened up the front room and on a Saturday night and Sunday night she lit the fire there. Her first suggestion that they should make use of this room in the only spare time they had in the week brought derision from Jake Yorkless; then after a time he had taken his place by the fireside in the horsehair armchair.

The only one who didn't make use of the room was Luke. In a way, she was glad of this for she herself couldn't have sat at peace for, wherever he was, his eyes would dwell on her; sometimes it was as if he were looking right through her without seeing her. At other times, across the kitchen table at a meal when he raised his head, his eyes would pierce her, and at such times she knew he was seeing her all right and that the resentment he bore towards her was corroding in him.

She had spoken to Barney about Luke and he had said, "Take no notice, he'll come round, he's bound to, he can't keep this attitude up forever. It was the same when he was a lad. He would go into the sulks for weeks on end, then one day he would greet you bright and smiling as if nothing had happened. You'll see," he said. "Just wait, he'll come round."

She didn't know if she wanted Luke to come round; as he was now she knew where she stood with him and she was on her guard against him.

She turned the bend in the road and there, only a few yards from her and also on foot, was the parson. She knew that at the sight of him the colour had swept over her face; it was burning as if the frost had seared her cheeks.

"Hello, Emma."

"Hello, Parson."

"How are you, Emma?"

She paused before answering, then said, "As you see, Parson." Then dared to refer to her condition, saying, "Nearing my time." It was an indelicate thing to say and she was surprised at herself, yet she had found that when she was in his presence there came a tartness in her tongue.

She had not come face to face with him for over three months now. He did not visit the farm and she no longer attended church. He had grown much thinner, yet his face looked prettier. . . . That was a silly word to apply to a man, particularly this one: handsomer it should be. Yet there was a ruggedness about his features that denied that description.

With some dismay she noticed that there were slight hollows in his cheeks. In her chatter Mary had said that he lived on hard tack in the vicarage and that Miss Wilkinson was neither one of two things, a good housekeeper or a good cook, but she had to work hard as she had no help to run that big place, and that she only stayed on in the hope of hooking him. It was known in the village that she had her sails fully set for him, and her almost eight years older. But as it was said in The Tuns, she had as much chance of becoming the parson's wife as Granny Frinton had and she was eighty-two. Mary had added it was a pity old Sir Peter had died because the parson hadn't been invited back there since, and his weekly visits to the House had assured him of one square meal at least.

The sparseness of him caused her to say, "Are you well?"

"Yes, yes. I am well, Emma. What makes you imagine that I am not?"

She cast a glance to the side before she said, "You have got thinner of late."

"Yes, yes, perhaps I have; but then I walk a lot these days. I got rid of the trap you know, the old horse was past it."

She hadn't known that, and she remembered the horse wasn't all that old. It was money again, he hadn't been able to afford to keep it. And it must mean too that the verger was out of a part-time job, and that wouldn't please him, because part of his work was to see to the horse and trap.

As she looked at him there returned to her the old feeling, so different from that which she had for Barney, and it turned into an ache that was sharpening itself into a stabbing pain which caught at her breath.

When she put her hand to the collar of her coat and gripped it, Henry moved a step towards her and, his voice full of concern, said, "What is it, Emma? Are you . . . ? Are you . . . ?"

For answer she gulped, drooped her head as any young woman of her age and condition should do before a parson, and muttered, "I . . . I must get back."

"Yes, yes, of course. Will you be all right? Or would that I come with you?"

"No, no"—she shook her head—"I'll be all right. 'Tisn't far now."

He was holding out his hand to her, not with any expectation of her taking it, but in a way that indicated a plea, which came over in his voice as he said softly, "If . . . if you should need me, you'll send for me, won't you, Emma? I mean—" He did not go on to explain what he meant, but now added, "I'll be thinking of you every moment, I'll be thinking of you till your time is over."

She found it was impossible to give him any sort of answer, even to say briefly, "Thank you, Parson," and she had to close her eyes for a moment so she wouldn't look into his face; then abruptly she turned from him and hurried away up the mud-ridged road, not taking care now to step over the ice puddles.

Barney was leading a horse across the farmyard and he left the animal and came hurriedly towards her. Taking her arm and lowering his head so he could see into her face, he said " 'Tis about?"

"No, no; I'm just cold."

"Oh, we'll soon put that right." He now called across the yard, "You Billy!" And when Billy Proctor poked his head out of the corn store Barney thumbed towards the horse, saying, "See to him." Then he followed Emma into the kitchen, and there he called to Mary Petty as if she too was at the other end of the farmyard, "Put that gruel pan on again, and look slippy." Then going to where Emma was taking off her cloak, he took the garment from her and, flinging it over the back of the settle, he said, "Sit yourself down. The gruel should be ready in a minute and a good dollop of rum in it will put you right." Now he bent down until his face was level with hers, and his voice lower, he added, "And skite the devil out of you whatever it be, one or t'other."

A few minutes later, sipping the laced gruel, she looked to where Barney was now sitting by her side and she said, "I'm all right. Go on . . . I'm all right."

"I can spare a minute." He smiled at her, a soft warm smile, and she was overcome with a feeling of guilt and betrayal and for a moment she felt that her only release would be to droop her head forward and let the tears flow.

But Mary Petty saved her with her tart remark: "My, my! some folks is lucky, pampered like ladies. Now there was me"—she nodded towards them both—"I nearly dropped me first in tatie field. 'Tis true." She jerked her chin upwards. "'Tis true as I'm standing here. I'd been in the field since five pickin'. 'Twas on nine and we were going to sit down for a break—five minutes we got for skimmed milk and a shive—and then bang! I was doubled up. 'Twas just as well the cart was ready to take the sacks back to the farm, for I got a lift and only got into the room just in time. 'Twas all over in an hour. Himself knew nothin' about it, he was away droving. And you know what he said when he came back three days later? I should have waited and hung on. Aye." Her head was bobbing up and down, a wide grin on her face now, seeing that she had got them smiling. "And you know something else? And I bet you won't believe this. That very night he sat down and reckoned up in his head, because he could neither read nor write, no more than meself, but he was sharp up here." She tapped her forehead. "He worked it out if I had one a year for the next ten years, not counting twins or triplets, how soon they'd be in work, for the quicker they were in work the quicker his idea of having a place of his own could come about. I said to him, 'Would you like to exchange me for a stud mare?' an' he said. . . ."

She had never expected to laugh this day, and now she didn't know whether she was laughing or crying, but her body was shaking, as was Barney's, and the tears were rolling down her cheeks, and now handing the almost empty bowl to Barney, she rose to her feet, saying, "Oh, Mary, Mary." Then looking down at her husband, she added, "Go on. Go on, or else we'll be having the mister in to find out what all the nuration's about."

Still laughing, Barney patted her arm; then as he was leaving the kitchen he glanced at Mary, saying, "You're a case. You know that, Mary Petty? You're a case."

As soon as the door closed on Barney, Mary turned and, giving her full attention to Emma, she said firmly, "Fun and jokes apart, get yourself upstairs and put your feet on the bed, for if I know anything you're going to have a visitor sooner than you expect. It's in your face."

And Mary was right, the visitor came two days later after hours of agonizing pain and straining, during which at times Emma longed for death. Even when her daughter was put into her arms she felt too weak, too tired to hold her. For some time she was only dimly aware of Mary hovering over her and of the doctor talking about the difficulty of the afterbirth; then of someone holding a cup to her mouth and making her drink something, and she recognized what it was, for she had given her granny doses of laudanum to ease the cramp.

At one period she imagined the parson was in the room and bending above her and she put her hand up and touched his face; and then she went to sleep, and slept on and off for the next two days.

2

She was a fortnight in bed, and she was surprised to learn that she had nearly died. Mary had informed her there had been complications after the baby had come and that she was lucky to be in the land of the living.

She didn't fully realize how ill she had been until she attempted to walk, when she felt weak and had a job to put one foot in front of the other. She couldn't imagine that she had ever run and sometimes, when no one was looking, jumped the stile.

Barney assured her that her strength would return. He was very gentle with her, tender, and so proud of his daughter. There was an ache in her heart when she watched him holding the child, yet at the same time she felt comforted in the knowledge that she had given him something, repaid him in a way for his kindness to her. She marvelled at his kindness and consideration. He was so unlike the rest of his family that it would seem there was no blood connection between them. He showed none of his mother's characteristics and little of his father's, except that, like the mister, he was a good worker.

They had been snowed up for a fortnight, and afterwards the roads had run with slush and rain, and so the child was almost two months old before it was christened. Henry held it in his arms and named it Annie Yorkless. Barney had wanted the name Annie because he said he remembered his grandmother with fondness. When Henry placed the child back in Emma's arms, their hands had overlapped for a moment, and it was a moment of which they were both aware.

When, later at the church door, Henry looked at her he said with conventional politeness, "May she be of comfort to you both." But it was Barney who answered, saying, "I'm sure she will be, Parson, I'm sure of that. And seein' who her mother is she couldn't be else." He had cast a warm glance towards Emma, but she was looking down on the child, wrapping her up and covering her face against the bitter winds, thinking as she did so that she should be proud of Barney because he always acted with courtesy, he always knew what to say, not like some of the farmers' sons who were as gauche as the meanest of their hired hands.

On the drive back, Barney said to her, "He's a nice chap that parson. We're lucky to have such. Not many would have tramped out here every day for a week as he did when you were so bad. And you know what?" He turned and grinned at her. "You patted him on the cheek one day and called him Henry. I thought I would have died, I thought I would have died meself. But he didn't take it as a liberty as old Crabtree would have done. Oh, you had to know your place with old Crabtree. But he held your hand and soothed you, he was full of concern. He's a good man, no matter what they say about him in the village. The fact is he's too straight for them, gets under their skins, the hypocrites. But that's what they're calling him now. They say he had a hand in emptying the cellar all those years back 'cos he was against the drink, but that now he's doing it on the sly himself. That's what they're saying. Willowy Wilkinson put that around. 'Twas after he brought the young lady to see the vicarage, the one that he was going to marry. Huh!" He laughed now. "Wilkinson had had her eye on him, a good-looking young fellow like that and a gentleman into the bargain. She should have had sense to know that young parsons come from the class, and they marry the same. They may be poor but it makes no difference, they don't stoop. If they did 'twould never work. Something in the calibre. You get it in animals, horses particularly. Something you can't put your finger on except in the voices. Like the painter." He turned and grinned at her. "He even swears differently, doesn't he, the painter?"

She looked at him with fondness. She liked to hear him talk. He talked a lot, especially in bed. Sometimes she went to sleep listening to him talking and he laughed at her the next morning, saying, "I sent you off again." But there was always a lot of sense in what Barney said, especially in the fact that the class didn't stoop. Yet at the same time this fact caused a form of irritation for she knew for instance that Barney had a better thinking mind than some of the folks round about who considered themselves near-gentry. These were the ones that joined the hunt after the fox, these were the ones who had two to three hundred acres of land.

"The painter fellow's a funny bloke, isn't he? I had a crack with him yesterday. I was in the lower field and he was on the road coming back from Newcastle. That's where he said he had been, and he was three sheets in the wind. He had come back on the carrier cart and had walked from the village. Must have been paying his monthly visits.

Cheaper than keeping a wife, eh?" He turned and laughed at her, his mouth wide, his eyes portraying the familiarity that existed between husband and wife. But when he saw there was no answering gleam of amusement in her expression, his voice more sober now, he added, "Well, 'tis only natural. And he's never touched on the village lasses. Not that there's much to choose from there, I'd say, if you go by looks. But then again—" Once more there was a note of amusement in his voice as he ended, "looks ain't the question in this matter, shut your eyes and hope for the best as they say."

"Barney!"

"Oh, all right." He pulled a face at her, then grinned as he added, "You sounded like Miss Wilkinson there in Sunday school. It's gone down, the Sunday school, they tell me. Now if you were to take it up, by! they would get stuck in the doorway."

And so it went on, and she listened to his bantering knowing that he was happy. With the exception of one cloud on his horizon, his sky was clear and full of promise. And the cloud was the man in whose veins his own blood ran.

It was on the day that she first took the child down to the painter's that she met up with James Fordyke. She had not come face to face with him since the time of the cholera, and now there he was riding his horse across the corner of the field of ripening barley. She had the child in her arms or she would have taken to her heels and run, but what she did do was to shout, "See what you're doing!" She called at the top of her voice, and it was loud enough for him to check the horse and look in her direction. He now brought the animal round and, instead of taking it to the edge of the field, he brought it straight across towards her, and she stood gasping for breath as she watched the animal treading down the growing shoots. They'd had two hard winters, they'd lost sheep and lambs, the milk yield was down, moreover, so was pig flesh in the open market, and you couldn't get more than one and sixpence for a fully dressed hen. Yet in the weekly paper she had read yesterday that the hungry forties were over and a golden era was dawning for the industrial areas which included the Tyneside, and this might stop people rushing off to the gold diggings in California, and that the Bank of England had a lot of money in it and so interest rates would lessen; also that the working man was happy and contented now that the loaf had been reduced to sevenpence. The rest of the world had gone mad with revolutions and things but England under good Queen Victoria was a haven of peace and an example to the world.

Well, her private comment on this had been, they must have missed their part of Tyneside for there had been talk of doing away with Billy Proctor's services. But she had stood out against this and said that, as the cottage was hers, if they dismissed him she'd put him in there. So determined had been her attitude that Jake Yorkless had passed over the idea.

But this five acre field and the ten acre beyond had been cropped for the first time. They had worked on the land for two or three years previously, clearing it of stones and tilling it, then leaving it fallow to the frost to cleanse it, and the result had been this promising crop. And there he was mowing it down.

And now he was sitting above her glaring at her.

"Did you speak to me?"

"Yes, I did." She added to her offence by not saying sir. "You're taking your horse over a clean crop, 'tis against all rules."

"Whose rules . . . who made the rules?"

She paused for a moment, lost for words, her lips rubbing against each other. She lifted the child from her left to her right arm, then said, " 'Tis a known fact that you don't cross, don't take animals over ripe fields. You wouldn't take it over your own land."

She saw his hand twitching on his riding crop; then bending towards her, he growled, "You forget, madam, that this is my land."

" 'Tis nothing of the kind."

" 'Tis nothing of the kind." His voice mocked her tone; then his voice in a growl again, he said, "I rent this land to Yorkless. If my memory serves me right he owns nothing but thirty acres and he pays yearly rent on fifty. I can recall it tomorrow if I wish, and I just might. Yes, yes"—he straightened in the saddle now and his head moved slowly up and down—"I just might, young matron, and that will teach you to keep a civil tongue in your head and to learn how to bend your knee and to address your betters when they deign to speak to you. What you need, madam, is a taste of one of your own whips."

On this, he kicked the horse viciously in the sides, and it plunged away down the perimeter of the field, leaving a churned path in its wake, and she stood for a moment swaying as if she were about to fall. She was even so affected that she went and rested her back against the dry stone wall. What would they do if he took the land away? And all through her. He had looked at her as if he hated her, loathed her; and this had all come about because she had afforded a little entertainment for his father-in-law. It was strange the trouble that those whips had brought into her life; and she wondered, were she to burn them now, if their influence would die away. Yet she knew she could never burn them, they belonged to her dada. They were the only things she had that recalled to her that at one time she had a father, and a mother, and that she hadn't always lived on this farm where peace was an elusive thing. It was there hovering outside herself, sometimes in the form of Barney, sometimes in the form of her child, but always overshadowed by Luke. That was strange. As she saw them now there seemed no difference between her brother-in-law and the master of the Hall. In her mind they merged and formed one person from whom emanated evil. . . .

She was still shaking when she reached the cottage.

"Is that you, Mary?" Ralph Bowman called from the inner room, and when she answered, "No, 'tis me," he appeared in the doorway, his face bright, his smile welcoming, saying, "Well, hello stranger . . . strangers. So this is it, is it?"

As he took the child from her arms he said, "What is it? You're shivering."

"I've had an encounter with Mr Fordyke."

She now proceeded to tell him what had happened and when she had finished, he said, "He's got no bloody right to cross sown fields and he knows that. 'Twas a form of aggravation and if it went to the justices that's what they would say . . . or should say, but they're all hand in glove. Yet I don't know if there's many would take his part, not even in his own class."

A few minutes later, sitting opposite to her, a hot drink in his hand, he said, "What perhaps you don't know, Emma, and it just came about in a roundabout way seeping downwards from Miss Noble to Mrs Atkins and through his mightiness the butler, then Pearson the steward and down through the stable-hands et cetera until it reached The Tuns, is that had the old man lived, Sir Peter you know, you were going to be asked up there to be trained as a lady's-maid. Some said it was Mrs Fordyke's idea and some said it was Miss Noble who suggested it to her because she was getting on, Miss Noble I mean, and she saw you as a bright young lass able to read and write, educated as it were by Henry. Then of course came the cholera and all that was knocked on the head. But that wasn't the only thing that soured Mr James Fordyke, for the old man had left everything, every penny to his daughter, and tied it up in such a way, and very cleverly too, that only she could touch it. They say it was a very bizarre will: She had a personal allowance and she could draw any money for living expenses but nothing to enhance the house or to reduce the mortgage that was on it or anything appertaining to the upkeep. They say his will was like an act of parliament. The old fellow knew what he was doing and whom he was dealing with, for 'tis known that James Fordyke has gone through two fortunes, whispered in ways best not talked about, so the man you met this morning is a very frustrated human being, Emma, and likely he was taking out of you what he wanted to take out of his wife. But it won't do him any good to cut off Yorkless's leased land: the rent can't be all that much but it's still something, and what's sure is he can't employ men to work it. And another thing that must be an irritant to him, he used to spend most part of his year up in London. He had a place up there they say. Now that is gone and he's stuck here. Awful life for him. Poor soul!" He grinned at her; then leaning towards her, he added, "Don't let it worry you. If he tries anything about the land, all you've got to do is to go and see Mrs Fordyke. After all, it is she who holds the whip hand there. Talking of whips"—his smile widened now—"what became of all those whips you had?"

"They're still there under the roof."

"Henry and I were talking about them the other day. You wouldn't know how to use them now, would you?"

"Oh, it would come back; you never lose the knack."

"No, I suppose not."

He looked now to where the child was lying in the corner of the big chair and after a moment he asked, while keeping his eyes on the bundle, "Are you happy, Emma?"

Her answer did not come immediately; then it was truthful. "In a way," she said.

He turned to her and he repeated, "In a way?"

She nodded. "Barney's good to me, kind, I couldn't wish for a kinder, but there's a feeling in the house. 'Tis Luke, he hates me. You can—" she closed her eyes now and moved her head from side to side— "well, sort of smell it. The only time I'm free of it is at night. Even then you're aware he's across the landing and 'tis as if his eyes are piercing the wall. Sometimes I . . . I find him standing staring at me and I haven't known he was there."

Ralph Bowman looked at the young girl sitting opposite him. She didn't look like the mother of a child, although she did not any longer appear like a young girl untouched, something outside nature; there was about her now a stronger appeal than that which had lent fascination to the girl, she was a woman with a quality that caught at a man's breath, all the more so because she was unaware of it. She was still not as yet conscious of her own value. No mirror had reflected her beauty, or if it had her eyes had been closed to it. It pained him to sit here looking at her. Did she know she had altered his life, made him want to go on living because, once dead, he would no longer be able to see her, hold her in the heart of his eye? . . . He had an advantage over Henry, because he could gaze on her when she was no longer present. And Luke. Oh yes, he could understand Luke hating her.

He bent towards her now and said quietly, "You've got to accept, Emma, that people will either love you or hate you. And there'll be no happy medium where you're concerned, particularly with men. And they only hate you because they are not able to love you, because there is something in you that has repulsed them, you can see through them, and it comes over in a kind of disdain. . . ."

"I don't disdain anybody. 'Tisn't in me to look down on anybody."

"Oh, don't delude yourself on that point, Emma. We all disdain somebody; there's always somebody lower than ourselves. You would have to have your nose in the mud before you could say to yourself, there is no one I look down on. 'Tis a natural feeling, not conscious all the time. Take Henry for instance. He appears to the outsider to be the humblest fellow on God's earth, whereas half his time he is scorning this one and that one. His saving grace is that he knows it. By the way, I don't think we'll have Henry with us much longer. Did you know he's applying for another parish?"

The constriction in her throat impeded the words that she would have used in polite astonishment and so she just stared at him as he nodded quietly at her, saying, "He's had it in mind for some time. Of course it all depends on the bishop, and the bishop may find it difficult to fill an uninteresting little hole-in-the-earth like Fellburn village and hereabouts. Then again the bishop might think him too good to lose in this quarter, for although some of the diehards have transferred their allegiance to Gateshead Fell, he's brought in a number of the villagers who had never been inside the church, except when they were christened. Unfortunately though, these haven't any money, and the plate is barely covered at the week-ends."

Ralph rose from the chair now and, walking to the window, he looked out of it as he said, "If my persuasion will carry any weight he'll remain here. He's the only friend I've got, the only friend I want. He's a good man, is Henry." He turned and was looking at her again. She had put on her shawl and had lifted the baby from the chair and he slowly walked towards her, saying, "What he's always needed is a wife, someone on whom he could lavish that mountain of affection that is within him; but I doubt that'll ever come about now. You know what I believe, Emma? I believe that everybody in this life is offered one chance of happiness, real happiness, and if they let it slip by they can never hope for anything to fill its place."

He was being cruel, and he knew he was being cruel, but that in a way he was not intending it for her, he was explaining something to her, and she knew what it was. She said, "I came down to say I'll be startin' next week, that's if you want me."

"Thank God for that." His manner changing, he now grinned at her and pushed at her shoulder with the flat of his hand, saying, "If I want you? How do you put up with Mary's chatter, she never stops?"

"Well, likely she's given you all the village news."

"Yes, she has that." He laughed again. "And the latest is, Miss Wilkinson slapped Miss Bonney's niece. Apparently the dressmaker's had the young miss staying with her. Eighteen she is and buxom, and she acquired the habit of visiting the vicarage at night, about eight o'clock and it on dark, saying she wanted some advice from the parson. And when it was the third time within a week, Miss Wilkinson apparently administered advice with a clout across the lug. . . . Oh! the things that go on in that village. Since Mary's been coming here I've never bothered to read the Newcastle newspapers. As she said yesterday, love runs through that village every spring like a dose of senna. Anyway, Miss Bonney's niece has now taken her departure."

As Emma went out the door she turned and with a small smile playing round her lips, she said, "Miss Bonney's niece, I understand, paid you a couple of visits too. What a pity you hadn't a housekeeper to slap her across the lug."

She went down the path to the sound of Ralph's laughter, and then his voice came to her: "The poor girl was only wanting practice, she'll be scared stiff of the proof."

The painter did her good. She was fully aware now of how he felt about her as she was of Henry's feelings for her. She could and she did call him Henry to herself, and her mind sometimes sang his name, but she had to be careful that she didn't think about it while in bed in case she called it out. But in bed she felt comforted: if she had to have a compensation for love in this life then God had been good to her and given her Barney.

"What the hell does he mean by it! Going to stop us renting the land come Michaelmas." Jake Yorkless appealed to his three sons who were standing round the kitchen table. "Sending Pearson the steward, and out of the blue, no reason or rhyme, just to say his master says come

Michaelmas he wants the land. And where does that leave us? Thirty bloody acres. Back to where we started, all me grandfather had almost a century ago. Why? Why?" He spread out his hands before them.

No one spoke for a moment until Luke, thumbing over his shoulder to where Emma was stirring the fire, said, "Better ask her."

"What's she got to do with it?"

Luke thrust out his chin at his father, saying, "Ask her, or ask her husband there." He thumbed towards his brother now and Barney, his face grim, said, "What do you mean? What are you up to?"

"Well, didn't I hear her tell you that she had seen Fordyke riding across the barley and she had told him he shouldn't do it?"

Jake Yorkless now brought his gaze on Emma, where she had turned from the fire and his voice was quiet as he asked, "You told him he shouldn't ride through the barley?"

"Yes, I did. You go mad if one of the bullocks gets into the field, and you were going to shoot Pearson's dog, you said yourself, if it cut across that way to the river again."

"But Mr Fordyke, he wouldn't have gone ridin' through it."

"Go down and see it, Da." Jake now turned and looked at Barney, and Barney went on, "One corner's flat and there's a path wider than this table right through the middle of it. I was waiting for you to find out for yourself."

Of a sudden Jake Yorkless dropped on to a wooden chair and, again looking round him, he said, "But surely he wouldn't take the land off us for that?"

"You've got his answer." It was Luke speaking again. "It's known he's a vindictive bugger, and anybody with any sense would have gone carefully, but no, somebody has to ride him, so much so that he must have been in a blazing temper to send his steward straight over here."

"I'll fight him. I'll go to the justices."

"A hell of a lot of good that'll do, he's one of the justices. What you want to do is make her go and apologize to him."

"She'll do no such thing."

The twin brothers were facing each other now like enemies, which they had become. Then Barney spoke again: "As Da says, we can fight him in court. But she's not going on her knees to him or anybody else."

"You'll lose in court." They all turned and looked at Pete. Pete rarely had an opinion about anything, at least that's what they thought, but now he went on, "It's a waste of time, land's his, just let to us, waste of money going to court. There's nowt you can do about it. Better to make the best of what's left."

It was a long speech for Pete, and for a moment it seemed to take their minds off the issue. Then Barney said, *"I'll* go and see him."

"Why should *you* go?"

Barney glared at Luke.

"Because Da there doesn't want to go. Do you?" He looked at his father and Jake, staring down at the table now, muttered, "Likely lose me temper."

Turning and confronting Luke, Barney said harshly, "And I'm the next in charge."

"Aye, by a few minutes. That's another thing I'd like to air: we should be equal, twins should be equal."

"God in heaven! shut up will you at this time." Jake had sprung to his feet. "If Fordyke gets his way there'll be nowt left to be equal about. Go on you Barney, and see what you can do. And as she won't apologize for herself, apologize for her."

Emma was about to make some retort but Barney gripped her arm and led her from the room.

Up in the bedroom, as she watched him change into his Sunday suit, she said to him, "You . . . you don't blame me for goin' at him for crossing the field?" And looking at her, he said soberly, "No, I don't blame you; but it would have been better if you hadn't met up with him and we never knew who did it, 'cos he's vindictive, he's known to be vindictive."

"I'm sorry, Barney."

He smiled weakly at her now, saying, "I'll have to tell him that, although the lie'll stick in me teeth. But don't worry." Putting his arms about her he kissed her on the lips, then said, "If the worst comes to the worst we'll have to pull our horns in some way and do different planning. But still, we won't go into that until I come back. Be a good lass." He patted her cheek, then went out; and she sat down on the edge of the bed and bowed her head over the solid wooden footboard and chastised herself for having such a ready tongue.

Barney came back and they knew what the answer was before he spoke. His father followed him into the kitchen, and he had just begun to speak when Luke came bursting through the door, saying, "Well, what happened?"

"I didn't see him. I got no further than the steward who had delivered the message. His master he said had gone into town, but it would be no use seein' him for he was firm on the point that he was taking over the land. And what's more, he's fencing in Openwood and the last of the common beyond."

"He can't do that."

Barney looked at his father saying, quietly now, "He can; there's been a law or some such passed: if common land lies within a man's boundary he can fence it in."

"There'll be murder done if he does that."

Barney now looked at Luke and said, "And where will that get them? Anyway"—he unloosened the narrow white neckerchief that showed above the top of his grey collarless coat and, pulling it from his neck, he turned to his father and said, "The sheep will have to go, but not before the back end. We'll get a better price for them then. In the meantime, I think it would be wise to try and clear the stone fields."

"Don't talk so bloody soft."

Barney rounded on Luke now, crying, "What else is there for it? You tell me."

"Those fields are full of boulders and stones for two foot down."

"So was the bottom field at one time, and the dip paddock, but I can remember seeing Granda clearing those."

His father's voice cut in between the two of them now, saying, "Aye yes, but it took all of two years, workin' every odd hour of the day and night, moonlight nights, until we dropped."

"Well—" Barney's voice was calmer too now as he leaned across the table and, looking into his father's face, said, "There's four of us now, hale and hearty, an' Emma there can lend a hand; Billy will do most of what's to be done in the yard."

"I've said it afore, Billy'll have to go at the end of the year, can't afford to keep him on eight shillings a week. Anyway, he's past a good day's work, he'll have to be put out."

"But he's not bein' put out." It was the first time Emma had spoken and they all turned and looked at her.

"Well, what plans have you got for him, missis?" Jake's tone was sarcastic.

"Well, as I said afore an' all, he can have my cottage, and it is my cottage, and as I'll be workin' as good as any man, I should deserve some kind of wage an' I'll take it in the form of grub for him."

They were all looking at her with open mouths. Even Barney was stunned by the fact that a woman . . . no, a chit of a lass after all, should expect pay for being a wife instead of being thankful to God He had seen fit to place her in such an advantageous position. It was beyond even him. He turned away and walked up the kitchen, through the door into the hall and he could hear his father's heavy hobnailed boots screwing round on the stone floor and making a screeching sound as he cried, "Let me get out of this an' all."

But Luke remained for a moment, glaring at her with a look of such ferocity that she turned from him and, going to the basket that lay to the side of the hearth, she picked up the child, although it was still asleep, and pressed it to her.

When the kitchen door smashed closed, it seemed a signal for Mary to come out of the long larder where she had been washing down the shelves. She said nothing, but she opened the back door and threw the bucket of dirty water into the yard where it trickled towards the channel that took the slush from the byres at the other side. Then having closed the door, she thrust the bucket noisily under the shallow stone sink before turning to Emma and saying, "Some how-d'you-do! Might as well try to move mountains as clear those two fields, I would say. Talkin' of getting rid of Billy, they'll be gettin' rid of me next, eh?"

"Not if I can help it, Mary. If I'm to be in the fields I'll need someone in the house to see to her"—she patted the child's back—"and the meals and such."

"You're right there, they'll still want feedin'. But I'll tell you what. You can put it to the mister if you like. I've got three youngsters, six, seven and nine. Dickie, he's the nine-year-old, he was down the pit till recently, till all the stink started about bringing the bairns up. Some of them are still down sayin' they're twelve, but they have still two years to go. But Dickie's small. He was on the bogies, pulling through the low drifts you know. They like the little 'uns in there. Well anyway, he's out now. Bird scaring, a penny a day when he can get it. The other two have been stone pickin' for Mr Rice, down at Gateshead Fell, but that's finished."

Emma looked at Mary. "I . . . I thought there was a school starting and they had to go to school," she said. "The . . . the parson. . . ."

"Aw! school. I ask you, what good is schoolin' gona do for them? It's not gona put any bread into their mouths. Besides, they know how many beans make five. And what's more, they can tell every coin up to a pound. Nobody's going to dupe them. Not that they'll ever earn a pound a week in their lives. But what I'm gettin' at is, they're sturdy, the three of 'em, an' used to bendin' their backs all day, and I'd like to bet, atween them, they'd do the work of two men, but they'll be worth more than a penny a day. My Dickie could get as much as five shillings a week doing overtime, but there'd be nowt like that here, I know. Billy was telling me he's never had more than eight shillings a week in his life. And there's my Ned grumblin' 'cos he only picks up twelve, unless he does a bit on the side, an' who's to blame him? Anyway, ask the mister for tuppence a day each. How's that? Do you think he'll rise to it?"

Emma knew her father-in-law would not rise to tuppence a day for the young six-year-old boy, but she would. Even after burying her granny decent, she still had quite a bit left of the painter's money in the bag under the rafters in the cottage. And along with that there were her granny's savings which she had discovered after her death in a little locked box at the back of the cupboard bed. She had always imagined her granny spent all she earned on the smuggled liquor when she could get it, but it hadn't been so, and the painter must have been generous to her an' all, for in the box she had found an assortment of coins, mostly silver. But there were four sovereigns among them and the whole amount had come to nine pounds. She felt guilty about her hoard at times because she had not even mentioned it to Barney. So she now said to Mary, "I'll ask him for a penny a day for each of them and I'll supply the rest, but keep it to yourself."

Mary's eyebrows moved up; her eyes became circles of amused light and there was admiration in her tone when she said, "You're young but you've got your head screwed on the right way. I wish I'd been as wise at your age. Aye, I do. 'Tis well to have friends."

Mary had gone down the kitchen and through the door before the implication in her tone dawned on Emma.

Almost dropping the child into the basket, Emma ran the length of the room, thrust open the door and caught hold of Mary as she was about to mount the stairs and, pulling her roughly round, she said, "I don't know what you think, not really, but let me put this straight to you, Mary: the money I have, which is very little, was—" She was going to say, "was given me by the painter for sitting for his pictures," but someone like Mary would not believe that, because sitting for a picture wouldn't be classed in the light of work to her, so she ended, "I found in my granny's box, she had saved bits and pieces over the years. I used some of it to bury her decent. There's a little left."

"Oh. Oh well, lass, but I meant nothin'. Well, I wouldn't, would I? I wouldn't think bad of you. But I can understand your granny havin' a bit put by. Oh aye, yes I can, workin' for the painter all those years."

She withdrew her arm from Emma's grip, saying now, "I'm sorry if you mistook me meanin', and I wouldn't upset you, not for the world I wouldn't, 'cos you've been decent to me. No, I wouldn't upset you." She stepped backwards up one stair and stared down at her mistress who was but a chit of a girl, yet a woman in so many ways, and she thought, astonishing it was that she should defend her honour with such spirit, it wasn't usual in one her age. 'Twas her foreign blood, she supposed;

they always said in the village she was different because of her foreign blood.

She turned and went quickly up the stairs, and Emma returned as quickly into the kitchen.

What were they saying in the village now? Her granny had gone and she was continuing to go to the painter's . . . that she had taken her granny's place in his bed? That's what had been in Mary's eyes.

The world was a dirty place.

She stood for a moment shaking her head. No; no, it wasn't. The world was beautiful, it was this thing that went under the heading of love that was dirty. And yet it wasn't, it wasn't. Her mind was at war within her. You could have love without it. Deep within her there was a spring brimming over with love. It was strong and at times ran fierce, but it could never rise to the surface. But oh, oh, how she wished it could. . . . This was bad thinking, but it was the only comfort she derived from this spring.

But this was no time to dwell on such things, what she must think about at the present was stones. Strangely, somehow the two things seemed connected, for the spring at the moment was assuming that weight of a boulder inside her.

3

"It's a lovely day. You should get out, take a walk. In the winter you're always saying you'll feel better when the warmer weather comes, and then when it does come, what do you do? Stick in that room." Henry jerked his head back towards the studio, and Ralph Bowman laughed as he said, "It's the weather, man. I just don't like weather of any kind. When they invent something else to keep us going I'll take advantage of it. Anyway, up till now it hasn't done me any good."

They laughed together now; then Ralph, in a high voice, cried, "You're the one to tell me what to do for my health's sake, walking in all weathers soaked to the skin. I don't believe you can't afford to run the horse and trap. If you stopped spreading your cash around you could. And you're blind, you know that? That Nolan fellow for instance, he's never out of The Tuns. As for the Stoddarts, within minutes of your departure your silver shilling is filling a can to be carried home by one of your youngsters whose mouth you'd hope to fill with bread."

A wry smile came on Henry's face. "By! By! you seem well informed for someone who doesn't like to go out in the fresh air. You must have had visions."

"No, simply a good runner. When Emma can't come she sends Mouthy Mary."

"Oh. Oh, that explains it. Anyway, the little I have to give away wouldn't mend the horse's harness let alone buy him oats. And you know, Ralph"—his voice dropped to a deep serious note—"things are bad all around. I don't suppose Mary's brought you the latest news of what happened yesterday on Newcastle quay?"

"What was that?"

"Oh, just a boat-load of emigrants leaving for the United States of America. A lot of them from Allendale way. All the result of a strike."

"Yes, yes, I read about the strike in the *Newcastle Guardian*. But it's their own fault, they must know they can't fight men like Beaumont. I'm sorry though to know they're emigrating."

"And they weren't the only ones. And one incident on the quay will always stick in my mind: there was the weeping and wailing of families, but some men, standing apart, booed two poor individuals who were getting on to the boat with cries of 'Dirty blacklegs!' I heard later that the miners had threatened them with death, even said that they had dug graves ready for them and that they didn't know their time, whether it would come night or day. I couldn't believe it."

"Oh, I could. Most pitmen are barbarians, else who would take their children down into the mine with them, and them hardly shortened. Anyway, I wouldn't worry too much about them. Look at Mary Petty and her brood. Dragged up by the scruff of the neck and all hale and hearty. It seems some children thrive on muck. Put them in a mansion nursery and half of them would have been dead before five."

"Half of them are dead before three in the towns. I think they survive out here because there's a little more space and the air is fresher. . . . Well, if I want to survive I'd better get to my bed."

"You look tired, Henry." Ralph had walked to the door with him.

"Yes, but naturally tired, otherwise I'm as fit as a fiddle."

"Well, I can't see you have anything to brag about there, you're all skin and bone."

"It's the thin ones that last longer. Isn't it a lovely evening? Look at the mist coming over the hill! I love this time of night; the worries of the day seem to seep away with the light. Of course"—he turned and grinned at Ralph now—"they come back full of vigour with the dawn. Anyway, I'm off. Take care. I'll see you sometime next week, if not before. Good-night, and get inside before the mist falls."

"Good-night, and yes, Father, I'll get inside before the mist falls."

At this, Henry walked away smiling. He walked slowly, savouring the evening. At the end of the bridle-path he climbed the small incline leading to the stile, intending to take the footpath through Farmer Hudson's field which would eventually bring him out at yon side of the village. But from his position on the rise he saw in the far distance a number of figures still working in one of the lower fields. Farmer Yorkless and his sons must be still at it. Would she be there? For answer the afterglow of the setting sun seemed to illuminate the stretch of land reaching from the village to the river, and from this height he could espy a steely gleam of water, but what the afterglow showed up more clearly was the dark heads of men and the cotton-bonneted one of a woman.

It was no conscious decision that turned him from the stile and caused him to leap the low wall and make his way in almost the opposite direction to that which would lead to the village, but as he came nearer the group in the field he saw that they were leaving, for a man was leading a horse on to the narrow road. He could just make out that the animal was pulling a kind of sledge, behind which, at intervals, three figures were walking; but the bonneted woman still remained in the field.

He crossed a wide field, leapt another stone wall, and dropped into the pasture beyond and made his way towards the figure. She was stooping, and he saw that she was putting cans into a basket, and as he approached her from behind he saw her whip off her cotton bonnet, then put her hand into the crown and use it as a towel about her face.

"Good-evening, Emma."

She almost left the ground as she turned round to him, and he saw that her face was streaked with dirt and sweat and the hand that gripped the bonnet black with soil.

"Oh, I'm sorry if I startled you."

"You did, Parson." She was gasping slightly. "One minute there was nobody here and the next minute"—she gave a little laugh—"there you were."

He repeated, "I'm sorry," then added, "You look very tired. Why are you working so late?"

For answer she flung her arm wide. "It's got to be cleared if we want to plant. Another week I should say and it'll be done."

He narrowed his eyes in the fading light and looked around the field. The walls looked uneven where boulders of all sizes were piled roughly against them. He turned to her again, saying quietly, "What a colossal task."

"Yes"—she nodded at him—"I think that's the word for it, colossal task. I never thought to see the end when we started. It's not so bad when it's dry but last night it rained and the earth gets sticky." She looked at her glary hand. "'Tisn't too easy. Still"—she turned and picked up the basket—"that's how it must be. But some good frost on it this winter and we'll have taties in it next spring. God willing." She smiled a small smile and he answered it, saying, gently, "He will be."

There was a tightness in his throat. It hurt him to see how she had to work like any peasant woman, even harder for they had set hours. But she was a farmer's wife and there was no six till six or six till eight for such wives.

"Let me carry that basket."

"No, no." She pulled it away from his hand. "It's all mucky."

"Mucky or not, give it here." He tugged the basket from her. The tone of his voice was different, it had a rough note to it like Barney's had at times. She walked on, he by her side, silence between them now, until he said, " 'Tis a beautiful evening, don't you think?"

"Yes, yes it is." She moved her head, looking about her as if she had only now become aware of the soft air falling with the night; then as if to herself she said, "By! it's been a scorcher." Then glancing at him, she added, "This afternoon we were all wet through."

His eyes caught her glance and held it as he said softly, "You shouldn't have to work like this, Emma. And the child, she alone must take your strength."

"Huh!" She made a small sound as she looked at him and the smile on her face held a sadness not untouched with pity and a flicker of criticism: "And the child," he had said, "she alone must take your strength." Sometimes he seemed like a being from another world. He lived on the outskirts of the village, and his mind, she felt, must be on the outskirts of real living. What about the women who had child after child, some of them born in the tatie fields. He was so dear, so wonderful, so clean and beautiful to her, it was like balm to her body just to look at him, yet at times like now he seemed so young. Although he was just about old enough to be her father, of late she seemed to herself to be older than him. And this feeling would come over her sometimes at night when lying awake, and she knew she was betraying Barney by her thoughts. Yet the desire in her then was only to hold this man's head against her breast like one did a child, like she did her child.

In the light of day she wondered how she could think such things; but the light of day was going now and her thoughts as she looked at him were beginning to run riot. She'd have to get back among them, among those four men who in their different way forced her to acknowledge that she had a life to live and in order to live it she had to work and sweat and even groan under its weight, as she had groaned many times this day carrying the rocks to the sledge.

Now, as if she couldn't wait to continue this life of labour, she put out her hand and, gently tugging the basket from him, she said, "I . . . I must hurry, I've things to do. And Mary will be wanting to get away home. You'll be cutting across here?" She pointed to the opening in the stone wall, and he stopped and said, "Yes. Oh yes. Well, good-night, Emma."

Stepping two paces back from him, she nodded towards him, answering, "Good-night, Parson." And with this they parted.

He did not hurry across the field, nor did he raise his eyes to the beauty of the fading afterglow, he looked at his feet walking between the ridged cattle imprints and the tufts of thistle here and there. If it had been day he might have said to himself: This is a dirty field, Hudson is

an indifferent husbandman, but it was coming night and, denying his ob-
servation to Ralph that the troubles of the day slipped away with the
twilight, his were presenting themselves to him as if the dawn had
changed places with the night. And now he was asking of God why the
ache in his body seemed to increase with the years; and indeed, not
only with the years but with each new sight of her. A minute ago he had
looked on her, her face streaked with dirt, her nails broken down to
the quick, her hands black with mud, the bodice of her dress showing
great arcs of sweat beneath her oxters and the dress itself clinging to the
clefts of her breasts, and her beauty had shone through it and almost
blinded him to the fact that she was no longer Emma the girl but Emma
the wife, and the longing to touch her had become almost irresistible.

Of a sudden his pace increased. He would go home, he told himself,
and when it was sufficiently dark he would go down to the brook where
it deepened beyond Openwood and there, lying in the water, his ache
would ease. His father used to tell him and his brothers after a day of
running wild during the holidays to get themselves into the river and
cool their capers. They had been innocent capers, easy to cool, but the
caper that was running wild in him now would, he felt, heat the water.

As he neared the outskirts of the village his head jerked upwards at
the sound of loud voices and cries coming from the end of the main
street where the inn was situated. Mr Turnbull's son Billy was standing
on the kerb in front of the grocer's bottle-glass window and he called to
Henry, "Skull and hair flying along there, Parson, the night. 'Tis likely
the pit blokes, being the night of the pays, can't get rid of their money
soon enough. All they'll have left the morrow will be thick heads and
empty bellies."

Henry nodded to him and passed quickly on down the street, noting
that Peggy MacFarlane was at her cottage door, as was Mr Farrow the
carpenter at his, with his wife and members of his large family around
him. And Mrs Farrow was having a job to restrain the older ones from
leaving her side to get a closer view of the fray. There was no one outside the butcher's shop, but then Mr Mason only opened it twice a
week. But he could see Mason's wife and his daughter Lily, the one
who made him uneasy with her staring, through the parted lace curtains
at the window. In the fading light he could not really distinguish their
faces but he knew it to be them, peering, as he himself was now, towards half a dozen men bashing each other on the cobbled square.

Coming to a halt some yards away he wondered what to do, but told
himself it would be little use appealing to them, the noise they were
making would drown his voice. Yet the next minute he heard himself
yelling, "Stop this! Stop it! Do you hear?"

Almost before he finished speaking a man was hurled backwards and almost fell at his feet. His opponent, staggering towards him was yelling, "Think you own the bloody place. Could work you off your feet, you Fellburn nowt you! Come to the Phoenix and you'll see what work is." And the man lifted his foot and went to kick the prostrate one but was halted by Henry rushing at him and grabbing him by the arm, crying, "Don't do that! Do you want to kill him?"

The pitman who was dressed in his best, wearing a bright-coloured neckerchief with a red handkerchief dangling from the breast pocket of his coat, stood for a moment slightly amazed at being confronted by a parson, easily recognizable from his black garb, high collar and flat hat; but he was no respecter of churchmen and so he made to throw this new opponent off, crying, "Take your bloody hands off me, ranter!"

"I will, when you decide to go home."

"Who the hell do you think you're talkin' to, eh?" He made another effort to loosen Henry's grip, but when he couldn't he became filled with a sudden fury and with his free arm he struck out and caught Henry a resounding blow on the side of the head which knocked his hat off and caused him to release his grip on the man's arm and to stagger back from him. Then, as he told himself for days afterwards, he didn't know what possessed him but the next minute his own fist shot out as it hadn't done since he was a lad sparring with his brothers, particularly with George who could box as well as a booth man. In fact, George had had a whipping from their father once because he had challenged a booth man. And now there was no one more surprised than himself when he saw the miner stretch his length on the cobbles alongside the man he had himself floored only a while ago. Then Henry's anger was replaced by a moment of terror when the pitman lay prone and still.

Now there was movement all around them: the others had stopped their sparring and were bending over the two prostrate figures, and George Tate and Tom Bessell were looking into his face. Tom was saying, " 'Tis you, Parson?"

He didn't answer for a moment but gently rubbed his clenched fist with his other hand for the pain in it from contact with the pitman's jaw was radiating up to his shoulder. And when another man shouted, " 'Twas the parson. 'Twas the parson, I tell you. Look!" he seemed to come to himself, and now he asked Tom: "The man . . . is he? . . . is he?" and he bent over the pitman.

When the man made a queer groaning sound, he closed his eyes and muttered a short silent prayer.

George Tate was yelling, "Carry them in . . . carry them inside." And combatants from both sides came and picked up their respective member and carried him into the inn. And Henry followed, because he had to know what injury he had done to the pitman. He recognized too that the other man was Willy Stoddart. Well it would be, wouldn't it? But the little pitman must have given him a mighty blow to knock him senseless because Willy was known to be a tough fellow.

Willy was groaning loudly now and holding the back of his head. The other man too was sitting up. They had propped him against the wooden settle, but his face was all askew, and now he was holding his hands to it and making moaning sounds, and it was Mary Petty's husband Ned who, looking at Henry, said in a voice filled with awe, "You've knocked his jaw out, Parson."

"Knocked his jaw out? No, no." Henry shook his head.

"Well, look!"

Henry looked closer and saw that Ned Petty was right, he had put the man's jaw out. "Dear God!" he said. "Go and fetch Doctor Rainton."

He hadn't given the precise order to anyone in particular, but Eddy MacFarlane said, "Aye, aye; better get the doctor. But 'tis all of two miles away." And he turned and looked at one of the other two men who were kneeling beside their mining companion. "You had a hand-cart, hadn't you?" he asked in a conversational tone, as if a few minutes earlier he hadn't been at this particular man's throat.

The man looked up and nodded before saying, "Aye."

"Well then, put him on the hand-cart, and on your way back home to Birtley call in at the doctor's. Best thing, save time."

The other man, answering as civilly, said, "Aye, you're right. And it would be on our way, as you say. Aye, it would."

Strangely, they all seemed to have sobered up somewhat, although Willy Stoddart was being plied with ale to refresh him.

Within minutes they were all outside again. The pitman being assisted on to the flat barrow looked up at Henry without the slightest animosity in his eyes, and Henry said in a low voice, "I'm sorry. I'm very sorry I've hurt you."

The pitman raised his hand as if in salute, at which George Tate turned to Eddy MacFarlane saying, "Go along of them, Eddy, and see what the trouble is. Parson'd like to know . . . wouldn't you, Parson?"

"Oh yes, yes." Henry nodded at the publican. "Yes, I must know."

There were eight now standing outside the inn watching the small cavalcade zig-zag its way up the road, one man pulling the barrow, and the man behind being assisted by Eddy MacFarlane. Then as they all turned to go back into the inn, they stopped as if governed by one mind and peered through the swinging lantern light at Henry.

"We'll send you word along, Parson, when we hear," George Tate said, and Henry answered, "Thank you, Mr Tate. Good-night."

A chorus of good-nights came at him now: "Good-night, Parson. Good-night to you, Parson. Good-night, Parson."

There were men among them whom he had never seen in church, but for a moment he felt himself to be nearer to them than to most of his regular parishioners.

Entering the front door of the vicarage he was greeted by Lena Wilkinson saying, "I didn't go, I was worried; you were late."

"I'm sorry I kept you, Miss Wilkinson. You mustn't wait for me. Please don't do that." His voice sounded stiff even to himself and then she answered as stiffly, " 'Twas only through concern; you never know on nights with strangers about, and them coming in from across the river pinching and stealing. Crosby's had four chickens gone last night."

"I'm sorry, but I must insist: you are not to wait. Good-night, Miss Wilkinson." He pulled the door wide now and stood aside while she lifted her cape and bonnet from the antlered hallstand, and when she passed him and went out into the night without further words, he felt a moment of contrition. Why couldn't he be pleasant to her? But no, he knew what pleasantness would lead to in her case.

He closed the door and drew the bolts and went through the candle-lit hall into the long gaunt kitchen, through the scullery and to the back door, which he found already bolted. He did not then make his way straight upstairs, but picked up the candlestick from the hall table and went into the sitting-room.

In the daytime the straight-back chairs and hard brown leather couch seemed to offer no comfort and he often likened the atmosphere to a monk's cell, only in a monk's cell you did know why you were suffering the austerity, it was for Christ. But here he knew he didn't suffer for Christ. He found no joy or penance in ugliness, and every room in this vicarage was ugly. Yet the Reverend Blackett lived in sumptuous conditions compared to this, and the bishop and his underlings over in Auckland lived in such style that the only thing seeming to be missing was a harem.

Oh my God!—he put his hand to his head—he was protesting about so many things these days. Vindictive in fact. At one time he'd had great high hopes of serving God, now in the secret cells of his mind he was asking himself if there even was a God to serve. And these cells were not impregnable any more, for his thoughts must have seeped through them because he knew his sermons were not pleasing his congregation.

He had faced up to himself. He knew he was not a good man and that most of his time he was living and preaching a lie. Apart from the ethics of his religion he was breaking so many commandments, daily, hourly. . . . Thou shalt not covet thy neighbour's wife.

If a man strike you, turn the other cheek. And what had he done this night? He had struck a man to the ground, and he would not be able to go to bed until he knew of the consequences of his blow.

It was no good, he would have to see the bishop, talk to him, tell him exactly what was in his mind. . . . But not all. Oh no, not all, only that which concerned the church. The coveting of his neighbour's wife had nothing to do with the bishop, for it was only in his mind and would never bear fruit.

His head was aching from the blow he had received and he didn't feel like writing anything in his diary tonight, but through force of habit he went over to the window where his desk was placed and, opening his coat, inserted two fingers into a small pocket in his waistcoat from which he took a key and then opened the bottom drawer in the desk. From there he lifted up a thick black book and he began to write in it.

The book was a third filled with closely written work and now, starting on a blank page, he wrote:

God, You are a jester. You know that, don't You? You are a jester, a sadistic jester, for why else do You give to Your priests the power to love in concentration. You ordain us to love all mankind, then You confront me with a human being, one who has such magnetism in her that dilutes . . . nay, eclipses all other feelings. You did it with Abelard and Donne and countless others, and to men like Augustine and Erasmus You added the power to explain Your method of working.

Your idea of justice is irrational. You state that those who sin and do not chastise their bodies in repentance will eventually find that this life is but a spark in an ever-erupting volcano, which is eternity, and in it they will burn forever, and all because they have loved and could no longer deny that love. Yet You who made us in your image, and gave us our natures, also gave us the power to love and the instrument with which to express it in ecstatic exaltation.

I ask You, are You a God? Or have I been worshipping man?

And I answer my own question; if the kingdom of God is within man, then man reigns over that kingdom and man is God and God is man; and now I know I have been afraid of man and not of God. And where does this leave me? Only with the knowledge that I'd rather be afraid of You as God as of man, because man has used Your name to stamp his laws and give power to the baseness and greed within him. He uses Your name to feel righteous in his own eyes. Is this not so?

As I await Your answer my mind tells me I only think like this because of the frustration born of my tethered love; but no, that is not true, for from the day before I was ordained, You will remember, I knelt in the chapel in the dead of night asking You to show me the way, repeating, "I believe, help Thou my unbelief."

Was there ever such a self-revealing statement written in Holy Writ: 'I believe, help Thou my unbelief'?

Following this, his pen became still for some minutes. Then he closed the book, locked it away and returned the key to his waistcoat pocket and, folding his forearms on the desk, he laid his head on them as he muttered, "Oh God!" . . .

It was almost two hours later when a thumping on the front door woke him. Blinking the sleep from his eyes, he picked up the almost guttered candle and staggered to the door and, pulling it open, saw through the swinging lantern light Eddy MacFarlane panting and peering up at him. He was saying, " 'Tis all right, Parson. Doctor pushed his jaw back an' strapped it for him. I'll bet he'll think twice afore he strikes out at a parson again, eh? What do you say?"

What Henry said on a long-drawn-out breath of relief was, "Thank you, Eddy. I'm glad it's no worse."

"It'll keep his mouth shut for a time, I should say. Got to go careful, the doctor said. Good-night, Parson."

"Good-night, Eddy. And thank you."

"You're welcome. Best journey I've ever enjoyed, that." He was about to turn away but then he stopped and, putting a hand to the side of the door stanchion, he leant forward and in a hissing whisper said, "Done you more good in the village an' thereabouts than all the sermons you could preach, that blow, Parson. And I'm tellin' you, better than any sermon you could preach." He jerked his head upwards now and, turning about, ran into the night; and Henry, bolting the door once more, leant against it and there came into his being a rising of laughter. It was loud and he knew it touched on hysteria and he checked it; then pulling himself from the door, he looked upwards, saying aloud now, "I had to break a man's jaw to get a standing in the village. Your ways are indeed strange."

4

"Eeh! the village is agog. And not only the village, they tell us it's all over Birtley and Gateshead Fell. Parson Grainger, they're sayin', is somebody to be dealt with. A fellow who could bust Gerry Gordon's jaw with one blow is no pulpit pap preacher. But mind, there's some in the village who are sayin', tut! tut! tut! Them are the ones who don't like his sermons. Well, when you come to think of it, he does talk a bit funny, doesn't he? Our Bella came back one Sunday sayin' the parson said there was no hell, not the fire and brimstone hell. Now would you believe that? Well, old Parson Crabtree used to make me smell the brimstone when he was up there in that pulpit when I was a lass. But our Bella said that Parson Grainger said, 'twas us ourselves that made the hells. She said he said we made hells for ourselves and for each other, and there was no worse hells. Well, she was all puzzled 'cos in Sunday school Miss Wilkinson had told them all they're bound for hell, the lot of 'em, and that was just for scrumping apples and pinching eggs. Of course the eggs our Bella nicked were all addled, the hen had been sitting on them for a week. I said to her, 'Haven't you any sense not to know that you only have one egg in a nest at a time, that's if you want to eat it without a chicken inside?' Anyway she was fuddled in the head about this hell business. An' she wasn't the only one, there was a lot of talk in the village about it. Well I ask you, Emma, if you hadn't to come to a hell just think of the things you would do, just think of the things that would happen. And what about the rich? Now if they're gona sit pretty all their lives and not suffer for it, well where's the justice in that? I mean they're havin' their heaven here, aren't they? And if there's no hope of us having one in the hereafter, what's the purpose of it all? That's what I said to Ned, and even he, thick in the top as he is, could see that parson had gone astray in his jabbering. And then there's this latest business. Well, you wouldn't believe it, I'll bet there'll be some strange faces under that pulpit on Sunday. But lookin' at him, you wouldn't think he would break somebody's jaw, now would you? One straight blow, our Ned said, and up that pitman went, soared through the air like a shot duck an' landed plonk, with his bottom jaw trying to pick his nose. I mean it's hard to take in, isn't it? It's unbelievable, 'cos a man with his ideas, you know odd talkin' ideas, they don't usually have a punch in them, do they? Eeh! 'tis unbelievable."

And so thought Emma: it was unbelievable that Henry could break a man's jaw, that he would even attempt to do such a thing; and only the night before last she had looked on him, as they stood in the road, as someone who had no conception of real life. The word she thought of for him was idealist. Yet no, that wasn't right. Nor was mystic. Oh no, not mystic, there was no faraway look in his eyes. She couldn't put a name to what he was, she only knew how she felt about him, the sensation the sight of him created in her, how she longed to touch him or he to touch her. Even when she had grabbed the basket from his hand she had made sure that her fingers were well away from his. Yet here was Mary telling her that he had broken a man's jaw, and that now the village was for him. People were funny, odd. It was a good job she hadn't time to sit and ponder, or else things would worry her.

She said to Mary, "I'm off now the milking's done. Wash your hands mind, Mary, before you touch anything in the dairy. I've left two dishes ready for skimming."

"All right, I know what to do, lass. But 'tis Sunday, and I think you should give that field a miss the day, the stones'll still be there the morrow."

"Yes, that's the trouble, they'll still be there the morrow." She now stooped and picked up the gurgling child from the basket and having placed it in the crook of her arm and partly on her left hip, she took up a basket of food from the table and made for the door, and Mary opening it for her said, "Hello, Mister Pete. What you after?"

Pete didn't answer her but said to Emma, "Ready for the field?"

"Yes, as you see." Emma nodded at him.

Lifting his arms towards her now, Pete said, "I'll take her. I want a word with you."

Relieved of the child, she now carried the basket in both hands in front of her and walked slightly ahead for the length of the farmyard. Gauging they were now out of both sight and earshot of Mary, she stopped beyond the big stone barn and, looking at Pete, said, "Anything wrong, Pete?"

She had come to like Pete, because she felt he was for her: he neither sided with Luke nor went against him, he was neutral as it were, saying little, but when he did it was to the point. She was beginning to realize that they underestimated the intelligence of this fair-haired, rough-looking, twenty-year-old young fellow. She watched him tracing his finger through Annie's hair as he said, "I thought I'd see what you think of it, Emma."

"Think of what, Pete?"

"Me goin' for a sailor."

"Goin' for a sailor? You mean . . . you mean joining a boat?"

"Aye; aye, just that."

"But why?" Even as she asked the question she knew what his answer would be.

"Well . . . well, with fields going ain't enough work, not even enough for Da, Barney, and Luke."

"Your . . . your father won't like it."

"He'll say he won't, but on t'other hand he'll be relieved."

She continued to gaze into the rough face. Yes, there was more in Pete than anyone suspected.

He humped the child from one arm to the other before saying now, "Big field's nearly cleared."

"When were you thinking of going?"

He was looking towards the ground now as he said, "Soon. There's a boat sailing next Saturday. 'Tis in dock now. I saw the mate yesterday night, he was in The Tuns. They're wanting hands, he said. Good ship, he said, going to the Americas."

"But . . . but you've never been to sea, I mean never been on a boat."

"I know, but 'tisn't that I haven't wanted to, Emma. Any spare times, Sundays like, I've made for Newcastle quay, like Billy used to take you, you know, but further along where they unload. It's always packed along there."

He now looked her fully in the face as he ended, "Thought I'd see how you took it, Emma, 'cos you've got a head on your shoulders. Think I'm right?"

She studied him for a moment, then smiled softly at him as she said, "Yes, Pete, I think you're right. 'Tis a hard life they say on these ships, but you'll see different places, see the world. I . . . I think it will be good for you, Pete."

She watched his face stretch into a great smile; then nodding at her, he said, "Good enough for me then, Emma. I'll tell them."

"You'll have to be prepared for squalls." She was smiling at him now, adding, "And that's before you hit the German Ocean."

" 'Tis good that, Emma, 'tis good. You've got a good way with your tongue. Learned, that's what you are."

"Oh no"—she shook her head—"I'm not learned. I wish I was."

"Well, some folks think you're learned." He nodded his head briskly at her as they walked on now. " 'Tis said in The Tuns that you read the same books as the parson. Now that's something. You must be learned if you read the same books as the parson."

Learned. The first books he had loaned her were stories from the Sunday school shelf, always about a good little girl and a good little boy. She had liked only three of the big books he had loaned her. One was called *Mansfield Park,* the others were written by a titled gentleman called Scott, one was *The Lady of the Lake,* and the other was called *Kenilworth.* It had taken her a long time to read these books because the print was small; even when her granny had, after much persuading, allowed her a candle under the roof she was often too tired to take advantage of its light. And she hadn't been able to read much in the presence of her granny, for the sight of her reading had always seemed to irritate her granny and she would keep talking at her about the events of the day which were mostly filled with animosity against her mistress. No, only very ignorant people would put the stamp of learning on her.

She glanced at Pete. She would miss him as she wouldn't have missed his father or Luke had they said they were leaving. . . . Oh, if only Luke would take it into his head to go to sea, then life would take on a peace which, as the Bible said, was past understanding.

Voices had been raised. Jake Yorkless, Luke, and even Barney had tried to dissuade Pete from, as his father said, taking this mad step. Everybody knew that except for the captain and the chief officers life was hell for the crew. But Pete was quietly adamant. He said he could but try.

It would be a long try, his father said, two years away and once that boat had left the dock he might as well consider himself manacled, for he wouldn't be a free man until it docked again in the same spot.

But Pete went into Newcastle and signed on as deck-hand on the *Fullmer.* And on Saturday gone, the three men had dressed in their best and accompanied him to Newcastle quay; and afterwards, lying in bed that night, Barney had said to her he never knew he had been fond of Pete until he saw him walking up that gangway with that canvas bag on his shoulder.

More to make conversation than to know the answer, she asked Barney, "Did you envy his going? I mean, would you like to have gone with him?"

"Oh! Emma." He pulled her into his arms with such force that she gasped for breath. "Would any man but an idiot exchange you for a trip on the sea, even as a captain? Oh! Emma. Emma. When will I convince you that I think I'm the luckiest fella alive? I had to wait for you, and as you grew older each night became an agony that burnt me up. But"—he chuckled deep in his throat now—"I've slaked my thirst and I'll never tire of doing it. Not for me the Laura Nixons or the Peggy Mac-Farlanes. I pity them that seek such relief. And then you ask me, do I envy Pete? Aw! Emma. Emma."

While he slaked his thirst once more she let her mind roam to things that might have been but would now never come about.

It was Monday morning and Billy Proctor was brushing one of the horses down in the stable. He was working sullenly. He had been on this farm since he was a boy, and he knew now that if it hadn't been for Emma he, as he put it, would have been thrown out on his backside and likely ended his days in the workhouse.

Emma had said to him, "Just do what your hands will allow, Billy." Well, his hands wouldn't allow him to do much, nor yet his back, every bone in his body ached. But then it had been so for many a year, but he had worked with good grace ignoring the pain. But now the pain was uppermost, brought to the fore by ingratitude, was the way he saw it.

Emma passed him on her way to the big barn. She did not stop to give him a word, she was in a hurry; there was a lot to do, and she must get back into the house before the child woke up. Mary had gone down early to the painter's. He wouldn't like that, but she herself was too busy today to see to him.

She intended to bring some oats back to the stable and, while she was in the big barn, throw a bale of hay down from the upper storey because she would need it later to fill the nests. She had said to Barney only yesterday that she thought the hens were starting to eat the hay because she was always filling the boxes. But as he said, and as she well knew, it was the red cock strutting about like a lord that scattered the hay. He was a character, was the red cock. The only time he acted in the manner of a known cock was when he was tending to his wives, other times he would race round the field very much like a colt that had just been let out. Barney had a name for him. The crazy coon, he called him.

She half filled the sack with oats, then leaned it against the old mill-stone which had once graced the mill that stood to the side of the bridle-path about half a mile from Mr Bowman's cottage. When the mill was burnt to the ground, leaving only one room at the end with a loft above, Jake Yorkless, his father, and two horses had brought the millstone to the farm, thinking to make some use of it. They had rolled it on its end into the barn and brought it to a standstill just below the platform that extended over one third of the barn. Whatever use they had hoped to put it to had not materialized, except that it was used for sharpening scythes and such implements.

Emma climbed the ladder to the platform above. She went to the far corner where the bales of hay were stacked and was about to pull the top one down when she stifled a cry as Luke appeared round the end of the stack with a pitchfork in his hand. He seemed amused at her fright and he muttered, "Nerves on edge?"

She made no reply and he turned and pulled a bale on to the floor in front of her feet, not to help her but to impede her way. Then after staring at her for a moment, he said flatly, "Nowt's gone right on this place since you came into it. Do you know that? I've said it afore and I'll say it again, you put a spell on it, you've got an evil eye . . . a foreign evil eye. You helped to knock me mother off." She clamped on her lips to prevent a retort and he went on, "Now you've talked Pete into taking to the sea. You'll not be happy until you get rid of me da and me and then you'll have the place to yoursel'."

As she turned her back on him and bent down from the waist to pick up the bale, it happened. Lifting the pitchfork, he thrust it into her buttocks, and the scream she let out caused him to screw up his face and yell at her, "Didn't kill you! Soft you are in some parts, soft you are."

She stood for a moment, her hands pressed tight to her bottom; then gasping, she turned her head from side to side as if in search of a weapon, and she saw it, one that she could handle. It was a piece of thick rope with a frayed end. She sprang towards it and with lightning speed she had gripped the end of it and given it one swirl about her head before bringing it fully across his face.

Now it was he who screamed and the sound was like a roar of an injured beast, and like a beast he sprang on her and bore her to the floor, where they rolled together tearing at each other, until at last he had her spreadeagled, his body on top of hers. And now her terrified eyes were looking deep into his throat for his wide-open mouth seemed like a lion's jaws, and she knew terror as she had never known it before.

When she felt his teeth go through the lobe of her ear she screamed to the heavens. Then they were rolling again. Now she was tearing at his face with her nails, but even as she did so she knew she was weakening, his weight was too much for her.

At one period when she managed to free one hand she stuck her thumb into his eye, and when his head went back she screamed, "Barney! Barney!" And almost immediately it seemed that her cry had been answered for the weight was dragged off her leaving her limp and gasping and covered with both Luke's and her own blood. For a moment she thought she was going to slip into unconsciousness; then the growls and the curses to the side of her brought her on to her hands and knees from where she was again knocked on to her back by the two struggling forms.

It was as Jake Yorkless came running into the barn that the locked figures reached the edge of the platform and before a cry could escape his lips he saw his eldest son topple over. There was a dull bone-crushing thud, then a strange stillness.

With a mixture of horror and incredulity he looked to where Barney hung backwards over the millstone for a matter of seconds before his body slid slowly and quietly on to the floor of the barn. He now lifted his head and looked to where his other son was dragging himself back from the edge of the platform; then his gaze moved from him to see his daughter-in-law kneeling further along the platform looking downwards. Her whole face appeared to be covered with blood.

Then the silence was broken as he let out a great oath and, dropping on to his knees by the prone figure, he straightened out his son, calling loudly now, "Barney! Barney!"

When there was no response to his appeal he looked towards where Luke was staggering down the ladder and he cried at him, "You bloody, bloody madman! You've killed him. You've killed your brother."

" 'Tweren't me. 'Tweren't me." Luke was standing apart now, shaking his head. " 'Twas her. 'Twas her. Look at me face."

As Luke drew his hand over his bloodstained face, Jake Yorkless turned his gaze upwards again to where Emma was now descending the ladder. Having reached the bottom she still clung to it for a moment before she tottered towards the millstone and there, dropping on to her side near her husband, she now cried, "Barney! Barney!" Then she was tearing at his jacket, her good ear against his chest.

Turning her eyes to look at her father-in-law and her voice merely a whimper, she said, "He's . . . he's breathin'. Get . . . get the doctor."

"You!"—Jake Yorkless was bawling at Luke now—"come and give me a hand to get him into the house."

"*No! No!*" Emma flung herself across the prostrate form, crying, "He won't touch him. I won't let him touch him." Then she looked towards the door to where Billy was standing and she yelled to him, "Go to the

Hudsons', Billy. Tell them we want help. Tell them to ride for the doctor, and send Tony. He'll help. He'll help."

Neither Jake Yorkless nor Luke made any protest at this, but she, with growing strength, got on to her knees now and looking at her father-in-law she cried, "Take him away." She thrust out her hand towards Luke. "I tell you, take him away."

When Jake Yorkless didn't move, her voice in a scream came at him again, "I tell you, get him out of this, or I'll do something to him. I'll stick the pitchfork into him like he did me."

His eyes widening, Jake Yorkless looked towards his son, and he said, "Pitchfork?"

"Yes, that was the start. He . . . he stuck the pitchfork into me as . . . as I bent down."

"Bugger me!" Jake Yorkless's face screwed up and his eyes became almost lost in their sockets as he stepped towards Luke.

Stepping back from him, Luke yelled, "I only did it after she gave me this"—once again he drew his hand over his bloodstained face—"with the pulley rope. How would you like it across your face?"

"Get out!" Jake Yorkless jerked his head stiffly to the side and Luke obeyed him, backing slowly towards the open door of the barn. But there he stopped and, almost screaming now, he said, "Whatever's happened she's to blame. There's no luck where she is; she'll be the death of us all afore she finishes. Mark my words. Aye, mark my words."

For some moments after he had disappeared into the yard his father stood looking towards the door. Shoulders rounded, his head hanging, he had the pose of an old man. But then, seeming to pull himself together, he turned and walked back towards the millstone, to where Emma had raised Barney's head and had it rested against her knee.

Looking up at her father-in-law and her voice and her attitude now depicting her age, she muttered as a young girl might, "I didn't start this, 'twasn't me. Believe me, mister, 'twasn't me."

He gave her no answer but continued to stare down on them both; then with a shake of his head he turned slowly away. . . .

It was twenty minutes later when Alec Hudson and his son Anthony arrived, and during that time Emma had had to fight a great wave of sickness and faintness that threatened to overcome her. Her body was aching as if it had been pummelled by a mallet. But there was a different pain in the side of her face. The blood had clotted around her ear and there was something dangling from it. She daren't, however, put her hand towards it, but when Alec Hudson came into the barn he stopped in his stride and, looking towards her, he said, "My God! girl, what's happened to you?"

And for answer she said, "Have you got the doctor?"

"Andy's ridden for him; he should be here in a short while. Shall we get him into the house?" He was looking down on the prostrate figure.

"I don't know. He . . . he hit the stone when he fell." She lifted a weak hand towards the stone. "He hit it with his back. I fear . . . I fear—" She drooped her head forward.

"All right, lass. All right. Come on, get to your feet."

It was when the kindly man's hand came towards her and she felt herself being assisted upwards by him and his younger son that the wave of faintness became so great that she sank beneath it and dropped into peaceful blackness.

Twice she had begun to emerge from the blackness but each time sank back again into it. The first occasion because she told herself she didn't want to face the day; the second time through pain, something was happening to the side of her face. The third time it was Mary's murmuring that brought her up, and the soothing feeling of warm water on her neck and chest. She lay savouring the comfort of it for a while until, full realization sweeping over her, she jerked her body in an effort to rise.

But Mary's hands kept her down. "There, there," she said. "There, there. Quiet now, till I get you dried."

"The doctor?" Her mouth seemed stiff, her whole face seemed stiff.

"He's upstairs."

"Barney."

"You'll know in a short while. But you've got to prepare yourself, lass; least that's what I think 'cos me sense tells me that you can't fall backwards on to a millstone and bounce off again whole."

"Oh." She put out her hand towards her ear and felt a bulge there, and Mary, nodding her head at her now as she tossed the towel aside and buttoned up the front of Emma's dress, said, "You're going to be short of a lobe, lass. It was hanging, he had to cut it off. In the name of God, how did it all happen? But quiet now, quiet, there'll be plenty of time for talk after."

Not that Emma had any intention of talking, she only wanted to get up and go to Barney. At that moment, however, the doctor came into the room.

Doctor Rainton was a big man with a small voice and a gentle manner. He bent over her, saying, "How are we now?"

"I'm . . . I'm all right, doctor." Her words came out on gasps; then she added, "Barney. What's wrong with him?"

The doctor straightened his back, moved his lips one over the other for a moment, then, bringing his chin into the collar of his grey tweed jacket, he said, "You'd better steel yourself, Mrs Yorkless. Indeed yes, you'd better steel yourself."

"He's . . . he's not?"

"No, he's not dead, and I don't know as yet whether he's going to die, at least soon. But what I can tell you is that his back is broken and he is paralysed."

She put her two hands up to her face, then moved the one quickly away from her left cheek and placed it on top of the other that was across her mouth, and the "*No! No!*" that was yelling inside of her, did not escape, but her eyes stretched as far as the pain in her face would allow.

"He . . . he can move his head and his right arm, but that is all as yet. And . . . and he has regained consciousness. But I have given him some medicine; more I shall leave you, which will keep him from thinking for the next few days. The realization of his condition will definitely come as a shock, and it is this that we have to be prepared for. It is a tragic happening; his father tells me he was so sure-footed and cannot understand how he slipped off the platform." He had now bent his head towards her and his eyes were asking the question of the words he had just uttered: were they true or false? But she did not answer the question, she was too numb. Yet her mind was asking, if this was the story that the mister was putting about, how would he account for Luke's face, because the frayed rope had drawn blood and he would be scarred for some time. And then, her ear. But that didn't matter, what mattered was that Barney, dear Barney was paralysed and all through her screaming for help. Yet if she hadn't screamed, what would have happened to her? Would he have taken her there and then as he lay on top of her, his body screwing her into the platform? No, no; the desire that was in him at that moment wasn't for her body but for her life. He had wanted to kill her. She had seen it in his eyes and she knew that as long as she lived and while he was alive, she would fear him. There were some things she could stand up to, but not such a hate as was in her brother-in-law. And what was the end to be?

When she shivered violently and her head dropped back on to the hard rolled horsehair bolster, the doctor, turning to Mary, said, "Stay with her, see to her. She needs to sleep too. I'll leave you something that will make her sleep."

On this Emma raised her head with a jerk, saying now, "No, no, doctor. I want no more sleep. I'll be all right. In a short while I'll be all right."

And she knew she must be all right, and now, in order to speak to the mister, for she'd have to ask him . . . *no,* tell him that his murdering son could no longer stay in this house. He had a woman over at Birtley who would no doubt welcome him. Moreover, if the mister made any bones about it she wouldn't lift another hand inside the house or outside it, she would see to her husband and her child and that would be all; to cook for, or sit at the table with, or even look at that fiend of a man, never, never again.

As she swung her feet to the ground and sat up the doctor stood above her, amazed at one so young, who had just come through some great physical struggle, if her torn ear and bruises on her face, neck and arms were anything to go by, yet who could show such resistance to the pain she must be suffering. But then women were strange creatures, all different and no accounting for them. But this one had foreign blood in her, Spanish blood he understood, and Spaniards he also understood were a fierce people, as their conquering history showed.

All he could say to her now was, "Go easy. Go easy. I shall be back in the morning."

And her answer to this was simply, "Thank you."

Mary escorted the doctor to the front door and when she came back into the room and saw Emma standing supporting herself against the head of the couch she cried at her, "Oh, you're a silly young bugger. Don't push yourself, lass, you can barely stand on your feet."

"I've got to stand on me feet, Mary," Emma said quietly. "I'll have to stand on me feet." And to this, after a moment's pause, Mary raised her eyebrows, then looked down towards the floor, muttering, "Aye lass, I suppose you're right. You'll have to."

5

Emma stood at the side of the bed holding Barney's hand, looking
down at him, and the pain in his eyes was almost too much for her to
bear. It was five days now since his body had hit the stone and only this
morning had he seemed to take in the fact that his life was broken and
never again would he walk. He could move his head and his right arm,
but the rest of his body was dead. It was as if he had been dismembered
and all that was left was the part of him that recognized his dismember-
ing and could brew the horror and the pain of it.

"Why couldn't it have taken me altogether?" His voice was a croak.

"Don't say that."

"But what use am I, Emma? Oh Emma"—his head moved slowly on
the pillow—"what use am I? Do you understand what has happened?
I'm no use, in no way, I'm no use."

"You'll always be of use to me." She now sat down on the side of the
bed close to him and his lips trembled as he looked up to her and
asked, "Why had it to happen? Why? What have I done to anybody
that this should happen to me?"

When she did not answer but bowed her head, he remained silent;
then his voice stronger, he said with bitterness, "He's always been mad.
If he couldn't get his own way, he . . . he made somebody pay for it,
but mostly Dan, because Dan was the weakest. Why he should go for
you though is beyond me. But no." Now he closed his eyes tightly and
repeated, "No, 'tisn't beyond me. I wanted you and he's resented it; you
were young and clean and lovely, not like the trollops he's favoured
since the first urge took him. And he couldn't get at me, so he got at
you." He opened his eyes and asked quietly, "Where has he gone? Da
wouldn't tell me, but I know he's not here, I can feel that he's not here
any longer. Funny that, but I suppose 'tis because the same blood flows
tightly through both of us."

"As far as I know he's gone to that Laura Nixon outside Birtley
township, and Billy says he's working on a farm down Lamesley way."

Pressing his head back into the pillow, Barney gritted his teeth together, then said, "I hope his time there is short and he soon goes to hell and the devil sticks a pitchfork into him and lops off his ear."

She started slightly; she hadn't told him about the pitchfork or her ear. But now he opened his eyes and said, "I know, the doctor told me. Da tried to hoodwink him and me an' all, but the doctor's no fool. I'm glad you marked him. He was always vain about his looks, thought he was pretty. Well, doctor says you did a good job on him, and for that I'm grateful."

"Oh. Oh." She bowed her head and almost whimpered now, "I'm not proud of it, Barney. I didn't want to mark him or anybody but when the prongs pierced me flesh I too went mad for a minute. He says I hit him first but I had no reason to." She looked at him now and, moving her head slowly, she said, "I never liked him, I couldn't like him, but ask yourself, would I take a rope at him out of the blue like?"

"Don't distress yourself; and I say again I'm glad you did it. But Emma—" He was now gripping her hand and she watched his lower jaw tremble before he brought out, "About us, do . . . do you know what this means? I . . . I love you Emma; I've always loved you; but . . . but never again will I be able to show it. Never, never." His lower jaw was wobbling, his eyelids were blinking and when the tears burst from his eyes she took him into her arms, crying, "Oh Barney. Barney, it doesn't matter, it doesn't matter, not that. Don't please, don't cry Barney. Barney. I . . . I can't bear it if you cry."

She had never thought to see this broad strong young man shed a tear; nothing in life she imagined—if she had even thought of it—could be of such pain as to make a man cry, especially this one.

Her tears now mingled with his and as his cheek pressed against her lacerated ear which was hidden now by a pad under the white cap she had taken to wearing, she did not wince, and when his whispered words coming as if through a layer of blankets pleading now, "Say you'll not stop loving me. Say it'll make no difference," she lifted her face from his and as she blinked the streaming water from her eyes and gazed down on him, it came to her that never yet had she spoken the word love, never once had she said to him, 'I love you, Barney'; he had just taken it for granted that she couldn't have married him otherwise. But now she said slowly and firmly, "I'll never stop loving you, Barney; not till the day death separates us will I stop loving you."

"Oh, Emma. Emma." His face was screwed up, his eyes tight, his lashes dripping, the water running from his nostrils over his lips.

Her breasts heaving, she withdrew her arms from about him and, taking up the corner of her white apron, she gently drew it around his face saying as she would to the child, "There, there, my dear. There. There, no more now, no more."

When his crying had eased and he lay staring at her, he asked, "What are we going to do? I mean, how are we going to manage?"

"Leave that to me, I'm very good at working things out. And Billy's had a new lease of life." And now she forced a smile to her lips as she said, "And . . . and Mary has stopped talking and is filling the time with extra work. It's all arranged. That side of it's all arranged. Now lie still." She made a slight movement as if to bite her lip on the words but rose from the bed, saying, "I'm goin' down for your broth and to make sure that your daughter hasn't wrecked the kitchen. I'll bring her up in a little while." She bent over him now and pressed her lips tightly to his; then straightening herself, she touched his cheek lightly with her finger before turning and hurrying out of the room.

She didn't go immediately downstairs but went into the closet where the linen was kept at the end of the landing, and there she laid her head on her arms on the slatted shelf, and the sobs attacking her afresh, she cried the agony out of her. And when at last she could cry no more she reached out and, taking a towel, she wiped her face vigorously with it. When she had finished she did not prepare to take it downstairs with her or fold it up and put it back on the shelf, but, holding it in both hands, she smoothed it out and stood looking down on it.

God has strange ways of working; but his punishment wasn't just, He made the innocent pay for the guilty. A minute ago she had said to her husband she would love him until death separated them, and this she must do, no matter how long that be, or how the body burned to be eased. The last time he had slaked his thirst, as he named his loving, she had let her mind drift away from it and had asked herself how the parson would have gone about the same process; but, as she knew then, the answer to that would remain a mystery. She knew now only too clearly that never again would any thirst be slaked on her, and this was the penalty God was extracting from her for letting her mind rest on another and a particular another . . . one of His chosen, like in the Bible. She was, in a way, being made to pay for committing a sacrilege.

PART FIVE

The Daughter

1

Pete sat to the side of the single bed in the sitting-room of the farm-house. To the parson who was seeing him for the first time since he had left home thirteen years earlier when he was already a man, he seemed to have grown to twice his size, not in breadth, for he was sparse of flesh, but for some reason in height. He was even taller than himself. His voice too had changed; no longer was it slow nor was he hesitant with words. This apparently was his fourth visit home, and as on the other occasions so now he was holding his audience riveted with his tales, and neither of his two listeners was concerned that he exaggerated.

"You have to see it, the river in London I mean. I have no words with which to tell what it's like. Newcastle is like a plaything to it. Wide it is past Greenwich, and so full of ships unloading and loading with everything you could put your mind to. The river's packed but the quays is crammed. You know, out foreign parts I once saw an ant-heap almost up to the ceiling." He raised his head and his arm simultaneously and the eyes of both Barney and Henry followed the direction. "'Twas crawling alive with billions of 'em. Well, the London quays, 'tis like that, with yards and docks and cranes and houses. Aye yes, livin' dwellings all jumbled up together. And I thought when I last saw it, which was but a week gone, I had never seen no port in the world so full of franticness, an' when inshore no such mixture of rich and poor. There's poor enough around here; you know that, Parson." He nodded towards Henry, and Henry answered, "Yes, indeed, Pete. Yes indeed, I know that only too well, and I have thought that parts of Newcastle would be hard to beat. But from some of the things you have told us before, there are many worse places."

"Oh aye, Parson. Oh aye, many worse. And 'tis the children that make it worse for them. And"—he grinned widely now—"worse for your pocket if you're not wary. Oh aye. An' 'tis no use to pity 'em, that's fatal: give to one and you have 'em on you as thick as that ant-heap I was tellin' you about. An' the children are not the only ones who rook us, we sailors. One of me mates last trip was beaten up an' was only saved from death by our captain and his brother. They nabbed the culprits but what did they get from the judges? Hardly anything, so our captain said, but the same day a man was sentenced to penal servitude for stealing half a crown from the housekeeper of a rich man, an' he did it for bread for his bairns. There's no justice, not in London city."

During Pete's pause for breath Henry said, "But you seem to like the sea more and more, Pete."

"Oh aye, I like it, Parson. I wouldn't say more and more. But I didn't like it at all as you've heard"—he now laughed from one to the other—"those first two years. Oh no! I longed for this room and me bed upstairs. When the skin came off me hands as they stuck to the frozen rails, I thought to myself, Pete Yorkless, you were considered a mutt back there in the village, an' they're right."

"You were never any mutt, Pete." Henry's face was straight now. "It would be a fool to himself that would put such a name to you. You know what I would say of you?"

"No, I don't, Parson, no I don't."

"Well, I would say, Pete, that you have it in you to be a writer."

The roar of laughter that Pete let out echoed round the room, and his shoulders were still shaking as he said, "You be funny, Parson, You be funny. Here's me can but write me name and count a bit, and you say to me I could be a writer. You meant of a book, didn't you, Parson?"

"Yes, I meant of a book, Pete. And there is plenty of time yet for you to learn to write."

Again Pete's head went back. "Never me, Parson. I haven't a head on me shoulders like me brother there." He thumbed jovially to where Barney was propped up against a pile of pillows set on a wooden frame. "Now, you have learned him to write, good and proper; and read an' all. And he was telling me only last night, weren't you, lad?"—he pushed his closed fist in Barney's direction—"that in a way you saved his life, I mean from goin' barmy, you've given him somethin' to think about. Why, he talks an' natters like a gentleman, he can even match yourself now."

"He can that. Yes, he can that." Henry was laughing at him.

"Well then, well then, get him to write your book."

"Not a bad idea either." Henry looked from one to the other. "You keep telling him your tales, Pete, and he'll put them down."

Barney now thrust his head back in the pillow and gazed upwards. His face had changed little over the thirteen years since he had broken his back, but his hair had receded from his brow and the side-whiskers that come down to below his cheek-bones were in contrast to the brown on the top of his head, being almost white in parts, and the effect lent premature age to his face.

He turned his head slowly now for his brother was speaking again and as he listened to him, he thought, the parson's right. 'Tis a great pity he can't handle a pen, for his words create pictures before your eyes. Listen to him now: "Frozen mits and hard tack an' maggot meat can be forgotten for a moment at certain times. Have you ever seen a four-master going before the wind, Parson?"

"No, never, Pete."

"Then it's somethin' you should hope for, 'tis somethin' that affects every man on board from the top to the bottom, be they good 'uns or bad 'uns, decent men or murderous bullies. They stand still and look at a sight like that. You can't see it on your own boat, but on one passin', there you have the picture. You talked about me writin' a book a minute ago, Parson. Now that never entered me head, but it has done to paint a picture. Oh aye. But not being able to paint a picture, nor know how to start, I took up whittling, for you have a knife always to hand and wood for the picking up, and as you have seen I haven't done too badly." He now pointed to the mantelpiece on which stood three small carvings of sailing ships.

"Not too badly?" Henry shook his head. "They're splendid! Splendid."

"I'll do you one on my next trip should you like, Parson."

"I would indeed, Pete. Oh, I would indeed."

"I've done a number"—Pete was now nodding towards Barney—"an' I've sold them. What do you think about that?"

"I think there's more in you than meets the eye. Always have done."

"You may be right there"—Pete was nodding and laughing at Barney —"chief mate gave me half a crown for the last one."

"You'll soon be a rich man." There was a trace of tiredness in Barney's voice now, and as Pete said, "Me? No, I'll never be rich, but I'm savin' me money, an' for a purpose." He nodded knowingly. Then seeing that Henry had risen to his feet, he said, "You on your way, Parson?"

"Yes, Pete; I think Barney's had enough chatter for one day."

"Aye, yes. They tell me once I get started I forget to stop." He again thumbed towards Barney.

Looking at this brother of his, Barney could not believe that at one time this was the man whom, truth to tell, he had considered a little dull in the wits, kindly but nevertheless not as bright as his age demanded.

Henry now moved up the side of the bed and bending slightly forward said to Barney, "I may not be able to look in tomorrow, Sunday being my working day"—he pulled a face—"but likely Monday."

"Thanks, Parson."

As Henry made to go out of the room, Pete, also nodding towards Barney, said, "Leave you to rest for a while, eh, and get me hand in outside. The only thing is, once I start out there among them the feeling comes back and I ask meself should I or shouldn't I go?"

"You can't help yourself, the sea's got you now."

Barney smiled gently across the room to this strange seafaring brother, and Pete, nodding as he followed Henry, said, "You're right. Yes, I think you're right."

The two men crossed the hall and went into the kitchen, there to see Emma, her hands pounding a large lump of dough on a floured board on the kitchen table. "He seems tired," Henry said; "I wouldn't let him do too much today."

Looking up at him, Emma said quietly, "He won't take much notice of what I say. Anyway you started it."

They now exchanged a quiet smile and Henry said, "Yes, I have that on my shoulders, and I feel guilty at times because I get more enjoyment from it than he does."

And as she thought, I too, she took her doubled fist and almost rammed it into the middle of the dough; then lifting it up, flicked it over and kept her eyes on it as she answered his good-bye.

When Pete said, "I'll go and tackle that bit of dry-stone wall, Emma," she said, "Will you Pete? Oh, thank you." And then when he asked, "Where's Annie?" she answered, "Down at Mr Bowman's."

"She works regular down there now?"

"Well, she dusts and that, but I still cook for him. Anyway, she prefers that to doing anything around the yard."

"Well, she would, she is but young," said Pete as he opened the door to go out.

Emma paused in her pummelling and looked towards the small window and into the yard. She was worried, and it was a strange worry, a worry she couldn't put a name to, or at least she wouldn't put a name to. The worry had begun about two years ago when Annie was eleven. Up till then life had taken on a pattern, a smooth if painful pattern. The pattern was set within weeks of Barney's accident: the parson was then calling twice a week and he asked Barney if he would like to hear some stories, stories of adventure, those written by Sir Walter Scott, and Barney out of politeness had answered, "Yes, Parson."

At first, she hadn't sat in on the readings for she couldn't waste time. Mary continued to do her utmost, having taken over the household, the cooking and the seeing to the child, while she herself attended to Barney's wants, his main demand being for her presence. But Billy Proctor's energy had soon flagged, and so for most of the day she had to be outside, helping with the milking and churning, seeing to the pigs, the chickens, and in the seasons helping with the crops. They no longer had any sheep and their cows only numbered eight, but she had trebled the heads of poultry and those of the pigs, and this in some way made up for the loss of the sheep and lambs. Her day started at five in the morning and very rarely ended before ten at night.

It was the parson, too, who suggested that they bring Barney's bed downstairs in order, he said, to afford Barney some interest, as one of the two windows in the sitting-room looked on to the yard. But she had known that this suggestion of his was also to save her legs up and downstairs to the bedroom, necessitated by the carrying of meals, water and slops.

Besides the reading of stories, the parson brought newspapers, and as time went on she was amazed to hear Barney referring to national and world-wide events. At night when she lay down by his side and when all she wanted was to drop into deep sleep to ease her weariness, he would say such things as "That Napoleon the Third is starting something. If we don't watch out there'll be revolutions here. Wealth's badly divided; Parson himself says so." Another time it would be, "Navy's gone to pot. Cutting down all round, them up there. Big piece about it in the paper this mornin'. One mornin' we'll wake up and find the Frenchies have swum across."

At other times it was the Russians. "Maniacs them Russians. Parson says they're after India now."

There were times when she would force herself to stay awake and listen to him, for although his knowledge was fragmented he was talking about places he hadn't even dreamed existed a few years ago, and although she could never get interested in the events of the day other than what was happening about her she felt proud and pleased that he was learning.

Then there were evenings in the summer when Ralph Bowman came up. His first visit had amazed her for he had never been known to enter any house in the village or thereabouts; and sometimes when the parson and he were with Barney there would issue from the front room great gusts of laughter. At these times the mister would be sitting in the kitchen nursing Annie. He had quickly grown very fond of the child. And he might look at Emma and smile or pass some remark such as, "Must have been mustard in that joke." He himself spent very little time with his son. Sometimes days would go by before he went into the front room; and then their conversation would be brief: "How are you, lad?"

"All right, Da."

"Been a nice day." Or, "A cold 'un."

"Aye, it has. How's things?"

"Goin' good."

"Stone field doing all right?"

"Aye." Sometimes: "Fine. Barley straight as a die." Or, "Oats middlin', but 'tis the weather. Good-night."

"Good-night, Da."

Emma felt that the only pleasure the mister now got out of life was through his grandchild, and she returned his affection equally. Strangely, like her grandfather, she would spend no time with her father. Even when she was small and Emma put her on the bed to kiss him good-night she would dutifully do this but scramble into Emma's arms again, or, as she grew older, on to the floor. She had always been a pretty child and big for her age, but now at thirteen years old she could have passed for much older. The buds of her breasts were already risen; her buttocks were forming fast; but it was her face that gave the impression of age. Her eyes were large, almond-shaped and pale blue in colour; her brows followed them in the arc; her nose was small; her mouth too was small but full lipped; her face was round; her skin like her hair very fair; and as she grew she promised prettiness but no beauty. Her manner was pert, saucy. She could be amusing, especially when there were men present. Although she attended Sunday school she had no special girl friends, but she always made a point of coming back with Jimmy Petty. Jimmy was Ned Petty's nephew, and when the boy's father and mother had died of the typhus, Mary had taken him into their overcrowded home, and from when he was seven Jake Yorkless had employed him on the farm, with a starting wage of sixpence a week, till now at sixteen years old he earned seven shillings together with his food and one pint of skimmed milk a day to take home, as well as three eggs and half a stone of potatoes a week.

Annie had followed Jimmy around from the first day he had come to the farm and he hadn't seemed to mind until lately, when he had become surly. Annie had, in fact, complained that he had pushed her and cheeked her. The first time she complained was about six months ago when she came into the house saying petulantly, "I don't like that Jimmy Petty." And Emma, on her way down the kitchen carrying a tray into Barney, said over her shoulder, "You're late in finding that out, aren't you?"

But when she arrived back in the kitchen she heard a commotion in the yard. Going to the door, she saw the mister wagging his finger threateningly in Jimmy's face and saying, "You lift a hand to her again, my lad, and it'll be the last hand you lift to anybody. You hear me?"

Jimmy didn't answer, he just hung his head; but he didn't move until the mister cried at him, "Get back to your work or else I'll let you have me hand across your ear in advance."

It was later on that day that Emma went into the cowshed and drew Jimmy aside and said quietly, "Did you push her, Jimmy?"

"Yes, missis."

"Why did you do it?"

When he hung his head and didn't answer she said, "I want to know, Jimmy. Why did you do it? You won't get wrong if you tell me, but I must know."

Slowly he lifted up his head and muttered, "She's always pushing me, missis, and . . . and when I was gatherin' the apples she took the ladder away and I nearly fell on to the roof."

The gnarled old apple tree, whose age nobody knew, grew by the side of the house and one of its branches touched the roof near the fanlight in the same attic that ran off the room where she and Barney had slept during those first months of their marriage.

Still muttering and his head hanging again, he went on, "I had to hang on the end branch. I was frightened, and when I got down, well, I pushed her."

She looked at him. After a moment she said gently, "Well, if she annoys you again, Jimmy, don't touch her, but come to me. Do it on the side, you know what I mean? and . . . and I'll deal with her." He looked up into her face saying, "Aye, missis. Thank you, missis, I will."

Jimmy was a good lad, a hard worker; of late he had been doing the work of a full-grown man; and what was more he was quiet and sensible. The parson spoke highly of him. He said that he was bright at his reading and writing. The parson had once tried to persuade Mary to let him go to the new school in Gateshead Fell, but Mary wasn't for it. Three shillings a week then was three shillings a week and most of her family were married and away making homes of their own now, and since, she said, it took Ned all his time to work for his beer the family was kept mainly on what she earned and the wages coming in from her fifteen-year-old, who was her youngest son, and from Jimmy.

When had she become afraid for her daughter? She couldn't actually put a finger on the time: she had been pleased to see her nestling in the mister's arms and he patting and stroking her. Her father could have patted and stroked her, but she seemed to want nothing from him. It had been some time before Emma realized that her daughter was drawn to vitality; even a sick animal did not evoke her pity, but she would race with the dogs, roll with them in the grass as if she were a puppy herself, and she would disappear at times when she knew the hunt was on. One day about two years ago she was missing for a whole morning and she found her perched on a wall waving to the riders as they passed her. The fact that she didn't care anything for Mr Bowman showed further there was this tendency in her to avoid all contact with sickness of any kind, for Ralph, as she had come to call him, could now feel so low that he spent his days in bed. She had been deeply saddened one day only last week when he said to her, "I never thought dying would take so long. If I had I would have assisted it earlier on when I had the courage. But now, strangely, I'm appreciating the days."

She liked Ralph. She had found out something a long while ago: not through any spoken word or look that had passed between them had he indicated that he loved her, yet she knew he did; if only in a way, she thought, that he might have done had she been his daughter. Nevertheless, it was love. But it was a different kind of love altogether from Henry's. Henry's love was in his eyes, in everything he did for Barney, in his wading through snow, hail and rain just to come here and be near her and allow her to be near him without question. She felt, at times when she let herself think about it, that Barney's accident had come as a sort of blessing for them both. It was a dreadful thought, but nevertheless it was true. She had come across a word of late that seemed to fit their position, sublimate was the word, it sort of meant you replaced one thing by another. Well, that wasn't quite right, you gave up one thing for another. And no, that still wasn't right, but she knew that the word fitted the position she was in with regard to the needs of her body and the presence of Henry.

When later she went in to Barney he said, "Did you ever see such a change in a man in your life as in our Pete?"

And she laughed as she answered, "Never. And talk, he'd talk the hind leg off a donkey, and you remember you could hardly get a word out of him at one time. I suppose it's because of all the places he's been and all the sights he's seen, and . . . and living with strange people."

"Yes, yes, I suppose it's that, but I've been thinkin' of late that a man hasn't got to go abroad to see sights and learn things, there's lots of things happening round here you know, Emma, that we know nothing about."

"Yes, I dare say." She straightened the quilt at the bottom of the bed.

"Durham for instance. Amazing the things that happen up there. As the parson said only t'other day, one is apt to think that the only things that take place is where there's industry. But each man has to live his

life, and his life is the most important thing he has and so there is happenings all around him. He's good at explaining things is the parson."

"Yes, yes, Barney, he is that."

Barney now moved his head on the pillow and more to himself than
to her he said, "Wonder he's never married. Some woman's missin' a
good man, for he's very presentable, isn't he?"

This time she didn't answer, "Yes; yes," but went across the room to
a small table on which stood a basin and ewer, and, taking up the ewer,
she poured the remaining water from it into the dish, then went to walk
out of the room when he stopped her, saying, "Mary says that Miss
Wilkinson is still breakin' her neck for him. She gets worse, Mary says,
makes herself a laughing-stock. Huh! As if he would take anybody like
her. She should have the sense to know he could only marry the class,
for he's a gentleman. He only has to open his mouth for you to know
that. But some women get queer fancies into their heads, and if I
remember rightly he was going to be married once. Do you mind that,
Emma?"

"Yes, Yes, I mind that."

"Do you know what happened?"

She paused a moment and drew a deep breath before saying, "As far
as I recall the house wasn't to her liking and the parish didn't seem up
to her standards."

"Well, well!" He paused and narrowed his eyes at her as he looked
across the room, asking now, "What's the matter?"

"Nothing, why do you ask?"

"You . . . you look peeved."

"I'm not peeved."

"No, no, you're not peeved." His voice had a flat note and so,
quickly now, she put down the ewer on the floor and went to him, and
bending above him said, "I'm all right. What makes you think I'm not?"

He stared up at her, his face sad. "I don't know, just something that
came over me. Couldn't say really, something in your face because you
know, Emma"—he gripped her hand with his one good one—"I know
every shade and flicker of your eyes. When you're not here I'm still
seein' your face. And, Emma . . . Emma—" He pulled her closer towards him until their breaths were mingling, and his voice now low in
his throat, he said, "I . . . I know what you must be goin' through.
Yes, I do, although me meself, I . . . I have no feelings left that way
except in me heart, and that is full to bursting for you. But t'other, God
yes"—he closed his eyes tightly now—"I have a good memory and because of it I know what you must be feeling."

There was a lump in her throat, her eyes smarted and she had to gulp before she was able to say, "You're wrong then, you know nothin' about it. You're creating a worry that's not there, at least not in me. It makes no difference, it doesn't matter; just as long as you're here, that's all I want."

His eyes were wide now, staring into hers, and his voice held a note of resignation: " 'Tis a strange life we lead," he said, "but we lead it as best we can, don't we?"

"We do. We do." She bent closer to him and put her lips on his, and he held her tightly in his arm for a moment before pushing her away and turning his head to the side; and she left the bed, walked across the room, picked up the ewer and went out into the kitchen. And there she wiped the tears from her face with a swift rub of her hand as she saw Mary entering by the other door.

Mary stopped and looked at her closely for a moment; then said, "Something wrong?"

"No. Well, nothin' more than usual. He . . . he gets sad at times."

" 'Tis to be expected. You've got somethin' on your plate, I must say that for you. And now I'm gona add to it, and not afore time. 'Tis Annie. She was with Mr Luke yesterday again, I saw them. They didn't see me. Somethin' passed atween them, a little parcel of some kind he gave her, an' . . . an'—" Mary could not go on to say, "she threw her arms around his neck and kissed him," that would have been too much, and so she simply said, "You did warn her, didn't you?"

Emma's jaws were tight: she could hear the grinding of her teeth through her skull. Warn her? She had warned her not once, not twice, but a number of times. What was wrong that she should have a daughter so wilful? The girl was like no one she knew: not her own mother or father, not herself or Barney, not her grandmother Dilly Yorkless, but from somewhere she had inherited a strain, a bad strain. She was a liar and she was inclined to favour. . . . Her mind jerked away from the word men. "I'll deal with her," she said.

"Well, Emma, when you're dealing with her, I've got to say this: tell her to stop pestering our Jimmy, else I'll feel inclined to skite her across the lug meself. The lad's worried an' he doesn't know what to do, because as he says the boss won't believe a word against her. You've got a handful there, Emma. I'll say that, you've got a handful there."

Emma took no offence at Mary's attitude: this wasn't a situation of mistress and maid, Mary was now an elderly woman and Emma had looked upon her as a sort of substitute-mother right from the time she had come to work here, when nobody else would for fear of the cholera.

She passed her now without a word and went out into the yard. Making straight for the store room, she called sharply, "Annie! Annie!" But there was no answer. Next, she went into the cow byre. Jimmy was swilling out and she asked, "Have you seen Annie, Jimmy?"

"Saw her goin' to the barn a minute ago, missis."

As he jerked his head in the direction of the barn she turned from him and went hastily down the yard. There was no one on the ground floor but she heard a rustle from above. Quietly she climbed the ladder and as her head came above the platform she saw Annie on her hands and knees in the far corner pushing something behind a broad stay-beam. As Emma pulled herself on to the platform, Annie swung round from the corner, jumped to her feet and, dusting the straw from the bottom of her dress, said, "You want me, Ma?"

Emma walked close up to her and, looking down into her face, she said, "Yes, I want you. What did I tell you some time ago about . . . about speaking to a certain person?"

"I don't, Ma. I don't."

"Don't lie, Annie!"

Emma had yelled, and now she hung her head and closed her eyes tight; then taking a pull at herself, she lowered her voice as she said, "You're lying, Annie. I know you are lying. You were talking to your uncle yesterday."

Annie shook her head, then flounced round, pushed her thumb into her mouth and began to nibble on it.

"Look at me!"

When her daughter refused, but shook her shoulders, Emma said, "What have you got in that corner?"

Now Annie swung round, saying, "Nothing. Nothing. I thought I saw a rat there and I looked down."

"Stop it, stop it, girl. You say you're afraid of rats and mice, would you go hunting them?" And she pushed her to one side and now made for the corner of the loft. But Annie raced before her and crouched down beside the beam, saying, " 'Tis nothing. They're nothing, just bits . . . bits."

Gripping the collar of Annie's dress, Emma jerked her to the side; then bending down, she pulled the straw away from behind the sloping beam and saw four small wrapped packages, and as she lifted them up, Annie made to grab them from her, crying, "They are mine! They are presents."

Emma swung round and tore open one of the four parcels, to disclose a string of gaudy glass beads. She had seen many such on the stalls at the big fairs when she was a child, and similar tawdry wares at the Gateshead market and at Newcastle hoppings.

The next small parcel displayed two hair-slides decked with bows of ribbon. In the third were three handkerchiefs, and these made her ponder because they were of fine lawn with soft lace edging. When she opened the fourth parcel she almost dropped the others for this disclosed a locket, a heart-shaped locket with a yellow chain that wasn't made of brass, nor yet was the locket.

She swung round on her daughter who was now standing with her hands gripped tightly behind her back, and holding out her arm with the locket hanging from her index finger she demanded, "Where did you get this?" Then she yelled, "Answer me girl! Where did you get this?" But Annie didn't answer.

Maddened, Emma threw the locket and the rest of the packages on the ground and, almost springing at her daughter, she gripped her by the shoulders and shook her till her head wobbled, stopping only when she herself had to gasp for breath.

Looking into Annie's face, she said, "Tell me! where did you get that locket, and . . . and the handkerchiefs?"

"Uncle . . . Uncle Luke."

Again she was shaking her. "Your Uncle Luke could not have bought you things like that, girl. The hair-slides and the beads, yes, but not that locket and chain and handkerchiefs. Where . . . where did you get them?"

"I . . . I found them; they . . . they had dropped on the road. They . . . they were in a little box. I opened the box and . . . and I took them out and threw the . . . the box into the ditch. I . . . I can show you, Ma. I can take you, Ma. I'll show you."

Emma released her hold on her daughter, she had been gripping her so tight that for a moment she had a job to straighten her fingers. Then she drew in a long slow gasp of air and let it out before saying, "Well, this is one time you'll prove if you're a liar or not."

"I . . . I can. I can, Ma, I can. I'll show you." Annie was running towards the ladder now, and Emma followed her. She followed her out of the barn, across the yard, through the gateless gap in the wall, along the lane, down the hill until they reached the coach road, then some way along it Annie dropped into the ditch and began searching. Presently, looking up with real fear on her face now, she said, " 'Tis gone."

"Oh!"—Emma stood above her—"you're wicked. Do you know that? You're a wicked girl. There was never any box."

"There was, there was, Ma." Annie began to scramble along the ditch; then with an almost joyful cry she held up a small wooden box about three inches in diameter. It was covered with velvet which had once been blue but was now discoloured. Scrambling out of the ditch, she pushed it at her mother, saying, "There . . . there. And that's where I found it." She pointed along the road.

Emma stood, her head bowed. She was feeling faint with relief: it didn't matter so much now about her lying over Luke, but the implication of that lovely locket and those handkerchiefs had been terrifying. She thrust out her arm now and pulled her daughter towards her, saying, "I'm sorry, dear, I'm sorry, but . . . but I was worried. Yet nevertheless"—her tone changed—"you promised me you would avoid your Uncle Luke, and you haven't, have you?"

"No, Ma. But then, you see he stops me and speaks, and he's nice."

"Your Uncle Luke is not nice, he is not nice, Annie. I've told you that before, he's not a nice man, and when he speaks nicely to you it isn't because he likes you."

"He does, he does." Annie had pulled back from her now.

"What makes you think that?" Once again there was a stiffness in Emma's tone.

"Well . . . well, I know. You . . . you always know when somebody likes you, or doesn't like you. Mr Bowman doesn't like me and me da doesn't like me."

"Oh, that's wicked, Annie; your da loves you, and he's hurt because you don't spend time with him."

"He's sickly."

"Yes, yes, of course he's sickly. His back's broken so he's bound to be sickly, but that doesn't stop him loving you and needing your company. Promise me you'll go into him more and talk to him."

Annie hung her head but after a moment she muttered, "All right, Ma."

"Come on, let's get home." As Emma went to put her arm around her daughter the sound of galloping hoofs stayed them. A coach was coming. They couldn't see it as yet but they knew it must be nearing the bend in the road.

The sound of galloping dropped to a trot and round the corner came a coach and four, and on the sight of it Emma drew Annie from the road back on to a patch of ground where the verge widened and the ditch narrowed, and they were standing there close together when it passed them and they both saw clearly the faces within: James Fordyke was sitting at one window and his lady at the other. It was many years since Emma had looked on either of them but the lady she recognized immediately for she had scarcely changed. The man showed his years for his face and neck looked fatter than ever; only his eyes were as she remembered them, and for a flashing moment they looked into hers, and she had the idea that he smiled at her.

The coach passed and she turned and put her arm around Annie again, but the girl, staring like someone dazed after the coach, murmured, " 'Tis lovely, isn't it, Ma, the coach?"

"Coaches are just things," Emma replied tartly; " 'tis people that matter. Come, let's get back."

As they walked Emma couldn't get the idea out of her mind that Mr Fordyke had smiled at her, and not unkindly . . . But why would he do that, when he still kept the land enclosed and spitefully made no use of it for it was full of tares and weeds which blew into their own field? But what matter, her mind was easy with regard to Annie. Dear God! that locket had frightened her . . .

Later that night she knelt by Annie's bed and, taking her daughter's hands tightly between her own, she gazed down at her through the candlelight where she lay, her hair rippling over the pillow like sunlight on water and her blue eyes like pools beneath, and she said to her, "You know it's a sin to tell lies, don't you, Annie?"

"Yes, Ma."

"And you do tell lies, don't you?"

There was a pause. "Yes, Ma."

"Well now, I want you to promise me, promise me on God's honour. Do you know what that means?"

"Yes, Ma."

"Well, promise me that if your Uncle Luke speaks to you again and you can't but answer him back, you'll come straight and tell me. Now will you promise me that?"

"Yes, Ma."

"Honest?"

"Honest, Ma," she said, and made a cross on her breast as she related the promise: "Cross me heart if I tell a lie and hope the devil takes me when I die." Looking down at their joined hands and knowing how worthless such words were, Emma murmured, "That's only a children's rhyme, Annie. You're a big girl, you're thirteen, you know the difference between right and wrong, don't you? . . . Don't you?"

Annie didn't answer, and Emma shook the hands within her own, saying in a low whisper, "I've told you, haven't I, the things you must not do, and how you must not let men touch you except to take your hand; and what to expect shortly when your time comes and not to be afraid, haven't I?"

"Yes, Ma."

"Well now, you'll remember all this, won't you?"

"Yes, Ma. I do, and I don't let them touch me. They want to, but I don't."

"What? Who?"

Annie tried to pull her hands away from the grip that was holding them, as she said pettishly, "Well, I don't know who, just boys, men. I . . . well, I know they want to touch me but I remember what you said and . . . and I don't let them."

"Who has wanted to touch you?" Emma's words were spoken slowly and hard now and Annie, flouncing on to her side said, "Nobody, nobody. I just thought, the things they say . . . an' well—"

"The things who says, girl?"

"Well, anybody I speak to." Annie's voice was loud now, her tone almost defiant, and Emma, releasing her hold of the tugging hands, rested her elbows on the bed and bent over her forearms for a moment before rising and saying, "Go to sleep. Good-night."

"Good-night, Ma."

About to close the door, Emma stopped suddenly for she imagined she had heard her daughter giggle: she stood staring at the candle, her eyelids flickering like its flame in the draught from the landing. After pulling the door closed she still did not move away but put her ear to it: there was no sound; it must have been imagination.

2

"She's a little scut. Whatever way you look at her, she's a little scut."

Henry, standing with his back to the fire, his head bowed, muttered, "I'm afraid you're right, but how has it come to be, with a mother like Emma and a father as nice as Barney?"

"A throw-back likely, but wherever she's got it from, she's got it bad. She has the makings of a whore."

"Oh!" Henry shook his head vigorously now. "Don't say that, Ralph. She's at the age when life is stirring in her as it stirred in all of us, whether we like to admit it or not."

"Last thing I'd think a parson would admit." Ralph slanted his gaze towards Henry, and to this Henry answered, "Christ was human." Then added, "You know, I often think about that: how did he manage the problem?"

"I don't know"—Ralph was laughing now, his head back against the pad on the rocking-chair—"but I'd like to bet, if you had been one of the twelve you wouldn't have reigned long, not with your ideas. It's a wonder you don't let them slip through that pulpit of yours."

"They do, but in a different form." Henry's mouth went into a quizzical smile now. "I've got to be careful, and every time I'm careful I despise myself. I wonder sometimes how long I can keep it up, with my true feelings about things."

"You wouldn't have kept it up this long, let's face it, if you hadn't been tied to the farm."

Henry didn't answer, but swung round and looked down into the fire now, and Ralph said, "I'm sorry; that was a winding punch."

"Not more than I deserved. I despise myself for that too. But man"—he turned again and faced Ralph—"I cannot help myself, I've got to see her. Years ago I thought once she was married that would be that, I'd get her out of my system; and then when I found her marriage made no difference, I prepared and applied for another living. You remember? Then Barney's accident happened, and God forgive me"—he turned his head to the side and gritted his teeth for a moment—"I welcomed it in a way, because I thought that the poor fellow was going to die. And I made up my mind that no matter what the village might say, or the bishop, or anyone else for that matter, I was going to ask her to be my wife. I was quite prepared to leave the church if there were any fuss. And then he doesn't die, but, base individual that I am, I invented a way in which I could see her two or three times a week, and which would bring no censure on either of us. And so it has gone on, and will I suppose to the end, for Barney could outlive me with the care he gets. Here I am, forty-seven years old and as the years go on the difference in the age between Emma and myself seems to widen. When she was sixteen and I but thirty-three the difference didn't seem all that great, but now she at thirty, a beautiful woman, more beautiful than she was as a girl, and I feel I am galloping towards old age. . . ."

"Nonsense! You haven't even reached your prime. Do you ever look at yourself, man? You look in your early thirties. Forty-seven indeed! Nobody would take you for that, and the best thing you ever did I think was to get rid of your pony and trap, for you must be the only man for miles around that hasn't got a paunch, and you have the stature of a soldier. . . ."

"Only because I haven't had to use my hands like other men."

"Ho, ho!" Again Ralph's head went back. "Only to break a fellow's jaw. By! you know, that's talked about even yet, so Mary tells me. But speaking of Mary leads me back to Jimmy. There I was sitting to the side of a bush, sketching the old ruined millhouse, when along comes Jimmy and her. They were on the towpath and when they weren't but half a dozen yards from me but couldn't see me, he turned on her, bawling at her, 'Get yourself away, you brazen bitch! You'll lose me me job. And if you do that I'll not go quiet, I won't keep me mouth shut, I'll tell the mister what I know you're up to.' And then she turns and says to him, 'Do it, and he'll knock you flat.' Then . . . then you know, Henry, she actually stepped up to him, almost pushed her bust into him, she did. It was like watching a whore at work, a real seaport trollop with no shame. And you know what she said then?" He looked at Henry who moved his head slightly. "She said, 'You're soft; I dare you to touch me.' Yes, that's what she said. I felt like getting up and taking my hand and swiping her across the face. I never take in all Mary's chatter, but a short while ago she told me that Mrs Pringle—you know, her husband's a drayman; they live just off the coach road going into Gateshead Fell—well, apparently Miss Annie had set her sights on him: waylays him at every possible chance. But after what I saw with my own eyes, I'd believe anything. And no wonder that the schoolmistress wrote to Emma, saying that she thought her daughter needed special tuition. My God! yes, she does. If Emma had been wise she would have used one of her whips on her."

"It wouldn't have done any good."

"No?"

"No. Some people are born with the desire whole in them, in others it matures through growth, except where it's forced by necessity, you can see that in the back streets of Newcastle any night of the week. There is a company of good men and women who travel those streets at night trying to save the brands from the burning. The Reverend Stoker's one of them. He says if he has one success in a year he praises God. He thinks the only cure is to feed and house them, but he admits that once they start, some at the age of nine, food and shelter only satisfies them for a time. I think the best thing that could happen to Annie is to get married as soon as possible. It's a pity in a way that Jimmy has no fancy for her, it would be a solution."

"Only for a time. A girl such as Annie would never be satisfied with one man. . . . Are you off then?"

"Yes; and thanks for the dram."

"Oh, you're welcome . . . you hypocrite." Ralph punched at the air in Henry's direction and Henry, a half smile on his face, said, "Yes, that's the right name for me, fits me like a glove."

"Go on with you. Get out. You're too good to be true. You always put a doubt in my mind and make me feel I should turn to something. Not religion. I don't know what, only something. Go on, get out. And by the way, tell Emma I'm running short of bread: she shouldn't cook so well and I wouldn't eat so much."

"I'll tell her." They nodded at each other, and Henry went out, bending his head and leaning forward against the strong wind. And like this he walked for most of the way, until he reached the stile and as he made to cross it he saw in the distance Emma standing on the rise. She had her hand over her eyes shading them against the sun, and she was calling, "Annie! You Annie!"

He left the road and crossed the field, leapt the dry-stone wall and so came to the bottom of the rise where she was still standing. She had seen his approach and was waiting for him, and before he came up to her she called, "Have you seen Annie?" And he shook his head, saying, "No, not today. Where is she supposed to be?"

She did not answer until he was standing facing her and she put her hand flat on her head to secure her starched cap as she said to him, "She was supposed to be feeding the hens and doing her morning chores, but the hens haven't been fed nor anything else done, and it is

now three hours since breakfast when I last saw her. She didn't come in
for her break."

"I'll go and look round by Openwood. It's full of cowslips, she likes
gathering flowers. She may be there."

She nodded, her face puckered with anxiety, and as he made to move
hastily away she said, "Have you been to Ralph's?"

"Yes"—he turned towards her again—"I've just come from there.
And don't worry, if she's not in the wood I'll take a walk along the
coach road." He was thinking of what Ralph had said about Mrs Pringle's husband: if the man was a drayman he would use that road on his
way between Gateshead Fell and Birtley.

For a while she watched him walking away, then turned and scanned
the country around her. There was a deep fear in her that Annie was
nowhere in the vicinity. Over the past years, as she had watched her
daughter grow, she had fought the mounting idea that her child was
wanton, that there was something in her nature that was bad, not evil
bad like the badness in Luke, but body bad like that which was in low
women. But her daughter wasn't yet a woman, she was not yet fourteen,
that was in years, but to look at her and to note the size of her bust and
the roundness of her buttocks, anyone could be forgiven for taking her
for someone of a marriageable age. But where was she? Dear God,
where was she?

She hurried down the slope, then running, made her way back to the
farm hoping that she would find Annie sitting in the kitchen having her
dinner or teasing her grandfather, if you could call it teasing, sitting on
his lap and playing with his whiskers. She had tried to stop her from
doing this, telling her that she was no longer a little girl; but the reply
her daughter always gave her was that her granda liked it. And she
knew the mister did like it; he was in a way besotted with her, too much
so. That, too, had made her uneasy.

There was no sign of her on the farm. Jake Yorkless met her in the
yard, saying, "Well?"

"I can't see hilt nor hair of her."

"God almighty! she must be somewhere. I'll go to the wood."

"The parson has gone there."

He stopped and looked at her.

"I met him on the hill."

"What about the painter?"

"Parson says she's not there. I'll go to the village." She now ran
across the yard and, pushing open the lower sash of the window, she
leant forward and said to Barney, "We can't find Annie."

"Can't find her, what do you mean?"

"Well, she's not"—Emma was yelling back at him now—"anywhere. I'm going to the village." She watched him let his head fall back on to the pillow in a manner which indicated his frustration, then she pulled down the window and began to run again.

The sweat was oozing out of every pore when she reached the village street and she stood for a moment with her hand pressed tight into her side to ease the stitch that had seized her. The first person she spoke to was Ann Turnbull: she was shooing some birds away from the top of the bags of pulses displayed on a slab of wood resting on barrels just below the bottle-glass window.

"Have you seen my daughter, Mrs Turnbull?"

"Annie?"

"Yes, Annie."

"No. No, Mrs Yorkless. I saw her on Sunday in church; then again going down the street to Sunday school in afternoon, but not since. But look, there's Lily." She pointed across the street to where the butcher's daughter was coming down the three steps leading from the shop, and Emma, saying, "Thank you," hurried across the road.

Lily Mason was of her own age; they had been to Sunday school together for years. She was still unmarried and was now as fat as a porker. She said to her hastily, "Have you seen my Annie, Lily?"

And Lily called back, "Seen your Annie, Emma? Not the day. Why? She done a skip to the fair?"

The fair. Yes, there was a fair on the Town Moor in Newcastle. But she would never go all that way on her own, never, and without saying a word. She had been to Newcastle and Sunderland and Durham, but she herself had always taken her.

"Fair's very attractive for young 'uns"—Lily was grinning down on her now—"and she's spritely, is your Annie. Huh! I'd say." She jerked her head and chuckled, and Emma turned away as Ann Turnbull shouted to her, "Try The Tuns, a number of them's in there at this time. Some of them'll likely have seen her. Or look, there's Miss Bonney. She's just come off the coach at the crossroads and heavy with material, been to market, looks like, p'raps she saw her on the road."

Emma now hurried towards the prim little dressmaker, calling to her well before she came abreast: "Have you see my Annie, Miss Bonney?"

"No. No, Mrs Yorkless. I have not seen Annie since . . . when?" She stopped and cocked her head to one side as if the answer to her question would come out of the air; then looking at Emma again, she said, "A week yesterday. That's it, I saw her a week yesterday when she was talking to the gentleman."

"The gentleman?"

"Yes, he was staying at the inn, on holiday I suppose. But as you know, I"—she shook her head vigorously and the pompoms hanging on the velvet ribbons from her bonnet danced against her rosy cheeks—"I never frequent The Tuns, never. But that was the last time I saw Annie. Yes, I had been to Mrs Freeman's to measure her for her new bodice and it was on my way back that I saw Annie and the gentleman in conversation, enjoyable conversation. They were laughing together and I remember I said, 'Good-day to you, Annie,' and the gentleman doffed his hat to me, and I bowed to him. Yes, that was the last time I saw Annie . . . and. . . ."

"Thank you. Thank you, Miss Bonney."

Emma was again running along the street, towards The Tuns now. Talking to a gentleman, laughing with a gentleman. That locket, those handkerchiefs. She had never been able to find any other present she might have received.

She herself had never been in The Tuns, but without hesitating she pushed open the door to be confronted immediately by what seemed to be a sea of eyes. There must have been twelve to fifteen men in the main bar and each one had turned and stared at her, some with their moustaches still in their beer glasses. It must have been the way she burst into the room.

They made way for her as she came to the counter where, addressing George Tate, she said, "Have . . . have you seen Annie?"

"Annie?" The publican screwed his face up at her. "You mean, your Annie?"

"Yes, yes."

"No, no; never set eyes on the child, not for days, even weeks. Me not going to church like." He looked round his customers and laughed, and some of them laughed with him. "But why should you think I've seen your Annie?"

"I . . . I can't find her. She's been missing all morning. By the way—" She glanced to each side of her now before moving closer to the counter and saying, "You . . . you had a guest staying with you?"

"We still have two guests staying with us"—he thumbed up towards the ceiling—"a Mr and Mrs Watson. Like this part of the country they do. Come every year. Have done for this past six. . . ."

"I mean a gentleman. Er . . . a lone gentleman?"

"Oh, you mean Mr Gardiner. He left this morning first thing. Well, not all that early, but he caught the nine o'clock coach going through."

"Where to?"

He pursed his lips. "Well, as far as I know back to Newcastle.

Traveller he be, so he said. Doing business in Newcastle. Went into the city every day he did from here. Why?"

She was gripping the counter now and looking down into the bubbles of froth on it and seeing for the first time the myriad flashes of colour radiating through them. When of a sudden the colours faded she knew someone had passed the window and temporarily blotted out the sun.

She lifted her head and looked at Mr Tate. "Thank you," she said and turned away, and the men in the bar moved aside and let her pass.

She spoke to no one else, and she walked back to the farm, not running any more. Mary met her in the lane outside the gap in the wall. She waited until she came right up to her before speaking, and then her voice was a whisper as she asked, "Any word?"

"No."

They both walked into the yard together. Emma couldn't see Barney through the window so she knew his head would be back on the pillow. As they neared the kitchen door Jake Yorkless came out and he looked at Emma, and she looked at him. Then she shook her head, and now he demanded, "Didn't you see anybody who'd had a glimpse of her? She just couldn't have disappeared."

She looked him full in the face now as she said, "She was seen talking to a strange man; he's been staying at The Tuns this past week."

"What does that mean?"

"What do you think it means?"

"God in heaven!" He took a handful of his grey hair as if he was going to pull it from the roots, and now he yelled at her, "She could speak to a man in the village and that wouldn't be a sign that she was going to disappear."

"I'm afraid in this case it was."

"How do you make that out?"

"I don't know, only Miss Bonney said they were laughing together. And it wasn't in the village, it was well out of it, near Freeman's, and Freeman's is well away."

He now bent towards her, his fists clenched by his sides, and said, "Are you meaning to imply?"

Still unflinching, she looked back into his face as she said, "I'm implying nothing from that incident, I'll just let you judge for yourself, but what I will tell you is, that if she is gone it hasn't really come as any surprise to me."

"*What!*" She watched him bring his lips back from his teeth and she thought for a moment that he looked like a horse that was about to neigh. And, yes, he did have a face somewhat like a horse. But now his neigh was more like a bellow from a bull as he cried at her, "You're an unnatural mother, that's what you are. She's but a bit of a lass, an affectionate, lovin' bit of a lass."

She dared to answer him, still in a steady voice: "Yes, affectionate and loving all right, but with a twist. And inside she's no bit of a lass. And—" Now her voice was almost as loud as his and her manner as ferocious as she almost bent her body double as she leaned forward screaming, "And you are a blind, thick-headed, stupid, ignorant old man."

From the corner of her eye she watched Mary clamp her hand over her mouth, and as Jake Yorkless drew his fist up to strike her she screamed at him, "You do. Just you do, mister, and I'll promise you I go up those stairs to that attic and bring down one of those whips that I haven't touched for years and I'll make you dance this yard, because now, let me tell you, I've put up with enough from you and yours since I entered this yard: first your wife, then your son, then you encouraging my daughter from she was a child to defy me, petting her in a manner that no man should, except a father, and then not even him. You can pet a little lass, a baby, yes . . . a child, yes . . . but not a girl that's growing up fast into a woman. So let me tell you, mister, I've stood enough from you and yours. The only decent one among you is crippled"—for the moment she had forgotten about Pete—"and if it wasn't for him I'd walk out of this place this minute. So I'm tellin' you, watch out."

They were both shaking with their anger and she outstared him until he swung round and marched across the yard.

She was swaying on her feet as she passed Mary; then she covered her eyes for a moment before going into the kitchen, through it and into the sitting-room.

Barney was waiting for her and he moved his head on the pillow, then brought it upwards, and when she stood looking down at him he said, "I heard it."

"Then that'll save me wasting words, won't it?"

She was amazed at her own manner now towards him.

"Why do you think she's . . . she's done it?"

"Don't ask me why I think she's done it"—she was bawling at him now—"she had it in her. She's always had it in her."

"Look . . . look, don't shout, Emma, don't shout . . . but . . . but just think. What's gona happen to her?"

She had turned away from him; now she swung herself back and, almost glaring at him, she cried, "Whatever happens to her, she'll enjoy it."

"God Almighty!" He brought his hand up, his fist clenched, and beat it against his brow, saying now, "What's come over you? Our daughter's gone God knows where and to what doesn't bear thinkin' about, and you say she'll enjoy it."

She came back to the bed and now taking his hand gently from his brow she opened out the clenched fingers, then stroked his hand, saying, "You are bound to have seen quite a bit from the window over the years: you know how she's carried on, running after Jimmy; you've even checked her yourself from pawing round the parson."

"That was years ago."

"No, it wasn't years ago. Anyway she continued to do it until he slapped her hands."

"The parson slapped her hands?" There was anger now in Barney's voice, and she said, "Yes, and rightly. He did it gently but firmly, and because of it she's never liked him since."

He moved his head slowly and bit hard down on his lip before saying, "What if she suddenly turns up and has just been to the fair, or someplace, with this man?"

"I'll be surprised, but I won't recall any word I've said this day."

He put his head back now on the pillow and through his gritted teeth said, "I wish I was dead."

Then his eyes sprang wide as her voice came to him quietly now, saying, "That makes a pair of us, for you couldn't wish it more than I do at this minute." And on that she turned about and went into the kitchen.

Mary was standing at the open door. She was rolling the corner of her coarse apron between her two palms and she said to Emma, "I don't want to tell you this but I think I'd better. Our Jimmy said he saw Annie talking to her uncle last night, and on his way home one night during the week he saw Mr Luke with the man who was lodging in the inn, not the one who has his wife with him, 'cos they come often and are known, but this man was a stranger. He was clean-shaven and well put on, Jimmy said, not like a gentleman, but not like a working man either. They were coming out of the bar together and they stood on the cobbles and talked a bit. Then Mr Luke went on his way towards the Lamesley road an' the man went back into the inn. Well, for what it's worth I thought you'd better know."

Emma said nothing for a while, then quietly she asked, "Will you go and tell mister what you've just told me?" And Mary said, "Aye, I will; but he might aim to hit me an' all."

"I don't think so, but I think he should be told, and I can't do it."

Mary went to turn away, but she turned back as quickly and asked under her breath, "What if she should turn up, like if she had been to the fair or something?"

"That's what her father's just said, and we'll have to wait and see, won't we?"

"Aye, that's all we can do, Emma, wait and see."

They waited all that day and the next; then Jake Yorkless put on his Sunday suit and went into Gateshead Fell and spoke to the justice. And when he returned he seemed to have aged still further.

Sitting down on the settle without even taking his hat off, he looked at Emma and, his tone subdued, he said, "They tell me it's happenin' all the time. The justice said that people should look after their daughters and not let them wander. He said there were people like that man at the inn, respectable soft-spoken men who act as go-betweens. He said he would pass word on to the dock authority. When they get reports like this they search the ships before leaving port, at least those that are suspect of taking lasses abroad."

"*What?*"

He blinked his eyes and repeated, "Of taking lasses abroad."

Emma now took her first finger and thumb and pressed them tightly on her eyebrows, moving them backwards and forwards over the bones as if aiming to remove a picture from her eyes. Her thoughts hadn't led her that far, not for her to be shipped away. Oh God! No, not that. But would it be any worse, for what would happen to her in a brothel here?

She brought her hand from her face and it trembled as she extended it towards her father-in-law as she said, "Luke . . . you know about Luke talking to the man, you've got to go and ask him what he knows."

Jake Yorkless straightened his back suddenly and, taking off his hard hat, he threw it on to the settle beside him, saying, "Confront our Luke with that! He may not be the best of men, but he'd never stoop to that, not his own flesh and blood, 'cos after all she is his brother's child. No, no; me go to him, after me telling him to get out? What do you take me for, woman?"

What did she take him for? She would like to tell him and say, a coward inside that big rough frame. He would strike young Jimmy or he would strike her, but the idea of coming to blows with his son was another thing. There was a name for men like Jake Yorkless: he was boast inside, as her granny often said and truthfully, full of wind and water, but no guts.

She went from him and into the hall and up the stairs and into the bedroom and, opening the wardrobe door, she took down her Sunday coat, and from a hatbox on top of the wardrobe her Sunday bonnet; then took off her boots and put on a pair of shoes.

When she stood ready she looked in the mirror as she tied the bonnet strings under her chin, making sure to pull it slightly to the left side in order to cover her lobeless ear. Her skin looked white, not creamy as it usually appeared; her eyes had dark rims below them; and she thought, I'm old before my time. But what does it matter how I look? Then turning from the mirror she closed her eyes and joined her hands together and prayed: Lord, help me to keep my temper when I see him, and help me to find her and bring her back. Yet even as she made the last request the pattern of life it presented to her made her shiver.

She had timed her visit to the evening. She rode on the flat cart from the village towards Birtley, and the driver stopped before the outskirts and she walked down the narrow winding road to the hamlet of Lamesley. She did not know exactly where Mrs Nixon lived. It was Mary who said she had moved from Birtley township to the adjoining hamlet.

As she passed the church she saw a woman coming out of the side door and she approached her, saying, "Could you tell me please where a Mrs Nixon lives?"

From the immediate expression on the woman's face, her slightly lowered lids, the pursing of the lips, she knew that the name had not met with favour and there was a slight motion of the head that wasn't quite a wag but sufficient to cause the lady's straw hat to slip further down on to her brow, and when with an impatient movement she said, "Mrs Nixon or Miss Nixon, I suppose it's all the same, but she lives over there"—she pointed—"about a quarter of a mile distant."

"Thank you. Is the house on the road?"

"The house you refer to is merely a cottage, and you won't be able to miss it, you'll be able to recognize it by its neglect and dilapidation."

"Thank you. Good-day."

"Good-day."

At another time the woman's manner would have brought from Emma an amused chuckle: she was evidently the parson's wife and she was what one would expect a parson's wife to be like. Her mind swung away from the woman and her position and she asked herself how she would begin. What would she say to him? What if he wasn't in yet from work? Would the woman let her into the house and allow her to wait? By the sound of it, it was a shambles.

Within yards of the cottage she saw that the parson's wife, or whoever she was, had not exaggerated in her description of the habitation. The railing fronting it was down in parts, what had once been a little garden in front of the cottage now appeared like a dump, for rubbish, ashes, bottles, and pieces of ironwork lay scattered about, the only clear part being the path to the cottage door.

Her heart was thumping so violently that she almost became afraid she would have a seizure; she could feel the sweat running down from her oxters as she lifted her hand and knocked gently on the paintless wood.

The woman who opened the door was a surprise in all ways. She was tall, her face and hands were clean, her capless hair tidy, and although her blouse and skirt were gaudy they fitted her well. What was more surprising still, she appeared near her own age.

It was she who spoke first, saying, "Yes, and what do you want?" She stretched the "you," then leaning forward to get a better look at Emma, she emitted a long, "Oh!"

"I'm Mrs Emma Yorkless. I . . . . I wondered if I might speak with Luke?"

"Mrs Emma Yorkless. *Oh my God!*" The young woman shook her head from side to side, her mouth wide with laughter now. "Of all the visitors on this earth, you're the most unexpected. And you want to speak to Luke? Well, all I can say, you're not without spunk. Well"— she sighed—"he should be here any minute. Come in." She pulled the door wide and, having slowly passed her, Emma was once again amazed at what met her eyes, for the room, unlike the garden outside, was neat and showed comfort. She moved her body as she looked round it, and then she was startled by the woman's high laugh, saying, "Surprised, are you? Asked your way down there, I'll bet." She jerked her head in the direction of the hamlet. "Bad name I've got down there, in more ways than one. And I won't let them across the door, keep them guessing. Drive them mad I do, with piling muck outside. Sit down." She pointed to a brown leather chair to the side of an open fire which had a hob in front of it and an oven to the side, both brightly blackleaded, the hearth in front being whitewashed and framed by a brass fender.

As she sat down the woman said, "I hope you're prepared for sparks, because if there's anybody alive that Luke hates more than another in this world it's you. And it's the first time I've had a good look at you. I've seen you from a distance once or twice. But you know"—she lifted her shoulders high round her face—"you don't look the tartar that you're made out to be."

"I don't think of myself as a tartar." Emma's voice was stiff, and the woman laughed and said, "Nobody does. But you've done things to Luke that no man could stand for and. . . ."

"I did nothin' to Luke, only in self-defence."

"You marked him. He'll carry the scar till the day he dies. They say you're clever with whips, and yet, lookin' at you—" She shook her head now, no smile on her face as she ended, "I would say you were the last to hurt anybody. Yet who can tell what's under the skin? I know that. The skin's the biggest liar on God's earth. Anyway, what do you want with him? Has your man gone, I mean died?"

"No, but . . . but my daughter's gone."

The woman now leaned her head towards Emma and narrowed her eyes as she said, "The young lass Annie?"

"Yes, Annie."

"You say she's gone, what do you mean by that? She's run off?"

"No, not run off, she's been enticed off by some . . . man."

"And you think Luke's got somethin' to do with that?"

The woman's voice had risen sharply; there was anger in her tone now and she ended, "By God! you're askin' for trouble if you confront him with that."

"I'm . . . I'm not blaming him, but I feel that he might be able to lead me, or tell me something about the man who enticed Annie. He . . . Luke was seen talking to him."

"Luke talks to everybody who'll talk to him: he tells them the story of his life, how he's lost his inheritance to the farm and . . . and separated from his family through a woman. And that woman's you; that's what Luke would talk about to that man or anyone else. Oh God above!" She turned and went to the window now and drew the lace curtain aside, saying, "Here he comes. Well, if I were you, missis, I would go very careful. I know Luke an' I know what he's capable of."

"So do I."

With these words Emma had risen to her feet and the two young women confronted each other for a moment before turning to the door to watch it being thrust open. And there was Luke. His gaze was directed towards Emma and, strangely, there was no surprise on his countenance. Without speaking he took off his hat and threw it onto a backless wooden settle, then slowly took off his coat and did the same with that, and now in his shirt-sleeves he came across the room towards her, and if he had screamed at her, or had gone to strike her, the fear would not have been as great as it was when, with a note of laughter in his voice, he said, "Why! hello Emma. This is a pleasure. Isn't it, Laura?" He did not look at the woman as he spoke. " 'Tisn't every day we have visitors. The front garden puts 'em off. Didn't it put you off, Emma?"

Her name had ended in a high note of enquiry and she turned her eyes from him, drew in a shuddering breath and said, "Stop playing games, Luke. You must know the matter is serious or I wouldn't be here."

"Yes, yes, I understand that, Emma." He was now stroking the red weal on his left cheek that ran from his ear to the corner of his mouth. It was a faint mark but nevertheless noticeable.

"You . . . you know a man called Gardiner. He was staying at The . . . The Tun . . . Tuns." She stammered on the word and when he nodded at her without speaking further she said, "Annie is missing. There are those who have seen her with this man and also those who have seen you talkin' to him."

"I've been seen talking to a man who was staying at the inn." He had now turned his face fully towards Laura Nixon, and went on, "Now isn't that strange? Somebody's seen me talking to a man who was staying at the inn."

"Stop acting, Luke." She had forgotten about her prayer to God asking Him to control her temper, and now she was yelling, "Annie has been taken away by a man and you know what that means."

Now the Luke she knew was facing her. In an instant his face was transformed. His sudden rage had turned it almost purple and he bellowed at her, "Don't you dare talk to me like that, Spanish Emma. I'm in me own house. And let me tell you something, the news you have brought is the best I've heard in years, but it's not unexpected. Your daughter's a whore, a little ready-made whore. She takes after her mother. But then her mother hadn't the nerve to come into the open, she concealed it running after the painter and the parson till she nabbed me brother. But every inch of you's a whore. Laura here is classed as a whore but she couldn't hold a candle to you because she was made into one. You were born one. But your little daughter . . . well, she wasn't afraid to show her wares. Do you know she even offered them to me? She had a fancy for older blokes and I bet at this minute she's making some old fellow very happy. . . ."

"*Shut up, you!* You're a devil, that's what you are, and I know now you're in it. Whatever happened to her you were a part of it, and just to get at me."

"Now you be careful. You say anything like that again and I'll go to the justices. Aye, by God I will. I'll go to Mr Fordyke. Yes . . . Mr Fordyke, that's who I'll go to and he'll take me case up for me, for he's got as much love for you as I have, 'cos you gave his son a taste of the whip, didn't you? Very handy with the whip, aren't you, Emma? And you know something?" His voice dropped to the bantering tone he had assumed when he first saw her. "You were very foolish to come here on your own, very foolish, for now I've got you alone it could be my turn. I've got one out in the yard an' could skin the hide off you. Oh aye, Emma, I could skin the hide. . . ."

"Leave her alone, Luke." The woman had caught hold of his arm now and she turned to Emma, her voice grim, saying, "Get out. Get out."

Like someone drunk Emma stumbled towards the door, and she opened it but didn't close it behind her and Luke's voice followed her, yelling to the woman, "I haven't started to pay her off yet. I'll do for her, I tell you. If it's the last thing on this earth, I'll do for her."

She stumbled out through the broken gate and into the road.

Beyond the bend she stopped and leant over a low dry-stone wall, muttering to herself, her thoughts and words all jumbled up, asking God why? What had she done that this should come upon her? Why should a man hate her so?

As the turmoil in her mind lessened it left one thing outstanding and clear: he had been the instigator of Annie's going, and he knew what was happening to her and was taking joy in it. She had been mad to seek him out; she should have known, past events should have warned her. But what could she do about it? Could she go to the justice? No, she had no proof. And as he said, he himself could go to Mr Fordyke and find an ally.

And now she must go home and lie. She must lie to Barney and to the mister, for as weak as she imagined the mister was, she knew that were she to tell him his son had purposely sent his only grandchild, his beloved granddaughter, into a life of . . . what was the word? sin, horror, degradation, he would in all probability try to kill him.

She did not wait for the carrier cart—in any case this would not pass within the next hour or so—but she set off to take the long walk back to the farm. Before reaching it, however, she had faced the awful truth that the horror of the situation was being felt much more by those Annie had left behind than by Annie herself, no matter what was happening to her, for there was something in her daughter that needed men far beyond a woman's natural desire.

3

The summer passed and the autumn came and the thick morning mists that covered the land were no heavier than the gloom that pervaded the house.

Emma had experienced tension before Annie had gone, but now the weariness that tension creates had dissolved into apathy, and not only in her, but more noticeably in Barney and his father. Although Barney was deprived of mobile life, his voice at times had been vibrant, but now when he spoke it was in a level, listless fashion.

As for Jake Yorkless, he worked as he always had done, hard; he ate as he always had done, gobbling his food in order not to waste time; but the spare time that he had he no longer spent in the kitchen but would sit in the late evenings in the tack room making tallow for the candles or repairing harness.

Emma herself had always been overworked, but now her workload had increased because she had to fit in the little that Annie had done and also do part of Mary's work.

Mary's legs had become very swollen and so she couldn't make the return journey every day but had been forced to cut her time to three days a week; even so, she had to be met at the bottom of the lane by the cart, and then dropped in a similar way in the evening, which meant late work harnessing the horse and bedding it.

As the winter drew on Mary did not always manage to make her three visits a week, as during this particular week when the snow was lying thick. Emma this morning was making Barney comfortable and answering his question of what she was going to do without Mary's help by saying, "What cannot be done must be left undone. The animals come first; after I see to the meals." She did not mention her attendance on him for that had to be done whatever else went by the board.

"When do you think the parson will be back?" he asked, and she answered briefly, "I've no idea."

"He's been gone nearly two weeks; his sister will either be better or have died."

"Yes, I suppose so."

He turned his head and looked at the snow-smeared window, saying now, "I . . . I miss him. He's become sort of . . . well, necessary to me. He seems to bring the world into the room. You know what I mean?"

She bent over him to fasten the top button of his shirt, but she didn't say, "Yes, I know what you mean," because what Henry brought to each of them was so different, but she thought, if he had the power to read my mind would he still welcome him? There was a small derisive laugh echoing somewhere inside herself as her inner voice said, "He'd forbid him the house." Men were odd; all men were odd, even Henry. Time and time again he'd had the chance to touch her hand, an action which would have been like balm on her tormented spirit, but he hadn't done it. He would open doors for her, carry trays for her, take them from her hands, but he would always avoid contact with her, even when there wasn't a soul in sight. Sometimes she thought God stood between them, his God, for she had little use for God or prayer now. What had God ever done for her but taught her in deep measure the meaning of frustration? She knew that if Barney were to die tomorrow her life would be no different from what it was today . . . at least with regard to what lay between the parson and her.

During the past months her thoughts had turned bitter towards him. At one time his presence had been enough; to sit for a few minutes in the room of an evening doing her mending and listening to him talking to Barney had been sufficient; but not any more, particularly since Annie had gone. It was as if her daughter had left her wanton desire behind her for lately she herself had tossed and turned so much that she had kept both herself and Barney awake, with the resulting consequence she had said she would sleep upstairs for a time; and some irrational part of her had known and experienced an added hurt when he raised no objection to this.

It had been the first Christmas since Annie was born that there hadn't been a child in the house, and the holiday had passed as a normal day except that Alec Hudson and his wife called on Christmas Eve to see Barney. But their stay had been short and, naturally, without jollity.

The waits had not come up from the village this year, and Mary had explained to her, if it needed any explanation, it had been discussed down below but that under the circumstances they had thought the better of it. . . .

*

It was now evening on this bleak day. The house was quiet and the meal was over. Jake Yorkless had gone to the tack room as usual; Jimmy had left the farm before darkness set in, in case there was another heavy fall of snow that would prevent him getting back to the village. It wasn't yet time to settle Barney down for the night, and for the countless time that day she filled the kettle from the pump and set it on the hob. Then she blew up the fire with the bellows to get some red-hot cinders to put into the warming-pans, for the mister liked his bed warm. And now she stood undecided, one arm stretched out against the mantelshelf as she stared down at the fire, asking herself should she sit down for a few minutes before she washed the crocks; but immediately deciding against it because, she told herself, once she sat down she would have a job to get up again, she was so tired, physically tired. The work was wearing the flesh off her bones, her skirt was hanging slack at the waist now. Her waist had always been narrow but of late she'd had to put a tuck into her skirt band. This would not have mattered so much if her mind had been at peace, but, with the combination, she wondered how much longer she could go on. She felt old and worn out. Here she was just turned thirty and she didn't care if she were to die tomorrow, or this night even. What was there to live for anyway?

Her hand left the support of the mantelshelf and her body jerked round as a tap came on the kitchen door. She heard the kicking of feet against the boot scraper. There was only ever one person who knocked on the kitchen door like that.

He entered hat in hand, having banged this against the wall, and she moved forward towards the table and leant against the edge of it.

"Hello, Emma."

There was a long pause before she could answer, "Hello, Parson."

"Have I startled you? I'm sorry."

"No, no, not at all. But what brought you out on a night like this?"

"Oh, I've been cooped most of the day."

"You . . . you've just got back . . . I mean today?"

"About four o'clock."

A little warmth came into her heart. He had arrived back at four o'clock and now it was only twenty minutes to seven and he had come all the way from the village on foot. It must have taken him an hour at least because the drifts were high in parts. She almost sprang round the table, saying, "Let me take your coat. Come up to the fire and I'll get you something hot; there's broth in the pan."

She went to take the coat from him but he said, "Just a minute," and putting his hand into a large inner pocket, he brought out two flat wrapped parcels, one of which he handed to her, "That is from my sister."

"For me?"

"Yes," he laughed, "for you. It mightn't seem of much value but she treasured it."

"Is she?"

"No, no; she's well on the mend again. But I was telling her about you, and she thought you might like it. I must warn you it is nothing much to look at, but she always found its contents very helpful and very precious."

Swiftly she unwrapped the paper and saw a much worn soft leather-bound book, and opening it at random she gazed at it for a moment. Then lifting her head to him, she said, "They're poems."

"Yes, an anthology of poems. She's had it since she was a girl."

Pressing the book against her breast, she gazed at him for a moment. She was deeply touched and found it hard to speak; then she said, "She must be a nice person . . . lady, so thoughtful to . . . to give me this." She patted the book twice with her hand. "Will you tell her when you write that . . . that I thank her and I'll treasure it as much as she did."

"I will. I will, Emma. This too is a book." He put the other brown paper package on the table. "It's for Barney. Much different from poems; it's a book of puzzles that exert the mind. It was in our school-room long before we made use of it. I don't know from where it came or who thought the puzzles up but none of us boys ever managed to solve them all. I . . . I think Barney might find it useful to fill in a little time."

She moved her head slightly. "Yes, yes," she said; "I'm sure he will. Look, come to the fire. I'll pour you some soup out. Come and get warm."

A few minutes later he was sitting on the settle to the side of the fire and she was standing before him holding out a tray on which was a bowl of broth and a spoon. He put his hands on the tray but did not actually take it from her, but staring into her face that was just slightly above his now, he said, "I'm so glad to be back, Emma."

The tray trembled between them. It was like a declaration of love and her voice was a whisper as she answered, "And I'm so glad to see you back." She did not add "Parson".

He now took the tray from her and placed it on his knees, and looked down into the broth.

She turned away towards the fire. Had she ever felt bitterness towards him? Had she ever wanted to die? If she had ever seen love in a man's eyes she had seen it a moment ago. It was enough; she'd survive on it.

4

The winter, like all winters, was hard. The hope was for the spring, and when it came it was wet and wild. The earth was heavy to plough; the horses became bogged down to their knees in the marshy parts. The yard was awash with mud: it tramped into the kitchen and from there to the hall and, as Mary could no longer go down on her knees to scrub the stone floors, Emma had to do it.

It was the middle of May before the weather changed. The fields drained, the yard dried, the sun shone, and she had opened all the windows in the house to let the air through. She had even opened the door into the attic with the fanlight in the roof. It was seldom she went under the roof. It was generally bare for Dilly Yorkless had had little enough furniture to fill the house, let alone storing it in the attic.

Emma paused a moment and looked about her. There were her whips, dust covered. She picked one up and smiled to herself. The mice had had a feed of the leather-bound handle. The wooden handle of another had been nibbled too, also the end of the thongs. Next, she unrolled the belt of knives and took out one of them from its sheath and laid it across her palm. It conjured up the picture of her father. His memory was dim now and that of her mother almost non-existent, and the travelling show folk seemed like shadowy characters in a half-forgotten dream, coming and going with no substance. She thought for a moment with welling sadness how different her life might have been if her father had lived: she herself would have travelled over a large area of the country; she would have lived in the open; she would have been brought up with compatible people, people who became friends; she would have become expert with the whips, and perhaps the knives too. Instead, what had happened to her?

Oh, enough of back thinking.

She rolled up the belt and laid it down near the whips. Somebody ordered your life. Whether it was God or the devil, she didn't know, but whoever it was, you had to go through with it. There was a saying that

God made the back to bear the burden, but to her mind He didn't make the back, He simply made the burden, and the burden either broke your back or strengthened it, it all depended on who you were and how much you could bear.

She went to the roof fanlight. It hadn't been opened for years, and she had a job to get the sneck out of the staple. And when she succeeded she had to make another big effort to push the frame upwards. She could hardly see through the glass. The weather had kept the outside clean but inside hadn't been touched, not in her time anyway. She told herself she must bring a bucket of water up here and clean it; it would let in more light.

The window pushed outwards. She pulled down the iron rods at the side that supported it, then she found she was looking into the branches of the old apple tree, and she smiled to herself. The buds were full. Oh, it was lovely to see new growth again. And from this angle she could see over the fields, and right along the track to where it dropped to the coach road. . . . There was somebody coming towards the farm. She screwed her eyes up against the sunlight, moved her head to get a better view through the branches. The figure disappeared from view for a minute or so, and when she next saw it she cried aloud, "Pete! Why, Pete." Now she was racing out of the attic, through the bedroom, across the landing and down the stairs, and she stopped for a moment to push the sitting-room door open and to shout to Barney, " 'Tis Pete! 'Tis Pete!"

"Pete?" His head moved quickly.

"Yes; I saw him from above."

She met him in the yard and actually put her arms about him and kissed him, a thing she had never done before, and he cried at her, "Well, well! Emma, after that I'll come home every week."

He looked about him. "Nothing's changed," he said. "Never will. How are you, lass?" He put his arm around her shoulder and when she didn't answer but bowed her head, he lowered his too and tried to look into her face. In the excitement of seeing him she had forgotten what lay over the house, until he had said nothing has changed.

"Barney, he's still all right?"

"Yes." She turned and pointed, and when Pete saw his brother's head as if it was resting beyond the window sill and his one arm raised in the air he waved back to him, then made hurriedly for the kitchen, saying, "Where's Da?"

"In the stone field I think. . . . Pete." They were in the kitchen now. He had dropped his kit-bag and he had thrown off his straw hat, and now looking at her straight face he said, "Somethin' wrong, Emma?"

"Very wrong, Pete. I'd better tell you afore you see Barney."

And she told him. Half-way through the telling he had dropped into a chair; when she finished he didn't speak, his head was deep on his chest. After some moments he raised it and, looking at her, he said simply, "She was lively that way, Emma."

And she answered, "Yes, she was, Pete. But . . . but God help her. She wouldn't know what she was in for."

"Aye"—he shook his head slowly—"God'help her. Indeed, God help her. I've seen them . . . lasses." He closed his eyes tightly, and jerked his head, then rose to his feet, asking now, "How did Barney take it?"

"It's altered him."

"Wouldn't be human if it hadn't. And Da?"

"Well"—she looked to the side—"all I can say is, I think it's affected him worst of all. He's . . . he's become strange. He . . . he doesn't stay in the house at nights, just to sleep."

"God almighty! the things that happen." Then looking at her closely, he said, "An' you're changed an' all, Emma. You've lost flesh. What about help?"

"We have Jimmy. I don't know what we'd do without him. But . . . but Mary only comes part-time. It's her legs." She watched him sigh deeply, then say quietly, "The justices? Was nothing done in that quarter?"

"Well, I went in every week for two months or more, but I could only see the clerks. I somehow got the impression they didn't think it was an unusual case, in fact one said the week that . . . Annie disappeared another child from Birtley was missing an' all. And one from Durham. The Birtley girl was younger than Annie. There are different people, private people, bestirring themselves about such happenings, and they did find one young lass trussed up in a sailor's bag. 'Twas on a foreign ship but it was an English sailor who carried the bag. You can't believe it, can you?"

"Oh aye"—Pete was still looking downwards—"I can believe it all right, Emma. Sometimes I've been sick to the heart at the things I've witnessed. Half the people round about don't know they're born; they think that when they see the poverty and the slums that's it, but there's some things that take place. . . . Aw, to hell!" His head came up with a swing. "Enough's enough. I'll away to see Barney."

She watched him stride up the kitchen and out of the door. Could there be worse things than had happened to Annie? . . . But she didn't know what had happened to Annie, and even Pete had suggested that Annie was different. Oh yes, she was different all right.

*

During the next few days a little lightness came into the house: Pete's presence, his tales of the sea, his cheery manner helped them all; especially so did it affect his father, and Jake Yorkless took to sitting in the kitchen again.

It was on the last Thursday in May, a day that heralded summer. Emma was walking across the farmyard with Henry. He had been sitting by Barney's side for the past two hours listening to Pete's crack, and Pete, she knew, had gone out of his way to make the parson laugh, and laugh he did.

He chuckled now. "There's a big streak of the comedian in Pete, don't you think, Emma?" he said.

"Yes, he has a way of taking one out of one's self."

"Indeed he has. And I never cease to marvel at the change in him from when he was a young man. Of course, he's still a young man but so different. Yet what do we know really what another person is like? We hide most of our selves within ourselves." They had stopped by the gap in the farmyard wall: the long twilight was deepening; he was looking at her averted face as he added softly, "Don't you agree with me, Emma?"

She did not turn to him but continued to stare over the fields as she answered as quietly as he had asked the question, "Yes, I agree with you. But then it must have always been so for everybody, because if people really spoke the truth about what was inside them life would be unbearable. You have got to bury things within you, bury them alive so to speak if you want to go on living. I mean"—she looked at him now, her voice taking on a brisker tone—"it must happen to everybody."

"Yes, yes, Emma, you're right." He nodded slowly at her. The sound of a cow mooing came from the byres. This was followed by a fluttering and cackling in the distance: a hen must have decided to change its place on the barks and so had caused an uproar.

He broke their silence by saying on a light note, "You know, you've given me an idea for my next sermon: What is truth? or Our hidden selves. Sounds like one of those stories in the new magazines, don't you think?"

"Yes. Yes."

"I have difficulty in finding subjects for my sermons, I mean suitable ones, because were I to express my true ideas from the pulpit, I'm afraid they would not be welcomed." There was a little laughter in his voice now, and she answered it in the same vein by saying, "I'm sure they wouldn't; I'm afraid you'd get your marching orders."

"To tell you the truth, Emma, I'm surprised I haven't had them before now. And it isn't for want of some people trying, so I understand."

"People would find fault with God." Why had she said that? Because she was one of those who of late had made a habit of finding fault with God.

He laughed outright now and said, "You're right, Emma, you're right, but I'm sure He's used to it. Now I must away, if not it will be dark and some highwayman will set about me and rob me of my purse and my jewelled watch and my rings." He held out his bare hand, his fingers spread towards her, as he ended, "You heard about the hold-up outside of Durham of a private coach?"

"No; I haven't heard about that."

"Well, it happened four days ago. So now I must away in case it happens to me." He paused and, his voice dropping, he said, "Good-night, Emma. I'm glad to see you looking a bit brighter."

"Good-night." She could not add "Henry" and she rarely now addressed him as "Parson". . . .

Henry walked slowly homewards, and the night was well set in when he reached the vicarage. He could see the dim reflection of a light shining through the curtains in the sitting-room, which meant Miss Wilkinson had departed, and he thanked God for that. Time and again when he went out visiting and told her he might be late and not to wait she would nevertheless be there to greet him, her face stiff with disapproval, her tongue wagging like a mother at an errant child: "Why didn't you wear your overshoes? . . . You haven't a muffler on . . . You're soaked to the skin . . . Why didn't you eat your meal tonight? . . . Isn't it cooked well enough for you?"

How had he put up with her all these years? Because, he supposed, he was too lazy to bother; or truth to tell, oh yes, let him speak the truth to himself, too afraid of the rumpus her dismissal would cause in the village, and all because he knew that it wasn't every housekeeper who could take Sunday school and play the harmonium for the children. Nor one capable of playing the church organ if she had got the chance. But Tom Bessell never gave her the chance these days; he had even threatened what he would do to her if she touched his organ. . . . He sometimes wished he had the courage of Tom where she was concerned.

He let himself into the house, took off his coat and hat, then went to the kitchen and into the pantry and there poured himself out a glass of milk from the metal can. He carried it to the sitting-room and after placing it on the desk he sat down, took his keys from his pocket and unlocked the bottom drawer. He took out the leather-bound book and he unlocked its brass clasp.

He sat looking down on a blank page telling himself if he were to do any writing tonight it should be to prepare his sermon. But she had looked better tonight, happier; he must think of her for a few minutes and then he would get down to work. So he began to write:

My dearest Emma,

It did my heart good to hear you laugh; you have been so sad of late. I have seldom seen a smile on your beautiful face since Annie left, yet when you do smile the pain in my heart grows deeper, because then I have to restrain myself from putting my arms about you. I must tell you, Emma, that I dreamt last night I had you in my arms and was holding you tightly and I felt no sense of sin, only of exaltation. It was the most strange experience, for I knew that God was pleased with me.

I seem to have come to terms with Him of late, Emma, for as you know I've asked Him time and again why He allows evil. But He has shown me time and again the goodness and strength that is born in people who have suffered evil, like yourself for instance, for since Annie has been gone I have detected a new strength in you, not physical, no. Would that it were partly that to help you over your tasks for it pains me deeply to know the work that you have to contend with. And how thin you have become under it; the flesh seems to have dropped from your bones. Yet it has left you more beautiful still.

You said tonight that we all carry secrets, and that is so true, but I wonder if there are any others as heavy as ours. Of course we all imagine, as individuals, that our body aches and heartaches have never before been experienced, yet in our case I do not know of a parallel where two people have met so frequently over the years. How many years, Emma? It is fourteen since you were married, but I loved you before that, from the first moment I saw you on the coach. As a father loves a child then, but not so later. No. And yet not one word of love has passed between us: we speak only with our eyes. We rarely touch hands. I avoid that for I cannot trust myself. And so it will go on I suppose until the end of our days and no one shall know about you and me except Ralph. And he loves you too but in a different way perhaps. Nevertheless he loves you, and if circumstances had been different in his situation he would have married you. Would I rather have had that, he as your husband? No, I don't think so. I would have been jealous then because he has a mind and you would have learned from him. Yes, indeed I would have been jealous of that, for I have always been your teacher.

Abelard and Heloise were much luckier than we, my dearest, because they experienced love in its fullness before the church parted them. Strange that. I've always thought it strange the cruelty latent in the church, physical and mental. They have practised it down the ages; what religion has slaughtered more than Christianity?

Another of my torments, Emma, is the Blessed Trinity. I can be thankful that you do not suffer in this way too. You do not say to God: "If You sent Your beloved Son to earth, You would expect the enemies He made through His goodness to slaughter but not His followers to do likewise and in His name. Since no one suffers alone in any form and since every experience has been experienced before, would that I could meet someone of like mind and we could talk this matter over. I cannot go too deeply into it with Ralph for he will not have it that You exist at all, and in my heart I know You exist. What I cannot understand is Your ways. But then, if I did I too would be God."

It is strange how when I write in this little book I talk to Emma and God on the same level. Am I blaspheming?

As if in answer to his question there came the sound of thumping on the front door and he jerked so violently that he toppled the inkwell. As he jumped to his feet he righted the brass stand and sopped up part of the ink with the blotter; then pulling out a handkerchief, he quickly dabbed on his fingers before lifting up the lamp and going towards the door. There he withdrew the bolts, then pulling the door wide he peered through a lantern light at a woman standing before him. She had a shawl over her head but although it did not hide her face he did not recognize her as one of his parishioners until she spoke, saying, "I'm Mrs Pringle, Parson, from along the road." And he said, "Oh yes, yes, Mrs Pringle," his groping mind telling him she was the drayman's wife. Neither of them had ever been in his church and he was surprised to see her now and to feel that she had any need of him. He said quietly, "Is there something wrong? Is there anything I can do for you?"

" 'Tis me man Alf, he's right poorly. He was kicked in the leg by a horse last week gone an' has been in a fever. He's had doctor but it got no better, an' then the night he asked for you. I wouldn't come 'cos I thought he was ravin' 'cos he's no man of God, don't believe in it, says God done nowt for him, but he kept on askin' for you. He said he hadn't gone off his head, just wants to talk to you."

"In that case I shall come and see him. Step in a minute."

He stood back. She put her lantern on the step before passing him, and with her head back she stood peering round the hall. Quickly now he left her after placing the lamp where it would give light to both the hall and the sitting-room. He hurried to the desk, locked the book, placed it in the drawer and then locked the drawer and returned the keys to the inside pocket of his waistcoat. Going into the hall again he put on his coat, picked up his hat, lit a lantern for himself, and once more opening the door, he said, "Shall we go then?"

As he locked the door on the outside she said, "You ain't got a trap now?"

"No."

"Nor a horse?"

"No."

"Act as poor as we then?"

"I'm afraid it's no act, Mrs Pringle, it's a necessity."

She swung her lantern and saw him smiling. And now she caused him to laugh gently as she said, " 'Tis right what they say, you're a queer chap. 'Tis likely 'cos you're like no real parson that my Alf wants to see you."

"Very likely. Very likely."

When he entered the cottage he stopped himself from pulling out his handkerchief and covering his nose with it. It was the usual cottage, one room, a scullery off, and a space under the roof. There were two beds in the room. In one was a huddle of small bodies with heads at the top and bottom of it. Two dogs were lying to one side of the fireplace; at the other side was another bed and the man lying under a patchwork quilt looked asleep. His cheeks and chin were covered with heavy whiskers, the growth of days. His eyes were sunk into his head and his hair was matted with sweat. It was evident he was in a fever and the first thought that came into Henry's head was typhoid; he had heard of odd cases of it in the city.

The woman now pushed a stool towards him and as he sat down she leant over the bed, saying quietly, "Alf. Alf, I've brought him. He's here."

Slowly the sunken eyes opened and, after a moment of dazed staring, recognition came into them. The man's hand came slowly out and it gripped Henry's as he said, "Not afraid to go, understand? Not afraid to go. Don't want no blessin', but trouble on me conscience. . . . Never should have done it, but five quid is five quid with mouths to feed."

He now turned his gaze on his wife and, taking his hand from Henry's, he motioned her to go; and she, after looking from one to the other, shambled out of the room.

"Take your time. Take your time," Henry said, quietly now. He watched the man moving his tongue over his dry lips; then, his voice throaty, the man mumbled, "The lass, Annie Yorkless . . . know where she is."

When he stopped and gasped for breath Henry bent nearer to him, suffering the foul breath on his face as he strained his ear to hear more.

"Shouldn't . . . shouldn't have done it. No, shouldn't have done it." He lay with closed eyes, saying nothing further, and Henry said urgently, "What shouldn't you have done, Mr Pringle?"

Slowly the eyes opened and the whisper came: "Taken her to that house."

"Which house?"

"The one in Newcastle."

"Can you tell me the name of the house?"

"Aye, aye." Again there was silence until Henry urged, "Please, please, Mr Pringle, give me the name of the house."

"What? Oh aye. Eight. . . ." His voice faded away and Henry repeated what he thought he had heard, "Eight Motherwell Row, did you say?"

Again the man spoke, saying, "Aye, aye. Nowt to look at on outside . . . plenty in . . . good guise, old bitch an' her family with the bairns, some never seen . . . upstairs."

"What is the name of the people?"

"Name? . . ." The man was gasping again. "D'know, just Ma. Big fellows there. Stall in the market. Cover . . . cover. Polis no use . . . too many nobs . . . back-handers. . . . Dry . . . dry . . . drink."

Henry looked about him. There was a mug on the table, next to a ewer. He went to it and as he poured some water out two small heads raised themselves from the foot of the other bed and the sight of them evoked the usual response against the poverty he encountered daily, Dear God! Dear God! He couldn't gauge in the dim light how many children were in the bed, six or eight; yet they were luckier than some. Oh yes, far luckier.

He returned to the man and, lifting his head, placed the tin cup to his lips. When his head was on the pillow once more, the man gasped again: "Not afraid to go. Never had no use for parsons, want no blessin', just . . . just want me mind easy."

When the head began to toss on the pillow, Henry said quietly "Rest easy, your conscience will be at peace now. Rest easy." But in his heart he said: God, forgive him for only You can. Then rising from the chair he went across the littered room and tapped on the door leading into the scullery, and when the woman opened it he said quietly to her, "I would attend to your husband: he would find some comfort if you sponged him down with lukewarm water."

"Aye"—she nodded her head—"I'll do that, though I can't see 'tis much use. He's goin' an' he knows it, an' what am I goin' to do with that squad?" She pointed towards the bed. "Seven of 'em and only two fit to work yet."

He looked at her coldly for a moment before saying, "Should it be necessary I shall see that you have help."

" 'Tis kind of you."

"Good-night."

"Good-night, Parson. I hope you find her."

He had half turned away from her; now he stiffened and, looking at her over his shoulder, he said, "You knew of this?"

"I knew he was up to somethin', you don't get five sovereigns for picking your teeth."

"Who else is aware of this, I mean in the village?"

"No names, no pack-drill as he used to say." She nodded towards the bed. "An' me, I don't want me face bashed in, an' 'tis better that Alf goes now for he'd go anyway if it were found out he snitched."

Henry stared at her in bewilderment. He had imagined he knew everything that went on in his parish. Hadn't he found out about the smuggling of the liquor? Wasn't he aware of who committed adultery once their husbands went on the droving journeys, and of the men who took advantage of the journeys? Wasn't he aware that his verger was a hypocrite, as he was also aware that there were good God-fearing people in the village? As he stared at this dirty dishevelled woman he felt like a child who was being laughed at because of his ignorance. And likely that's what many of them did, laughed at him behind his back, because he knew so little that went on below the surface behind the smiles and nods and "Good-day, Parson". They paraded to church on Sunday in their best and some of them, he was sure, tried to live life at its best, but there were others, and he must now think these others were in his village and they had enticed a child into corruption.

He turned from her and, picking up his lantern from near the door, he went out into the night. But he did not hurry towards home. He knew he could do nothing until first light. It was no use going to the farm now, and even when he did go they could not just up and march to this house in Newcastle. He must think. But first he must get a little sleep for he was very tired.

Life as a whole, he was finding, was tiring. People were tiring. He wished he was miles away. There came over him a longing for his childhood home again: the serenity of his father's face, the caring love of his sister, the comfort of the timbered house sitting comfortably in the centre of the now overgrown gardens, and the softer air and the softer atmosphere of the south country. He had been here, what was it, twenty-four years? and the land was still alien to him. And the majority of the people. Yes, he had to admit the majority of the people too.

He had imagined through his vanity that the episode outside the inn had changed their attitude towards him, made them see him in a different light, but not really. In their minds he was still someone who could be duped. Yet he was not the only one who had been duped. The innkeeper had been duped over his guest Mr Gardiner, at least he hoped he had, as others in the village had been duped by the civil, nice-spoken man.

Oh, let him stop thinking, let him get home and lose himself in sleep for a while and forget that he was the minister of a parish, and forget that with the light he must go up to the farm and give them the news . . . give Emma the news. What would her reaction be? He didn't know, he only knew in this moment that he wished he had never set eyes on Emma Molinero the child who had led him to become obsessed with Emma Yorkless the married woman, for then he would no longer be in this parish, but in some place more compatible, in a house less large and more comfortable, and with someone to see to his needs who was the antithesis of Miss Wilkinson. . . . Oh! Miss Wilkinson. That woman was really getting on his nerves.

It was a quarter to seven the following morning when, walking out of the drive into the road, he ran into Miss Wilkinson, and she, staring at him and with her mouth slightly agape, said, "My! we're up afore our clothes are on this morning. Are you going on a call?"

"Yes."

"Who's dying?"

"No one as far as I know, Miss Wilkinson." Though as he said it he thought of Alf Pringle.

"You haven't had your breakfast?"

"I've had a hot drink."

"What time am I to expect you then?" He had passed her and she was talking to his back.

"In an hour, or a little more," he called over his shoulder.

"You haven't got a coat on and the mist is thick."

He walked quickly on. He had been aware for some long, long time of Miss Wilkinson's feelings towards him and of her ultimate intention, and to this intention he always said to himself, "Over my corpse, and not even then." Yet, having said that, part of him was sorry for her. Her

history was that of thousands of other women: she had looked after her
parents until they died, then at quite an early age became housekeeper
to his predecessor and now, well into her fifties, himself and the vicarage were all she had in life; not forgetting the Sunday school, for the
power she asserted over the children was that of a frustrated mother.
He knew that she was laughed at behind her back by the villagers, and
that her feeling for him was a joke amongst them and had been for a
long time.

The morning was misty, but when he left the coach road and as-
cended the hill the sun came out and the whole world seemed bathed in
a silver glow. He stood for a moment letting its peace fall upon him; but
even as he did so his mind was asking what would be the outcome of
this day.

Well, it was no use standing here, he must go and set the outcome in
motion.

The first person he saw as he entered the yard was Pete, and Pete
stopped in his tracks, narrowed his eyes through the thin mist that was
still hanging around the farm and said, "That you, Parson?"

"Yes, Pete."

"My!"—he used the same threadbare term that Miss Wilkinson had
uttered—"you're up afore your clothes is on this mornin'."

Henry made no comment but asked briefly, "Where's Emma?"

"Oh, she's back in there." Pete pointed and jerked his head towards
the farmhouse. "Seein' to Barney she was little while gone, but she'll be
makin' the meal now I should think. Anything wrong?"

"I don't know how you'd look at it, Pete, but I . . . I think you had
better come indoors for a moment, I have something to tell you. Where
is your father?"

"In the byre."

"Would you care to fetch him too?"

Pete said nothing, but his head moved slightly to the side as if in an
enquiry; then he turned and went towards the byre. Henry crossed the
yard and opened the kitchen door without knocking and so startled
Emma that she almost dropped a bowl of porridge she was placing on a
tray, and she, asking the same question as Pete, said, "What is it?
Something wrong?"

"I have news about Annie."

Emma gripped the corner of the table with her hand. "She's not . . .
not?"

"Dead? No, no. But . . . but I have found out where she is."

"Who from?"

"I'm . . . I'm afraid I can't tell you that, Emma, but. . . . Oh, here is Mr Yorkless."

Jake Yorkless came into the room followed by Pete and they both stood staring at him for a moment. Looking from one to the other, Henry said, "I have found out the whereabouts of Annie."

"*What!*" Jake Yorkless took a step forward then added, "Where?"

"As far as I can gather she's in a house in Newcastle. I think it's eight Motherwell Row or something like that. Do you know Newcastle well?"

"I don't know it at all 'cept the market."

Henry now looked at Pete, and he, going to the table, pulled a wooden chair from under it and sat down and nipped at his lip before he slanted his eyes up towards Henry and said, "I know it a bit and—" His eyes moved away as he continued, "the district she's likely to be in."

When he next spoke he was staring up at Emma and he said, "There's Bucketwell Row. Used to be big houses, sailors' boarding-houses now supposedly, captains and such, not common lodging houses. They stand well back, bordering on fields at one side if I remember rightly. How I know about it is—" He glanced from one to the other now with a shamefaced look on his countenance, adding, "Had to go and find captain once, went along of chief mate."

He now turned his head sharply and looked at his father who was striding up the kitchen, and he called to him, "Where you off to, Da?"

"Where the hell do you think I'm off to?"

"Don't be so daft." Pete got to his feet. "You've got as much chance of getting in there as I have into the Queen's bedchamber." He turned and gave a quick apologetic look towards Henry, then went on, "They've got bullies who'd smash you up as quick as look at you."

Jake Yorkless turned slowly about and, his voice grim now, he said, "Well, what do you propose to do? Just stand there?"

"No, no. But give me time to think. Give us all time to think. There's one thing certain, us two alone would be less than useless, we've got to have help."

"Alec Hudson, and Joe Mason, and. . . ."

"No, no, Da. You would set the village alight by asking any of them for help, an' the flame so to speak would spread into Newcastle afore you could say water. Whoever was in on this is still in the village. Am I right? Am I right, Parson?" Pete was looking straight at Henry now, and Henry hesitated before saying, "I . . . I would say you're right, Pete."

"God Almighty!" Jake Yorkless came slowly up to the table now and sat down heavily and bent his head over his joined hands. And there was quiet in the kitchen for a moment.

Emma herself hadn't moved, but it was she who spoke now. Looking at Pete, she said, "What do you think should be done, Pete?" And he glanced at her while he nipped the end of his long nose between his thumb and the knuckle of his first finger; then, as if speaking to himself, he said "We can do nothin' in the daylight, that's for sure, and we'll want to know where we're goin', that's for sure again, and we'll want lads with us who know the ropes of them places." He turned now and looked fully at Henry as he ended, "A man could be murdered and thrown in the river and not be missed, so to speak. It's happened, when they get too inquisitive like, because there's big fellows behind some of those places. 'Tisn't only the madams who run them. Look"—he got abruptly to his feet—"I'll go in and have a walk round, and I know two or three of me shipmates'll be glad to flex their muscles in a little bit of a bust up. There's the donkey-man, Johnny Robson: he's doin' watch on board time her backside's being scraped . . . the boat you know." He nodded at Henry who said, "Yes, yes, I know." Another time he might have laughed, but this was no time for laughter, and Pete went on, "And Carl. He's a square-head . . . Swede, the size of a house end. He lives out Denton way, married a lass out there. I know his house, I've been there. And then if we could get Ratty Mullin. But he's in South Shields, down the river. He's not the size of two pennorth of copper but he's got hands on him like a pair of sledge-hammers. I've seen what he can do with them an' all. If I could get the three of them, something might be done."

"I would come along."

"What!"

Now Pete actually laughed; then bowing his head and wagging it from side to side, he said, "Oh, Parson, you don't know what you're sayin'."

Henry's voice was stiff as he answered, "I know what I'm saying all right, and I've been known to use my hands on occasions."

"Aye, aye, you might, Parson, but I bet me life you've never seen anything like them on the waterfront, not the bully boys who take care of the madams. Anyway, too many can be worse than too few at times, and believe me, Parson, I know what I'm talkin' about. Anyway"—he turned and looked at his father—"the place's got to be found first, if there is a Motherwell Row. Might turn out we're on the wrong track. So the best plan I think, Da, is for me to get meself over there now and see what's to be done. What d'you say?"

Jake Yorkless didn't speak for a moment, but he put his hand up and ran it through his grizzled grey hair before muttering, "Well, you seem to know all about it, so the quicker you get movin' the better." And he now rose from the table and, passing them, went into the yard again, and Pete, his voice quiet, looked at Emma, saying, "I'll change me things and have a bite afore I go. By the way, we'd better not let on to Jimmy, and certainly not Mary or else you may as well get the town-crier out."

She nodded back at him and watched him go up the kitchen and out into the hall before she turned and looked at Henry and asked quietly, "How . . . how did you find out?"

He hesitated for a moment before moving to the table and standing to the side of her, when he said, "It wasn't a confession, so I can tell you. But don't tell the others, please. The man Pringle took her there."

"Pringle?" The word was a whisper.

"Yes."

"Who's behind him?"

"He didn't say, but it's someone from about I should think."

"Luke?"

"I would hate to think that, but I don't know. One thing I do know, if Pringle hadn't been near death's door and wanted to clear his con-science we wouldn't have heard anything; it was obvious he goes in fear of the instigator or the instigators of this business."

"Dear God." She lifted up the bowl of porridge now in both hands and she looked down into it as she said, "If . . . if they get her, what will she be like? Will she ever be able to live a normal life again?" And she slowly turned her eyes towards him; but he could not answer the question, the only thing he could do was to shake his head.

She now went to the stove and scooped the porridge back into the black cooking-pot which she then pushed into the centre of the fire, and as she stood stirring it she said, "Have you eaten?"

"No," he answered; "but I . . . I don't feel like breakfast."

Presently she pulled the pan on to the side of the hob again and when the surface of the porridge subsided into slow plops she turned once more from the fire, saying, "I meant to go down to Ralph's this morn-ing, but I don't think I'll be able to now. Would you be passing that way today?"

"I'll make it my business, in fact I'll drop in on my way back."

As Henry was speaking Pete re-entered the room. He was once again in his sailor's clothes and Henry said to him, "You won't have any idea when you'll be back, Pete?"

"Well, not quite, Parson. I can round up Johnny Robson any time and he'll get somebody to stand in for him, and Carl, he'll be about somewhere, he likes fixing things in his house, but Ratty, well, I'm not sure where I'll find him. He's likely the one that'll take me time. And then I've got to look round the place. S'afternoon at the earliest, Parson, I should say."

"I'll look in around teatime. Good luck, Pete."

"Thanks, Parson."

"Good-bye, Emma."

"Good-bye."

After the door had closed on him she looked at it for a moment before turning again to the stove. She emptied two ladlefuls of the porridge into a bowl and when she placed it before Pete he said to her, "You know what you'll have to do, Emma, don't you?"

"What do you mean?" she said.

"Well—" He picked up the milk jug and poured milk over the porridge before saying, " 'Tis on a year she's been gone, and if you do get her back she won't be the same as when she left, you'll . . . you'll have to understand. . . ."

"I know that, Pete."

"And there's another thing that's just come to me mind. They . . . they may have moved her on."

"Yes, I've thought of that an' all."

"But nevertheless, we've got to hope she's still there and chance gettin' her out. But it's going to be risky business, for it's no use gettin' the polis in on this. You understand?"

"Yes, Pete. And Pete, I'll be going with you."

He bounced in his chair and almost choked on the porridge. "Begod! you won't," he said; "not if I know anything, Emma."

She stared at him quietly. "I'm going with you," she repeated.

"And I say you're not, Emma. You've got no idea. . . ."

Now, her voice raised, she almost yelled at him, "I have got an idea, my mind's full of ideas of what's been happening to her every day, every night since she left. Nothing I could see or hear in the future can come up to what I've already thought. I almost go demented at times with ideas. And so Pete, whoever you get to go along with you, I come too."

"Oh my God!" He put his hand to his brow now, saying, "The lads wouldn't stand for it, there'll be some roughin' up."

"Pete." Her voice was quiet now and he looked up at her and she said, "Perhaps that's one of the reasons why I feel I should be there, for if there's fighting she . . . she may be frightened and. . . ."

"Oh, Emma—" He sighed and drew in a long breath as if begging for patience before he said, "If she's been there a year, you've got to face it there'll be very few happenings that she'll be afraid of, a fight least of all I should imagine. I'm sorry . . . I'm sorry to have to put it like that."

She turned from the table and went to the sink, and she stood looking over it and into the yard before she said quietly, "In any case, I'm goin' along of you. You needn't tell your mates, I'll just be there on the cart."

There followed a silence before she turned and, walking past him, said quietly, "Now I'll go and break the news to Barney."

5

Dusk was deepening when Pete drove the flat farm cart down on to the bridle-path and from there to the coach road. Everyone in the village knew he was home on leave from the sea and no one would question his driving the cart at that time of night. He could be on his way to The Tuns or into Birtley for a spree; but as he turned towards Gateshead Fell the few people he passed guessed that his revelling was going to be enacted further afield, for it was known that he favoured a drink and a sing-song.

He was half a mile out of the village when he came across the parson supposedly taking an evening stroll, and the parson took his seat beside him on the front board. It was unusual that he wasn't wearing his clerical hat, and no white collar showed above his collarless jacket. Another half-mile along the road, Jake Yorkless and Emma appeared from behind a hedge.

With regard to the presence of Emma and the parson, there had over the past two hours been the most heated arguments. Pete had pointed out to Henry that they might all end up in . . . the clink, then what would he do about it? As for Emma, her very presence might put a spanner in the whole works.

Henry's answer to all the talk had been that someone would be needed to stay with the horse and cart, you couldn't just leave an animal standing unattended in the middle of a street at night. So, if nothing else, he could be in charge of it and if any questions were asked he could say he was waiting for someone, which was true.

Emma's answer had been brief: "If you don't take me along of you, I'll simply follow you."

And so it was a half an hour later that they passed over the river by the High Level Bridge and into Newcastle. Their next stop was opposite the station, where Emma saw three men emerge from the gloom into the light of the lantern swinging from the side of the cart. One had great bulk, another was of medium size, and the third had the figure of a boy with a wizened face above it.

They didn't attempt to get on the back of the cart but the middle-sized man spoke to Pete, saying, "Set are we?"

"Aye, all set." Then as Pete went to urge the horse on, one of the men catching sight of the hooded figure sitting in the back of the cart leant over the side, saying, "Who's that?"

Without turning round, Pete answered, "The mother."

"In the name of God!"

" 'Tis all right. 'Tis all right, Johnny; she knows what she's doing."

"I hope so. Begod! I hope so."

The cart moved on and Emma could make out the three figures taking up their positions behind it, and as she looked at them she wondered how the big man was going to get through the back window which Pete had said wasn't all that big. The place they were making for was Bucketwell Row as Pete had imagined, and, as he had told them earlier, there was no hope of getting an entry in the front way. Through standing a man a couple of pints of ale he had been able to gather from him that one of the streets in which he regularly played the mouth-organ was Bucketwell Row and that number eight was a kind of special house. No customers during the day; the madam went out sometimes accompanied by a couple or so of young lasses, supposedly her grandchildren. Her sons were hefty fellows; one had a barrow in the market, for cover as much as anything, he thought. 'Twas at night time the custom started there, and not just ordinary customers, the man had said, toffs most of them, he thought. There had been raids on some of the houses round there by the polis but to his knowledge number eight hadn't been touched. Perhaps after all, he said, it was still a family house for these houses had at one time all been family houses, the homes of the moneyed merchants. He remembered one being occupied by the family of a cheesemonger; and he had a bacon factory an' all. And the clog-maker from number six had only moved out within the last ten years. And in number three there had lived the owner of the paper mill in Scotswood. The Row had been quite fashionable at one time. It was still fashionable—the man had laughed—but not in the same way.

Pete had seen that the top windows were barred; likely the windows of a one-time nursery now put to good stead, he had said. And he had almost given up the idea of gaining an entry when he had taken a walk through the fields at the back which bordered the courtyards. It had been one chance in a thousand that as he was passing the back door of number eight it had opened and a middle-aged woman swept the dirt from the yard outside into the field. He had hurried up to her, saying, "Could you give me a drink of water, missis, I'm as dry as a fish?" She had looked him up and down in his sailor rig-out before saying, "You lost your way?"

"No"—he smiled at her—"but I see so much sea water that I like to walk on a bit of grass now and again."

She had stepped back into the yard and looked about her, first one way and then the other, then said, "I'll give you a drink but stay where you are." And when she disappeared, he stood on the step and peered into the yard and almost opposite to him he saw what looked like a kitchen window. It was a sash window and could be easily opened with a knife, that is if it wasn't nailed. But then it wasn't likely to be nailed because further along the yard he saw a similar one and this was open a few inches both at the top and bottom. Yet, as he had said, they had to be prepared, there could be blocks at both top and bottom to stop them being opened any further. If that was the case, then the only way to get a door open was to create a commotion outside and he hoped they hadn't to do that, there would be plenty time for that once they were inside.

The woman had returned with a tin mug full of water and she stood with the door in her hand shielding the yard from him; and when, having drained the mug, he handed it back to her and, smiling, said, "Thanks missis, that was as good as a draught of beer," she said nothing but went so quickly to close the door that he almost tumbled back on the grass. It was, Pete said, as if she was regretting her hospitality and was afeared of what she had done.

One thing, he noticed, was that there must be comings and goings from that back door for there were two paths worn in the grass. One led across the field, the other round the corner to the front of the house. This he imagined had once been a right of way until the stile had been removed and railings put in its place.

The horse was struggling to pull the cart up the cobbled street, and the three men had to put their hands to the back of the tail-board and push. At the top of the incline Pete had to drive the horse on to the mud pavement to give way to a coach and pair. The driver yelled at him and he yelled back like any Newcastle drayman would, an oath punctuating each word.

A short while later Emma knew now by the smoothness of the cart that they were in a field and her heart began to beat so hard against her ribs that she had to press her hand tight against her breasts.

When the cart stopped with a jerk they all dismounted, except Henry, and she heard Pete say softly to him, "Take it over by the hedge, you'll be nearer the road that way. But whatever happens, stay by it. Do you hear me, Parson? Don't come into anything, please."

She did not hear Henry's answer because of the scrambling in the cart and knew they were gathering up the lengths of rope they had cut earlier in the evening.

The cart had moved away and they were in darkness now. There was no moon as yet and the wind had come up. It attempted to take her hood back from her head, and as she put her hand up to keep it in place Pete took hold of her other arm, whispering urgently now, "You stay by Da, remember? And if there's any big shindy, get back to the cart and tell him to drive away."

She made no answer. They were now close against a wall. She heard a slight scuffling and she knew that the small man called Ratty was scaling it.

It seemed that the next minute she was being pulled through a doorway and she knew by the feel of the hand she was beside the mister; then she was encircled by the men, all standing perfectly still. In a lull of wind she heard a slight grating noise. Following this, there came a thump between her shoulder blades. It was the signal that the window was open and they were going in. For a moment she was almost paralysed with fear, and her other emotions were so mixed that it was impossible for her to tell herself what she felt about the coming encounter . . . if there was to be an encounter.

Then she and the others became absolutely rigid as a muffled cry came to them. As if of one body they stood huddled round the window waiting for what to her seemed like an eternity; then the small man's voice which seemed much larger than himself came hoarsely to her ears, saying, " 'Twas an oldish wife, I fixed her."

The next minute Emma was being dragged shoulders first into a dark passage and when she was on her feet she was pressed slowly forward towards where in the distance was a faint light coming through an open door.

When she entered the kitchen of the house the lamplight seemed so bright that she had to blink her eyes tightly against it. They were all in the kitchen now, the five men and herself. Beyond the table was the bound and gagged figure of a middle-aged woman, her eyes staring out of her head in abject fear. Then she herself knew an added fear as she saw the man called Johnny draw a knife from under his coat, and the tall fair man bring from a pocket of his jacket a short piece of wood that looked like a stick with a nob on the end. Then they all became rigid again as the kitchen door opened and a young woman said, "Meg," before her mouth went into a scream that was choked before it reached its height. Pete, who had been nearest the door, had sprung at her. His hand round her mouth he dragged her inside and within a split second he had pulled a rag from his pocket and rammed it into her mouth; then as if she had been a bale of hay he whipped her off her feet and threw her face down on to the floor. And Johnny Robson, jumping forward and acting as if the rope in his hands was greased, had the girl's legs and arms trussed up almost as quick as it had taken Pete to gag her.

One thing penetrated Emma's whirling mind: it was that the girl's stifled scream had not brought any one to her assistance, and so screams or squeals perhaps were a natural sound in this house. But within a minute her thought was disproved.

Two abreast, the men had moved through the kitchen into the hall, followed by Jake Yorkless and she herself close on his heels. She had only time to take in that the hall was a large one with broad stairs going up from its middle, for coming rapidly down the stairs was one man while another was emerging from a room at the far side of the hall.

A confusion of muffled blows and yells followed. She was rammed against the wall near the kitchen door, her way blocked by the Swede and Pete and the man seemingly bigger than the Swede throwing his fists left and right; further in the room the other two sailors were fighting with the second man. As she eased herself along the wall to get away from the flailing arms, she saw a woman standing at the far side of the room. Two girls were near her, one with her mouth wide open. Perhaps she had screamed but the noise in the room had drowned it. As she now rushed towards the stairs she saw the woman turn towards the girl and strike her across the face with such force that the girl fell on her back.

She was half-way up the stairs when she was almost pulled down again by a fierce tug on her skirt, and as she gripped the bannister and swung round there was the woman below her, her fist raised again. Emma took in that she was elderly, well into her fifties, and what she did now was instinctive, for she lifted her foot and kicked the woman in the stomach and she herself almost let out a cry as she saw the figure tumbling back down the stairs.

She was on the landing now: Or was it the gallery? For there were railings round it and before her was a square area with doors leading off.

Two pedestals stood close to the wall, a lamp on each, and the light from them showed up the thick red carpet covering the floor. There had been no carpet on the hall floor, only some form of linoleum. There were pictures on the walls here too. For one frantic second she stood in the middle of the landing looking at the array of doors. The sound of the fighting downstairs had become dim, just a series of gasps and groans. She swung round twice as if she were in a game and had to choose a door; then springing forward, she turned the handle of the door nearest her. But it didn't move and as she listened for a moment she thought she detected a moan or a whimper.

The next door she tried wasn't locked and before thrusting open the door she paused for a second, her body so taut that she wouldn't have been surprised if she had screamed herself. But the room was empty. There was a lamp, though, burning near a bed and her mouth fell into a slight gape at the luxuriousness it showed.

Hearing from across the landing voices like those of children at play, she turned swiftly around. The door to this room wasn't locked, but she did not thrust it open; quietly she eased it forward and what she saw brought every feature in her face stretching as if away from itself. The man was elderly but the total ages of the three children in bed with him wouldn't have reached thirty.

She closed the door and leaned against the wall for a moment, and as she did so Pete appeared on the landing and slipped across to her and whispered, "Well?"

She made a slight movement with her head, then again he whispered: "Have you tried them all?"

She moved her head and gasped, "Not those two." She pointed, and as she did so she noticed for the first time the stairs leading upwards. Pete too looked towards them. Then, jerking his hand forward, he ran from her and as he mounted the stairs she made her way across the landing to another door, and it was as she went to open it that she heard the giggle. It swung her around and brought her for an instant frozen to the spot; the giggle had come from beyond the door opposite and it was a well-remembered sound.

She didn't seem to hurry as she made her way towards the door and her mind was telling her that if it was locked she must run to those stairs and scream for Pete. She put her hand on the handle, but she did not ease the door quietly forward because open or locked she meant to get into this room, so she thrust at it and it sprang open, and there before her stood her daughter.

Annie had been halted in her running, but her running had definitely not been in fear for her face was alight with laughter, as was the man's. They were standing a yard apart now, staring at her as if she were an apparition, and as she stared back at the two stark-naked figures, that of her daughter, different yet still her daughter, and of a man of whom the recognition burst something in her mind, she knew that if she had been carrying a knife she would in this instance have thrown it with her father's aim into his fat white body.

"Ma!" The word held amazement.

As Emma tore off her cloak and rushed at her daughter, the man also rushed towards the bed and, taking up a silken cover, pulled it around himself; and then he stood glaring at her, the hate in his eyes almost matching that in her own.

But now she was struggling with her daughter, trying to keep the cloak round her until, rage overcoming all her other momentary feelings, she grabbed Annie by the hair and dragged her out of the door on to the landing. But when she saw Pete come running down the far stairs, she pulled the door quickly closed behind her. If Pete saw who was in there, there would be real murder and he would hang. Oh yes, he would hang.

She thrust the struggling figure of her daughter towards him, saying, "Carry her." And after one glance at the naked shoulders and arms pushing out from the cloak, Pete grabbed up the slight body and made for the lower stairs.

Stumbling after him, Emma looked down into the hall. The woman was lying where she had fallen at the foot of the stairs, her skirts well above her knees and one leg twisted underneath her. But she was conscious, and her face didn't look that of a woman but of a devil. The two girls were crouched in a corner and on the floor lay three men, one appearing to be motionless; the big man was half propped up against the wall, his hands tied behind him. His legs likewise were tied, and there was blood streaming down the side of his face. She remembered that when he had entered the hall he had been dressed in only his shirt and trousers. Now his shirt was in ribbons hanging down over his belt and there was a trickle of blood oozing out from a spot near his ribs. The third man on the floor was the mister. He lay on his side, his hand to his head, and his hair and his hand were covered with blood. The three sailors all looked the worse for wear, but Pete called to Carl, saying, "Here, take this one. Put her in the cart. I'll be with you in a minute." And to Johnny Robson and the small man, he said, "Give me da a hand; I'll be there in a minute." Then going across to the woman lying at the foot of the stairs, he bent over her and said, "You filthy old bitch, you! Now listen here. If those lasses on the top floor aren't set free, them that wants to, and the bairns sent back to where they came from by the morrow night, I'll have every bloody decent-minded man off that Newcastle waterfront up here and if nothin' else we'll burn you out, even if we've got to swing for it. Do you hear? And you needn't bring your friends the polis in, back-handers'll be no good in this case." He thrust his foot against her shoulder, and as she spun round on the linoleum she groaned aloud. When he went to repeat the process, Emma pulled at his arm, saying, "Pete. Pete, come on. Come on."

They did not go out the way they had entered because now the heavily barred front door was open, and so they walked through it and into the darkness.

The street was still, there wasn't a movement in it; if the rumpus had been heard the other residents were minding their own business, likely thinking it was the police who were doing some investigating because they wouldn't all be blinkered or bribed.

The cart was standing in the rough road bordering the field. The mister was lying flat in the back of it and in the light of the cart lantern Emma saw that Annie was still struggling in the Swede's arms, but Pete, taking in the situation, dragged her from him and standing her on her bare feet in the road shook her by the shoulders as he hissed down into her face, "Stop it! you little bitch you. Stop it, or you'll get my hand across yer lug."

She became quiet; and he hoisted her up into the back of the cart; then, turning to Emma, he said, "Get yersel' up, lass."

Emma eased herself over the tail-board and next to her daughter, and she closed her eyes tightly as if through a stab of pain as the girl shifted her body away from her and pressed it against the side of the cart. Dimly she heard Pete saying to his mates, "See you in the mornin' then, at the Bell, round twelve. And ta . . . thanks." There were muttered words and then the cart rocked as Pete pulled himself up into the seat beside Henry, and they were moving once more.

Emma leant her head against the side of the cart which rocked from side to side with the motion, and her thoughts rocked with it. What now? How was she going to keep her? How was she going to control her? This wild thing who hadn't wanted to be saved from a life of degradation and iniquity. Never until the day she died would she forget the look of joy on her daughter's face as she had first opened the door of that room and seen her with that man. Dear God, that man! Only she and Annie knew his identity. If she once let that slip the world would explode. Yet, oh how she wanted to bring him to justice, to see him standing in a court of law exposed for what he was. She had said a court of justice, but there was no justice, there was nothing, nothing in this life but pain, work and frustration . . . and beastliness.

They were now passing through one of the main lamplit streets of the city and she turned her head in amazement and looked at her daughter who, from being crouched in the corner of the cart, was now sitting upright, her head strained over the side, presumably taking in the shops and houses shown up in the lamplight. The action which in itself was simple seemed to set the seal on the creature her daughter had become. No . . . not had become, had always been.

6

They were all in the sitting-room. Pete and Emma were standing but Jake Yorkless was slumped in a chair. His head was bandaged, and every now and again he leaned it to one side and placed his hand over his ear as if to ease the pain. But no one of them was looking towards the bed where Barney lay, his head turned to the side, his eyes fixed on his daughter who was dressed in last summer's frock, and the change in her was shown, if by nothing else, by the fact that the hem of her dress barely reached the bottom of her calves and that her breasts were straining the buttons at the front. But for the men gazing at her, the change was more apparent in her voice and brazen attitude, for now she was yelling at them, "I'll not stay. You can't make me. I hate it here. I always hated it here. It stinks. Mud, animals, smells and . . . and it's on you all." She now jumped back towards the fireplace wall as Jake Yorkless made to spring from his chair only to be held back by Pete, saying, "Steady. Steady. Watch your head," and he pressed his father back into the chair for he was already holding his head in both hands now as he muttered, "She's gone demented."

"No, she hasn't gone demented, she knows what she's saying."

They all looked towards Emma now where she stood supporting herself against the back of the horsehair chair, and she went on, still quietly, "You've got to face up to it, all of you, there's no difference in her now from what there was before she left. It was there then, but you closed your eyes to it, all of you." Her moving gaze settled on Jake Yorkless, and he held it for a moment before drooping his head and muttering, "God Almighty! That this should come upon us. The village will be alight by noon."

"It needn't be." Emma's voice was quiet. "It can be said she's come back on her own, she just walked in late last night. She's been no further than Howdon staying with some folks, friends of yours." She nodded again towards Jake Yorkless. "I've told her what to expect if she says otherwise." She turned and stared at her daughter, and Annie returned her look defiantly, as she had done half an hour ago when Emma had said to her, "Open your mouth as to who was your companion and your granda or uncle will swing. You understand that, don't you?" And Annie's answer had almost driven her to lift her hand and fell her daughter to the ground, for she had said, "I like him. He's nice. He buys me nice things, scent and that."

They had been standing in the room that had once been used by Barney and Luke. It was situated above the sitting-room and she'd had to clamp her hand tightly over her jaw to stop herself screaming, but she hissed, "Shut up, you dirty little trollop you!" And the helplessness of the situation almost overcame her as Annie retorted fearlessly, "I'll not shut up. And you can't keep me locked up forever. He'll come for me; you'll see."

Then overwhelming rage overriding all her other emotions, she had sprung forward and gripped her daughter by the shoulders and had shaken her till her head wobbled. And when she ceased, the girl had leant against her for a moment gasping and she thrust her from her, but had then leaned towards her, saying, "You've got to promise me one thing, just one thing, and I won't lock you in. Don't mention his name downstairs. If they ask you for names, or who took you there, say you didn't know them by name. Just that, you didn't know them by name." And she stopped herself from adding, "Only by the sight of their nakedness." Then she had stood looking down at the girl, her fair hair tousled like that of a child about her face, her blue eyes wide, her red lips in a wet pout. Like this, she still appeared the child, and no doubt she acted the child, but beyond that face there was a woman, a ravenous woman that had come into being a long time ago.

As she lay wide-eyed in bed waiting for the dawn, she had tried to find excuses for this girl who was part of her, because she herself knew only too well what suffering the frustrated urge of the body could bring to a woman. At times you longed for your body to be separated from your mind, yet she knew it was in the mind that the longing started. Pictures of love conjured up by the mind seeped like a poison into the bowels and there brewed the torment. Oh, she knew all about the longings of the body. But they hadn't attacked her until she had become a woman.

But when did one become a woman? This was the question she had asked as she stared into the blackness of the night, and when the answer had come to her, from birth, when you first suckled the breast, she had tossed her head against the idea, for that smacked too much of the painter's reasoning. Oddly, her mind would always call him the painter when she connected her thinking with him.

At one point during the night she had argued with herself. Who was she to condemn, what about the parson? . . . Dear, dear Henry. This disparity in their ages now seemed little; yet hadn't she loved him from the first time she set eyes on him, when she was seven and he twenty-four years old? What about that then? Oh that was different, different, the parson was a man of God. . . .

The parson was a man. And wasn't she reminded of the fact every time their eyes met, so much so that they didn't even dare touch hands.

At first light she rose and went in to her daughter, and after their encounter she then brought her down to face her father and the others, for what had to be said amongst them had to be done before Jimmy and Mary put in an appearance.

During the whole proceedings, Barney did not open his lips, his head lay sideways on the pillow; like the rest of his body, it too could have been dead. His eyes were unblinking as he stared at his daughter, and she had hardly looked at him since coming into the room. And her words upstairs concerning him were still ringing in Emma's ears, for she had said, "I don't like me da. I never did, 'cos he's sickly." If there was anything more needed to confirm that this girl was so alien as to make her think that she hadn't been born of her own flesh, it was this utter lack of compassion. As she stared at her daughter now she wondered what she was going to do with her, what life was going to be like in this house from now on. She would have to watch her every move.

When Barney's head moved on the pillow and lay straight, his eyes staring upwards towards the low ceiling, Emma went to her daughter and, taking her arm, she pulled her out of the room, across the hall and into the kitchen, and there she said, "You'll help Mary in the house. You're not to put a foot outside this door today, do you hear? Leave me to do the talking. And—" She leaned forward to look hard into Annie's eyes and, her voice low and grim, she said, "And if I find you making up to Jimmy, I'll take you up into that attic and I'll whip the hide off you meself. Do you hear?"

But if only Jimmy would take her and marry her. That would be a life-saver. But Jimmy was no fool, he had resisted her for years and now he wouldn't likely touch her with a barge-pole. As wouldn't any other lad in the village. They might take advantage of her nature. Oh yes, they would do that all right, and she'd be only too willing to let them. But marriage, no, because most of them had mothers, and as mothers they weren't fools, they would put two and two together as to where Annie Yorkless had been over the past year; and her return would certainly be linked up with her grandfather's bandaged head and Pete's black eye and busted lip. No; people weren't fools.

She was turning away from her daughter when Annie let out a long yawn and to Emma's amazement she saw the girl stretch her arms well above her head. It was as if she had just awoken from a long and un-troubled sleep; it was a natural action, but under the circumstances it caused Emma to turn away and walk into the kitchen, her shoulders stooped, her whole attitude one of hopelessness.

As she entered the yard Jimmy came through the gap in the wall, and he touched his forelock, saying as he did so, "Morning, missis."

"Good-morning, Jimmy."

"Gona be another fine day."

"Yes, yes, I should think so."

He came abreast of her now, saying, "Riders out early this morning. Must have been up afore their clothes is on." He laughed.

"The hunt?" There was a slight note of surprise in her voice.

"Well, no not at this hour, but lady from the House is out and about. Saw her jumpin' stile further back and she's makin' for this way. She'll be along in a minute, should say. I've seen her out ridin' in the mornin's afore but not as early as this. She must like gettin' up better'n I do." He grinned at her, then went on towards the tack room.

She was about to turn and go into the byres when she saw a horse and rider filling the gap. She stopped in her stride, turned her head and stared towards them, and when the rider's hand was lifted in a beckon-ing motion she made no move towards it. If Jimmy hadn't told her who it was she would have recognized her, and she knew why she was here. It wasn't until she saw her dismount with the intention of leading the horse into the yard that she herself moved.

Emma came to a stop about a yard from Kathleen Fordyke. Neither of them spoke for a moment; then Kathleen Fordyke said, "May I have a word with you, Mrs Yorkless?"

Emma gave her no answer but continued to stare at her until she saw the woman bow her head and mutter in a broken voice, "It is terrible that I should be called upon to do this." Then after a moment, lifting her head, she added, "Will you walk with me a little way along the lane?"

Emma glanced back into the yard. It would be better to comply than to stand here because if Pete or the mister saw who the early morning visitor was they might start asking questions.

For answer Emma now walked out through the gap and Kathleen Fordyke, picking up the skirt of her riding-habit in one hand, took the horse's bridle in the other and slowly now began to walk down the lane. Neither of them spoke until, after some distance, they rounded the bend when Kathleen Fordyke drew the horse to a stop in the shadow of a clump of trees. And now facing Emma, she said, "I . . . I don't know how to begin. I only want you to know that I'm not doing this for my husband's sake."

The question, "Then whose?" was on Emma's lips but she didn't voice it, she only stared at the woman in front of her for whom she had held kind memories over the years.

"I . . . I am here to plead for your silence, Mrs Yorkless, as I said, not for my husband's sake, but for my sons'. They have both grown up into fine men with excellent careers, and . . . and this has been a source of comfort to me, seeing—" now she swallowed deeply in her throat before she ended, "who their father is. Fortunately, they have developed traits of my own father whom you will remember was a fine old gentleman. Well—" She now began to pick nervously at the fabric of her riding-habit, an action similar to that of plucking a chicken, and for a moment Emma felt pity well up in her for this woman and she could have stopped her talking at this point by saying, "Don't worry, I don't want this made public no more than you do, because I have a care for my brother-in-law and even . . . however little the regard I have for my father-in-law, I would not wish to see him suffer through what he might do to your husband"; but she remained quiet, listening to the refined voice saying, "My eldest son is to be married next month. His future wife is of high standing, her . . . her mother is a lady-in-waiting to the Queen. They are a truly religious family, and should any . . . of . . . of this matter be voiced abroad, then I'm afraid there would be no marriage, and . . . and John is in the army, his career would be affected too. My other son Peter is also engaged to be married. They have both taken time in choosing wives and Peter's choice is . . . is"—again she swallowed—"is similar to that of his brother. It is because of them that I am here, and . . . and not because of how the scandal would affect my husband for—" Her head came up and her chin wobbled slightly and her words seemed to tumble out now as she said, "He . . . he deserves horsewhipping, and . . . and not only now. Your daughter is not the first. Oh no, no." Her head now moved from side to side. "You are a married woman and I can say this to you as one to another, he and I have never lived together in that way since my second son was conceived. It was then I discovered his predilection. I was for returning to my father at that time, but he, my husband, swore it was but a slip and that there was nothing other than a fondness that he felt for . . . little girls. He hoped our second child would be a daughter. I thank God he wasn't. Later, again I was about to leave him but on the advice of my father I stayed, for as he said a reason must be given for our separation and would I be able to stand up to the exposure of my husband's weakness? I knew I wouldn't. The disgrace would have been too humiliating. And my husband at one time said—" She turned her head away now and, taking her hand from the rein, she drew it down the horse's neck as she added, "It was a sort of compulsion he couldn't conquer and that the only happiness he had in life was when he was with the young, and . . . and that he meant them no real harm."

"*No real harm.*" Emma's voice disturbed some birds in the trees behind them and as they fluttered noisily away she put her hand over her mouth. It was the first time she had spoken and she had yelled. But wouldn't it make God in heaven yell, this woman, this lady, to say that such men as her husband meant no real harm to young girls and little children? She felt sick.

"Oh, Mrs Yorkless, I can understand how you feel, I can. Believe me I can, but I beg of you not to take this matter up, not to expose him. He . . . he has promised it will never happen again, because although he is what he is, he is very fond of his sons and would not willingly hurt them, especially their careers."

Emma closed her eyes for a moment: Dear God! He would not willingly hurt his sons, especially their careers. . . . They thought differently, the gentry, they didn't think about their lives, they thought about careers.

"He has said he will return the land to you and . . . and even make it freehold. . . ."

She only just stopped herself from yelling again, but her voice now came from deep within her as she said scathingly, "You can tell him I want none of his hush money through the land. He took it from us out of spite, well, he can't buy me with it now. I want none of it."

There was silence between them for a moment; then Emma watched the head in front of her bow low and when the muttered words came to her: "I feel humiliated to the soul of me," she had the instinctive urge to put out her hand and touch the woman and say, "It's all right. You needn't worry," because it wasn't good to see a woman of this standing brought low. And what she must have felt when that white slug of a man crawled to her in the night as he must have done, begging her to be the means of shielding him from exposure.

It was of no comfort for her to realize that the rich could also suffer the torments of the damned, even more so than ordinary folk for they stood to lose more, position, respect, the being brought down from high places, from pinnacles. The poor had no pinnacles to cling to, so really their suffering was more of the body than the mind. But here was she herself, and she wasn't of the gentry and her suffering was all of the mind.

As she couldn't stand to witness any more of this woman's pain she said, her voice still stiff, "You need have no worry. Up till now, anyway, I've told no one and I've warned my daughter what will happen to her grandfather and her uncle should she mention your . . . husband's name, because then I wouldn't be responsible for what would follow, especially from her uncle. But you can tell him this from me, that my silence only holds as long as he makes no move towards her, nor pays one of his cronies to do so."

"Thank you. Thank you, Mrs Yorkless. And . . . and I can promise you there will be no repetition. . . ."

"How can you, if he's got an obsession like that?"

Emma watched the head droop again and the voice was merely a mutter now as the woman said, "You're right; but . . . but I swear to you he will not come near your daughter again." The head lifted now. "May I add this: if ever you or yours are in need of help which I could provide, you have only to approach me. It is strange"—a sad smile now touched the lips—"you know, if my father had lived you yourself might have been in a different position altogether. He talked of you often. He recognized your intelligence and felt that something should be done for you and was intending to do it after your second visit, but then . . . well"—her shoulders moved slightly—"God's ways are strange."

Emma could not stop the words spurting out: "And man's more so."

"Yes, yes I agree with you, man's more so."

They stared at each other; then Kathleen Fordyke said again, "I'll be forever in your debt, Mrs Yorkless. Now I will go. Good-bye, and thank you." At this she led the horse slightly forward, then looked about her for a place from which she could mount, a tree stump, or a gate, and after a moment's hesitation Emma stepped forward and, joining her hands together, she bent her body, indicating that she would act as a hoist. But Kathleen Fordyke shook her head, saying, "No, no, Mrs Yorkless. Thank you." As Emma straightened her back and her hands dropped to her sides, they again stared at each other and as equals for in a strange way Emma knew that the woman in refusing to use her as a hoist had lifted her momentarily up to her own level, and on this plane there rose in her for this woman a feeling of respect that outweighed all other emotions at the moment.

She stood now watching the rider and horse walking up the lane. Then she turned and walked slowly back into the farmyard.

Pete was at the far end, about to go into the barn, and as she herself went towards the kitchen door it opened and the mister came out, saying, "Pete's yelling for you." And then he added, "Me head's burstin', and what for, I ask you?" He glared back into the kitchen and Emma said, "Wait, and I'll bathe it for you."

"It's been bathed; it's no good; it feels as if the fellow's boot went inside it. I'll have to see the doctor."

She stayed a moment watching him go across the yard, his shoulder hugged up to his ear. Last night the big man had kicked him in the head as he lay on the floor and she had been told that the man would have repeated the action if the little fellow hadn't jumped on his back and knifed him.

Last night was like a bad dream, a mixed-up nightmare. Had she really seen men battling with each other? And had she ever lifted her foot and kicked an old woman in the stomach? And her eyes ever witnessed what they had when she opened those doors?

But it was no nightmare, as the figure sitting to the side of the fire-place reminded her. Her daughter wasn't sitting like an unruly child hugging her knees, but rather like a woman, her left hand under her right oxter and her right hand gripping her left arm; and like this she was rocking herself backwards and forwards.

"Set the breakfast."

When Annie didn't turn her gaze from the fire Emma barked at her, "Did you hear me?"

The girl now getting to her feet said, "Aye, I heard you, but I'm not gona do any work. I'm not used to it anyway. And I hate this place. It . . . it. . . ."

"Yes, I know how it smells," Emma interrupted her; "it smells of the earth, and that's a clean smell, and you're goin' to help keep it clean, because now you're goin' to set that table and then you're goin' to get a bucket in your hand and scrub out the hall and then this kitchen."

"I'll not."

"Oh well, we'll see if you won't. Take your choice, it's either that or locked in your room with bread and scrape. And you'll have plenty of time to do nothing up there, for I'll take the mattress away and your clothes. But you won't mind that, will you? And anything else that might give you comfort. Now I'm going in to your father and when I return I'll know if you've made your mind up or not."

With this, she turned abruptly and went out of the kitchen and into the hall, and from there she heard Barney shouting, "Emma! Emma!" As she opened the door he had his mouth open ready to yell again, and now he demanded, "Where've you been?"

"Outside; there's things to see to."

"Aye. Aye." His head stopped moving restlessly on the pillow as he said quietly now, "It's come to a pretty pass, by God it has. I've had the worst night since this happened." He now lowered his lids and looked down the length of his inert body. "I couldn't sleep, and of all things I kept thinking about love." He glanced at her. "It became strange, for in the darkness I imagined I could see it. It was a funny experience. It looked wider than the world; it had so many strings to it and all tangled up with other strings, like hate. Love's near hate, you know, Emma." He slanted his eyes again towards her. "I loved me ma at times, but at others I hated her. And me da an' all. Aye, I loved him once. And then there was our Luke. That was a different kind of love, but strong, it was like loving meself. Natural, I suppose, with the same blood running in our veins. Yet here I am, hating him with a feeling stronger than any love I ever had for him. The parson says it's no use hanging on to retaliation, it only wears you out. Well, our Luke left me nothing to wear out but me mind and as long as that works I'll hate him. Then there was you, Emma." Again his eyes were turned towards her, and he now kept them fixed on her as he said, "I think I loved you from the minute I first saw you, but there came a time when I hated you. Aye, I did when wantin' you and couldn't have you and you burnt me up so much that you came between me and me wits. Pictures of you blotted out everything I was handling, whether it was milking, mucking out, herding the sheep, or ploughing. As the earth used to spurn the blade as I went up the furrow and showed itself naked, so I would see you, an' because I couldn't ease meself on anybody else, with you in me mind, I began for a time to hate you. You never knew that, did you?"

She did not even shake her head, but stood staring at him, thinking, He's talking just like the parson, taking things to bits and looking inside them.

When he looked away from her and up at the ceiling he said quietly, "And there's the love you feel when your child is born and you hear its first cry. That's somethin' different altogether, as is the hate you have for her knowin' she's gone wrong. Why?" His head jerked upwards, his eyes glaring at her. "Knowing she comes from us two ordinary living folk, I say again to you, *why?*"

As she saw the tears spurting from his eyes she could bear no more, she swung around and rushed from the room.

7

Henry wrote in his book:

It has been a beautiful day; the sun has been very hot, too hot. What a pity we have no power to moderate the weather. Last week it rained incessantly for days; added to which the wind blew and a lot of the crops looked devastated. This week the sun has shone, but again the weather has shown no happy medium. It's like a capricious child, all sunshine or tears. Which brings my mind to Emma and Annie. I say brings, but is my mind ever free from the former? She is looking so care-worn, she has no flesh on her. And that child . . . no, she is a child no longer, not even a girl. Yet she is not a woman. God help her, for she is the essence of all mythology: she is Venus and she is a Gorgon, for the child is ugly inside. When I spoke to her, she answered me like a woman of the streets. What's to be done? What is Emma to do with her?

Emma is quiet now; she has very little to say to me. She has told no one what she witnessed upstairs in that house, except, as Pete said, to say that the girl was with a man.

There is so much unhappiness around me, and in me too. The bishop detected it yesterday. "Are you well?" he said. "Yes, my lord," I answered. Then he said, "You seem troubled. Is there anything you wish to tell me about your parish?"

"No, my lord," I answered. "Very little happens in the village"— and that was a lie—"things go on as they always have done." And to this he replied, "Then it's a happy situation." Oh, if only I could have given the answer, "It is not a happy situation, my lord, neither physically, mentally, nor spiritually, and since my spiritual welfare concerns yourself, I must tell you that I no longer feel a man of God. . . ."

Yet that would not have been right: it isn't that I no longer feel a man of God, but that I no longer feel able to accept all the doctrine that man has put into the mouth of God, or, coming nearer to earth, into the mouth of Jesus. His enemies crucified Him, but his friends split Him up into so many denominations that religion has become like a parliament, one party fighting for power against another.

He dipped his pen in the inkwell again and was placing it on the paper when his hand flew half-way across the page, ending in a scratch and a blot, and he swung round in his chair to see Miss Wilkinson standing in the middle of the room. Still turned towards her, he put out his right hand and closed the book as he said, "I thought you had gone some time ago?"

"Well, I was doing the church for the morrow with the flowers'n things. Mrs Wilson's hurt her hand and you can never rely on Lily Mason, and I was short of a vase. I . . . I came in to see if I could get you a drink?"

"No, thank you. I've already had my evening meal, you know."

"Yes, I know; but that's a long time ago and I just thought you might be thankful for a drink."

"No, thank you, Miss Wilkinson. It's very kind of you, but I'll have nothing more tonight."

She didn't move, but said now, "I've mended that rent in your coat. I don't know how you managed to do that."

"I told you, I caught it on a thorn bush."

"Yes, yes, you told me."

Still she didn't move. And so, turning to the desk again, he took up the book, placed it in the drawer and locked it, then as usual put the key in the inside pocket of his coat, and as he turned back to her she said, "You know what they're saying in the village, an' round about, about the latest?"

"What is the latest, Miss Wilkinson?"

"Well, you know as well as I do, about Annie Yorkless being back, don't you?"

"Oh, that." He jerked his chin upwards and closed his eyes for a moment, saying, "Yes, yes, everybody knows that Annie's back."

" 'Tis a funny business that, don't you think?"

"That she's back? She likely got homesick."

"That's all in me eye an' Granny Martin."

For a moment he felt inclined to laugh. Anyone else could have repeated that saying, but coming from the prim Miss Wilkinson, it wasn't in keeping. However he managed to keep his face straight as she went on, "Homesick? Well, I wonder if it was her that gave her Uncle Pete his black eye and split lip, or knocked farmer Yorkless half daft, as Mary Petty says, for he's gone around holding his head for days. And it all happened on the night she was supposed to return home. People are not stupid, you know, Parson, nor blind, and things link up. The latest comes from young Simon Tate. He was out rabbiting the very next morning and what does he see? The lady of the manor, Mrs Fordyke herself, and Emma Yorkless in deep conversation. And not at the farm, but along the lane, hidden like, and this just turned six in the morning. I bet you didn't know that."

She now nodded at him, and when he remained silent she went on, "'Tis the opinion of many in the village that young Annie Yorkless has been in service of some kind through the influence of Mrs Fordyke, that Emma, wanting to push her daughter on, took advantage of the times that she was invited up there by the old man to do her circus tricks and got the girl set on with some of her ladyship's friends."

"Don't be silly, woman. Have you forgotten that Annie went missing."

"She was supposed to." Miss Wilkinson's voice was stiff and her hands joined at the band of her black serge skirt showed the knuckles to be white where the bones were pressing against her skin. "It was all a tale."

"Why? In the name of God, why? Have they worked that out?"

"No, but they will." Her head was nodding at him now. "They're not the fools that some people take them to be."

"I'm surprised at that then, Miss Wilkinson, because only a fool would suspect there was any connection between Annie's disappearance, or her return, and the Hall."

"You needn't get yourself in a frazzle, Parson, I was just telling you what's been said, thinkin' you should know 'cos . . . 'cos it's my opinion"—and now she made one deep obeisance with her head—"that you close your eyes and your ears to lots of things that should be stretching them."

"That is enough, Miss Wilkinson."

Her mouth went into a tight line; then as if it were being drawn by a thread, it puckered, causing the lines of her skin to appear like channels running from her nose. Swinging round, she made for the door and from there her voice came back to him. "I don't know why I stay here," she said.

And he answered her, "I don't know either." His words halted her for a second, and then the door banged on her.

Sitting down at the desk again, he leant his elbows on it and covered his face with his hands. He said he didn't know why she stayed, he knew all right, and she had given herself the place she desired, acting like a nagging wife in all quarters of the house except his bedroom.

After rising to his feet he walked to the window. It was open, and, looking out into the darkening night, he drew deeply on the soft warm air. The window was at the front of the house and faced the drive, and now he bent sharply forward as he saw a figure coming down the drive. He knew that step; he knew the height of her; if she had been walking in a battalion of women he would have recognized her. Within seconds he was at the front door holding it open, looking down at her as she mounted the three steps.

"Emma."

"I've been to see Mary, she's . . . she's in a bad way. I couldn't get down until now, with things to do and that . . . and I thought that if you weren't busy, I might . . . I might—"

Her words were low and hesitant and he held out his hand towards her, saying, "Come in. Come in."

When he had closed the door he pointed towards the sitting-room, saying, "It's many years since you were in this house, Emma."

"Yes it is. The last time I came to Sunday school, I think."

They were in the sitting-room now and she looked about her. She considered the farm to be rather comfortless, though the cushions and covers and mats that she had made over the years during the long winter evenings had added a little warmth here and there; but this room was stark, not that the furniture wasn't good, she could see that the chairs and tables were made of either mahogany or oak, but everything in the room appeared heavy, brown and drab. The floor was covered with brown linoleum and even the mat at the fireplace was brown.

"Sit down." He had drawn a chair forward towards the window, and he added, "The light's fading, but I never light the lamp until I must, I like the twilight."

After he was seated opposite to her they became silent while they looked at each other, and then she turned her head from him and gazed out of the window as she said, "I . . . I suppose I shouldn't have bothered you, but when I was in the village, well, it suddenly struck me—" She was looking at him again as she finished rapidly, "I had to speak to someone, talk to someone about it. I promised I wouldn't but I can talk to you and it will never go further. There was no chance up there; anyway, I couldn't talk about it up there."

When she stopped for a moment he said softly, "Something else has happened?"

"No"—she shook her head—"it's already happened, it's filling my head both night and day. I thought if perhaps I told you, it would . . . well . . . Oh I don't know." She put her hand to her throat.

"Does it concern what you saw upstairs in that house?"

"Yes," she nodded at him; "but not only that, it's . . . it's who I saw, the man I saw Annie with and the condition they were in."

"Luke?" His voice was merely a whisper, but she shook her head quickly, saying, "No, no. I could have understood it more if it had been him. No, it wasn't Luke. But he was in on it. Oh yes, I know that, he was in on it. No, it was—" For a moment it appeared that there was a stoppage in her throat and that only by gulping quickly could she get rid of it, and after a moment she released the name from her lips, "Mr Fordyke."

Slowly his body bent towards her, his mouth opened, his eyes narrowed, his mouth closed again before he said softly, "Emma, do you know what you're saying?"

"Yes, I know what I'm saying."

"*Mr Fordyke?*"

"Yes, Mr Fordyke."

"You couldn't have been mis. . . ."

"No, no, I couldn't have been mistaken. He hadn't a stitch on him, but I not only recognized him, he recognized me, and for the moment was frightened out of his life, so much so that he crawled to his wife and she came to me early that following mornin' and begged for my silence. And although I promised her for her sake and that of her sons, who I understand are about to be married, I still want to stand in the village square and scream his name out aloud. Can you understand that?"

He made no answer but he got to his feet and walked away from her to the end of the room, where he stood for a moment before turning towards her again; and as he looked down on her bent head he thought: A few minutes ago I scorned the villagers through Miss Wilkinson, thinking them a lot of ignorant tactless fools, but, as many of them were apt to say, they knew how many beans made five, and in connecting Annie with the Hall, they had been on the right road but had gone off on the wrong track.

Emma raised her head, saying softly, "I had to tell someone."

"And who better than me? But it's lucky Pete didn't know of this, or else the business might have been more serious than it is."

"Yes." She looked towards the window again, saying now, "I miss Pete; he was such a help in all ways. I wish he'd come back to the farm, but I doubt now that'll ever be for he's met a young lady. She's the sister of one of his shipmates; they live in London. He talked quite a bit about her. I think he might be serious, and should he marry he'll dock there and we'll see less of him than now."

"Yes, that's possible." Henry nodded at her; then said, "I talked with him yesterday for a few minutes while he was waiting for the carrier cart. He says it will be a short trip this time, just a few months perhaps, a year at the most. His face is still badly bruised and I asked him if there would be any comment on board. He laughed and said, 'They only comment on you after shore leave if you return with a clean face and your hair still on.' He has a sense of humour, has Pete."

He now took the seat opposite to her again and asked, "How is she?"

"Still defiant, and lazy; she works only because if she doesn't I lock her up. What am I going to do?"

When she held out her hand as if in plea towards him he instinctively grasped it. It was the first time since she had married that he had touched her hand, and the feeling that went through him was as if he had plunged his arm into fire yet without experiencing the agony of burning. Her hand was rough, the palm hard, but from it he was now drawing a feeling that coursed like fire through his body.

He whispered her name softly now, saying, "Emma. Oh Emma." And she remained still, not answering, simply staring through the dimming twilight into his face. Then as if she had been stung she jerked her hand from his and, springing to her feet, she turned her back on him, saying, "I've got to go, it's getting on late."

When he made no response she turned again and saw him standing with his head deeply bent, and she said, "I'm sorry."

"So am I." He was looking at her now and he repeated, "So am I, and for so many things. Yet, no, I take that back, I'm not sorry that you came into my life, nor that you're still in it."

"You should have moved on to another parish," she said quietly.

"Yes, it would have been wise, I suppose, but the price of wisdom in this case would have been too great." He sighed. "I'll walk a little way with you; we'll go out through the back."

As she followed him out of the back door and through the large overgrown garden she was quite aware why he had chosen this way: they could reach the coach road without passing through the village; there was only one cottage on the way, that of old Janet Crosby and she was bedridden most of the time. They could of course meet someone on the road, but it was hardly likely at this time of night; the model citizens in the village went to bed with the dark to save oil; the others, at least the male section of them, would be in The Tuns.

Having reached the coach road, they walked not close but not too far apart. They were like a couple out for an evening stroll and as such he remarked on the weather. "It's a beautiful evening," he said, and she answered, "Yes, it is. And it was a very red sunset, which augurs good for the morrow."

"Yes; yes, indeed."

As they turned from the coach road on to the lane that led to the farm, she wanted to say, "Don't come any further," but such was the longing in her to lengthen these moments alone with him, to walk with him like this, that she made no protest. But half-way along the lane he stopped and, turning to her, said, "I'll come no further, Emma. I . . . I think I'll cut across the fields and have a word with Ralph. I haven't seen him for three or four days."

"I saw him yesterday."

"How did you find him?"

"Not too bad at all. He's . . . he's like a creaking door, I think he'll go on for ever."

He paused, then said, "I would like to think so."

The twilight had almost gone; their faces were veiled with the coming darkness, the slightest move and they could have fallen against each other, and as if he had suddenly become aware of the danger, as she herself had earlier on, he stepped back from her, saying, "Good-night, Emma," and, turning abruptly, hurried away across the field.

Very soon he was lost to her sight and, as she was wont to do when greatly distressed, she clamped her hand across her mouth before she too turned and forced herself to walk towards the farm whereas the urge in her was to throw herself into the grass and to cry her heart out at the hopelessness of her life at this present moment and the fear of what this hopelessness might drive her to in the future.

There was a light in the cottage and Henry, after tapping on the door, went to open it, but finding it locked, which was unusual, he called, "You there, Ralph?"

After a moment the door was opened and Ralph, dressed in a thick rough dressing-gown although the night was so warm, said, "Yes, I'm here; where do you expect me to be? And what's brought you out at this time of night?"

"I was taking a stroll to calm my nerves and I saw your light in the distance. What are you doing up so late?"

"Oh, I can't sleep these nights and I find it's much more comfortable in front of the fire."

As he took his hat off Henry turned round and looked at the door, saying, "You never used to lock it. Have you had an intruder?"

Ralph sat down in his chair, pulled the dressing-gown over his knees, and arranged its lapels over his chest before saying, "Not yet; but it's prevention."

"What do you mean?"

Ralph put his hand into his hair now and scratched his scalp for a minute before saying, "You've been up above these last few days?"

"Yes, the day before yesterday."

"How did you find Lady Annie?"

"Much as I told you in the first place, defiant, if not more so."

"Who's keeping an eye on her?"

"Well, now Pete's gone there's really only Emma, because Farmer Yorkless is in a bad way. That blow to his head is becoming serious; I think there must have been some internal damage done."

"Where are they sleeping her?"

"Annie?"

"Who else?"

"Well, as far as I know in the upper room. And Emma locks her in at night."

Ralph now put his head back and laughed, repeating, "Locks her in at night. By! if ever there was a born madam in this world, she's one. I thought they were made by circumstance, or came to it by the evil touch of man. . . ."

"Look, talk plainly, Ralph. What are you getting at?"

"Only that our dear little Annie manages to escape her prison at night."

"No!"

"Oh yes. There you've got"—he jerked his head now—"the reason for the locked door."

"She's been here?"

"Not exactly; but she certainly had it in mind."

"Explain yourself."

"I will, Parson, I will," Ralph said mockingly. "It was around one o'clock this morning. The old machine here"—he patted his chest—"was working at top speed. I got up to have a drink. I passed the window there"—he pointed—"the moon was shining and at first I thought: Ralph, you've done it at last; you've died, old fellow, and here's one of the angels come to guide you to your heavenly home, because there, coming along the road, was what I took at first to be an apparition. Then, as the saying goes, my eyes nearly popped out of my head when it paused at the gate and I recognized the angel. She had grown certainly, but no one could mistake our Annie, could they? I don't know what she had on her feet, but I do know what she had on her body, and it was simply her nightgown. Of course, the night was warm, but as you yourself know a cold mist can roll up in a second. Still, I don't suppose that would have affected dear Annie, for there she stood at the gate deliberating. Yes, I'm positive of that, she was deliberating whether to come in or not. Fortunately, she moved straight on and I breathed again, because, Parson"—his voice was still mocking—"I cannot give you my word that I would have been able to withstand her charms at that time of. . . ."

"Shut up!" Henry was on his feet.

"Oh, don't sound so shocked. It isn't like you."

"I am not shocked, I am only defending your character against your opinion of yourself."

"It's very kind of you, Henry, it is." Ralph looked at his friend, a half-smile on his face, then said seriously, "In my opinion it's a great pity they ever brought her back. Emma had enough on her hands without this. And I'll tell you something, Henry, while I'm on. I'm worried about that girl, Emma I mean. I fear she's at breaking point. And no wonder. And the visitors are not helping. She was telling me yesterday she's being plagued: she didn't know she had so many well-wishers, she said; people that she's hardly spoken two words to hereabouts dropping in on her just to say how pleased they are that she's got her daughter back, and wanting to meet the daughter."

"She said nothing about this to me."

"Well, you're not her only confidant and she's likely afraid you'll go to your parishioners and tell them to mind their own bloody business or else you'll name them from the pulpit for lack of charity."

His bantering tone changed again and he added, "Have you heard anything further about the house in Newcastle?"

"No; only that when the police went the following day after being notified of what happened, they found the whole house empty; stripped of furniture, too, not a stitch of anything in it."

"Amazing. Yet not so. That madam would likely have a number of such going, and willing hands make labour light, so they say. Anyway, what do you think should be done about the midnight strolls?"

"Emma will have to be told."

"Yes, I thought of that, but how can she prevent her, short of tying her up? You know what I would do if I were her?"

"No."

"I'd let her get out during the daytime and go back to where she's been for the past year, because if anybody was made for it that girl is. And you'll never alter her, not in this life."

If only because of his calling, Henry should have protested loudly at this, but he said no word because he knew that what Ralph had said was absolutely true. Annie, only God knew why, had been made for that kind of thing. Yet he did not want to connect "that kind of thing" with the midnight strolls for he remembered that her mother, his dear, dear Emma had been in the habit of taking midnight strolls.

As if Ralph had just that moment picked up his thoughts, he said, "Funny, but Emma used to take midnight jaunts when a girl, didn't she? Yet it would seem it's the only thing she's passed on to her daughter and our dear Annie is not going to waste the trait if she knows anything about it. I wonder what will happen if she meets up with someone, say one of the poachers, or the moler." He began to laugh now as he ended, "You know, she'd be disappointed, for at the sight of her in that white nightie they'd take to their heels and run, especially if they'd just left The Tuns."

8

Emma had imagined that nothing more her daughter could do would have the power to upset her further; yet the news that Annie had been walking the countryside in the middle of the night in her nightgown raised such anger in her that she felt capable of murder. However, she had warned herself that shouting and yelling, and shaking and slapping, had proved of no avail, she must try other tactics, she must try to reason with the girl.

And that's what she had been doing for the last half-hour or so. Annie was sitting on the edge of the pallet bed in the attic, her ankles crossed, her knees sticking up at an angle so that her calves were exposed making Emma want to interrupt her reasoning and say, "Pull your clothes down, girl. That's how boys sit." And she might have done so except she felt that her daughter would have laughed.

When she had confronted her with the fact that she had been out at night, the girl had answered calmly, "Well, you won't let me out on me own during the day, will you, Ma?" And when she had come back sharply, saying, "I should have thought you would have been used to being locked in by now," Annie had retorted, " 'Twasn't like that at all, I wasn't locked in."

And now Emma had become reduced to pleading: "Annie—" She leant towards the girl saying softly, "Won't you try to be different? Try to act like other young lasses of your own age, just until it's time for you to marry?" Her words were crushed by the thought, who would marry her? Who would take her on? No one from around here, that was certain. But she ended, "You could be married when you're fifteen."

Annie made no response to this and Emma straightened herself and asked now, "What makes you do it? Why?"

The girl lifted her head and for the first time her face looked serious, as her voice sounded when she said, "I don't know, Ma; I've always felt like this. I want . . . well, I want"—she shook her head—"I don't know how to put it."

Emma's own head now moved slowly from side to side and, her gaze directed to the bare wooden floor, she said, "It's bad, Annie, it's bad."

"No, Ma."

"What!" Emma was looking at her daughter now through narrowed eyes. "You don't think it's bad?"

"No, Ma. . . . And Ma—" Annie uncrossed her ankles and, drawing her feet under her, she half knelt up and leant towards Emma, saying in a tone that held a plea and seemed to ask for understanding, "I . . . I liked it there. I did, I did, Ma. Don't look like that, Ma. 'Twas a nice house and 'twas warm; it had nice furniture and lovely curtains and we had lovely things to eat."

"Oh, Annie. Annie." Emma's head dropped on to her breast and Annie said, "We weren't locked in like you think. Well, at least I wasn't, or Alice or Rene, and Mrs Boss took us out. . . ."

"Mrs Boss?"

"Well, she was called the boss an' we called her Mrs Boss. And she did, she took us out on a Saturday. We went to the market, and once"—her face spread into a wide smile—"we went to the Newcastle theatre. Eeh! it was lovely, Ma, beautiful, the ladies on the stage. And we were dressed up to look like ladies an' all."

"Be quiet, Annie! Be quiet!" Emma's face was screwed up tight.

"But Ma, I'm just tryin' to tell you. And Fordy, Mr Fordyke, he was kind. I liked him, Ma."

Emma rose hastily from the broken-backed chair, crying now, "Shut up! Shut up!"

"Ma! Ma!"

The cry halted Emma as she reached the low door of the attic that led into the bedroom and, with her hand on the sneck, she said, "Yes, what is it?"

"Ma"—her daughter was behind her—"don't lock me in, please Ma. I promise I won't go out at night. Honest to God I won't go out at night." Slowly Emma turned round and faced the girl and she repeated, "You promise?"

"Yes, Ma. But will you let me walk round in the daytime on me own?"

Emma swallowed and looked to the side, and Annie said, "I won't go far; I just like to wander the fields."

"Have I your word that you won't run away again?"

"Yes, Ma."

"And you won't go near the village?"

"Oh no, Ma." Annie's voice was louder now. "I won't go down there; they don't like me down there, the women anyway."

Oh Lord, Lord, what was she to do? She had no choice; and so she said to her daughter now, "Come down into the kitchen and do the dishes and clean up; Mary's legs are too bad, she won't be able to make it for days, and I have your granda in bed this mornin'."

"All right, Ma." The voice was full of willingness. "And . . . and I'll dust the rooms if I can go out this afternoon. Can I?"

For answer, Emma nodded her head twice; then bending her back, she went through the door, and Annie followed her.

When they were on the landing Annie ran ahead of her down the stairs, and Emma stood watching her for a moment, the pain in her heart so great that she likened it to a crucifixion. . . .

"This all comes about of foreign blood." Jake Yorkless spoke from the bed in which he was propped up, his hand held seemingly now in a permanent position against the side of his head. "Nowt in my family that would bring out anything like this, nor was there in Lizzie's as far as I know but that foreigner of a circus man."

"He was a Spaniard, and he wasn't a circus man, and as far as I remember he was a good and respected man, and there's nothing in me that I have passed on to Annie. But if I recall what you said on the night of my wedding, that your grandfather tried his son's bride first, then I don't think you've got to look much further for the reason why your granddaughter is as she is. 'Tis known that these traits jump generations. . . ."

"By God! if my head wasn't in this state I'd give you the length of me tongue, if not me hand."

"You'd give me neither, mister, and you know it. I was pretty young when I took your measure. You made a brave show of going rescuin' Annie, but underneath you were like a frightened rabbit. You've always been like a frightened rabbit; if you hadn't been, you would have married me granny and not the tartar you took on although she had her belly full of you. Now, I've seen to your head, and the doctor says that you've got to rest." And on this she turned away and lifted the bowl of water from the washhand-stand, and as she passed the foot of the bed he said, "What's goin' to happen down yonder?"

She paused for a moment, looking over the brass rail as she said, "I don't know. Something will have to go, and it'll have to be the house, for we depend on the animals for our bread and there's no money to hire another hand, at least not that I know of. Do you know of any?" She watched his eyelids flicker before he replied, "How should I?"

"Well, you do the buying and selling."

"You know what I get and you know where it goes."

"I thought I did."

On this she turned and left the room, thinking as she went down the stairs, Yes, I thought I did, but Jimmy had come back from the market yesterday after delivering butter and eggs and milk and he had given her three shillings and sixpence more than the mister was supposed to get for the same amount of produce.

Her next task before she went outside was to go and see to Barney. When she entered the room his voice was querulous as he greeted her, saying "Here it is near the end of the morning and I haven't seen a soul. Where've you been? What's happenin'?"

"I told you, your father's in bed, the doctor says he's got to stay there, and Mary hasn't come, and she's not likely to with the state of her legs, so there's only me and Jimmy." She did not mention Annie's name to him as he hadn't spoken it since the morning he had talked of love that had turned to hate.

"What's to be done?"

She did not answer him in the same vein as she had answered his father but said, "Don't worry; we've weathered storms before, this one will pass."

"Not before they bury you."

"Well, you only have to die once, so they say."

Softly he said, "I get lonely, Emma."

"I know you do." She went closer to him and took his hand, adding, "I wish I could be with you more."

" 'Tisn't fair." His lips trembled slightly. "This place has turned you into a cart-horse, more so, because horses get their rest periods. 'Tis a good job you're healthy, with no aches and pains. They say the wiry ones last the longest."

If there had been a laugh left in her she would have bellowed. Did she ever have any aches and pains? Her body should be inured to aches and pains, yet when she dropped into bed at night there was a protest in every limb; but it was worse in the morning when every fibre of her being resisted rising from the bed. Did she ever have any aches or pains! But what were body pains compared to those of the heart? Oh, for God's sake, don't let her start on that tack at this time of the day, especially with all that lay before her. She was about to say, "I must get going, Barney," when his next words stayed her. "I don't want to see the parson today," he said.

"You don't want to see . . . why? I thought you looked forward more than anything to his readings and your chats and. . . ."

"Well, I just don't want to see him today." His voice had changed, the whole expression of his face had changed, and her voice changed, too, when she retorted, "All right, all right, you don't want to see him, so I'll tell him. I'll say to him, 'Parson, Barney doesn't want to see you. You've travelled this road for years now coming up here in rain, hail and sunshine, when many a time you must have had better things to do, but you just wanted to help somebody out. But now I've got to tell you that that somebody doesn't want to see you. No explanation, just that, he doesn't want to see you.'"

She was really glaring down at him when he came back at her, saying, "Well, what's the good, where's it gona get me, eh? All the readin' of books and discussin', discussin'. Discussin' writers and them what's running the country, not forgetting religion. Where is it gona get me? I'll end up in a box and the sooner the better." She did not now soften and say, "Oh, don't talk like that, Barney," but what she said was, "Yes, if that's how you feel, the sooner the better, for if you're just going to lie there like a stuffed dummy waiting for my flying visits then I agree with you."

She watched him turn his head to the side and mutter something, and when she said, almost demanded, "What was that you said?" he moved his eyes in her direction and, his voice loud now, he cried, "You're gettin' hard. You never used to be like this."

Her voice matched his now as she replied, "I never had a farm to run practically on my own; I never had another sick man upstairs; and I never had a daughter that is a. . . ."

She had almost said the word. What was she coming to, going for Barney like this? She should be able to understand and sympathize with his frustration, but at the moment she was carrying more burdens than her back could or would bear and if something didn't happen to relieve her then she would surely sink under them.

She turned and was at the door when his voice halted her, saying pathetically, "Emma." And now she looked at him and her voice quiet, even soothing, she said, " 'Tis all right, Barney, 'tis all right. I'll be back shortly."

And her burdens seemed immediately to be lightened when, in the kitchen, she saw her daughter scrubbing the table with sand and she was quick to notice there were no dishes in the shallow sink, and when the girl smiled at her, her face so fresh, fair and innocent looking, she wanted to throw her arms about her and hug her tight into her breast for she felt she had been given a sign: her daughter could change, her daughter would change; she would grow up and marry and be like other girls. Please God. Please God.

Jimmy came earlier and stayed later. Emma rose earlier and went to bed later. Annie did not rise before seven but from then until three in the afternoon she worked in the house and without a word of grumbling. But after that time she would go upstairs, wash herself, put on a clean frock, tie a ribbon in her hair, then go out whatever the weather. If it was raining she put on Emma's old cloak, if it was fine she went out as she was and with no covering on her head either of cap, bonnet or hat, which was a daring gesture in itself. But Emma did not reprimand her, for Annie had promised she would walk no farther than Openwood one way, to the coach road the other, and on the path that led to the river she would stop at the old turnpike. Sometimes she would be out for three or four hours. Out of curiosity, mixed with fear, Emma had one day followed her and for part of the time she saw that she sat on a knoll overlooking the coach road but some good distance from it, then she crossed the fields in the other direction and sat on the stile near the old turnpike.

Another time when Emma went out after her, if she hadn't caught a glimpse of the wind blowing Annie's loose fair hair above the grass she might have stepped on her had she walked on; but then she saw her rise from her elbow and place something round her neck, it was a daisy chain. The sight had caused Emma as much pain as if she had found her daughter out in another indiscretion. . . .

And so the summer wore on. Once or twice Emma had experienced the old dread and fear when Annie did not return till dusk; but these times were few and far between.

Jake Yorkless had become worse, and now there was talk of him being taken to hospital. Over the past weeks a lump had emerged behind his ear which the doctor said would need medical attention. Emma had to face the fact that she wasn't upset by this decision, for of all her tasks the nursing of the mister was the most trying, and the most thankless, for he never had a civil word for her and there was scarcely a time when she entered the room but he would upbraid her for being the cause of his trouble: if she hadn't had a daughter like she had this wouldn't have happened to him. He seemed to have forgotten that he had ever adored his granddaughter, and just as it seemed his son had, so he too had thrown off all responsibility for her; never once yet had Barney asked to see the girl, nor had she visited him or even mentioned his name; it was as if he didn't exist for her. One task she'd had to let fall from her shoulders and that was the work down at the cottage. She still baked bread for Ralph, but she had got a woman from the village to do the cleaning and cooking for him. However, she made a point of slipping in to see him now and again. At such times as when she was tatie or turnip-picking in the bottom field she'd fill a basket, hurry along the road with it and there have a few words with him. She had seen a difference in him these last few months and she thought it would be a miracle if he survived the coming winter; the disease was reaching its height and she knew that when he went she would miss him. He was someone she felt who had always been in her life, someone who had been kind to her and who had loved her. Yes, who had loved her, and still did. . . .

It was the beginning of November when they took Jake Yorkless into hospital. The day was biting cold. They brought him downstairs wrapped in blankets and laid him on the flat farm cart. Jimmy drove it and Emma sat in the back and tried to make the journey as comfortable as possible for the irate man, and irate he was. But she could understand more now his irritation, for the doctor had explained to her that he suspected there was something touching the brain. This kind of thing often altered a man's character, he said, but he would soon be himself again, they were very clever in the Newcastle Infirmary and the doctors there did all kinds of marvellous operations.

Last night she had tried to convey this to her father-in-law, but his response had been to tell her that she had always wanted him out of the way so she could run the place on her own, as if she hadn't been doing that for months now.

She had always liked Newcastle, that was until that night she had made the journey in the dark; now, all she wanted was to get out of it.

The ward they carried him into was a bare place. It had beds along each side with men in them, some lying prone, some propped up, all looking ill. The place smelt strongly of carbolic combined with the smell of a dirty floorcloth that hadn't been wrung out to dry: sour, arid.

A big woman dressed as a nurse told her to wait in the corridor for his things, and when they were later brought to her the big woman appeared again and said, "You can have a few minutes, that's all."

When she stood looking down on the man who had been her master since she was seven years old she did not chide herself because she could rouse no feelings of pity for him, for he had worked her hard all her life. She couldn't remember him giving her one kind word, and lately she had wondered at times how she had suffered him while tending to his needs . . . all his needs, for he had been completely bedridden for the past month. Yet she managed to say, "You'll soon be well; they're very clever here, as I told you."

"Bloody liars, the lot of them, you an' all. You want to see me finished, don't you? And 'tis all through you I'm here, don't forget that. If I die I'll be on your conscience. Just remember that. Got me clothes there I can see, sell them likely."

She turned away for she could stand no more and when she got outside the hospital gates and climbed up on to the seat where Jimmy was sitting patiently waiting, he looked at her and said, "Don't cry, missis, he'll be all right."

And she turned to him and slowly she said, "Jimmy, I'm not crying for the mister, I'm crying because I'm sorry for meself."

He smiled at her broadly now, saying, "Not you, missis, not you. Got too much gumption. Me ma said that an' all just last night. She said you must have gumption to put up with what's been shovelled on you."

She dried her eyes and smiled at him, then said, "Let's get back, Jimmy. . . ."

But his repeating of what Mary Petty had said was literally made evident when they entered the yard, for the first thing she saw was that the coalman had been and there on the ground near the coal-house was a huge load of coal.

"Crickey! that would have to come the day, wouldn't it?" Jimmy jerked his chin upwards. "And there's the milkin' and the horses."

"You see to the animals, Jimmy, and I'll see to the coal."

"No, no, missis."

"Yes, yes; you're better at the horses than I am, and they behave for you. Paddy made to bite me yesterday."

"He makes to bite me every day. He's a devil is that one, but he can pull. He's got his good points, and that's what we need him for, isn't it, missis, pullin'?"

"Yes, yes, that's what we need him for, Jimmy." She was making her way towards the kitchen door when it opened and Annie stood there bright-faced greeting her with, "You frozen, Ma?"

"Yes. Yes, I am cold. I shouldn't be surprised if we haven't some snow shortly."

Annie stood back, the door held wide, and Emma saw why: the table was set for tea; there was a plate of cut bread-and-butter, a dish of apple jelly preserve; there was the remains of the boiled bacon they'd had for their dinner yesterday; there were two cups and saucers set beside the plates; but best of all there was a tray with a single cup on it and a plate holding two bacon sandwiches. She turned and looked at her daughter. Annie's face was bright, like that of a child who had presented her mother with a surprise present. Again she wanted to put out her arms and draw her tight, but something held her back; yet she said with deep feeling, "Oh, that is nice. What a welcome! And is the tea mashed?"

"Yes, Ma. I poured the water on as soon as I heard the cart come in. It should be drawn in a minute."

"Oh, I could do with a cup of tea."

"I'll pour it out for you, Ma."

As she took her hat and cloak off she watched her daughter scurrying backward and forward between the fire hob and the table, and again she wanted to cry. Things would come right, there were all the signs of it. She didn't know how long they would keep the mister in hospital. Likely when he returned he would no longer be bedridden and perhaps his temper would be improved too. But that was in the future. Here she was drinking a cup of tea and eating bread-and-butter that her daughter had made ready for her. The load of coal that she had to move would appear light after this. . . .

Half an hour later she had changed into her working clothes, seen to Barney, and now she was about to tackle the coal, but because it was growing rapidly dark she lit a lantern, and as she did so Annie, coming to her side, said, "I'm going out for a little, Ma."

"But it's on dark, lass."

"I know, but I want a breath of air and I won't stay out long. I promise you. I'll just walk down to the road and along by the field. I won't be long. But I've been in the house all day and. . . ."

"All right, all right; but come back before it's real dark, won't you?"

"Oh aye, Ma."

"Wrap up well, it's enough to cut you in two now."

"Yes, Ma. I'll put a shawl over my head."

"Do that. Do that."

Emma went outside, and Annie now ran down the room and, taking a coat from a wooden rack that was nailed to the back door, she hurriedly dragged it on. The sleeves were much too short and the hem of it hardly came to below her knees. From another peg she took down a shawl which she threw over her head, crossed the ends over her breast and tied them in a knot at the back. Then she ran back to the kitchen door, but after opening it her walk was slow and it even turned into a saunter as she passed her mother who was shovelling the coal into wooden buckets at either side of her prior to carrying them into the coal-house and she said, "Won't be long, Ma."

"All right, all right, Annie." Emma had paused for a moment, and she shook her head, wondering again at her daughter's craze for wandering. Perhaps it was because she had been shut up in that place so long. Yet, in her own words, she hadn't considered herself as having been shut up; in fact, even before that business started she had wandered. Was that something she had inherited from her own line, from her grandfather who had wandered from one town to another, and from herself who had loved to wander when she was a child? Oh, enough that her daughter was changing for the good now. . . .

When Annie was through the narrow alleyway between the stables and the barn her sauntering ceased and she began to run, then skip, and the path she skipped along was not that towards the coach road but one that went off at right angles in the direction of the river and Openwood. Openwood was now wired off but the wire was obliterated by a dense growth of scrub that had been left uncut over the years. There were openings here and there where someone had forced their way through, likely poachers, and it was to one of these that Annie made her way, even though it was almost dark now.

She did not go through the opening but stood to the side, her head cocked as if listening, and when the sound of crushed undergrowth came to her she smiled and her smile broadened into a grin when a voice said, "You there, Annie?"

"Aye, Uncle."

"How's tricks?"

"Fine. They took me granda into hospital the day."

"Did they now? Did they now?"

"He's gona have an operation."

"Is he now? Is he now?"

The voice being thrown forward through the hedge appeared bodyless.

"Did you find them, Uncle?"

"I did, Annie. I did that."

"Did you tell her what I said?"

"I did that an' all, Annie. Yes, I did that an' all."

"And what did she say?"

"Well, what do you think, Annie?"

"She wants me back?"

"That's just it, Annie. She'd welcome you back, she thinks you're a fine girl. Oh, yes indeed."

"Where are they then, Uncle?"

"Well now, 'tis a bit difficult to describe and it's farther out than the last place, but I'll take you there, Annie, any time you're ready. But I'd leave it until the nights get a bit darker, say the first week in December and you'll be all set in afore Christmas. They have some high times at Christmas, don't they, Annie?"

"Oh aye, Uncle. Oh aye."

"Listen to me, Annie."

"Yes, Uncle?"

"We mustn't be seen together, not at all, you understand?"

"Oh yes, I understand that. She'd go mad, Ma would."

"She would indeed, Annie. She would indeed." The words came deep and soft and borne on laughter. "So caution's the watchword, eh?"

"Yes, Uncle."

"Well now, you come out for your jaunts mostly in the daylight, don't you?"

"Yes, Uncle."

"Well, one day I'll tie a bit of blue ribbon on the post just to your left, it holds the wire, it'll just be a tiny scrap so it won't be noticed. Now when you see that, get yourself ready for the next day. Rain, hail or snow, just walk out as if for a saunter and take the road to the river. And you know where the path leads to the top of the bank, it's the first place from where you can see the water and the jetties, you know that?"

"Yes, Uncle, I know the place."

"Then make for there, an' I'll be waiting. Now you've got that?"

She now repeated slowly, "The day after I see a bit of ribbon on the post here, I'm to make me way to the top of the bank overlooking the river."

"That's the girl. No grass will grow on you, Annie, you're sharp and you'll get somewhere. Oh aye, you'll get somewhere, Annie. Now I've got to be off, you get back."

"Ta, Uncle. Thanks."

"You're welcome, Annie, you're very, very welcome. Good-night to you."

"Good-night, Uncle."

She turned and ran all the way back to the farm. Emma was still shovelling the coal and when her daughter said, "I'll give you a hand, Ma," Emma straightened her back and said, "No, lass, you'll get all dirty. But I'll tell you what you can do, you can go into the dairy and do a bit of churning for me. You know what to do, don't you?"

"Aye, Ma."

"And then peel some taties for the dinner. There's those fresh herring the fishwife brought yesterday, I'll fry them when I come in; they'll be tasty."

"Aye, Ma."

Her hand tight against her thigh, Emma stood for a moment tensing her back muscles. Her daughter had offered to shovel coal with her. She closed her eyes and smiled to herself: God seemed to be at last paying attention to her prayers.

She attacked the coal with renewed vigour.

Three days later a man came from the hospital, knocked on the front door, then was directed by Jimmy to the farmyard and into the byres. There, facing Emma, he doffed his hat and said, "I'm very sorry to inform you, missis, that Mr Yorkless died this morning at half past eight. The operation was successful but apparently his constitution couldn't stand up to it."

9

Soft flakes of snow were falling when they buried Jake Yorkless, and there was a good turn-out at the funeral for he was of an old farming family and, as one of those present said later when seated round the kitchen table, one of the few freeholders hereabouts.

Not more than twenty people had returned for the meal; these included the pall-bearers of whom Luke was one.

They had brought the farmer's body from the hospital already boxed and he had lain in the hall on trestles for three days, his head bandaged like a mummy, only his eyes, mouth and nose evident. He was a weird sight and Emma had had to force herself not to look at him as she passed back and forth to the sitting-room to attend to Barney. As for Annie, once she was downstairs in the morning she wouldn't go back into the hall until she made for bed at night.

Emma couldn't stop Luke from attending his father's funeral or helping to bear his coffin down the lane to where the hearse waited on the coach road. Nor could she prevent him entering the house and sitting down to a meal. Only one thing she was glad about, Annie paid no attention to him, in fact she seemed to ignore him. She had not even answered his, "Hello there, Annie me dear," when he first came into the kitchen.

Now the mourners and sympathizers had gone and there he stood facing her across the table, saying, "I want to see me brother."

"You're rather late in the day wanting to see him, aren't you?" Emma answered.

"Things are different now, this is business."

"Business? What business?"

He poked his head towards her as he said, "The business of me share in this place."

"You must be joking."

"Oh no, Emma, I'm not joking. It's a matter called inheritance, and I'm equal to Barney in this."

"No, you're not." Her voice was deep and full of bitterness.

"Well, we'll see. Anyway, are you going to try and stop me seein' me brother?"

She knew that there was no way in which she could stop him seeing Barney. He was a big man, thickset, brutish looking now, any good looks he had had were long since gone, and she knew if she attempted to bar his way he would enjoy struggling with her. And so, after a moment's pause, she moved from the table and walked up the room, and he followed her through the hall and into the sitting-room. As she opened the door she called in an over-loud voice, "You have a visitor, Barney."

Barney lifted his head from the pillow and stared at his brother coming towards him, and Luke, coming to a stop at the foot of the bed, stared at the white face with the eyes buried deep in it and the brow receding well into the head that was now bald to the crown, and he said, "Well, hello there."

"What do you want here?"

"I should have thought it would be evident to you, brother, since you haven't lost your senses. As I told her"—he jerked his head towards Emma—"I've come to claim part of me inheritance."

"Get out. Get yourself out."

"Not afore we come to an understanding, for I don't suppose the old man had the sense to leave a will. I've been informed that as I stand I am due to me share and this business about you being the elder wouldn't stand up in a court of law."

"There you're wrong on both counts." Barney now lifted his thin arm and thrust one bony forefinger at Luke, repeating, "On both counts, because I am the elder and that stands, and the other thing is the old man did have some sense and after what he found out about you he made it his business to put it in writin'. You can go to Gateshead, to Hedley and Stocks, solicitors. They'll give you all the information you need. But I can tell you now what they will say to you: the farm was left to me, solely, and when I go I leave it to me wife. That's been seen to an' all."

Luke's face was a study. Emma expected to watch it becoming contorted with rage, but when he smiled the effect was much more disturbing than rage could have been. But there was no smile in his voice as he said, "We can all have lawyers, and I'll fight you for this. And anyway, how can she run the place on her own?"

"She's done it for a long time now and she'll do it to the end."

"We'll see, we'll see, brother. Oh aye, we'll see." His head nodding the while, Luke backed two steps from the foot of the bed; then turning suddenly about, he left the room, and Emma, after casting a quick glance towards Barney, ran after him.

In the kitchen she stood just within the hall doorway and watched him grab up his coat from the back of the settle, then take his tall hat from the hook behind the back door. When he had put it on his head, he tapped the top of it; then looking at her across the room, he said, "You'll be seein' me, Emma. Don't forget that, you'll be seein' me. Oh aye, bet on it, you'll be seein' me."

She was actually shivering as she leant against the door. She had no doubt in her mind but that she'd be seeing him, in one way or another she'd be seeing him. There was something frightening about Luke York-less, there was an evil in him, and she herself in some way always managed to bring it to the fore.

Well now, she sat down on the settle and looked at the fire, to all intents and purposes the place was theirs. Strange, but it was really hers for she would have to see to the money side of it now. She had said to Barney last night, "You could help me with this, I mean with the bills and things and the buying and selling." She knew she was quite capable of dealing with these matters herself but she had thought it would give him a new interest; but he hadn't seemed enthusiastic over the suggestion, there was an apathy about him that was getting deeper each day. Yet when he was going for Luke he had sounded like his old self.

But sitting here wouldn't get the work done. Yet oh, how she longed to sit for half an hour or so looking at the fire and thinking. At night-time, if she had attempted to do so, she would have immediately fallen asleep. She rose, saying to Annie, "Clear the table now and put the best china away, there's a good lass. I'm going to change."

Annie was very quiet. She had been so for days now, and she answered briefly, "Yes, Ma."

Ten minutes later Emma was in the yard making for the byres when Jimmy came hurrying down from the barn saying, "Can I have a word with you, missis, special like?"

She smiled at him as she said, "You can always have a word with me, Jimmy. What kind of a special word do you want to have?"

He pushed open the byre door and they went in and stood in the steamy dimness, and there, moving from one foot to the other and his head slightly lowered, he said, "I'm courtin' strong and I don't want to go on for years like some, and . . . and I thought, well, sort of killin' two birds with one stone, you need a man round here all the time like, don't you?"

She nodded her head. "Yes, you're right Jimmy, I do."

"Well, I wondered if you would let me have the cottage. I'll do it up meself and everything, so we could get married, Alice and me. An' she would be handy round about. She's in service in Gosforth, but she doesn't like it much. An' she doesn't want much pay. Well, she wouldn't expect it because you can't afford it yet, I know how things are, but we'd manage fine on what I get, if we had the cottage."

"Oh! Jimmy." She put out her hand and grabbed at his dirty square red one and, shaking it warmly, she said, "Oh, you're welcome, boy, you're welcome. But then you're no longer a boy, are you?" She laughed now. "And I'll be glad to see the cottage occupied again. Of course it's not much of a cottage. I thought little of it when I first saw it and it's pretty dilapidated now; it'll want working on both inside and out."

"Oh, missis, don't you worry"—his face was one broad grin—"I'll do that, nights after work an' Sundays. The parson won't get at me for breakin' the Lord's Day up here 'cos he won't see me. Not that he would say anything, not him, if he did see me breaking the Sabbath. What do you think?"

"I think the same as you, Jimmy. Well, go ahead as soon as ever you like."

"Well, the nearest I think would be Easter, 'cos she's tied you see, and her time will be up at Easter. Funny that, isn't it? They can throw you out at a minute's notice if you do owt wrong, but if you want to leave you've got to work your time."

"Yes, it is funny." Emma now leant towards him and in a mock-menacing tone she said, "But as soon as you're married I'll bond the both of you, ten years each."

It was a long time since the byres had rung with laughter. Although it was soon over and they both went on with their work and it didn't exactly efface Luke's threat, it lightened Emma's day, for the prospect of having Jimmy permanently on the farm she considered to be a blessing, especially if his wife should turn out to be a companionable lass. And there was the added thought that, being young, she would perhaps have a good influence on Annie. . . .

It started to snow in earnest the following day. The ground was frozen hard and so it lay, and in the afternoon Annie played snowballs in the yard. She threw one at her father's window and it spread across the pane and obliterated the shadow of his head behind the glass; she threw one at Jimmy, but he didn't stop and throw one back; then she ran out from the farmyard and across the field. But she was back within half an hour, her cheeks glowing, her eyes bright, her voice high as she burst into the dairy, crying, "Oh, it's lovely out, Ma."

"Well, get out again." Emma shooed her back towards the door.

"Look at your feet! I've just done this floor. We want no muck in here, go on."

Annie went out giggling, and Emma smiled quietly to herself. Her daughter was changing.

The following morning Emma awoke to a hushed world. Her shoulders hunched against the cold, she went to the window and peered out into the still black morning, black in the sky that was, and she had to look upwards to see it, for the snow had piled itself on the deep window-sill and formed a drift a third of the way up the panes. She screwed up her eyes and shook her head, shaking the sleep from her. If that window-sill was any indication they'd soon be cut off. She lit the lamp and quickly got into her clothes and went downstairs.

The hall was freezing. She glanced towards the sitting-room door. She hoped there were still some embers left in Barney's fire. In the kitchen she took the bellows and blew the slack coal to a red glow; then taking a newspaper from a box at the side of the fireplace, she opened it wide and placed it across the whole grate, and with her arms spread she held it like that until the centre of it became brown and was on the point of bursting into flames, when she quickly pulled it away and folded it up and replaced it in the box before lifting the black kettle from the hob and putting it in the heart of the now flame-licking fire. Following this, she went to the door and, after unbolting it, she gently pulled it open. But even so the drifted snow fell inwards. Pushing the door quickly closed again, she muttered to herself, "Good gracious! it must be deep. I wonder if Jimmy will make it." And she looked at the clock. It was turned six. On fine mornings he would be here by now. She was going to have a job if he didn't turn up. Oh, but he would. If it was at all possible he would.

She went back to the stove and mashed the tea; she then took a cup in to Barney. He was awake and he greeted her with, "The room's like an iceberg."

"I'll get the fire goin' in a minute. Here, drink this." Supporting his head while he gulped at the tea, she said, "It looks as if we are going to be snowed up. I'm worried in case Jimmy doesn't make it."

"What's to stop him? I used to go through drifts waist-high, in fact fell into them up to me chin. They've got things too soft these days."

She said nothing but she was asking herself what had happened to Barney to bring about this change. For weeks now he had been like this, his attitude almost like that of his father. He was hardly civil to the parson and she had to apologize to Henry for his behaviour. But Henry had said that it was understandable in Barney's case, a breaking point must come at some stage. It was all the outcome of frustration and she should be patient with him.

The only way she could be patient was to bite her tongue and say nothing. This she did now and, turning from the bed, she went to the fire and got it going. Following this she went upstairs and roused Annie. Her daughter was curled up like a ball under the bedclothes and when her head emerged she looked so pink and glowing and fresh, almost like a child again, the sight brought tears to Emma's throat and softened her voice as she said, "Come on, dear." It was a long time since she had called her daughter dear. Then she repeated, "Come on, dear. Time to get up. The snow's thick, you'll enjoy it."

"Oh Ma, it's cold."

"Yes, I know, so jump into your clothes, then have a hot drink and you'll feel fine."

For answer Annie pulled the blanket over her head again and wriggled her body, and Emma turned away and went down the stairs, and her face broke into a smile of relief when she entered the kitchen and heard a scraping at the back door and knew it was Jimmy with the shovel clearing a way out.

Opening the door gently, she said, "You've made it then."

"Aye, yes, missis. It wasn't too bad; it's just the drifts. But it's still comin' down. Won't be able to say it's not too bad by the night if it keeps on like this though."

"Here"—she opened the door further now—"step inside and have a cup of tea, you must be frozen."

"Oh, I wouldn't say no, missis. Ta." He kicked his boots against the wall, took off his cap and dashed it against his shoulders and arms, then stepped over the threshold and closed the door and stood with his back to it, saying, "I'll come no further, the heat'll drip me and it'll be all over the floor."

"It'll be all over the floor afore the day's out, Jimmy, you can depend upon that." She was smiling happily as she handed him a mug of tea, and as she stood looking at him drinking, the steam wafting round his pleasant square face, she realized that this youth was the only person in this place who had never caused her any trouble; in fact, his presence had brought a kind of lightness to her life, especially where work was concerned. And what was his reward? Ten shillings a week now and his rough food, with lately, a sack of potatoes at Christmas and the same of turnips, and in the summer all the apples he could gather from the topmost branches of the old tree. But then he had always had this latter perk since he was a lad because he was the only one who could get up there. The branches wouldn't bear the men and they hadn't a ladder long enough to reach. As he himself had grown older and heavier he had devised a way of climbing the tree and supporting himself against the roof. Even so, there were always a few apples he couldn't reach, and these had to be left until they dropped. But what dropped to the ground was the farmer's, even those that were bored by the wasps because then, as she remembered only too well, her chore had been to cut the good parts out ready for stewing and straining to make jelly, always supposing the sugar wasn't too dear. Otherwise, Dilly Yorkless used to put them in a vat with yeast and make a kind of wine that was like vinegar. She had never attempted to make it herself.

"I got a note off to me lass last night," Jimmy said. "Ted Conroy. He goes into Newcastle every day, he's apprenticed to a marble mason. 'Tis a good job that, because there'll always be cemeteries an' they'll always want headstones an' them that can pay always have marble. And he has to pass where Alice works so he's gona pop it in the back door. She'll be over the moon. . . . Well, I mustn't stand here jabberin', else the snow'll have blocked us in again." He handed her the mug, saying, "That's gone where it was needed. Ta, missis."

When she turned about, Annie was coming into the kitchen. She was yawning and stretching her arms above her head. Her hands at right angles to her wrists made her look as if she was giving an offering to the gods. . . .

Now what had made her think that? It was something that Ralph or Henry would say, in fact had said more than once about offerings being made to the gods.

"Come and get a drink. And I think you should stay in the house the day because. . . ."

"Oh no, Ma. No." Annie came hurrying towards Emma now. "Oh, let me go outside. I'll help to clear the yard. You know I love the snow."

"But it's freezin'."

"Oh, I can work hard enough to keep meself warm. Oh Ma, I don't want to stay inside, please."

"Well, it's up to you. If you don't mind gettin' wet up to the knees and chilblains on your hands."

"I've never got chilblains."

No, that was true, she never had. Her skin was without blemish of any kind. . . . What was she saying? She was not only thinking like a doting mother now, she was almost believing what she thought. Her skin without blemish. Dear God! Her voice was brisk now as she said,

"Well, you can go out later and help, but now there's this room to clean up and the beds to be made."

"Oh, I'll do me inside work, Ma, I needn't go out until this afternoon. But as long as I can go out for a bit."

"That's all right then. Get on with it. . . ."

And Annie got on with it. She had worked hard all morning, as Emma saw when she came in to make the dinner. She had even taken out the ashes, a chore she hated doing; but she hadn't attempted to blacklead the stove, she couldn't stand the sight of blacklead because of the mess it made on her hands. But by three o'clock in the afternoon it was impossible to see a finger before you, so thick was the snow falling. And now a wind had got up and part of the yard was as clear as if it had been swept by a broom while there were drifts six foot high against the barn and the byres.

Peering out of the window, Emma said, "You can't go out in this. You'd get lost."

"Don't be silly, Ma. Anyway, I won't go that far to get lost, I'll just walk round the yard or to the chicken run. That's what I'll do. I'll go and see if they're all right over there, will I?"

"You could fall into a drift, girl."

"Oh Ma, fall into a drift goin' to the chicken run! Anyway, if I did I could scream and you would hear me." She laughed, and then she stood staring at Emma while she picked at the nails of one hand with the fingers of the other.

Emma had never seen her do this before and she said, "What's the matter with your hand?"

Annie quickly drew her hands apart, looked at them and said, "Nothin' Ma, only I . . . I've got a snagged nail."

"Well, take the scissors and cut it off, don't stand picking it like that. Go on now."

Annie went to the table drawer and took out a pair of scissors and with these she clipped at her nail. Then swinging round, she faced Emma, saying, "I must get out for a little while, Ma, I feel choked up, I want air."

Emma stared back at her helplessly, saying, "All right, all right, you want air. Well look, go to the barn and take a scoop of oats down to the chickens. Spread it about, mind. And see what eggs there are; some of them are late layers. I got a good few this mornin' but they are going off. We'll have to wait for the young pullets I suppose. At this time of the year they don't pay for their feed, never mind their lookin' after."

"Yes, Ma. Yes, Ma."

"Now wrap up well. Put my old cloak on and put the shawl over the hood. And don't stay out long mind, because I don't want to have to go out in that and look for you."

"No, Ma."

A minute later Annie came down the kitchen. Emma's cloak fell to the caps of her boots, her face was lost in the hood and the shawl covering it. And then she did an unusual thing, she came round the table and, poking her face forward, she kissed Emma lightly on the cheek. "You're nice you know, Ma," she said, her eyes blinking as she looked at her mother. "You're nice you know." Then turning, she ran to the door, pulled it open and went out into the yard.

Emma stood, one hand on the table, one hand against her cheek. That was the first time her daughter had voluntarily kissed her in years. She was a strange girl, strange. But there was good in her. Oh yes. She had proved it of late; there was good in her.

It was dark and Annie hadn't returned and now the snowstorm had turned into a blizzard. Emma had a coat on, a shawl on her head and above that a split sack, one bottom corner acting like a hood and protecting her back as she struggled from one end of the farm buildings to the other shouting, "Annie! Annie!" As yet she hadn't called on Jimmy for assistance. She had warned Annie not to go near him, and for his part he had never needed any warning to keep away from her, but now staggering into the stable, she called, "Jimmy! Jimmy!" And he left what he was doing and came swiftly towards her and she clutched at his arm as she said, "Annie hasn't come back and the drifts are neck high in parts, see if you can make your way down the lane towards the road. She might have got stuck some place. I'll go by the chicken runs; she was going to gather the eggs."

Jimmy buttoned up his coat, and took his cap from a nail in a wooden stanchion. Then as he took his lantern from another nail he said, "If it isn't one thing it's another."

"Don't worry, missis; she's likely in a drift. She should never have gone out. 'Tis madness to risk out a day like this if you haven't got to. I was gona say to you meself, I would stay put the night and sleep in the loft 'cos if I don't I'll never get up here the morrow, by the looks of it."

"That would be a good idea, Jimmy. Yes, yes."

They were outside now and she said, "If it's too thick on the lane, come back. I might have found her at this end; don't you get stuck an' all."

"Don't worry about that." He went towards the gap in the stone wall while she turned and, with body bent almost double, made her way up the yard towards the passage that divided the byres from the barn, but this she found almost half-blocked with snow. When she eventually got through it was only by instinct that she found the hen crees, for the lantern did nothing but show up a circle of whirling flakes.

The wind had drifted the snow away from the front of the crees and when she pushed open the door and stepped inside there was a fluttering and a cackling and the birds jumped off the barks, then jumped on again. She put down the lantern on top of one of the egg boxes and stood quietly until they settled. It was peaceful in here and relatively warm. After a moment or two she moved along the row of egg boxes. There were a number of hens sitting in them and, putting her hand underneath one after the other, she felt to see if there were any eggs, and out of the twelve nests on one side and ten on the other she picked up six eggs, which in the ordinary course of events was very good for a late laying at this time of the year. But the significance of it was frightening. Annie hadn't been here. Even if she had intended to pick up the eggs on her return journey she wouldn't have taken the oat scoop with her, she would have left it here, and the lantern light showed no empty scoop.

As her mittened hand gripped the handle of the lantern it became still and her other hand went to her face as she thought, Oh no, she couldn't be, not as devious as that. No, she wouldn't believe it. No, she couldn't believe that that had been a kiss of good-bye, because then it would mean that all these weeks she had been biding her time while playing the reformed girl. No, if she believed that she would have to believe that her daughter was not only bad but evil, for if she had gone off again she would surely know her destination; she liked her comfort too much to chance wandering round Newcastle aimlessly, she wasn't that kind of a whore. . . .

Oh my God! what was she thinking? "No! No!" she cried aloud now, and once again the hens were startled. Her daughter wouldn't do a thing like that, she couldn't, not after the softness and sweetness of the past weeks. She pulled open the door and the wind brought a swirl of snow on to her and the hens fluttered and the cock protested. No. No. She kept repeating the words to herself as she struggled back to the yard. Her daughter was out there somewhere and she would find her.

Two of the eggs were broken when she put them on the kitchen table; then just as she was she went out of the kitchen, through the hall, and into the sitting-room. The lantern was still in her hand and it added to the glow of the oil lamp on the centre table, and she looked such a weird sight that Barney's body seemed to rise momentarily in the bed as he asked, "What is it? What's wrong?"

"Annie. She went out for a walk, she hasn't come back. I . . . I'm goin' out to look. Jimmy'll be here. I won't be long."

"Emma." His head was raised well up from the pillow now, his one arm extended towards her. "Don't go."

"I've got to."

"How long has she been gone?"

She paused a moment thinking. "Almost . . . two hours I should say."

"She's not worth it, Emma. There's a blizzard out there. It's been raging all day and all night. Haven't you noticed?"

"Aye; aye, I've noticed, but Barney, I've . . . I've got to go. I won't go all that far, and Jimmy's helping. Anyway, I'll tell him to stay put. Ring the bell hard and he'll hear it."

"In the name of God, Emma, how long do you intend to be?" He was yelling now.

She peered at him with a dazed look in her eyes. How long did she intend to be? As long as it took to find her daughter. But why was she bothering? As Barney said, she wasn't worth it. What was the matter with her? She put her hand up underneath the sacking and pressed her forehead. Her head was aching, she felt sick. But it was no use standing here. She turned and went out of the room, his voice calling after her, "Emma! Emma!"

As she opened the kitchen door, there was Jimmy. The rime was standing on his thick eyebrows and his lashes, and he gasped before he could speak, saying, "See nothin' of her, missis, and there's no foot-prints 'cos they're covered up as quick as they're made with this lot. Where you off to?"

"I'm goin' to look, Jimmy, and after you've tended the animals stay in the kitchen, will you? And when his bell rings, go in, go in to him."

"But, missis, you'll get nowhere in this."

"I'll get as far as Mr Bowman's cottage. She . . . she may have taken shelter there."

"I don't think you should go, missis." He put his hand tentatively out towards her, but she passed him, saying, "Do as I say, Jimmy. Do as I say." Then with body bent again, she was pushing her way towards the opening and into the lane.

Once when she found herself walking on practically exposed ground, she stood for a moment and shouted, "Annie! Annie!" But the falling snow seemed to whirl her words about her within a radius of the lantern; and so she went on, sometimes walking on a clear bit of road, the next minute she was in drifts almost up to her waist.

Sometime later she saw the old signpost sticking out of the snow, and she realized she had missed the path that cut off to the cottage. Perhaps it was just as well because she would never have got through that way, whereas there had been some kind of traffic along the coach road up till recently and in places the newly fallen snow was lying in hard packs, so the going was easier this way.

She wasn't aware of how long it took her to reach the cottage, nor of what was happening to her mind for at times she imagined the object of her journey was to see that Ralph had plenty of fuel inside and had enough food to see him through the storm.

She actually fell against the door and slumped on to her knees before she lifted her fists and banged on it. It was some minutes before it was opened, and then she felt herself being hauled inside. And again she fell to her knees and only managed to steady the lantern as it hit the floor.

"In the name of God! girl, what's brought you out in this?"

She remained posed, resting on her hands for a moment, before flopping to the side and looking up at him, saying, "Annie . . . I'm looking for Annie. Is she here?"

"Come on, get up. Come to the fire." And he helped her to her feet, saying now, "No, she isn't here, and not likely to be. Get that sack off you and out of those things."

"I've got to look, Ralph."

"You're looking no further until you thaw out." He was now seized by a bout of coughing and after wiping his mouth with a handkerchief he said harshly, "Go on, get your things off, woman. I've got some soup heating in the kitchen."

When he left her, she slowly took off her head shawl and coat. Another time she would have carefully shaken the snow off them in the hearth, but now she just let them drop to the side of the chair on top of the wet sack; then flopping down on to the chair, she leant her head back for a moment, closed her eyes and began to mutter to herself, "Oh dear me. Oh dear me." She wanted to go to sleep. That's all she wanted, just to go to sleep.

"Here, get this into you." She opened her eyes and reached out and took the bowl of soup and, putting it to her lips, she drank it greedily. When she had finished she handed him the bowl, then laid her head back in the chair again. She felt better now, more awake, but she understood how people could readily lie down in the snow and die. That's what her Annie had done likely. Oh yes, yes, that's what had happened. Her mind grabbed at the idea. Well, it would be better so than. . . .

Now her mind jumped, as did her body when there came a thump on the door, and she was on her feet and rushing towards it. She was right, she was right, the lass had found her way here. Ralph was beside her when she pulled the door open to see there in the lantern light the tall snow-covered figure of Henry.

Her body seemed to fold in two. She stepped back and watched him knocking the snow off himself right and left; then he was in the room, the door closed, taking off his hat and overcoat and these he dropped to the floor by the side of the door before walking to the fire. And all the while he had not given one answer to Ralph's rapid cough-punctured words: "Are you another mad one? What in the name of God has brought you out? Well, say something man."

Henry was bending over the fire, his hands extended to the flames as he said, "Let me thaw out a bit."

"Thaw out! You don't deserve to thaw out. Mad, that's what you are. I told you this morning I'd everything I needed."

"I know, I know." Henry now turned round, his voice sharp. "But I went up above"—he jerked his head backwards—"and Jimmy told me that—" He now turned his gaze on Emma and said slowly, "You needn't worry about Annie lying in the snow, she's gone, Emma. She's gone."

"Gone? What do you mean?" As if she didn't know what he meant she repeated again, "What do you mean? What are you saying?"

She watched him turn and look at Ralph, and he, taking a seat beside her now, put his hand on hers as he said, "She's gone back to where you took her from, Emma. She's been preparing for it for some time. You've got to face up to the fact that she's made that way and nothing on God's earth is going to change her."

"Preparing?" She swivelled round to the edge of the seat, her manner bristling now. "What do you mean, preparing?"

Again she watched the two men exchange glances, and now it was Henry who spoke to her saying, "She's been meeting Luke in Openwood for some long time. Billy the ratter saw them and heard them. He's a discreet old fellow, not a gossip, and he didn't say anything until a few days ago when he told Ralph here, and he said he thought you should know, but—" He stopped, and it was Ralph, his head hanging, who now ended, "I . . . I couldn't bring myself to tell you, Emma. In fact I made up my mind that I wouldn't tell you, because if she didn't go now she would go sometime."

There was a deep silence now in which you could almost hear the hush of the falling snow outside. Then a blast of wind, coming down the chimney, blew smoke into the room and Ralph coughed.

Emma sat back in the chair and after looking from one to the other she closed her eyes, and again the feeling came over her that she wanted to sleep, not only to ease a great tiredness that was on her but to shut out life, dirty life, body-aching, mind-bedevilling and soul-searing life. What was it for anyway? . . . *It was for living and working at. You must get back and see to Barney.* It was as if a voice had shouted loud in her head and she sat up straight, saying, "I've got to get back."

"I'll go with you, you'll never make it alone."

"You'll both have a job to make it. Why don't you stay, there's plenty to eat and drink inside?" Ralph jerked his thumb towards the kitchen, but it was Emma who shook her head, saying, "I must get back, there's no one to see to him."

She now began to scramble into her outdoor things, and when she put the sack over her head its warm wet weight seemed to drag her down and she pulled it off again.

Henry was standing ready at the door and saying to Ralph, "We'll go by the coach road, I think it'll be the safer." And Ralph answered, "Try to find the middle of it, because remember, there's ditches at both sides and they'll look solid enough on top."

Ralph had his hand on the latch of the door when he turned to Emma, saying quietly, "Face up to it, lass, and as soon as you can, for your own good."

Face up to it, he said, face up to the fact that her daughter was a sneaking, lying, filthy little bitch, that she had been smiling her angel smile on her for weeks now, while on her jaunts for air she had been meeting Luke. Face up to it, he said. He didn't know what he was talking about. She went through the door without giving him any word of farewell, and when she felt Henry's hand gripping her arm, his touch brought no fever to her body.

Close together now, their heads bent, they pushed as one against the snow-filled wind and, like the bow of a ship dipping and rising in the waves, they were walking on firm ground one minute then wallowing in deep drifts the next.

Emma had left the guidance to Henry and when he stopped and turned them about, their backs to the wind, she knew instinctively that he had lost all sense of direction. They should still be on the coach road, but the last drift they had gone through had taken her above the waist and he'd had to haul her upwards.

"I think we've come off the road," he yelled at her.

She made no answer but she lifted her lantern higher. He did the same, but the light showed them nothing but swirling snow, and a pinky white circle that turned to grey beyond the penumbra.

He had taken her arm again and once more they were stumbling on. Twice they stopped and leant against each other, his arm about her shoulders; but their closeness meant nothing now.

At one place the wind had almost cleared a path ahead, and when she felt the ridged hard ground beneath her feet she knew they were in a ploughed field. But which one? If it was their bottom field they had only to find the wired fence and it would guide them to the farm. If it was one of Alec Hudson's fields, then they were on the wrong track and going away from the farm.

When he hauled her on, she gasped, " 'Tis a field . . . a ploughed field."

And he yelled back to her, "Yes, I know."

When they came up against a post in the wire fence, she thrust her hands deep down into the snow beside it, and when she could feel only two wires leading from it she knew it wasn't their field. Jake Yorkless had put three wires round one field he kept for his few sheep, the other wiring that had been done under Mr Fordyke's orders had been a kind of mesh. They were, she knew now, on the other side of the road and going away from the farm and so she shouted, "Hudson's field."

Henry didn't answer but peered at her through the lantern light before gripping her arm again and leading her now along by the wire fencing. But when the posts ended abruptly she lifted her lantern high above her head and through its light she saw through a gap the dark blur some distance away to the left. She knew where they were. It was she who now gripped his arm and pointed. Then they were struggling through drifts of snow waist high, and when they came up to the ruined mill they leant against the wall for a moment gasping for breath.

Presently, pushing herself from the support of the wall, Emma gasped, "The . . . the door to the side."

The snow at the side of the building came only up to their knees but it had drifted through the partly open door, yet when they pushed it open it was as if they had come out of a raging sea and on to a beach, for they both dropped down on to the earth floor and lay flat for some minutes while they regained their breath.

Henry was the first to get to his feet. Going to the door, he kicked the snow to one side until he could push the piece of rotting wood back into its original position. But even then it hung drunkenly. Now lifting the lantern, he looked about him. He had passed this place literally hundreds of times but only seen it as a dirty ruin with a leaning chimney and a broken roof, the holes of which got bigger as the years went by as different villagers or farmers helped themselves to the old tiles, some of which were eighteen inches square and made of thick flat stone. He surmised that the whole roof would have gradually disappeared if the tiles hadn't been so heavy to get down.

The room they were in was about twenty feet long. There was a window at one end but only the frame of it was left and the snow had come through and piled up on the floor. There was a ladder leading upwards from the centre of the room to the floor above, but there was thin snow at the bottom of it which suggested that the upper storey was mostly open to the heavens.

Emma had risen to her feet and was standing beside him now. " 'Tis the old mill," she said. "Yes," he answered. Then looking down at her, he added, "It saved us."

Yes, she supposed it had, for they surely couldn't have gone on much longer outside. But what now? How long would they have to stay? Would they send people to find them? But how could Jimmy send any-one to find her? He was up there alone and had to see to Barney. But Henry. . . . Miss Wilkinson would surely report the parson was miss-ing. But perhaps not until tomorrow morning. They . . . they would have to stay here all night. She closed her eyes against the thought of what this would have meant at one time, but now it brought her no sen-sation at all. Her body seemed numb, her mind seemed numb. Was she ill? Or was it just the shock about Annie? Annie. Could one go to hell for cursing one's own. If she had run away immediately after she had been brought home she would, in some way, have been able to forgive her. But that she should act the part of the dutiful little daughter all these weeks while deceiving her, laughing at her . . . well, she wouldn't be human if she didn't feel devastated and bitter.

"You can't sit on the floor."

"What?"

"I said, you can't sit on the floor, you'll get your death . . . it's sod-den. What's through there?" He pointed to a door at the other end of the room, and she said, "An old scullery, I think."

She did not follow him but went towards the ladder and, putting her arm through one of the rungs, she leant against it. Even after some min-utes when she heard him enter the room again she didn't leave its sup-port, but when she heard the dull thud on the floor she turned her head and looked through the flickering light and saw that he had brought a door in and was placing it lengthwise against the wall.

He came to her now and, without speaking, drew her from the ladder and over the wet floor, and when they reached the wall he pressed her gently down on to the door. Then having fetched the lanterns, he blew one out before seating himself beside her.

Their backs against the crumbling wall, their heels stuck in the muddy floor, their forelegs raised slightly above it, they sat in silence for some minutes until Emma shivered and Henry said, "Here, take my coat."

But as he went to unbutton his coat she put out her hand quickly, saying, "No, no; you'll freeze. I'm . . . I'm all right."

He hitched himself closely to her now and taking her hands, he chafed them between his own, saying, "They'll start searching. It'll be all right, someone will soon come."

She looked at his face. It looked grey and pinched in the dim light, only his eyes looked warm. She could not see the colour of them but she knew his look was tender.

"No one will get through tonight," she said flatly.

He looked to the side and nipped at his lip before saying, "No, I suppose not." Then turning his head, he brought his gaze on her again as he said wistfully, "You know, Emma, this is the only time we've ever really been alone together. Even when you called at the vicarage and we walked along the road we were afraid of prying eyes. Now we are cold and exhausted and our only thought is for someone to come and rescue us. Strange, isn't it?"

Yes, it was strange, when she came to think about it: they would be here all night together sitting on this board, and what would be made of that? Oh, a great deal. The consequences made her stir. "Don't you think we could have another try, I mean at getting home? I know where we are now," she said.

"So do I, Emma, and we're half as far again from the farm as when we left Ralph's."

Yes, that was true. She nodded her head at herself. Anyway, it was silly to suggest that they should attempt to get back. She was so tired. All over she was tired, she just wanted to sleep, but if she fell asleep like this she would fall over. She said to him, "I would like to lie down, I feel very tired." She was looking into his face; his eyelids were blinking as he said, "Yes, yes; I'll pull it slightly away from the wall, it will give us more room."

He assisted her to her feet, then pulled the door a few inches from the wall, and when she sat down she hitched herself backwards, then lifting her feet up, she dropped on to her elbow before laying her head down, only to raise it, saying, "It . . . it breaks your back without a pillow."

"Try lying on your arm."

She put her arm underneath her head, then said, " 'Tis a bit better until I get the cramp."

She was surprised that she was talking in an ordinary voice for there was so much going on in her head, questions, answers, protestations, even swearing, and cursing; yes, cursing her own flesh.

"Sit down," she said now; "there's plenty of room." And he sat down, his hips against her side, and he reached out and took her free hand and again he chafed it. Then as he sat peering through the dim light of the lantern down the rank smelling desolate room, he began to talk. He talked about his boyhood and the happy times he had with his brothers and sisters. She had heard part of all this before but now he was talking about when he was a young man and her eyes became wide and she checked her wandering thoughts and brought her mind to him as he said, "I should never have gone into the ministry, Emma, I wasn't really cut out for it. I'm a protester by nature and I have come to the stage now when I don't know whether there's a God or not. I sometimes think that this life is all we have; then I am very, very sad because if it is I have wasted it, wasted the opportunities to live and love like an ordinary man should. You understand what I'm saying, Emma?"

"Yes, Henry, I understand." And she did understand, she had understood for a long time.

"When you came and said you were going to marry Barney, I should have said, 'No, you are not going to do any such thing.' But what did I do? In my weakness I pointed out all the obstacles to Ralph, and you heard them from the kitchen. I've never forgiven myself for that, Emma, and over the years time and again I've been going to leave this place to get away from the sight of you, the sight of your beauty, the sight of you having to work like a drudge, the sight of you living a marriage that was no marriage, the sight of you going through the torments of hell through your child. But I stayed because I knew that all this I could bear more than never seeing you again. Do you know?"—he turned and looked down on her—"Every night for years I have written to you, and about you. The last thing I do before I go to bed, I take out my book and I talk to it about the doings of the day, my feelings towards my vocation, which is not a vocation at all, but mostly I talk to it about you."

Every night he talked to his book about her. But he wouldn't do it tonight, for there'd be no need, they were here together, really alone at last, as he had said. And what did it mean? What did it portend? . . . Nothing. Nothing that was connected with love for him, the love that nightly burned her body, for at this moment she would have forsworn everything connected with her bodily urges for a dry warm bed, a hot drink, and the knowledge that her daughter was safely tucked up in her bed across the landing.

But what if no one came in time to get them out of this place and they died here? Well, they were in God's hands. . . . Oh! God. What had He ever done for her, or him for that matter. If he hadn't been a servant of God they would have come together. But now it was too late, and Henry knew it. Oh, yes, in his heart he knew it, for he had substituted a book for her.

Oh, she was cold, and so tired, so very tired.

She awoke in the dark. The lantern was out. For a moment she didn't know where she was, only that her back was numb, that her hip was aching, as also was her head. Oh, her head was splitting. Where was she? What had happened?

"It's all right, dear; the lantern went out. I . . . I think it must be near morning. Go to sleep."

When next she woke she pulled her stiff body further up the door and peered through a dim grey light and saw him coming down the ladder.

He came to her and dropped on to his hunkers and, taking her hands, he rubbed them between his own stiff ones, saying, "You're very cold."

"Yes." A shiver came over in her voice. "Did you sleep at all?"

"Yes. Yes, I slept. Come. I'd get up and walk about."

As he helped her to her feet she said, "Can't we make a move now that it's light?"

He didn't answer her for a moment but, taking her hand, he led her to the door and, easing it open a little way, he said simply, "Look."

And when she looked she saw a blank wall of snow; the drift had reached the top of the low door.

"I've been up above," he said. "It's unbelievable. It looks twice as deep as when we came in. It has stopped snowing but you can't see a post or a fence or a wall anywhere. Of course, we're in a bit of a hollow, which I suppose makes it worse."

She turned from him and hurried to the glassless window at the end of the room. The snow had fallen in for some distance but the whole aperture was blocked. Swinging round, she said, "But we've got to make an effort, Henry. We . . . we could scrape the snow from the doorway into here; the drift mightn't be that deep."

He didn't answer her for some seconds; then he said, "We could try. But looking at it from above, it looks pretty hopeless. Nevertheless, anything is better than sitting still; and we haven't any food. As for water, well, we're not short of that."

For the next hour or more they clawed at the snow, dragging it into the room until, both exhausted, they returned to the door and sat down; and there he put his arm about her, saying soothingly, "They are bound to come soon. They will know that we're missing by now, at least they'll know about me, which doesn't matter. But the men of the village, I'm

sure, will make some effort to search . . . headed by Miss Wilkinson."
He put his head down and gave a small wavering chuckle, and she said,
"Oh yes, Miss Wilkinson. She's very fond of you is Miss Wilkinson."

"And I've suffered from her fondness for years. You know something, Emma? I've been tempted to treat Miss Wilkinson like any married man would who has for years been plagued by his wife, and take the dinner she had served him and, if it was liquid such as stew, pour it over her. . . ."

"Oh, don't even make me want to laugh."

"It's funny, Emma, but I want to laugh." His voice was deep in his throat now. "I'm cold, I'm hungry, I'm stiff and tired, and at the bottom I'm in despair if we'll ever get out of this place before we are frozen to death, yet I am happier at this moment than ever I've been in my life. Just because I'm really alone with you at last. I've got my arm about you, you are close to me. If we get out of here I may never be able to hold you again and the memory of this will have to suffice, without happiness; but as for now, well, I'm holding you close to me, Emma."

In answer she simply leant against him; she didn't want to talk. The effort in moving the snow had taken her back to the exhaustion of last night. Her head was aching terribly; she felt she was in for a cold, and could one wonder at it? Her wet clothes had dried on her but the dampness seemed to have soaked into her very bones; she was shivering deep inside. She found herself trying to recall why she had come out in this weather. Then, like a knife piercing an already open wound, she remembered Annie. That's why she had to come out . . . Annie. And Annie now could be the death of her, and of Henry too. "We could freeze to death, Henry," she heard herself saying.

"No, no, my dear, nothing like that. I shouldn't have said that. Come, walk about, keep the circulation going."

As he made to pull her to her feet, she said, "No, Henry; I'm too tired, I'd like to lie down."

He did not speak for a moment; then he said, "Yes, you lie down, dear." And when she had lain down he took off his coat and put it over her, and she made no protest.

Kneeling beside her, he gazed at her. Her eyes were closed, her teeth were chattering. He looked about him helplessly; then suddenly pulling himself to his feet, he went outside once more and began to tear madly at the snow.

10

Six men working with shovels and a horse and cart to take the snow away had worked incessantly for two full days before they reached the farm, only to find that the parson wasn't there; nor was Mrs Yorkless. Later in the day, continuing along the coach road they reached the painter's cottage. He was safe and sound and warm, but he got into a state when he heard the news, and he told how the parson had left him two days before to escort Mrs Yorkless back to the farm. Mrs Yorkless had been out looking for her daughter, he said, but he himself had been able to tell her that her daughter had gone into the town some time previously.

"Well now," said the village men, "where could they be?" Two nights and two days. They would never have survived in this. Likely buried in a snowdrift. Farmer Hudson had lost fourteen fine sheep. Stiff as pokers they were when he dug them out, and not two fields from his house. This had been a storm and a half.

Well, they would keep searching. That's all they could do. One thing was sure: they were both lying somewhere near the coach road.

It was half past seven that evening that Florence Bessell banged on the vicarage door and gasped at Miss Wilkinson as she opened it, "They've found them. They've found them."

"Them?" said Miss Wilkinson as she let Mrs Bessell into the hall.

"Yes, Mrs Yorkless and him."

"I . . . I didn't know she was lost."

"Lost and found." Florence Bessell's mouth went into a wide grin. "And how were they found?" She nodded at Miss Wilkinson; then bending her head forward, she said, "Mr Bessell said he hadn't seen anything like it. There they were lying on the same boards, 'twined together like ivy round a tree. Couldn't have got closer if they had been forged together, he said, and as stiff as boards."

Miss Wilkinson put her hand up to her mouth, saying now, "He's . . . he's dead?"

"No, no. They took him to Mr Bowman's cottage, that being the nearest, 'twasn't very far from there. They were found in the old mill-house, you know. They must have taken shelter and made the most of it." She giggled now. "Eeh! this'll cause a stir. Mrs Yorkless; they took her back to the farm but she's in a bad way. Couldn't get her round. They've taken the cart for Mary Petty to go up and see to her. And if it hadn't been for her Jimmy, Barney Yorkless wouldn't have survived, so they say. Perhaps it's a pity he has, isn't it? Well, I must get off but I thought you would like to know." Her eyes narrowed as she gazed at Miss Wilkinson. Everybody knew what Miss Wilkinson thought about the parson. And she herself knew what her husband thought about Miss Wilkinson: she was an interfering nosy busybody and would have taken the organ position off him if she could have. Well now, she was glad she was able to bring her this bit of news. As she made for the door she said, "He'll likely be down in a day or two . . . when he thaws out. But he'll have something to face, won't he? because Joe Mason was one of them that found him, and George Tate another, and neither of them can keep their tongues still, can they?"

Lena Wilkinson would like to have said at this moment, "And you're another one that can't keep her tongue still"; instead, she said, "Thank you for letting me know."

When she shut the door on her visitor she stood a little way from it, her hands clenched at her waist. She knew it, she'd always known it. He was never away from that farm, supposedly reading to the paralysed farmer! Even when Emma Crawshaw was a girl he'd had his eyes on her. She hadn't been blind. He'd favoured her from the others, giving her books to read that were far above her class, and himself teaching her to write. . . . To write. That book he was always writing in and locking up. It was in that drawer. She marched into the sitting-room and stood looking towards the desk.

For the past two days and most of the night she had paced the floor of this house wondering what had happened to him, praying that he wouldn't be dead. Even if he was never to give her a kind look she still prayed that he wouldn't be dead. But now this, lying with that woman. She knew that bodies huddled together for warmth if lost in the snow, but Florence Bessell had implied something deeper than that. She turned quickly about now and went into the kitchen and, taking a strong knife from the table, she came into the room and after inserting it into the drawer she levered it backward and forward until she managed to loosen the lock, and when with one final tug the drawer opened she stood gazing down on the black leather-bound book with the brass clasp.

11

Emma knew she was lying in the kitchen, but how long she had lain there she didn't know. At times her body burned so much she longed to fling it into the snow, in fact she struggled to do just that; other times she lay in a half-world just conscious that Mary was hovering over her, and Jimmy too. She smelt Jimmy rather than saw him. Jimmy had the byres on him; it was a warm smell mixed with the taste of sour milk on the tongue. And there were other faces too that came and went before her vision; but she never saw Henry. She wanted Henry near, she wanted to feel his hand on her brow. She called out to Henry but he never came. Henry must have died in the old mill. She was going to die. She wished it would happen soon; she would wait though till after the snow went so they could get the coffin down the lane to the coach road. It was an awful business that. She couldn't see why they couldn't bring the hearse up to the yard. But no; it was all glass and the rocking on the rough road might crack it. That's what they said. Well, the coach road was rough enough in parts.

"Lie still, dear. Lie still. You're better this morning."

Was she better? Was she not going to die? She was very tired, she was very very tired. If you could die in your sleep it could be a good way to go, not knowing anything about it.

She continued to drift in and out of sleep. She seemed to float away on the subdued voices. Sometimes she could hear what the voices were saying; but it didn't make much sense to her. Mary was talking to someone down the kitchen now.

. . . "That Mrs Bessell was talking to her man, and Bett Skinner who was there doing the washing heard that apparently Mrs Bessell called at the vicarage the next morning and there was Miss Wilkinson having hysterics. As far as Bett could make out it was over some book or other she had found that the parson used to write in. Filthy, she said it was. Can you believe it? The woman's gone off her head: man starvation attacks spinsters like her an' they'll say anything. But Bett said there must have been other things in the book; blasphemous, Mrs Bessell said they were, not believing in God and things like that. Now I ask you, our Jimmy, can you believe it? People will say anything, make mountains out of molehills, like they did about finding them together. As I said, what did you expect them to do freezing to death, sit at each end of that sodden floor? Daft, that's what people are, daft. Not that I don't think they weren't fond of each other, mind. Well, he practically brought her here, didn't he. But as for hanky-panky, well he wouldn't get up to that, would he, not in his position. Although mind, I've often wondered about a man like him not being married, because he didn't look like an ordinary parson, white-livered you know like some, or barrel-round like others with noses you could strike a light off. No, he hadn't the face of a parson; nor the voice for that matter, not that I ever heard him preach. But that's another thing about him: because you didn't go into his church he didn't pass you in the road without a word. Asked after everyone of mine he did from they were nippers; knew them by name an' all. Anyway, there was hell let loose down there as far as I could gather yesterday, but more about him writin' something about potching the rum-runners years ago. Aye; aye; they're saying it was him, but they can't prove it like. An' he didn't say in his book where the stuff was. They've been turnin' over headstones in the night, they say. Eeh! the goin's on. Pity I wasn't there all the time, I'd 'ave got me ears stretched as to the latest. As for you, our Jimmy, you're like a clam."

"Enough talkin' when you're at it, Ma. By the way, how long do you think she's gona be like this?"

"Oh, it'll take some time to pull herself round. But I hope it isn't too long 'cos I want to get down home; I don't know what they're up to there."

"Oh, they're managin', they're big enough."

"Aye, you said it, three hulkin' brutes. Any road, I'll be shot of two of them this year and maybe then I'll be able to put me legs up . . . that's until their bairns start runnin' about me again."

Bairns running about. Emma saw a bairn running about: she was running all round the kitchen table, dancing as she sang:

> Two, four, six, eight,
> Mary at the cottage gate,
> Eating cherries off a plate,
> Two, four, six, eight.

She was bonny like a fairy. She was dancing up the kitchen. Now she had jumped on the bed and thrown herself across her and made her cry out against the weight.

"There! There! Come on, drink this. Open your eyes, that's a lass, open your eyes."

Emma opened her eyes and muttered something, and Mary said, "What is it, lass?"

"The book."

"The book? You want the book?"

"Yes." It was the breath of a whisper.

Mary turned from the bed now and, looking down the kitchen, she said under her breath, "She wants the book, the Good Book. It's in the sitting-room on his table; bring it."

A few minutes later Mary placed the Bible in Emma's hands which now looked white and soft, only to have it thrust slowly away.

Mary handed it back to Jimmy, saying, "She doesn't want it now."

"Ma."

Jimmy beckoned her from the bed, then said quietly, "You were talking about the parson's book; do you think she heard?"

"No, no, me voice wouldn't carry up that far."

"You could use your voice for a hunter's horn, Ma."

She pushed him now, saying, "Go on, get outside afore I clip your ear. Isn't there any work to be done?"

"Mary." The whisper came from the bed, and she hurried back to it and, bending over Emma, said, "Yes, me dear."

"What . . . day . . . is it?"

"What day is it? Well, the morrow's New Year's Eve, lass. And look, can you see, the sun's shinin'. Would you believe it? The sun's shinin' an' the morrow's New Year's Eve. It's got a nerve after the weather we've had lately. But there it is, lass. Can you see the window?" She raised Emma's head gently from the pillow. "It's gettin' us ready for the New Year and brighter things ahead. They would have to be brighter, they couldn't be worse than this one's been. Anyway there it is, the sun, and it'll soon have you on your feet. Nothin' like the sun for gettin' people on to their feet."

It was the second week in January when she put her feet to the floor and it was snowing again, but a fine thin snow, and Mary said it wasn't laying.

It was only with the aid of Mary's thick arm that she could stay upright, and when she reached the chair by the fire she felt faint with weakness. She had been in bed for more than a month and it was the first time in her life, apart from when she had the child, that she'd been ill, and now she was feeling so weak she doubted if ever her strength would return.

After a few moments she looked at Mary who was heating some milk on the fire and said, "How is he?"

Mary straightened her back and, her head jerking towards the far end of the room, she said, "You mean mister?"

"Yes."

"Oh, just the same. Well"—she suddenly lifted the pan from the fire and blew at the rising froth—"he's missed you. That's only natural. And he hasn't much to say, not even to Mr Hudson or his missis when they come in to see him, and you. But perhaps you don't remember."

Emma shook her head slowly, and Mary went on, "And then there's Tom Turnbull; he's been up twice. I nearly asked him what brought him 'cos he's a Nosy Parker if ever there was one."

"Mary."

"Yes, lass?"

Mary had poured the milk into a cup and was now sprinkling cinnamon on the top of it, and as she stirred it she brought it back to Emma, saying again, "Yes, lass?"

"The parson, was . . . was he here before when . . . when I didn't know anything?"

Mary drew a cracket from the side of the fireplace and placed it by Emma's chair; then putting the cup of milk on it, she turned to the fire again and, taking up the poker, she said, "Truth to tell, lass, I haven't seen hilt nor hair of him. But . . . but then it's understandable."

Some seconds passed before Emma said, "What's understandable, Mary?"

"Oh, lass, we'll talk when you get a bit better."

"Mary—" Emma put her hand out and clutched at Mary's skirt, staying her hurried departure from the fire, and now she said, "Please. I'm . . . I'm all right, but tell me what's happened to him. I'll only worry."

"Well"—Mary tossed her head from side to side—"there's nobody likes a bit of gossip more than meself, you know that, Emma, but down there it's all hearsay—he say, an' she say."

"Tell me, Mary."

Mary went to the seat placed at the opposite side of the fire and, sitting down, she lifted up her apron and began to smooth the bottom hem of it between her finger and thumb as she said, "'Twas all started by that skinnymalink Miss Wilkinson. She found a book of some sort that the parson had been writin' in, what they call a dairy, or a diary, I don't know which, but anyway he had been writin' in it every day for years apparently. And because she's always had a fancy for him, an' that's well known through the village, she has hysterics. So what does she do? She ups and sends it to the bishop."

"*No! No!*"

"Aye, lass, that's what she did. An' well now, the latest is, he's on the carpet, an' some say he's likely to get the push."

There was a long silence. Mary sat still plying the hem of her apron, her eyes cast down towards it, while Emma's gaze was centred on the heart of the fire.

It was when Mary suddenly said, "Drink your milk, lass, while it's still warm," that Emma looked at her and asked, "Was . . . was he ill too?"

"Well, he was out for the count for some days, I understand, but not like you. You got the pumonia an' more besides. I've seen pumonia afore, but the dose you had went to your head good'n proper."

There followed another silence; then Emma asked quietly, "How is Mr Bowman? Do you know?"

"Coughing worse, I understand from our Jimmy. I send him down now and again. Course I haven't seen him. Jimmy takes the bread down and gets his coal in an' does odds an' ends for him. . . . By! Emma, I've got to say this to you although it's like braggin' 'cos he's as good as me own, but you would have been hard put to it if it hadn't been for our Jimmy."

"Yes, I know that, Mary, and I'll be ever grateful."

"Well, you've started by lettin' him have the cottage; he's luckier than most at his age."

"It's nothing, the cottage."

"It's as good as what we've got except that we've got an outhouse and a lean-to. By the way, the mister was asking when you'd be able to get up. Do you think you could toddle in and see him in a little while?"

"Not today, Mary; I don't feel up to it yet."

And she knew she wouldn't feel up to it tomorrow, or the next day either. She didn't know how she was going to face Barney, for she wasn't the same person he had looked upon before the snowstorm. She would never be that person again. Those two nights and two days spent alone with Henry had changed her, but more so had Annie's craftiness, leading up to her desertion. That would leave a mark on her she'd never be able to erase.

*

It was three days later when she went into the sitting-room, and the change she saw in Barney's face was as great as the mirror showed her in her own; and there was no welcoming look in his eyes. He didn't speak until she reached the foot of the bed and had pulled a chair towards him and sat down, when he said, "Well, here we are then."

"Yes, Barney, here we are. How are you feeling?"

"Oh, me? I'm feeling fine. Lying here doing nothing all me life, just thinkin', thinkin'; what else could I feel but fine?"

"What's the matter, Barney?" Her voice was quiet. "What's making you like this? I've been ill, you know I have, or else I would have been about me duties afore now."

"Yes, I know you've been ill, and I know how you got ill. The whole countryside knows how you got ill, trapped in the old mill with the parson. But you didn't expect to be snowed up, I suppose."

She pulled herself to her feet, then hung on to the back of the chair as she said, "It's not true, it isn't. I was out looking for Annie. I went down to Mr Bowman's cottage thinking she might be there. I was half-demented. The parson came and he was to help me home. You will have heard what kind of a night it was. Well, you could see from the window." She pointed. "Do you think we stayed in there on purpose? We dug at the snow with our bare hands for hours." Her voice was rising and weak tears were raining down her cheeks now, but they did not seem to have any softening effect on Barney for he cried back at her, "Aye, and by all accounts you must have lain together for hours an' all. And he's losing his job over it, because he's been writing about you and him for years. They came up from the village bustin' to tell me, but I couldn't tell them it wasn't any news to me. Oh. Oh, you can look surprised. It was a long time afore I cottoned on. I used to think it was out of kindness for me condition he came and read his blasted books and talked his high-falutin talk. But no, it was so that he could eye me wife and more likely have it on the side afore you got to the mill. Or was that a meeting place?"

She wasn't aware that Mary had come into the room until she felt herself being turned about while Mary yelled at Barney, "You want somethin' for your corner, goin' on like that! You should be damned glad she stuck to you all these years. Another would have been off an' you would have ended up in the poorhouse hospital. If she'd had ten men, could you have blamed her? Who do you think you are, bawlin' your head off?"

"Get out of here! out of my house."

As the sitting-room door closed on them, Mary repeated, "Out of my house. Well, whoever sees to him from now on, it won't be me. Come on, lass. Come on." She led Emma forward, adding now, "Stop your crying, it's not gona do you any good. And when I get back to that village I'll skite the hunger off Tom Turnbull, you see if I don't. That's all he came up here for. I knew it, I knew it, because after he was gone that one was unbearable, like a bear with a sore skull, nothin' pleased him.

"There now. Sit down, sit down." She pressed Emma into the chair by the fire; then bending her face close to her, she said, "That parson should have married you years ago, an' him a young fellow full of stridin' life. It was bustin' out of him then. Yes, that's what he should have done, married you years ago, and you would have had none of this. 'Cos what life have you had? I'll tell you this, I wouldn't swop mine for it. No lass, I wouldn't, for you've been nowt but a skivvy from the day you stepped into this yard."

Mary was right. Oh yes, she was right; she was Mrs Yorkless the farmer's wife but she was still a skivvy and was likely to go on being so. Why hadn't she died in the mill? It would have been good to die there.

a very presentable man, so why did I frustrate myself by . . . lusting? Yes, yes, he did, Ralph." He was laughing now. "He used the word lusting, but tentatively. Why did I demean myself by lusting after a married woman, and she handicapped by an invalid husband?"

"You should have said that was the reason."

"You know something? I did in so many words. The poor man; he didn't know I was drunk with a kind of spiritual freedom. Anyway, he changed the subject back to my ministry. And at this point I told him I'd never voiced the opinions in the book from the pulpit. But he came back at me here, saying that it was impossible for man's inner beliefs not to seep through into the words of his mouth, and that there was a section of Christians who weren't blind believers, and it was they who would read between the lines; it was they whom I might set thinking. I said, wasn't it a good thing that they should think? And you know what his answer was to that? When one had faith one did not question. He pointed out that that was why the Roman Catholic church was so strong; they were taught not to question. He regretted, he said, that there was a tendency in our church today for a section of the flock to ask questions with regard to their faith. It wasn't a healthy sign, but one of sickness. . . . And more and more. We got in deep here, and I got the feeling that if I'd known him better I might still be in the ministry, for he obviously had a feeling for the poor. Yet, at the same time, I felt bound to ask him what the church really did for the poor, and pointed out the one and two roomed cottages from which the church drew rent, their assets being mud floors and dungheaps. I wished I hadn't liked him for then I could have let myself go. Anyway, by offering my resignation, I saved him the trouble of having to defrock me or having me brought up before a consistory court . . . or whatever.

"At the end he shook my hand and said he would pray for me, and his final words were, 'You should never have come into the church because you have never found God; you are really an agnostic.'"

Henry now looked at Ralph for a moment in silence; then holding out his hands again to the fire, he said softly, "I'm not, you know. I'm not. And if it wasn't for Emma I should feel an entirely new man at this moment."

"What are you going to do about Emma? Why haven't you gone up there and seen her?"

"First, what can I do? And the reasons I haven't been up are . . . well, I can't trust myself. The other is, I don't want to give the dear parishioners anymore fuel for their fires: I'm leaving, but she's still got to live here, and they are watching my every move. The funny side of it now is they are beginning to question Miss Wilkinson's sanity. Poor

12

"After I'd said my piece with regard to resigning he dismissed his chaplain with a nod, and the other God-fearing men, and then he bade me sit down, after which the business of the diary came up.

"He was very interested in the part about the liquor. He laughed. Did I actually remove it? And where was it now?

" 'Well, my lord,' I said, 'you've read the diary.'

"You see I had made a joke about that part, and I had never actually stated in my writing that we'd moved the stuff. The only clue he would have got from his reading was, I mentioned the number of bottles. It's a good job I didn't refer to the tomb of John Freeman Ellis. Anyway, I felt sorry for I saw he was embarrassed; he practically apologised for having read my diary. I've always known he was a gentleman, and a very learned one, but at our meeting I found him to be a very human one too."

"And then what happened?"

"Oh."—Henry swivelled round in his chair and held out his hands towards the fire before continuing with a smile,—"he began to talk. And he talked, and he talked, and he talked. How such men can talk!

"And they are good to listen to, even if you don't believe what they are saying. There he sat behind his magnificent desk, a great blazing fire in the grate, the room as sumptuous as any I have ever seen, much more so, and he spoke of the flock who had to be defended and protected. He didn't say from such as me, but somehow I got that feeling. Yet all the while, I knew he was aiming to be kind and understanding."

Henry now gave a deep laugh and moved his head and said, "There were parts in my diary that I'm sure he enjoyed, the parts where I spoke of my love for Emma. I recall I sometimes became quite flowery and poetic; it was my only outlet. He even touched on that. He said that he could not understand the liaison when it was open for me to take a wife. Here I was, he said, in the prime of life, still a very presentable man. Yes"—he smiled again as he nodded towards Ralph—"that's what I am,

Miss Wilkinson. I have it in my heart to feel sorry for her, and strangely I feel no animosity towards her for what she did. It would have had to come sooner or later. If this hadn't happened to bring the truth out of me something else would."

"You'll see Emma before you leave though, won't you?"

Henry's jaw tightened and the muscles of his cheek-bones stood out under the taut skin for a moment; then he muttered, "Yes, I'll have to."

"Does your father know you're coming?"

"Oh yes; yes." A little lightness came into Henry's eyes. "He says he's counting the days, as is Clare. He has great plans as to what we're going to do in the garden, at least what I'm going to do." He smiled wistfully now, and Ralph said, "What are you going to do? I mean with your life."

"I've been thinking about that. It would be pleasant just to spend the remainder of it at home just pottering. But then I might live to be as old as my father, and what a lot of time I would have wasted just pottering. One thought is very serious in my mind, it concerns writing. I'd like to put down all I think about God and man . . . and woman. And you know something, Ralph?" His voice took on an eager note now. "From the moment I left the bishop's palace I felt nearer to God than I've done since I was ordained; in fact I wasn't near to Him then at all; He was like the bishop and I the poor poverty-stricken peasant; He was someone afar off, someone that had to be looked up to; but strangely, and yes Ralph"—he nodded his head now towards the man muffled up in the chair before him—"I felt so near to Him that He could have been alongside me. You won't understand that."

"Who says I won't understand it? I have my own ideas about whatever is there; and to my mind it's here." Ralph now dug his fingers into his chest, and this resulted in a bout of coughing which left a pink stain on his handkerchief, and when it was over he went on, "I understand perfectly how you felt, and I believe you when you say you are nearer to God now than ever you'd been before. And I say to you also, hang on to that idea and use it. Write. And may I give you a word of advice?"

"Why ask, you'll give it to me whether I like it or not."

A chuckle passed between them, then Ralph said, "Write stories like you tell them, don't go in for the heavy stuff, theology, or philosophy. Well, if you must use the latter, weave it in, but you'll get more people to listen to you through a good story than any high-falutin pamphlet on the whys and wherefores of Protestantism, Catholicism, Mohammedanism, and all the other isms."

"I think you're right."

"I know I am. By the way, when do you say you've got to leave the vicarage?"

"The end of the month, if not before. I've got to the first of March anyway."

"Will you do something for me?"

"Anything. Anything, Ralph."

"Will you come and stay here a couple of days before you finally go from the place?"

"Yes." The answer was unhesitating, and he repeated, "Yes, of course I will."

"Once you're gone, Henry, you'll be gone for good; I won't see you again."

"Don't talk like that." Henry got to his feet. "Spring will soon be here. You've weathered worse winters than this. You always say that; you've said it every year that I can remember back."

"Yes, haven't I?" Ralph was laughing now, his hollowed cheeks puffed out, and he said again, "I'm a devil for repeating myself. And talking of repeating myself, I've got to say this. I've made out a little will. What I have is left between you and Emma. The only value is in the pictures, and—who knows?—some day you may be able to get half a dollar on them."

"Oh! Ralph."

"Don't say, oh! Ralph, like that, Henry. Let's face it. I've been lucky. Who would have thought when we met years ago that I'd still be here today? Now who would have thought it? I've been lucky in more ways than one, and one of them is in knowing you . . . and Emma."

It was too much to bear. There was an emotional breaking point, and he was near it. He would blare like any child any moment. He picked up the tray that held the two empty cups and went hurriedly down the room into the kitchen and, putting the tray on the little table, he stood with his body bent over it and, his throat full, he repeated, "Oh! Ralph. Oh! Emma."

It was the last Friday in February. Emma was about her duties again. Mary had returned to the village to attend to her family. Jimmy came early in the morning and stayed till last thing at night, sometimes working inside the cottage by lamplight. It had taken her days to get into the routine of the house again. When Mary was still here she had done the lighter work, breaking herself in as Mary called it, but now, when she had everything to do herself, she reached the evening feeling utterly exhausted. However, each day her strength increased and she'd made up her mind that what couldn't be done in the house must be left undone. She would see to the meals and attend to Barney and help where she could outside. And this she did. But the task that she found the most wearing was her attendance on her husband, for when he talked at all he talked at her; but most of the time he was silent and surly. He picked over the food she gave him, and when one day he said, "I could starve myself to death and then you could be rid of me," she had to clamp down on a retort for she knew she had no energy to waste on rowing with him. Yet at the same time she wondered how long they could go on in this way.

Then a little brightness came through the door late on this particular Friday. He threw his sailor bag in, took his hat off and flung it with dexterity on to the knob of the settle, then cried to her astonished face, "Well! where's me welcome?"

And Emma gave him a welcome. She ran to him, put her arms round him and kissed him, and he, holding her at arm's length, said, "Well now, that's more like it." Then his eyes narrowing, he added, "They're right. I heard down in The Tuns that you'd been through a bad patch, and it's told on you."

"Oh! Pete. Oh! I am glad to see you. Oh! there's no one, no one I'm more glad to see at this minute."

And at this minute she was actually speaking the truth, for Pete would lighten the burden of work, he would also do something of much more value, he'd cheer them up, bring a brightness into the house, perhaps he'd bring Barney back to his old self again.

"Come on, sit up; I've got some mutton stew here and there's new bread. I just baked it today."

"Now you're talking. How's his nibs?" He jerked his head towards the end of the room, and when her face clouded, he said with a change of tone, "I was only in The Tuns long enough to hear the bits and pieces. But things have been happenin' round here, I understand."

"Yes, Pete, things have been happening. Go and look in on him, and have something to eat, and then we'll talk. . . ."

And later Emma talked as she hadn't talked for many a long day. She told him all there was to know, and when she finished he'd said, "To think we went through all that to get her out of that place. And it was the means of doin' me da in an' all. Well, you can wash your hands of her, Emma, for good an' all. Some lasses are made like that. Oh yes they are. You wouldn't believe it, Emma, but they are. But about the parson. I'm sorry to hear about him. . . . You liked the parson, didn't you, Emma?"

She looked him straight in the face as she said, "Yes, Pete, I liked the parson. I've always liked him."

"More than liked, Emma?"

"Yes, Pete, more than liked."

"Is it true then what they were saying about you and him being found together in the old mill? Had you gone in there and got trapped?"

"No, no, Pete. Haven't I told you? He was bringing me back after I'd been looking for Annie."

"Aye. Aye, that's what you said, but one doesn't like to own up to these things."

She wasn't annoyed, not even slightly vexed, but she put her hand out and caught his as she said, "I can swear to you, Pete, there was never anything between the parson and myself."

"Well, if there had been I wouldn't have blamed you, Emma, for you've had a pretty scanty time of it with our Barney, the way he is. 'Tis a wonder you haven't strayed afore now; there's plenty round about who would have been ready and willing to help you. Anyway, the parson's leavin' they say?"

"Yes."

"And he hasn't been near you?"

"No. The last time I saw him was when we lay down so exhausted that we were prepared to die."

"You were?"

"Oh yes. It was two days and two nights. The cold was indescribable. And the wet. And no food. As you know, you can be blocked in here for weeks at a time. We had tried to claw our way out by pulling the snow into the room. You have no idea what it was like, Pete."

"Oh aye, I have, Emma; I've had me hands frozen to the rails and when I've pulled them off it's left the skin behind. Oh, I know what intense cold's like an' what it can do to you an' all. And now, Emma, I've got somethin' to tell *you*. . . . I've left the sea."

"*What? You mean for good?*"

"For good, Emma. An' that's not all. I'm gona be married."

"Oh! Pete." She held out her hands again to him. "Oh, I'm glad. Who is she?"

"Well, it's nobody hereabouts."

"No?"

"Oh no. It's the sister of one of me shipmates. I think I told you. An' that's not all. I've got a proposition, sort of, to put to you. But mind, it's just up to you 'cos either way doesn't matter to me. . . . Aw"—he tossed his head from side to side—"that's a lie, but I'll go along with whatever you say. How would you like me to come back here and give you a hand and bring Beth along of me?"

"Oh! Pete." She opened her mouth wide. "I . . . I'd like that better than anything in the world." And again she meant what she said at this moment. She was now shaking his hand up and down. "Oh! Pete. Not only to think of the work that would be off my shoulders but to have you about the place, it . . . it would be like the sun coming out."

"Aw, lass." His weather-beaten face took on a deeper hue. "I'm not as bright as all that."

"You would be to me, Pete. And oh! I'd welcome your wife."

"You'd like her, Emma. She's your sort: hardworking, down to earth. But she wants to get away from London. It's no place to live in, although they're decent enough folk. Her father's a gaffer in the docks and her brother works there an' all. It's a tight place to find work in, they tell me, but they would get me set on, havin' influence; that's if you didn't want me back here."

"I'll set you on any day of the week, Pete." She was smiling widely at him now. "And it would be share and share alike."

"Oh, I didn't mean that, Emma."

"Well, I meant it, because you worked all your young days here, slaved is a better word. We've all slaved."

"Aye; aye, we did slave, didn't we? But we were lads, then men, while you were just a bit slip of a lass. I never thought it was fair, but I kept me mouth shut. They used to think I was dim, you know, because I didn't say much. Took it all in and said nowt, because you couldn't get past me ma or me da. And then there was our Luke. He was a bad 'un from birth. Still is, by what you've just told me. Barney was all right though, Emma. But he's changed like, hasn't he?"

"Yes, he's changed, Pete. He doesn't look good."

"Has he seen the doctor lately?"

"Yes; I think the doctor went in to him when he visited me."

"Had he anything to say about him?"

"Not to me; but he said something to Mary about there being more deterioration. At times he can hardly lift his right arm now, and he's almost completely helpless. But"—she turned her head away—"I wouldn't mind that, Pete, I wouldn't mind what I did for him, if he was only civil."

"He's jealous, Emma. An' that's understandable; even in his state he could be jealous because he's still got his mind."

She looked at him now without speaking, and she realized that Barney must have confirmed what Pete had heard down in The Tuns.

She said, "When is the wedding to be?"

"Well, all depends, Emma. If it's gona be up there I'd have to stay in the parish for a certain time, I understand, and have the banns called. But as I put it to Beth, why not have it down here? An' she was all for that, havin' it down here, because she's not the drinking kind. Not that she objects to me having a pint or two, but her da and the lads can almost swim in it, and when they're full there's always high jinks. She's been brought up with it and I think she'd give her eye-teeth to get out of it. So I could lay it on that I'm wanted back here an' bring her down. Of course there'll be objections, but I hope they're sober when they're objectin'"—he now laughed and pushed his hand out towards Emma—"else there won't be much left of me for any weddin'. . . . No; they're all right really. But Beth's different. She's steady, and all she wants is a good home . . . an' me of course."

"Well, she'll get both here, Pete."

"Eeh! I can't believe I'll be comin' back. Me feet on solid ground again. Anyway"—he clapped his hands together—"for the next few days I'll get meself outside and give Jimmy a hand. He's done marvellous to manage on his own, and him an' me'll get along like a house on fire. But first of all this very night, I'll write Beth a note tellin' her to get herself ready. I can be up there an' back with her within three or four days going by the railway. Marvellous thing, trains; next best thing to ships. What am I talkin' about? I don't like ships any more. I don't really think I ever did, except when I was on dry land afore I had found out what they were like. . . . Well, am I sleepin' in the same hammock, Emma?"

"Yes, the same hammock, Pete."

"Well, good-night, lass."

"Good-night, Pete." She went to him now and kissed him gently on the cheek, saying, "I never thought to meet with any good in me life again. Oh, I'm so glad you're coming back, Pete."

He seemed too touched to answer, but he patted her shoulder, then turned away and walked up the room; and she went and sat down by the fire and, joining her hands on her knees, she dropped her head back and, looking up to the smoke-covered ceiling, quietly said, "Thank you, Lord."

13

Pete stayed five days on the farm and he worked like a Trojan outside. Sometimes she heard him and Jimmy laughing together; and it was a good sound. Yet when it happened she always turned her head in the direction of the sitting-room: Barney's hearing was still good and the sound must irk him. Yet he, too, seemed better for Pete's presence.

The night before he left Pete went down to The Tuns on the cart and brought back some bottled ale which he took into the sitting-room, and long after Emma had gone to bed she could still hear the murmur of their voices from down below, and her thoughts were that the ale had loosened Barney's tongue.

It was around seven o'clock in the morning when Pete left the farm to catch the carrier cart into the town. The sun was shining, the morning was bright and brisk, and Emma set him to the gate and wished him a safe journey, for to her the journey to London was as dangerous as a journey in a boat on the high seas. Her last words to him were, "I'll be counting the hours until I see you again, Pete."

She watched his figure marching away down the road. He was dressed in an ordinary suit, but his walk had a slight roll to it. It was a sailor's walk.

As she crossed the yard back to the kitchen door Jimmy called to her, "I'm goin' to miss him, missis. I'll be glad to see him settled back."

"You're not the only one, Jimmy. But he won't be long. Four days at the most, he said."

She went inside, and immediately the kitchen seemed different, and when later she lifted the breakfast tray to take in to Barney she thought, he will be different too—he had been civil-spoken to her whilst Pete had been here.

She placed the tray across his lifeless knees and, lifting the spoon, handed it to him. But he didn't take it; what he did was to grasp her hand and, looking at her, he said, "I'm . . . I'm sorry, Emma, I've been a bit rough on you." Then lifting her hand upwards he pressed it gently to his cheek.

The change was so sudden and unexpected that she could say nothing. The tears gathered to a great knot in her throat; she closed her lids tightly as he said again, "I'm sorry, Emma; it's taken Pete to make me see things more reasonable like. As he said, you've had one hell of a life with one and another of us, not countin' Annie."

"Oh! Barney. Barney." She drew her hand from him and turned away and stood with her head bowed, the tears raining through her fingers; and when his voice came to her brokenly, murmuring, "Emma. Emma, forgive me. I'll . . . I'll try to be different and . . . and understand." She couldn't bear it, and ran from the room, into the kitchen where, throwing herself on to the settle, she leant her head on her arm and cried until she could cry no more.

When at last she pulled herself upwards it was as if she had been washed clean of feeling. Her mind was at rest. The future lay clear before her: her life need not be that unhappy; she would tend Barney and love him; yes, in a way she would love him and comfort him; and as a stay she would have Pete and his wife, and Jimmy and his wife; and there would be times when she would forget altogether that she had a daughter. This would be the hardest task of all, but one which she must work at. She would not allow herself to think of the other person she must forget.

She went to the pump near the sink and after drawing a dishful of water she sluiced her face, dried it, then reaching up to the mantelpiece she took down a comb and pulled it through each side of her hair. This done, she took in one long slow deep breath, made her way back into the sitting-room and without any words sat on the edge of the bed and put an arm under Barney's head and held him to her.

It was as if Pete had taken the sun with him for a wind came up and brought rain with it; then it freshened still further and by the evening it was blowing a gale.

It was almost nine o'clock when she saw Jimmy's lantern swinging down the yard. He had been working on the cottage: he had done wonders with the inside; he had mended the doss bed and varnished and comb-grained the doors; he had brought up from the village an old broken cupboard, taken it to pieces and made a delf rack. By the time he'd finished, the cottage would certainly be fit to live in.

She bolted the door, emptied the teapot on to the fire to damp it down and stood back from it for a moment coughing as the cinder-smelling steam wafted about her face. Then picking up the lamp, she went into the sitting-room to say good-night to Barney; but finding he was already asleep, she quietly turned down the wick of his lamp to a mere flicker, then went up the stairs.

It was sometime before she went to sleep. As always, the doings of the day tumbled through her mind, and again as always she ended up thinking about two people, Annie and Henry; then finally, just before sleep, she thought, I wonder if he'll come and see me before he goes. The thought took her over into a dream.

It was the kind of dream she'd often had before: she was in the midst of people, all misty faced, and she was peering at them in the hope of recognizing one. At times she thought she saw her father, and when she imagined she was looking at her mother the face would turn into that of Annie and she would go and put her arms about her, only to find she was embracing a man.

Tonight the dream was following the same pattern and she had reached the point when she had her arms around the strange man when she screamed; and she ran from him and through the village, only to meet him again. When he put his arms about her, then threw her to the ground, she screamed once more and it wasn't like a dream scream when your mouth opens and no sound comes out, or that you've imagined that you've yelled to the pitch of your lungs only to wake up murmuring; now she knew she was actually screaming and that she was no longer in a dream but was actually struggling with a man. When his body came thumping on to hers and his hand was ramming something into her mouth she tried to bite on it; but the next instant her head spun as she received a blow to the side of it and she was only vaguely aware that she was being thrust on to her face.

She came to herself screaming in her head as she felt herself being dragged from the bed. Her hair was being torn from her head. She knew now she was being pulled into the attic and as she emerged from the darkness of the bedroom into the light of the lantern the terror in her almost caused her heart to stop, for she saw plainly now who her assailant was. Yet subconsciously she had known that from the moment in the dream when her own screams had echoed those of another.

The agony her body had endured in being dragged over the uneven floor boards was nothing to that of her mind when, as she lay on her side, he brought the lantern and, swinging it so close to her face that she thought he intended to spill the oil on her, he said, "Comfortable, Emma?"

Her eyes, wide like those of a trapped animal that knew it was about to die, stared back at him.

"Didn't tie you too tight, did I?" He took his foot now and kicked at her bare ankles where the rope was searing the skin. "Anyway, you won't mind that in a minute or two, you'll have forgotten all about it."

He now stood the lantern on the floor and, dropping on to his hunkers, he brought his face close to hers and his spirit-laden breath wafted over her as he growled, "You don't know how long I've waited for this minute, Emma, just you and me alone, nobody to interfere. Years and years I've waited for it, ever since you first toddled into the yard, I think. It was from that minute you blasted me life. Do you know that, Emma? You blasted me life. You separated me from me family; you turned me out of me home; you lost me inheritance that you are now handing on to Pete; an' you made me somebody to be pitied and scorned because I'd busted up me brother's life an' all. I've had to carry the blame for that. I just told him so downstairs. Did you hear him yelling? He was trying to warn you while I was giving him a kind of picture of what I was gona do to you. But he's quiet now; I saw to that. That's one chalk mark off me slate, 'cos he never liked me nor me him. But we would have got along if you hadn't stepped in. You should have seen his face when I told him what I was going to do to you after I had taken you. But you know something, Emma? I don't want you, not that way; not even years ago I didn't want you. Didn't mind lookin' at you or havin' a tickle, but you had no fire in you; not like Annie. Aw now, Annie's got fire in her. And I'll tell you something more, Annie's worth a hundred of you."

He now took the flat of his hand and brought it fully across the side of her face, and when her head hit the floor she again almost became insensible. But she came to herself when she felt his hand grip the front of her nightdress and with a savage tug rip it clean down to the hem, and there he had to use two hands to tear the calico apart.

"Skin and bone, not really a woman. Open your eyes, Emma; I'm lookin' at you."

"Well now." She knew by the sound of his voice he had turned from her; and slowly she forced her lids open and then her mind cried, "Oh! Jesus. Jesus," as she saw what he was about to do. He had taken the lantern to where the wall sloped and he was examining the whips that had lain in the corner for years. She saw him pick one up after the other before he appeared to choose what her dada had called the standard. This had a heavyish handle and a single strand of leather, broad at the top and narrowing to almost a thread at its end. It was very like the one she had used to whip the idol off the table in those far gone days up at the house.

He next picked up the belt of knives, and when he held the cloth case by its strap it unrolled and two of the knives dropped out and fell hilt first to the floor. Throwing the case down, he said, "We might come to you later."

Coming over to her now, he bent over her once more and pulled the gag, a dirty cloth, out of her mouth, and smiling at her he said, "It's easier to yell, Emma, and I want to hear you yell . . . scream, screech. It's a windy night and it's not likely that anybody's around at this time. Even if a fellow was poaching he would just take it for one of the owls, or a fox because you'll be screamin' like a vixen afore I've finished with you."

"Luke." His name trembled on her lips, and he said, "Aye Emma, what is it?"

"Pl . . . pl . . . please, do . . . do . . . don't do this, Luke, please."

"You pleading with me, Emma?"

"Yes, Luke, pl . . . please." As her lips trembled out the word and she looked into his contorted face an even deeper terror filled her, for what she saw in his eyes she recognized as madness. It wasn't only that he had been drinking, for he wasn't really drunk, but he was mad; and it wasn't only the madness of a moment she was witnessing, it was an insanity that had taken him over. She could smell it; it was almost tangible; and the fearfulness of it was in the seeming reasonable animosity of his next words.

"Oh, what a pity, Emma, you didn't think about pleadin' afore now. Funny; if you had, things might have been different. No . . . Emma—" His voice changed now and he jerked himself to his feet and, cracking the whip over the floor boards, he said, "I'm gona take payment for me life, an' for this." He pointed to the weal on his face. "Remember this, Emma? You did that with a rope. Well, just in case you had got rid of the whips I brought some along of me. But this one is better. Oh, much better." Again he cracked the whip. Then swinging round, he brought his arm in a lightning flash over his head and the end of the whip across her face.

As her body bounced on the floor, her screams seemed to deafen herself, and as the blood ran into the corner of her mouth he lashed out at her again and once more her body bounced. This time she rolled on to her face, her open mouth pressed against the dirty boards. But she wasn't there seconds before his foot had brought her on to her side again. And now he was flaying her. No part of her body did he miss. And when his arm became tired he stood gasping, his own body heaving almost as much as hers. But she was past hearing when he bawled, "That's only the beginning. An' don't think there'll be somebody comin' to your rescue, because I've arranged it. There's a note left for your dear helper to say you've gone to the painter's. How's that for thinkin'? And when they eventually find you and him I'll be miles away. And I've people to vouch that I'd been with them every minute for the past week, because I've made meself scarce, said I was goin' into Newcastle to look for a job and some place to kip. And of course that's natural since me and Laura broke up. The bitch! The bitch, to leave me. I'll do for her an' all. I will! I will. . . . Emma." He again pushed her with his foot, and when there was no movement from her he brought the lantern and held it above her. Her face was streaming with blood, the crossed lines on her breast, stomach and legs were oozing blood; the torn nightdress was now bespattered with blood and split in places and had ridden up beyond her thighs.

He took his hand and gripped her shoulder, shouting now, "Come on! Come on! You're not goin' as easy as that." Then when her head rolled to the side, he straightened himself, saying, quietly, "Well, rest a while. That's it, rest a while. An' me an' all. It's hard work lashing out. I don't seem to have your knack, Emma, but I'm not doin' so badly, am I? 'Tis hard work. An' me head's aching. Want a drink. Me head's aching."

And on this he threw the whip down and went and sat on the floor opposite her. His back against a box, he sat gazing at her wealed and bleeding body, as another man might have done at a picture that soothed his senses. And time went on and he continued to look at her, and the only movement his body made was when his jaw sagged. From then on his mouth remained open as if in astonishment.

14

It was the day for the market. Jimmy came into the yard around six o'clock. The first job he did was to water and feed the horses; he then put the mash on in the boilerhouse for the pigs; following this, he let out the hens earlier than usual simply to stop the cock crowing its head off; and before he started the mucking out of the cow byres and the milking he got the horse and cart ready for the market.

Later, on looking towards the attic he noticed there was a light showing dimly through the fanlight. But he had seen no sign of the missis, and market day she was generally trotting backward and forward to the dairy getting the stuff ready for the cart. And she always called him over about this time and gave him a mug of something hot. Perhaps she wasn't well. Perhaps the boss had taken worse.

He went to the kitchen door and tapped on it. When he received no response he pushed it open and stood looking round the kitchen. The fire wasn't blazing; the kettle wasn't boiling on the hob, as he would have expected to see; but the table was set for breakfast as it always was the night before. She couldn't be up yet.

But there was a piece of paper stuck in front of the jug.

He took a step further into the kitchen and went towards the paper and read his own name on the top of it. Picking it up, he saw that it said: Jimmy, been called to Mr Bowman's. Carry on as usual. I've seen to Barney. Don't trouble him. I'll soon be back.

He stared at the piece of paper, then he looked down the room to the far door before bringing his eyes back and reading the note again. She had written her husband's name calling him Barney. She never called him Barney, not to him, she always called him the boss, because crippled or no he still owned the place. And he had always thought it a nice gesture of her to refer to him as the boss. But here she was calling him Barney. But that wasn't all. The writing, it was big and scrawling. He had seen her writing before on the orders she had written out for him when he had taken the cart into Gateshead Fell for horse feed and such.

There was something funny here. And she said he hadn't to go in to the boss. Why? when he had looked after him those days when she was cut off by the snow, and for sometime after an' all, to help his ma out.

He turned about and left the kitchen. Then, going quietly along the yard, he stopped outside the sitting-room window. The head of the boss's bed had been placed so that he could see out of the window. Jimmy stood a pace back from the window, looking at it for some seconds; then leaning towards it, he pressed his nose to the glass and looked in. There was the boss in bed where he expected him to be. He looked asleep; yet no, he wasn't.

Jimmy moved his head against the reflected light, then cupped his hand over the side of his face and his mouth opened wide as he stared at the face on the pillow. The eyes were open, the jaw was hanging slack, and one eye was black and blue as if he had been in a fight.

He stood back, his doubled fist held tightly against his mouth now. The boss was dead. He was dead. And the missis? There was something wrong. He looked upwards towards the windows. Should he go in, and upstairs?

No, no, he must go and get somebody. There was something radically wrong here. But where was the missis?

He ran across the yard now towards where the cart stood. He had to go and get somebody, he couldn't tackle it himself. He was just about to mount to the seat when he stopped as he remembered something. The light, that light coming from the attic. He had thought it was the reflection of the rising sun spread through the branches of the apple tree.

He turned from the cart and ran across the yard to the side of the house; but there he stopped and, moving cautiously, he crossed the square of grass in which stood the old tree. Then backing two or three steps, he looked upwards, and yes, there it was. It was dimmer now in the broader daylight but it was nevertheless a light, and what was it doing in the attic. Nobody, to his knowledge, slept in the attic. Well, there was nobody to sleep in the attic, was there?

He looked up into the branches of the tree. He had skimmed up this old tree more times than he'd had weekly wages. He put his hands up and gripped the stout lower branch and within seconds he was standing on it, and from there he threaded his way as if up a known staircase to the top.

He wasn't quite on a level with the fanlight and the sun coming through the branches of the tree was still dappling it. He put his hand gently out and laid it on the roof, then brought his face round to the edge of the dirty pane, and through narrowed eyes he squinted into the room below. And what he imagined he saw almost brought him toppling backwards. He could see the dim outline, also dappled by the sun's rays, of a trussed naked figure on the floor. It was red in parts, and sitting not a yard from it, his back against a box, was the hunched figure of a man. And he recognized the man.

His lips formed the words, Eeh! God in heaven. Eeh! Then he was again moving cautiously through the branches. But once on the ground he seemed to cover it in leaps until he reached the cart; then mounting it, he cried, "Gee up there!" and the horse trotted out through the opening on to the lane, with Jimmy again urging it on: "Up! Up!"

At the coach road he pulled the animal to a halt and looked first one way and then the other. He had to get help. But it was a couple of miles to the village. Just along the road though there was the painter's cottage and the parson was staying there, and he was no weakling. This was the day he was leaving, so it was said; his ma said his big trunk had been sent on to the station yesterday.

Having turned the horse's head in the direction of the cottage, he put the animal into a fast trot, and when they reached the cottage he jumped from the cart almost before the horse had come to a stop. Tearing up the path now, he hammered on the door.

It was opened by the painter, with a shawl over his shoulders. "Oh, Mr Bowman"—Jimmy leaned forward, one hand clutching the stanchion of the door—"is . . . is the parson with you?"

"Yes. Yes, I'm here, Jimmy." Henry appeared by the side of Ralph.

"Oh! Parson. Parson, you've got to come, there's somethin' going on up there, bad. I . . . I think the boss is dead, and the missis." At this point he closed his eyes tight, drooped his head and shook it as if to fling off the picture in his mind; then on a gabble of words he said, "Luke Yorkless. He's got her up in the attic. She . . . she looked stark, stark-naked. She's trussed up and as . . . as far as I could see. . . . I . . . well, I might have been mistaken but . . . well, she looked as if she was bleedin' in parts."

For a second Henry and Ralph remained mute; then Henry rushed down the room, grabbed up his coat and was back within seconds, to find that Ralph had thrown off his shawl and that he too was lifting a coat from the back of the door. *"No! No! man. No! No!"* Henry bawled at him.

"I'm coming with you."

"No! I tell you. Anyway, what use would you be? You're in no fit state to. . . ."

"Don't waste words, Henry. I don't know what use I'd be, I only know I'm coming with you."

Henry looked from where Jimmy had mounted the cart to where

Ralph was now pulling the door closed behind him, and he shook his head. It was no use wasting time arguing.

He helped Ralph up on to the seat beside Jimmy and he himself jumped on to the back of the cart.

It was some five minutes later when they neared the farmyard, and before they went through the opening Henry called, "Stop a minute." He jumped down, went round to the front of the cart and, looking up at Jimmy, he said, "Had he a gun?"

"Oh, I couldn't see that, Parson; I just stayed long enough to see what I did. But he could have; he used to poach along of the moler, 'twas known."

"Come on, get down." Henry put up his hand and caught at Ralph's sleeve, then added, "Not you, Jimmy. What you must do is turn about and get into the village as quickly as possible and bring some help back."

"I've been thinkin', Parson, most of 'em'll be in the fields or away into Gateshead. An' Mr Tate's not much good with his fists although he's an innkeeper. And it being market day the butcher won't be there. And Tom Turnbull, well. . . ."

"All right. All right. Well look, go back the way you came and beyond to Farmer Hudson. Anthony will come along with him. Go on now; get away as fast as you can."

Before the cart had turned about he and Ralph had entered the yard. Henry opened the kitchen door and they went in quietly, and both stood looking about them for a moment before Henry said softly, "Stay where you are, he's dangerous." And Ralph answered as softly, "Well, I'll leave you to tackle the danger. By all accounts Emma will need some help."

Henry let out a quick short breath, then went cautiously up the kitchen and across the hall. At the foot of the stairs he hesitated and after looking towards the sitting-room he moved swiftly to the door, opened it, and went in. Ralph followed.

They stood looking down on Barney, and Henry moved his head in a pitying gesture, muttering, "He's mad. He's mad. This was his brother." He now looked at Ralph whose lips were spread from his teeth which were clenched, and he seemed to speak through them as he said, "He's been pummelled."

Henry looked upwards; then turning swiftly, he went from the room and up the stairs. Ralph followed more slowly but he gained Henry's side as he paused outside the bedroom door.

Henry knew the layout of the house; he had sat in this particular bedroom many times after Barney had first had his accident and he knew of the low door that led into the attic. Quietly now he gripped the handle and, turning it slowly, he pressed the door open; then on tiptoe, they both entered the room, and their eyes were directed straight to the bed. All the bedclothes were on the floor, and the patch quilt was lying under the window with a pillow near it. There were various articles of clothing strewn about the floor but the way to the attic door was clear.

Standing in front of it, he turned his head on his shoulder and listened. But he heard no sound at all. After nodding once to Ralph he leaned forward and with a jerk pulled open the door; then bending his length, he almost dived into the room, there to see a sight that was to remain with him to the end of his days. The sun was dappling the almost naked figure on the floor. It looked like an animal that had been trussed and badly slaughtered, and to the side of it sat the slaughterer.

The eeriness and horror of the situation was heightened by the fact that the man on the floor didn't move; that was until Ralph muttered, "Oh my God!" Then it was as if he had bellowed, for Luke's head jerked to the side and, looking at them, he smiled.

Henry spoke not a word. Within a second he was kneeling by Emma, and for a moment his hands hovered over her as if afraid to touch her. There was in him an agony as like to a crucifixion as he would ever know. When he loosened the ropes that bound her hands and feet it was as if the nails of the cross were being driven in to him and he was crying, Lord, why hast Thou forsaken me? for surely God was punishing him through the torn bloody body before him.

"He's mad. He's gone mad."

He was aware that Ralph was speaking but he paid no heed to him. Putting his arms gently under the contorted and blood-sticky limbs, he lifted Emma gently up and, holding her to his breast, he stumbled from the room.

15

She had lain in the kitchen for two weeks, but after the third day her mind became quite clear, and she was fully aware from then of what was going on and what was being said in whispered words or normal talk. She knew for instance that they had buried Barney, that the papers had been full of the tragedy, that people from as far away as Newcastle were taking Sunday trips to see the farm where the woman had almost been flayed alive. She knew that Pete had cried like any woman when he had looked down on her, and that the girl he was going to marry was nice. She was small and tidy in her person, but had a strange way of talking. She could understand little of what she said. She also knew that Luke Yorkless had been put in an asylum and they were saying in the kitchen that he might as well be dead, but she knew that for her he would never be dead, he would live forever all over her body . . . and her face.

Yesterday, when a strange doctor came from Newcastle he had ordered them to take off the pig fat muslin wrappings that covered her body up to the chin and said that all that was needed now was a light gown. She had seen her body, at least at the front. It had not shocked her because each lacerated piece of flesh was engraved on her mind, except those Luke had accomplished with his last effort when he must have turned her over on to her face . . . kicked her over.

Her face! It was only in the night that she put her hand up to her face and let her fingers follow the weals. She had asked Mary yesterday to give her the looking-glass from the mantelpiece, but Mary's answer had been, "There's plenty of time. And that one from Newcastle said they'll heal an' they'll fade. You'll hardly be able to notice them in time. You'll see, they'll vanish."

But the rope mark she herself had laid on Luke's face hadn't vanished. In his demoniac hate it had stood out like a piece of red cord.

She hadn't imagined that she cared overmuch about her looks. She had never been pretty, not like other girls. But Barney had told her so often in that first year of their marriage she was beautiful, and Ralph had told her she was beautiful; and Henry had told her she was beautiful that night in the mill when they thought they had been going to die. He had said her beauty had made him ache, that sometimes he couldn't bear to look at her for the pain her image had on him. And that night she had been glad she was still good to look upon. Tired out with work, her mind weary with grappling, that she could still be thought beautiful had been a great comfort. But now she was beautiful no more; nor ever would be in her life again.

She had heard Mary talking to Pete's young woman, saying, "She's lucky to have her sight. He likely only left her that so she could see his handiwork for the rest of her days; that's if he intended her to go on livin'. 'Tis a wonder that she's alive anyway."

Yes, it was a wonder that she was alive. And a pity, for if ever before she had longed for death she longed for it now. Henry's loving words could not soothe her. There was nothing standing in their way now, he had said; he was leaving and as soon as she was well enough to travel she was going with him. She would love his father and sister, and they would love her; and she would love the house and the country-side. . . . On and on he had talked, but not once had she opened her mouth in one word of reply of acceptance of the future he portrayed or of refusal to share it with him.

There was a great stillness inside her as if the world had stopped moving. It had come into being from the time she had regained full con-sciousness. Prior to this her mind in her lucid moments had been screaming out to the heavens a great *why*. And now this silence seemed to be the answer.

She looked down the kitchen. There was no one in it. Pete's girl was upstairs doing the room, Pete was outside with Jimmy, Mary had gone into the dairy.

Slowly she pushed the bed cover back and slowly still she brought her legs over the side. The stone was cool to the seared soles of her feet. With the support of the bedhead she pulled herself up, and the effect of moving was such that she imagined all the skin on her body had become brittle and was now cracking. Her head bent, she stood gasping for a moment before moving one foot in front of the other like a child at-tempting to walk. Painfully she made her way from the bed to the table, and after resting there for a moment she turned about and went towards the fireplace at the side of which hung the shaving mirror. . . .

The only thing she recognized about the woman's face looking back at her were the eyes, for below them, following the cheekbones, were two red weals that gave the impression they were the lower rim of a large pair of spectacles. On her left cheek the lines were so criss-crossed that they melted together. There were only two marks on her right cheek. These came down from her temple and curved beyond her lower lip to the middle of her chin.

She was hideous. *Hideous*. She turned from the mirror, her hands covering her face, her mouth wide open.

Oh no! No! No! No! She couldn't bear this. If she couldn't stand the sight of herself, how could other people bear to look at her? Why had God put this on her too? Why? Why? What had she done to deserve it? Knowingly she had committed one sin in His eyes, that was loving Henry, but to her it hadn't been a sin, no more than lust was apparently to Annie. God Almighty! what was she thinking? She'd go out of her mind. That'd be the next thing He'd do to her. Just to let her see there were worse things than losing your looks, He'd send her mad, as He had sent Luke mad so that he wouldn't have to pay the penalty for killing Barney.

As she reached the table the door opened and Henry stood poised for a moment before moving swiftly towards her, saying almost harshly now, "Why are you up? You shouldn't have attempted to get on your feet for another week or more."

She looked up at him into his face and, slowly turning, she pointed to the mirror; and at this he cried, his voice overloud, "Well! what about it? In time they'll heal. . . . Oh! Emma. Emma." His voice dropped and he put his arms about her, saying softly now, "Believe me, the scars will fade to nothing. And look"—he thrust his hands into his coat pocket and brought out a round box—"I went into Newcastle yesterday and saw a Doctor Fenwick, and he made up this ointment. This is specially for your face. He says it will soften the skin and reduce the weals in no time."

She put out her hand and laid her fingers gently on the box, then shook her head, and in a voice that was merely a croak as if from disuse she said, "Don't hoodwink me."

As they were the first words she had spoken during the past two weeks he smiled at her, saying, "Who could hoodwink you, Emma?" Then he added, "But I'm telling you the truth. Doctor Fenwick is a skin specialist. Now come on back to bed because you've got to get your strength up, and quickly, because I can't wait to take you home."

When she was once more in bed, he sat on the side of it and, taking her hand in his, he traced each finger gently with his own as he said, "I never, never thought we'd ever be together, Emma. And now the prospect of spending the rest of my life with you is so overwhelming I can't believe it's about to happen."

When she made no response he asked quietly, "You won't mind leaving the farm, will you?"

Would she mind leaving the farm? She never wanted to see this farm again, not in this life, or the next. She even startled herself when she said in a voice that was like a cry, *"Oh no! No!"*

"That's all right then. I've talked it over with Pete. He says if you pass it on to him then you must be recompensed in some way, but I said that I thought that you wouldn't want anything. Am I right?"

"Yes." She nodded her head twice: she wanted nothing from this place, she wanted to be away from it, to fly . . . fly away from it. Yet she couldn't fly away, not with him. It wouldn't be fair. She would be an embarrassment to him; he'd have to explain how she had come by her disfigurement. He'd always have to explain, and so many things. It was because of her he'd lost his ministry. Mary had said as much. She turned her head away from him now, saying, "I . . . I can't go with you, it's too late."

"Emma"—he brought her face gently towards him—"you . . . you don't care for me any more?"

Oh—she looked into his eyes—if she had ever loved him before, she loved him at this moment, and the weight of the love that was opening up in her was like a physical load pressing her body double, for now she was bending forward over the bed her face in her hands, and when he forced them apart and brought her round to him again he said, "Answer my question."

She stared at him while her tears followed the channels of the weals and spread over her face, and what she answered was, "I'm . . . I'm different now; I'll never be the same again, inside or out."

Once more he said, "Answer my question. Do you care for me still?"

"Oh! Henry; I can't go with you, it's too late."

"Emma, do you love me? Because if you do and you want to stay here, then I stay too."

"No, no; you mustn't stay here . . . oh no. Oh! Henry." Her head fell forward and when it touched his shoulder his arms went round her and he looked over her head down the kitchen to where the rain was streaming down the window and he said softly, "That's settled then. That's settled. Our lives here have run full circle because I, in a way, brought you here, and it's been left to me, and thank God for it, to take you away from this tormented house. And I promise you, Emma, that for the remainder of my life my main concern will be your happiness."

Raising her head from his shoulder, he now placed his lips firmly on hers; then stroking her hair back from her forehead, he said softly, "So it is sealed, Emma, so it is sealed, for life, what is left of it."

*

Three weeks later, Emma, dressed in a new cloak and a wide-brimmed bonnet that shadowed her face, was sitting by the side of Ralph. Their hands were tightly clasped and words were coming difficult to both of them. He coughed, wiped his mouth with a handkerchief, then turned to her, saying softly, "I'll have the pictures sent on . . . later."

"I hope it won't be for a long long time."

"It likely will." He coughed again, then smiled at her, saying, "You know me, I've been dying every winter since you first put your nose through that door. What is it, twenty-three, twenty-four years ago? Twenty-four years ago. A lifetime. But you . . . you Emma, you've got another lifetime before you and if anybody can make you happy he will. He's loved you from the first minute he saw you. And I did an' all." He now wagged her hand up and down. "Oh yes, I did, but"—he turned his head away as if in shyness now—"you knew the circumstances." Then looking at her again, he added in a whisper, "And what might have happened but for those circumstances?"

"Oh! Ralph. Ralph." She looked lovingly into his emaciated face and they both knew that this was the last good-bye. "Go now," he said; "he's out there straining at the leash."

He did not kiss her but brought her hand to the side of his face, and she, bending forward, put her lips to his brow and they held each other tightly for a moment. Then blindly she rose from the chair and went out of the cottage to where Henry was standing near the trap talking to Jimmy who was sitting in the driving seat, and after Henry had helped her into the back of the trap he said, "I'll be back in a minute." Then hurrying up the path, he went into the cottage and stood looking down at Ralph for a moment before sitting down beside him.

"I hate to leave you like this," he said brokenly. "If . . . if there was only some way."

"Don't be silly, man. We both know I'll be leaving myself in a very short time. But I want to say one thing to you, and that is, thank you for the friendship you've shown me over the years. I sometimes have wondered how I would have gone on without you . . . and your crack." He jerked his head and blinked rapidly. "If you'd been an ordinary parson, you'd never have stood the pace, but you were never an ordinary parson. You should never have been a parson; you know that, don't you?"

Henry couldn't speak, but what he did was put his arms about the muffled figure and, holding him tightly, he muttered through the tightness in his throat, "I've loved you dearer than father or brother."

"Go on. Go on." Ralph pushed him away, then turned his head towards the fire as Henry went out, the tears streaming unashamedly down his face.

The train was puffing noisily; the smoke was billowing down the platform enveloping them in cloud as if in mist; Pete and his future wife and Jimmy stood around her, and one after the other they shook her hand and wished her all the happiness in life; but it was Pete who kissed her, then whispered, "Don't worry. I'll do what you asked an' let you know if . . . if I should hear anything. Go now and be happy."

And she went, lifted up the high step by Henry, and then they were both standing at the window until the whistle blew and the train moved slowly out of the station. And when they had stopped waving they sat down side by side, their hands joined as they were to be whenever possible for the rest of their lives.

ABOUT THE AUTHOR

CATHERINE COOKSON was born in Tyne Dock, South Shields, England, in 1906. This river area, known as Tyneside, and its people provide the settings and characters for her many novels. And in the tradition of many great English novelists, Mrs. Cookson captures the mood of her settings with remarkable clarity. In fact, so successfully has Mrs. Cookson re-created this area that in 1968 she was the recipient of the Winifred Holtby Award of the Royal Society of Literature for the Best Regional Novel of the Year, and in 1974 she was awarded the Freedom of the County Borough of South Shields in recognition of her services to her hometown. Mrs. Cookson and her husband live in Northumberland, England.

Epilogue

EPILOGUE

On a day in June of eighteen ninety-three, a woman sat in the front room of a house in a respectable quarter of Newcastle. She was nearing her middle forties but with her slim body and babyish-looking face she could have claimed to be in her early thirties. She was reading the deaths column in *The Times*. Her late husband had always taken *The Times*, and because it set a sort of social pattern she hadn't stopped its delivery. She read again the words:

GRAINGER.—On the 4th June, 1893, peacefully, at the Towers, Burnside, Emaralda Grainger, two days following the decease of her husband, Henry Francis Grainger. Both greatly beloved of their son, Ralph Francis Grainger, and their daughters, Mrs. Elizabeth Scott Mather and Mrs. Mary Barrington. Funeral at Burnside Parish Church, the 8th inst., at 2 o'clock. They were inseparable in life, they are inseparable in death.

The woman got up and walked to the window. The paper hung slack in her hand, and as she stood gazing out on to the neat back garden her thoughts ran wildly back down the years to the day when she was sixteen and Bill had bought her out from Ma Boss's and had married her, actually married her. She was still wondering why to this very day, for he hadn't wanted all that much out of her, just snuggle and cuddle. And he had known of her side capers, but he hadn't minded as long as she was there. And she had stuck by him. Yes, she owed him that much, she had stuck by him until he had died in his dotage. But he had repaid her well, she was set for life. . . . and after all, what was life for but for living?

She now recalled the day that she'd first heard of her Uncle Luke flaying her mother, and it hadn't been till after Bill had brought her out. She'd felt dreadful about that and had gone up to the farm, but it was all changed and her mother had gone and her Uncle Pete wouldn't tell her where. But he had said he would let her ma know that she was all right and respectably married.

And now she was dead. And the parson was dead. And Uncle Pete was dead, and his young son was running the farm, so she understood.

She lifted the paper and again read the notice. Her mother had had a son and two daughters. She had a half-brother and two half-sisters, and now she knew where they were. . . . Well, they could remain there. She'd never be able to undo all the damage she had done in her life, but she would cause no more. But she could go down there to the funeral couldn't she? On the quiet like?

She turned from the window. No, no; the doctor was calling later in the day. He called every week to see to her heart. She smiled to herself: appearances had to be kept up. And then it was almost time for Jack's boat to be in, it could be any day now. She looked forward to that. He was her nephew . . . for the neighbours. He had to be to stay a fortnight or more at a time. It took all sorts to make life worth living, and life was for living according to how you were made. Aye, according to how you were made.

She laid the paper down on the table and went out of the room and across a well-carpeted hall and up the stairs and into a very comfortable bedroom and got ready to meet the doctor. . . .

Life was for living.